THE SATYR'S DANCE

Gary Dolman

REYNARD PRESS

THE SATYR'S DANCE

Published in 2016 by
REYNARD PRESS
West Lane,
Ripon
HG4 2NP

All Rights Reserved

ISBN: 978-0-9934208-4-9

THE SATYR'S DANCE

Also by Gary Dolman:

Red Dragon-White Dragon

The Eighth Circle of Hell

But wild beasts of the desert shall lie there… and satyrs shall dance there.

The Holy Bible, Isaiah 13:21

That which is below is like that which is above.

The Emerald Tablet of Hermes,
(Translation by Isaac Newton, circa 1680)

CHAPTER ONE

For a little less than a week now, the street performers of Harrogate had been joined by a travelling show, a freak show, which contained just a single exhibit.

Sometime in the night, one Thomas Wilberforce had parked his little horse-drawn van between the magnificent spa pump room and the Bogs Valley Pleasure Gardens. It was a prime pitch, squeezed-in somehow between Professor Bailey's celebrated Punch and Judy stall and that of an African salamander man. This latter had been particularly aggrieved by the intrusion, but although he could swallow a red-hot poker right up to its handle, he, like the professor, had said nothing. In private they would both admit to being a little wary, afraid even, of what Mr Wilberforce kept chained inside his gaily-painted van.

But now, at this late hour, Professor Bailey and the salamander man, the acrobats, the jugglers and the street-organ turners had returned to their lodgings. The Ailing, who came to the spa for its health-giving waters, had been driven indoors, into the hotels and the concert halls by the damp, chilly air, and the people of Harrogate had duly followed to minister unto them.

The town was silent and deserted. The evening mists, fed by the smoke of a thousand chimneys, had thickened and settled and cloaked the streets in a dense, dripping shroud of grey, pierced here and there by light, as the leeries[1] trudged the long lines of streetlamps and touched life to their gas. It was silent and deserted that is, apart from the occasional stirring of Wilberforce's old cob and the heavy and regular tap of a gentleman's walking cane on the stone flags of the pavement.

"Though I walk through the valley of the shadow of death," the gentleman muttered, slowing a little and glancing about, "I will fear no evil, for Thou art with me."

An emaciated dog raised its head at the words and for a moment its eyes beaded yellow. Then it seemed to catch another scent clinging to the moist air, something from the direction of Wilberforce's van that brought a low growl to its throat. It stared curiously for a time, and then laid back its single, tattered ear and skulked away into the shadows.

The gentleman halted and he too stared at the van. The words painted across the side, black and stark in the lamplight, confirmed he had found what he had been looking for.

"Wilberforce's Wonders of the Modern World," he read aloud.

His voice was stronger now, mocking even, as he took courage from the sound, and from the weight of the borrowed, pewter-topped walking cane he gripped tightly in his fist.

A sandwich-board, blistered and cracked across its middle, was leaning against the iron rim of one wheel. It was headed by the same words and the gentleman stepped up to follow the smaller letters beneath with the horn tip of the cane:

Esau:
An extraordinary Freak of Nature.
The long sought-for, but hitherto undiscovered link between
Mankind and the Great Apes of Africa.
Hours of Entertainment.
6d Admission.

The gentleman frowned. Under ordinary circumstances, he would have passed such a show with nothing more than a derisive snort, but today – today he was not so sure.

"Good evening," he called.

The cob snickered and swished its tail.

He jabbed the tip of the cane against the sandwich board. It rocked against the wheel – once, twice, and then lay still.

"Good day! Wilberforce, are you there?"

There was a shuffling from inside the van and the rattle of what might have been chain. A latch clicked somewhere above his head and a black shadow lengthened and spread, and became a door.

"Wilberforce, is that you?"

A face emerged above a frayed, collarless shirt, its irritated frown melting into an unctuous smile as Thomas Wilberforce caught sight of his visitor below.

"Last showing's eight o'clock sharp, and it's more than five-and-twenty minutes past now. I suppose I could accommodate you though, for a shilling."

The gentleman swelled.

"You're a thieving scoundrel. You should be grateful I'm not having you moved-on, or thrown into gaol even, for allowing… for allowing whatever it is you have in there to scare my poor daughter half out of her wits, never mind charging me double."

He fished irritably in his pocket.

"But very well, here is your wretched shilling. I warn you though, Wilberforce, I am a scientist, a naturalist. I'll not be taken-in by a fraud. Now, where is this so-called link to the apes?"

Mr Wilberforce reached down and grasped the coin, and his stoop became a low bow.

"Sir, fear not, this is no fraud. A certain learned and reverend gentleman once declared my creature to be, without question, a descendant of Esau of the Old Testament. A man of science, a gentleman-naturalist like your clever self, informed me that it could not be anything other than Mr Darwin and Mr Wallace's[2] missing intermediate link. Humbly I say to you that whatever it is, it is without doubt, the most marvellous creature in all of the world and worth, not just a shilling, but easily a hundred pounds from any gentleman's purse.

"Come with me, sir, that you may behold it with your own eyes."

He backed into his van as an eel might slide into its hole and beckoned.

A stepladder clung to the van on iron grips, its wooden steps worn and polished smooth by the soles of countless boots. It creaked wearily as the gentleman climbed up into the long shadow of the door and it creaked again as he stepped inside.

Mr Wilberforce was just turning back from one of a pair of bracket-lamps, whose light was swelling and reaching out into the space, conjuring shapes and shadows onto the walls that might have been a whole menagerie-full of exhibits. It certainly stank as much.

"You have a late viewer, Beast," he snarled, "A gentleman and a naturalist. Greet him now, but nicely, mind you."

The sharp rattle of metal on wood drew the gentleman's attention to the floor and the space between the oil-lamps, where a large shape was stirring and shifting.

"Good day, shir," a voice rasped.

The gentleman found himself staring directly into the depths of two black eyes, and he yelped and jumped back in fright. He gathered himself. Settled into a nest of rags and blankets was a creature – a beast. Whether or not it truly was a descendent, either of Esau or of Mr Darwin's apes, he could not even begin to say, but in that moment it gazed up at him with a fragility and a torment that was somehow almost human.

"Good day, Beast," he whispered.

The crown of his top-hat pressed against the planks of the roof and he reached up to remove it. The creature glanced up at the movement and the light caught on an iron collar fixed around its throat. Thank the lord that the ape-beast was chained.

And it was most certainly a species of ape, he noted with a scientist's discipline, quite as large as a man, with dark, matted hair of indeterminate colour, given the imperfect light. The hair was significantly longer on its head and face, which rather gave the effect of a lion's mane, and it was sitting in the manner of a gorilla with its hind limbs, surprisingly long for an ape, crossed in front of it.

The gentleman became aware of Wilberforce watching him with the rapt attention of a fairground pickpocket.

"There, sir," said the showman, "I trust you are not disappointed. Is it not, without any shadow of a doubt, the very greatest wonder in all of creation? It can talk in English, as you have just heard, and I could get it to read from the Holy Scriptures for you too – for another shilling."

The gentleman nodded and reached into his pocket.

"Do you have a name, Beast?" He addressed the creature directly, speaking slowly and loudly, careful to hide his fear, just as he had learned to speak to the savage tribes in Africa.

The creature rose suddenly to its feet and the van swayed alarmingly on its iron springs. A billow of acrid, animal stench followed the movement and the gentleman turned away his head.

"My name… my name is Eshau, shir."

Wilberforce's oleaginous face slid in front of it. "It means Esau – named for the first of its line. If you want it to talk at length, it'll cost extra, mind you. I have a lot of expense to keep it fed and decently clothed and all, a great lot of expense."

The gentleman tapped him aside with the thick shaft of his cane and stared again at the beast. His blood was pounding in his ears. Alice, his daughter, had not been exaggerating one degree. This was without question, without the slightest atom of doubt, the very greatest discovery of the age – perhaps of any age. It was a link; it was the very conjunction between a higher and a lower order of life.

"Mr Wilberforce," he declared, "My name is Joseph Malkin and I have made up my mind. I wish to purchase your exhibit, now, this very evening. I wish to purchase it for proper scientific study and observation."

He pulled his eyes from the ape-man standing as it was, wretchedly, in ragged trousers such as the meanest street urchin might wear, and stared instead at Wilberforce.

"Not just one hundred pounds from my purse, sir, but five hundred; five hundred pounds payable on my bankers, the Halifax Old Bank, the instant they open for business tomorrow morning. You can see their branch from the top of the hill, yonder. I am a director of that bank and my word, sir, is unquestionably my bond.

"Five hundred pounds." He said the words again, more slowly this time, allowing their sound to hang in the air between them like the apples of Eden. "I fancy it didn't cost you anything near that amount of money to procure yourself."

"That would be my own business," the showman murmured. He held Malkin's gaze for several, long seconds and then turned, allowing his eyes to wander around the cramped compartment as if he were looking at it for the first, or perhaps for the very last, time. His eyes passed over the sheens of mould creeping out from the shadows of every corner, past the dust-laden cobwebs festooning the walls, and came to rest on an old hand-bill tramped into a crack in a floorboard. Its message, faded and mouldering, affirmed once more how the creature, Esau, was indeed the greatest wonder in the whole of the Empire.

Wilberforce turned back.

"I might just be agreeable to selling him to you, Mr Malkin," he said, "But not for five hundred pounds. No, sir, I fancy he would cost you double that."

"Well then, let us make a bargain at one thousand pounds and shake hands on it, before you try to extort yet more from me. William Hales' inn is just over the way. Come, and we can draw-up our agreement there. I shall need a drink in any event, to wash the stench of this place from my gizzard."

CHAPTER TWO

"Mashter, nay!"

Esau the Beast staggers, and falls back against the planks of the wall behind him. In spite of his thick and shaggy coat, he shivers, and his legs tremble and spasm uncontrollably, unable to support him as the suddenly leaden chain drags him down into his nest.

"Lord God, pleash nay."

He has pleaded to his god Jehovah many, many times in the twenty-one years it has been since his mother first screamed and screamed for him to be taken away, but it is only the third time in his life that he has changed master. This master has been good. At least here, in this van, he has his daily bread. He has water too – even ale sometimes, when his master has been drunk and fallen asleep with a half-supped pot in front of him. The chain on his collar is long; it lets him move all around his stall, and it has a simple lock.

By day there are faces – human faces – peering at him over the half-door opposite. The men shout and jeer, as men have always shouted and jeered. The women stare or weep, or sometimes, like his mother, they too beg and scream for him to be taken away. And here, he has a Bible.

His Bible is his most precious thing. It was thrown at him by no less a person than a vicar, and it is much better than the mouldering, ragged book he was allowed at the workhouse. The very best times are when he can sit quietly in his nest of rags and lose himself in its wonderful words. As he reads of Jesus and Mary and dear, dear Mary Magdalene, he can make it seem as if the gawping faces aren't there at all, except when they hurl things at him of course; stinging farthings and stones and clods of mud they have kicked up from the ground. Whenever they do that, he knows he must lay his Bible gently aside and roar and pummel his chest just exactly as his master has taught him. He must, or else Master will shut the door tight and thrash him with his fists or a long, swinging loop of his chain.

At least here, in this van, he has but one master to thrash him. Before, in the old days, he was beaten by everyone.

Along with the thought, a line of angry, jeering faces rises up in his beast's mind and Esau remembers those years – the ones he spent in the union workhouse at Ripon. He feels the hair across his brow tingle and prickle with sweat and he rolls over and vomits down through the latrine-hole onto the grass beneath. The cool, moist air reaches up to soothe and comfort him, and he shivers again.

His master has gone out. He has gone with the gentleman who has offered a fortune for him, and now the oil lamps have spluttered and gone out too. In his beast's mind, the planks of his stall become the gloomy walls of the cubby-hole. It is the cubby-hole at the back of the workhouse schoolroom where he was taken and allowed to watch the human children at their lessons. The latrine hole is the hatch they had cut in the door in order to discharge their parochial duty to educate each and every child in their keeping, no matter how bestial that child might be. It is a tiny hatch, barely wide enough to let him see the blackboard, but more than enough for the sticks and the stones and the taunts of the pauper children, whenever the schoolmistress left the room.

"Shit-face! Shit-face! Shit-face!"

He was fortunate that the schoolmistress, Mrs Nudds, was not entirely comfortable with the parochial arrangements for Esau's education and for the fact that she seldom left the schoolroom.

"A freak he may very well be, Mr Greenwood," she would remark to the master of the workhouse, "But in every subject he excels the other scholars by some measure."

"But what is to be done with him, Mrs Nudds?" the master would reply, leaning forward and peering at her over the blued-steel rim of his spectacles, "What tradesman, street-organ turners apart, would want a monkey-boy for an apprentice?"

And to that, Mrs Nudds would have no answer.

One time, after Charlie Wintersgill had pulled Esau's hood back during prayers and Old Mother Richmond had screamed and fallen down in a faint, Mr Greenwood had stamped his boot. He had declared that his very dearest wish was that Esau's mother should have thought to take her monkey-child with her when she had flung herself into the boiling spate-waters of the Ure. Of course the master of a union workhouse had no business ever wishing for such a thing, and most especially not on a Sunday. So once Mother Richmond had been revived and propped back onto her bench, and once Charlie Wintersgill had been taken away to be thrashed, he had quite properly begged God's forgiveness for his outburst. But Mrs Nudds aside, the staff and the inmates of Ripon workhouse had heartily agreed with him; Shit-faced Esau would have been much better served if the river had indeed carried him off to Hell and to his father the Devil.

Mrs Greenwood, the master's wife and the matron of the workhouse, also had cause to beg forgiveness from God on Esau's account. Marian, the young woman cursed to give birth to the monster, had screamed and thrashed in her cot, whenever it was brought near to her. There had seemed very little prospect indeed of her being persuaded to feed or to take care of it. So Mrs Greenwood had taken the municipal nurse into a corner of the infirmary and in hushed tones had suggested that it might be quieted with laudanum and lime milk, and allowed to starve to death. It would be for the best. It really would. Such an unholy creature would surely die in any event, and this was the kindest way to be rid of it.

But Nurse Bupett had searched her conscience and found that she could not. Instead, she, in her turn, had begged forgiveness from God and put him to suckle on an imbecile woman that instead, he might live.

CHAPTER THREE

Esau's early years were coloured in shades of blue and grey: By the blue-and-grey gowns of the pauper-women, who would hiss and spit and lift away their own infants whenever he came near; by the greyed-out worsted stockings of the imbecile who watched over him, and by the blued, distempered walls of the female ward.

On what would be his fourth birthday, it was announced at breakfast that the workhouse was to be honoured by an inspection round by the lord, ladies and gentlemen of the Board of Guardians. It was to celebrate the opening of the new infirmary wing, and it would be led by their chairman, His Lordship, the Marquess of Ripon, himself.

In the weeks leading up to this momentous day, Matron rushed around the workhouse like the most zealous eschatologist, her panic increasing daily as she supervised every preparation. Their entire store of linen was laundered and freshly blued; all visible surfaces scrubbed and scrubbed again; fresh distemper put on the walls, and each and every pauper issued with a newly-sewn uniform.

Then, on the day appointed, the pauper-women and the children were lined up by their beds, reminded on pain of eternal damnation not to catch their uniforms on the freshly-blacked bed frames, and instructed to wait. Esau stood by his own blanket on the floor and waited too, sensing that something momentous was about to happen but unsure as to exactly what that thing might be.

A seeming age passed. Martha, the imbecile, began to mutter to herself, and then stopped and glanced inquisitively along the ward. There had been a muffle of voices from beyond the door, from beyond the edge of Esau's world, and the paupers stiffened and hushed. Esau felt a sharp cramp stabbing at his gut. The door opened and Matron entered the room. Her face was flushed crimson between her elaborately curled ringlets and she was speaking in a curiously high-pitched manner.

"This is the six-bed ward for infants and able-bodied women and girls above sixteen years of age, Your Lordship, Your Ladyship, sirs and madam." She curtsied to each class of guardian in turn, just exactly as she had been practicing in front of the big looking-glass by her bed.

"Very well, Matron, very well; everything here seems to be quite in order and perfectly satisfactory."

As he was speaking, George Robinson, the Lord Marquess of Ripon, seemed a little distracted. Both he and the Lady Ripon at his side were glancing down the ranks of paupers as if they might have been looking for something.

"And where is the hairy little fellow Mr Greenwood was telling us about?" Lord Ripon enquired.

Matron curtsied again.

"Oh, Esau you mean? He's right at the end, Your Lordship. We thought he would be happiest being close to

the stairs to the outside yard, with him being… you know…
half-monkey and all."

Lord Ripon raised his great, bushy eyebrows.

"Did you indeed?"

Esau stood, trembling, watching as the august party processed slowly down the ward, great ladies and gentlemen coming nearer and nearer, all with their eyes fixed down onto him. A second cramp caught his guts and twisted them, bending him double and forcing a cry from his lips.

"Oh, Lordy!" Martha the imbecile cackled suddenly through the dead silence, "It's gone an' shit itsen."

Lord Ripon held up his hand and the party halted.

"Your Lordship… Your Lordship, and Your Ladyship, I am… I am *quite mortified*."

Mrs Greenwood had once heard the words used by a great lady in Harrogate and in this moment they seemed to fit perfectly. "*Quite mortified*," she repeated for good measure.

She reached down and grasped a fistful of the longer hair at Esau's neck. With a sob, she forced him over, pushing his face again and again into the stinking mound.

"That's the ticket, Matron," a farmer-guardian growled approvingly, "Rub its nose in't. That'll larn it of its manners."

"Enough now," Lord Ripon snapped.

Matron pulled Esau upright. A gob of faeces clung for a moment to the matted hairs on his cheek, and then slowly peeled away and spattered onto the floor.

"The floors are stone and won't be spoiled from that," Ripon went on, "I dare say it will scrub away easily enough. Now, Mrs Greenwood, half-monkey, as you call him, or not, I see he has no cot to lie in."

Mrs Greenwood stared at the mess on the floor and shook her head in disbelief. A big ringlet at her temple suddenly dropped, giving her a curiously lopsided appearance.

"No, Your Lordship, begging your pardon, he hasn't, but that's only because there's no one as'll let their own child share with him. The inmates are all a bit a-feared of him, if truth be told, all excepting Martha but she has little Jenny with her already. Esau generally sleeps out on the landing and we bring his blanket in by day so he's not in folk's way."

Lady Ripon inclined her head towards her husband and whispered something. He nodded, and peered down his great grizzled beard towards Esau.

"Do you have a name, child?" he asked, not unkindly.

"Stand up straight." Matron nudged her knee into Esau's back. "Answer him directly and mind you call him 'Your Lordship'."

"Yes, sir, Your Lordship."

"That's a good little man. And what might that name be?"

"Dirty-Monkey, Your Lordship."

"More like Shit-Face now."

Martha's whispered observation could be heard distinctly over the paupers' sniggers and, as it transpired, her words were to prove prophetic.

George Robinson, Member of the Most Noble Order of the Garter, First Marquess of Ripon and Chairman of the Ripon Union Workhouse Board of Guardians raised himself up to his full height. He cast a glance towards Lady Ripon and wondered briefly whether it was the sight of the mess, or its stench, or the pungent scent from the delicate vinaigrette she was holding to her nose that had brought such tears to her eyes.

Then he said: "It seems quite apparent to me, Mrs Greenwood, and I have little doubt that my fellow guardians will agree." He turned his head to his left and to his right, just exactly as he might have done in the great House of Peers[3] itself, "That… Esau would be better suited to accommodation elsewhere than in a ward where all are hostile to him. Our wish is that you have him put somewhere where he might have a cell of his own, with a proper cot to sleep in. The vagrants' ward, perhaps? But mind that he isn't set to work there, or exposed more than is necessary to the other inmates. He is likely to have enough tribulation in his life without their tender attentions. Who knows what they might make of him."

An expression of deep pensiveness passed suddenly over his face and left it troubled and frowning. He reached up to touch a delicate golden pendant hanging at his breast. It was a locket, fashioned as a dove-descending, to commemorate his recent, and to some quite scandalous, conversion to Catholicism.

Lord Ripon turned and peered across the faces of his fellow guardians as they regarded him, at first without expression, but then with increasing curiosity. When he turned back, his benevolent, patriarchal air had gone, replaced by one of the gravest foreboding.

"The boy is no monkey, and he is most definitely not an ape. Every person here must remember that. He is hirsute, but that is all. I imagine his mother was also?"

"I beg your pardon, Your Lordship but I'm not right certain what that means," Matron said with a curtsey.

"My husband is asking if Esau's mother was hairy too," Henrietta, the Lady Ripon, explained.

"The women in the lying-in room said she was, Your Ladyship. Hairy as a Russian, according to Violet Wilcox, with a full set of whiskers."

She regarded the Marquess' own great, red beard. It was carefully brushed out so that it quivered with each movement of his chin.

"I thought as much," Lord Ripon declared. "Then I shall insist upon you and Mr Greenwood keeping a particular watch on him. There are dangers in this world far beyond the taunts and jeers of a work-yard. 'Satan transformeth himself into an angel of light,' Saint Paul reminds us, and you must be vigilant against those who would do the same – those who would make of the boy something he is not. Keep him away from the cathedral at all costs, Matron. Send him to chapel instead. Or better yet, bring him up as a Roman Catholic."

He felt the suddenly indignant glares of the other guardians on his back and ignored them.

"You must arrange for his schooling too, particularly in the Holy Scriptures, which may prove as much of a protection for him as they have for me. I am informed that he has wit beyond his years."

"He has, Your Lordship; why, he's as clever as the three wise monkeys all put together." Mrs Greenwood, instantly regretting her choice of words, bit her lip.

Lord Ripon grunted and then smiled down at the tiny figure cowering before him. He reached into his waistcoat pocket and pressed a silver half-crown into its hairy palm with a wink.

But his expression was dark as he led the party away, down the stairs, and out into the clean, fresh air of the exercise yard.

CHAPTER FOUR

It was said by the newspapers of the time that in illuminating its main street by means of water-gas, Mr Samson Fox had captured the very light of the Sun for Harrogate. What Mayor Fox perhaps did not understand, was that in order to provide fully for the needs of the town's visitors, it was necessary to keep at least some dark and shadowed places.

It is in one of these places, close to the entrance of the Bogs Valley Pleasure Gardens and not so very far away from Mr Wilberforce's freak show that a woman stands and pulls her shawl tight against the chill and the damp. She too is a mountebank, a street entertainer, but of the kind that creeps out at night to satisfy the needs of those for whom the jugglers and the acrobats are not quite enough.

A shadow, a silhouette blacker than the night around it, creeps towards her. At first glance, one might assume that it is human. Certainly it is as tall as a man, its height accentuated by its curious gait, which is high stepping and awkward, as if it might be unused to walking on such smooth and even pavements.

The woman hugs herself and leans forward, peering into the drifting fog. She catches sight of the figure and watches as it stamps towards her. Like an actress, she rehearses her lines, prepares her turn, and reaches into her pocket for the little bottle that will get her through the long hours until morning.

A scream – a woman's scream splits the night. It is smothered by a bellow of anger and of pain beyond belief and then once more there is silence. The mists seep back into the archway, and gently and mercifully cover the horror within.

CHAPTER FIVE

Even though he reads his Bible every single day until his eyes sting with tears and the blessed words swarm and merge until he can read them no longer, it seems that God does not listen to the pleas of his more lowly creations after all.

The morning after the fine gentleman came to look at him and to ask him his name, the half-door at the end of his stall was not thrown open as it always, always was. The music from the bandstand up the hill, which each morning seeped through the gaps in the twisted and broken planking and eased his soul, if soul he had, served only this day to mock him as he sat, cross-legged, in his nest and rocked backwards and forwards, to-and-fro. It was when they were playing the tune his master had once told him was called 'Heart of Oak' that the floor beneath him jerked.

And then it jerked again.

He froze. The van was moving. *They* were moving. They were moving-on. They must be. They were moving-on, away from this place with its crowds and its stinging farthings and its new masters that wanted to buy you for a thousand pounds. Yes, he could hear old Albert's hooves clattering on the hard stones of the road now. Thank the Lord! The van lurched to the side as it dropped from the kerb and the Bible slid from his lap, all at once reminding him of his faithless thoughts.

"Oh, God, Lord God, I am shorry, so shorry, that I did not believe on you."

He bowed his beast's head, so that the collar hurt his throat and he recited the Lord's Prayer, just as he knew they did each and every day in the chapel.

He had recited the Lord's Prayer a great many times and let the collar hurt his throat surely long enough to show God how truly sorry he was when the van stopped. Instead of Albert's iron-shod hooves, men's boots now clattered on the ground outside. They were Master's boots, he dearly hoped, his own master's. Please, Lord God, please let them be his own master's boots.

Their sound moved along the side of the van and a silhouette passed a knot-hole in the wall. It was surely his own master's silhouette that he has known these past seven years.

He was by the door now. But why was he there? Lord Jesus! Why was Master standing at the door and why was he sliding out the steps? They hadn't gone far. They hadn't gone nearly far enough to have moved-on.

The van creaked and swayed on its big iron leaf-springs and he heard the sound of Master's boots climbing the treads – five steps on the five treads. The long hairs on his shoulders lifted and tingled as he stared at the latch, as he waited for it to nod, and for the door to open.

Master might be drunk. Master might have the fierce, red eyes he had when he'd had whisky, when he would kick him and punch him and beat him with his chain.

Today they were moving on, so today wouldn't be a show day. Oh, Lord God! It wasn't a show day. Master always, always, got drunk when it wasn't a show day. He got as drunk as a boiled owl. Esau felt a bead of sweat picking its way between the hairs on his forehead and run down to sting his eye. He rubbed it away.

And then the latch did nod, and an instant later, the door did open and there was his master, standing there. Oh, thank you, thank you, Lord! His eyes were not fierce and red, like men's eyes got when they were angry with drink – like the tramp-major's eyes at the workhouse. Master's eyes were smiling as they had never smiled before. Thank the Lord that this day, he would not be beaten.

"Now then, Esau," his own master said, "I've sold you on. And a tidy sum I got for you too, I don't mind admitting. You're to have a new master now – a gentleman master." He laughed. "Mr Joseph Malkin is a man of *science* who is going to keep you in a *proper menagerie* and *observe* you – and make a king's ransom along the way, I shouldn't wonder." He laughed again. "But for a thousand pounds, he can stuff you and mount you on his parlour wall for all I care – you and that knackered, old horse with you."

Still chuckling, Wilberforce reached down and picked Esau's chain from the floor. He gathered a long, heavy loop in his hands and allowed it to sway menacingly by his feet.

The smile died.

"So hark you this," he said in a voice no louder than a hiss, "A thousand pounds is a thousand pounds. It'll set me up for life and I'll not be losing a farthing of it on any account of yours. So you'll do just exactly as I tell you and you'll mind your manners good and proper until I get my money and away. Or else, by God's truth, I'll kill you."

The chain cracked and growled on the floorboards and dared him not to believe it.

"Steady, man!" a new voice implored and Esau glanced across so quickly that the shackle on his collar jingled. It was the gentleman from yesterday who had asked him his name and who had tried to buy him – Lord God! who really must have bought him – for a thousand pounds. He was peering in through the open door, shaking his finger admonishingly, just as Mrs Nudds the schoolmistress used to do. "There is no need for brutality. It's God's creature too, after all's said and done."

Wilberforce snorted. He reached behind Esau's head and unhitched the chain from the wall.

"Did you hark what I said, Beast?"

Esau felt each plosive batting against the hairs of his ear in stale, beery breath.

"Aye, Mashter."

"Good, Esau, that's a good lad." Wilberforce's voice was bright now, loud and unnaturally cheery. "Now come with me and let us meet your new master. And you'll take care to remember exactly what I've told you."

The ape-man rose up on his long hind legs and was drawn out through the door and into the brightness beyond.

"Mashter!"

Esau cried out in the glorious, glorious sunlight, holding his great hands over his face to shield his eyes. The probing rays bathed him in warmth, bathed every part of him in wonderful, joyous comfort and in his beast's mind, there rose up the sudden image of Martha, the imbecile woman, lifting her own little Jenny into the light from the window and hugging her to her breast. The image faded, and he stumbled, dragged into the void by the iron will of his collar.

"Be careful, Tom Wilberforce; I won't have him damaged." It was his new master speaking again.

"It'd take a deal more than a trip down some steps to damage this one, begging your pardon, Mr Malkin. Don't you be fretting none on his account."

The collar was urging him to his feet now and he struggled up obediently. The blinding pain in his eyes was beginning to abate and tentatively he lifted away his hands and tried to look directly into the raw daylight. He blinked, and wiped his eyes, and blinked again, and the vivid colours and shapes coalesced into a face – his new master's face – gazing back at him and smiling as Your Lordship once smiled. Like *la belle Acarie*, Esau felt the circle in his palm where once a silver half-crown was pressed.

"Esau, my name is Malkin. Jo-seph Mal-kin," the gentleman repeated, tapping a fingertip on one of the fine pearl buttons of his waistcoat.

"Aye, shir," Esau the Beast acknowledged. He was transfixed; the iridescent sheen of the mother-of-pearl was beautiful beyond imagining. "Good day, Mashter Malkin."

"Upon my soul but he's intelligent, Thomas Wilberforce. Did you hear him just then? He's as smart as new green paint, learning my name and saying it, just like that."

He spread his arm towards a large and very handsome mansion, built in the classical style with a broad front pediment and great central dome.

"Esau, this is my home. It is called Bea-gle House and you are very welcome here. It will be your home too, in time, but for now, I am going to put you into one of my stables with Albert."

Esau glanced over at the elderly cob resting in his harness, one great whiskery ear turned back, alert to the tell-tale sounds that would augur yet another moving-on and still another day of toil. Then he realised that Master Joseph Malkin was still talking. It struck him as a very long time indeed for one person to have been speaking to him.

"Thomas Wilberforce tells me that you and the horse are great companions. I must say, that doesn't surprise me in the least. I've seen such friendships many times in the course of my various zoological expeditions. It is commonly known as *the fellowship of beasts*. So I'm sure you will feel much more settled being in with Albert until I can have a proper enclosure built to display you. So here, my fellow, come this way. Come this way, if you please."

The collar tugged and Esau allowed himself to be led away. The big flagstones on the ground felt chill on the soles of his feet, a chill that seemed to seep up his legs and slowly encircle his heart. He had taken a proper look at the house, at Beagle House, rising up before him and he remembered the shape of that great front gable all too well.

It was a workhouse!

He was going back to a workhouse, with its vagrants who spit at you, and its tramp-majors who come for you in the night, and its matrons, who push your face again and again into stinking mounds of shit.

"He's relieving himself, in his own trousers and all over my forecourt. I thought you said he was domesticated, Thomas Wilberforce?"

"It's just the excitement of seeing his new home, Mr Malkin." Wilberforce curled his lip and snatched back viciously on the chain. "Do you see? He's stopped already. He's gen'ly as clean as a vicar's cat, I swear he is."

"Well it's of no consequence, I suppose; the stone won't be spoiled from that and his trousers will need to be burned anyway. Come, help me to get him settled-in and then you can take your money and be on your way. Will I need a blacksmith to knock that collar off him?"

Wilberforce grasped Esau's scruff and pushed his head forward.

"There's a screw-lock on the shackle at the back of it. Do you see? It's over-complicated for him to work, but I've kept it well greased and it'll come off easily." He cast a doubtful glance at Malkin. "Are you sure you want to take his chain off though? A thousand pounds is a lot of money to lose if he takes himself off. And I don't give refunds."

Malkin waved away his words.

"I'm quite certain of it, thank you very much; chains are for fallen angels, not for creatures of God. And you needn't worry about him escaping; John Oates, my coachman, will be standing guard over him. He couldn't get away from him if he tried until Judgement Day."

He chuckled.

"But as I know very well: 'money sits atop the altar, that all may bow down to it', and if you're fretful over your thousand pounds, well now, let me give them to you directly. Then the risk of loss will be mine and mine alone."

A large bundle of banknotes was exchanged for a broad smirk and the swinging loop of chain, and Esau, still trembling, was led away to the side of the house. That was where the vagrants would be. He was a dirty, shit-faced monkey and just as at Ripon, he would be locked up with the tramps.

CHAPTER SIX

It seemed to Atticus Fox that the long-case clock in the hall must have become filled with treacle, so slowly was the pendulum marking away the seconds.

He glanced down from his window to the dainty cup-and-saucer his wife held on her lap. It was still brimming with tea, quite as full as it had been the last time he checked.

"Atticus," cried Lucie Fox, "You are quite setting my nerves on edge, hopping around like, like, some great dancing elephant. We are expected at two o'clock sharp and it won't even take us fifteen minutes to walk up to Beagle House."

Atticus retreated to his chair.

"I'm sorry, Lucie. It's just that I've never seen Joseph Malkin so excited in all the years I've known him. Proof-positive of the Theory of Natural Selection, he tells me. Proof-positive of it! What a day this could be."

"Well then we shouldn't want to spoil it by arriving early and having to suffer Lady Victoria for any longer than we need, should we?" Lucie sipped serenely at her tea.

Atticus swirled his own dregs around the bottom of his cup and his quivering reflection smiled up at him. His wife, as ever, was correct; it would be impertinent to arrive early, even at the house of his oldest friend. But it would be a folly greater still to be accosted by his wife.

In the event it took no more than ten minutes to walk up to the head of the Stray, that two hundred acres of open parkland, which served both to open up the heart of the town and to interconnect its many medicinal wells and springs. There, the Malkins' mansion rose up behind a terrace of modest stone cottages like some great, dome-headed schoolmaster peering over his schoolroom desk.

A barrel-organ turner stood, watching their approach. He began to wind his instrument and a tiny monkey, dressed in a little red tunic and hat, scampered down from its lid. It sat in the grass, tethered at its wrist by a lanyard, with a tin mug in its hand and its fangs bared. Atticus buffed a pair of pennies against his sleeve and threw them down for the creature to find. He returned the organ-grinder's grin with a polite tip of his hat and hurried past, before the monkey found his coins and came screeching and biting for more.

Ahead of them, a maid waited between the big carved-stone gateposts of a driveway, a shawl clutched at her throat against the ever-present breeze in this part of the town.

"Thank the lord," she muttered as the caterwaul from the street-organ abruptly ceased, then with a curtsey: "Good day to you, Mr and Mrs Fox. Master's expecting ye. He said it would save time if I took you both straight round to the stables, rather than going up to the house."

"That is an excellent idea, Susan," Lucie replied drily.

The parlour-maid grinned. Out of the butler's earshot, she, like most of the servants, referred to Mrs Payne-Malkin as 'Lady Victoria' and she rather suspected that, in private, the Foxes did too.

They followed her along the carriage-drive, to the side of the house, where the big York-stone flags gave way to the more utilitarian cobbles of the stable yard. A man they recognised as Mr Oates, Joseph Malkin's coachman, was standing stiffly and self-importantly by a loosebox door. He was holding an enormous gun against his shoulder as if he might have been a guardsman at Buckingham Palace.

"Lordy-me, look at him!" the maid muttered under her breath. Then as they got closer: "Mr Oates, I have Mr and Mrs Fox to see Master and that… that thing he has in there."

"The zoological specimen you mean, Susan? Very good, thank you; I'll take them from here." He stamped the hobnailed sole of his boot smartly against the cobblestones. "Good afternoon to you, Mr and Mrs Fox. If you would both care to go straight in, Mr Malkin will be pleased to receive you."

He rattled back the bolt of the stable door and swung it wide.

"Thank you, Mr Oates." Atticus' eyes were two huge circles of anticipation. He took his wife's arm and led her inside.

"Upon my word, Atticus and Lucie Fox!" Joseph Malkin pulled a big gold watch from the pocket of his jacket and caught the light from a tiny skylight onto its face. "Is it really that time already?"

He was standing ankle-deep in freshly-griped straw and it rustled softly as he turned and lifted down an unusually thick, pewter-topped walking cane from a hay rack.

"I am grateful to you for the loan of your cane, by-the-by, Atticus. *Thy rod and thy staff it surely comforted me.*" He paused to smile at his own joke, "Although I'm thankful I had no need of it in the end. You never can know though, can you?"

"Indeed you cannot," Atticus agreed.

"Is it a Masonic pattern? You mentioned it was once your father's? I couldn't find any marks."

"I had them polished out."

"Oh, I see. Why ever would you want to do that? But never mind; never mind. Lucie Fox, you must forgive me for dragging you round to my stables instead of sending you up to a comfortable chair in the drawing room as a proper host should. I recalled you were trained in nursing, you see, and I rather selfishly realised how valuable your insights into relative anatomies might be to my observations."

His grin faltered and became almost rueful.

"Besides which, you would have been entertaining yourself. The Dame – Victoria – is as thick as black treacle with my architect, Gerard Prêtre, and they are presently engaged in plotting how best they might outdo our friends and neighbours by making Beagle House the very grandest in Harrogate."

"I should be very happy to help you in any capacity I can, Mr Malkin." Lucie returned his smile graciously. "Now, I believe you have something quite astonishing to show us."

"Upon my word, but haven't I just!"

Malkin turned, and rather in the manner of Mr Wilberforce before him, said: "I appear to have come into the possession of what is, without doubt, the most marvellous discovery in the whole of the natural world.

"My dear friends, may I present to you nothing less than Alfred Russel Wallace and Charles Darwin's hitherto missing link, the very coming-together of mankind and the great apes."

With a flourish, he swept out his arm towards one corner of the loose box. There, an elderly cob was standing, dozing, with its great, whiskery head hanging low and its eyes half-closed. But then, beside its thick, mud-caked forelegs and peering up at them from a nest of straw, they saw it.

"Great heavens above!" Atticus cried and Lucie gasped in astonishment.

Malkin chuckled and clapped his hands together with delight.

"Yes, yes, exactly so; the beast is a wonder of creation, is it not? It has a given name too, which is Esau, and it will respond to simple commands. Please observe: Esau, I should like you to greet your visitors, Atticus Fox and Lucie Fox."

With incredible speed, the creature leaped to its feet and bellowed. The cob jerked its head in surprise, its hind hooves slipping and skiting on the straw-strewn bricks. Esau pounded his fists on his chest, and bellowed again, curling his lips back just exactly like the little monkey on the Stray but revealing not fangs but a handful of surprisingly small teeth between enormously thick gums.

"Esau, stop!" Malkin cried. The beast froze and stood watching them, its black eyes uncertain and suddenly wary. Oates exploded into the doorway, his great gun level and steady in his hands.

"You're quite safe," he declared, patting the barrel with his twisted and work-worn fingers, "This is a 4-bore elephant gun; it would stop a rhinoceros."

"Hold your fire John Oates," Malkin snapped, then: "Atticus Fox, Lucie Fox, please pay the closest attention to what I am about to say to you: Stand perfectly still; make no sudden movements, and do not, under any circumstances, stare directly into its eyes."

The seconds stretched out and, mindful of Joseph's warning, Atticus and Lucie made only brief, darting glances towards the animal. It was clearly some species of ape, and yet somehow, not an ape, fully two yards in height and covered in thick, unkempt hair. Unlike the smartly-dressed monkey on the Stray, Esau wore only filthy, ragged trousers, which barely reached to his knees.

As the seconds became minutes, and glancing warily between Oates' gun and Atticus' walking cane, the creature sank slowly back into its nest, pulled a heavy book from out of the straw, and began to rock to-and-fro.

"Good work, John Oates, thank you." Malkin cautiously reached out and pushed the thick muzzle of the coachman's gun down towards the floor. "You may step outside now."

"Very good, sir."

After the stable door had shut after him and they heard the bolts rattle home, Joseph added: "Excellent man, that. He came down from Halifax with Victoria – almost like a part of her wedding dowry. Cool as iron, an excellent shot, and a thoroughly competent naturalist in his own right. I insist he comes with me on all my expeditions."

He glanced over towards the beast.

"It seems our specimen has settled down again. Shall we proceed?"

Malkin drew a tiny, leather-bound notebook from his pocket and thumbed rapidly through the pages.

"Atticus, I shall appoint you as my official scientific recorder and ask that Lucie assists me with the observations."

He passed the notebook to Atticus, hooked his thumbs into his waistcoat pockets, and stretched tall on his heels.

"I hypothesise," he declaimed, as if he might have been addressing the great halls of Burlington House[4], "that our specimen represents an ancient, but hitherto unknown, species of man. I propose to name this species *Homo sylvestris* – the wild-man."

"Bravo!" Atticus murmured as he scribbled furiously in the notebook and Malkin beamed.

"We have an adult male; John Oates and I measured it earlier today at precisely six feet in length between pegs. It is covered entirely in dark hair, which is around four inches in length, except around the head and neck, where it is longer, approximately eight inches long, and the palms of the hands and soles of the feet, where there is none. The eyes have dark-brown irises – very dark-brown irises – verging indeed, almost on black. And, Atticus, you might want to make a particular note of this: The specimen possesses visible, white *sclera*, which is what Lucie Fox will know is more commonly called the whites-of-the-eye. This is wholly untypical of the great apes and rather more characteristic of the human eye. It also appears to possess a very high degree of intelligence, this being amply demonstrated by its ability both to read English and also to speak simple words of the language, although with poor enunciation."

"Quite incredible," Atticus exclaimed, shaking his head in wonderment.

"Indeed it is, and furthermore, John Oates and I have observed that it walks in an upright fashion with little, or indeed no, reliance upon its knuckles for support."

Malkin unhooked a thumb from his waistcoat and held up a grave and learned forefinger.

"I declare that the species *Homo sylvestris* is indeed the missing intermediate link between the higher orders of primates and man himself, which Charles Darwin, Alfred Russel Wallace and others have suggested previously in their own scientific works."

"This is a sensation, Joseph." Atticus was breathing heavily, aware that here, in this little, leather-bound notebook, he was recording nothing less than an entirely new chapter of human history. It was, in its way, perhaps a greater scientific work even than Darwin's *On the Origin of Species.*

"Sensational, incredible, you call it? Yes, Atticus Fox, it is all of that, and more. It could be surpassed only, perhaps, by the discovery of the link between mankind and God himself." Malkin stretched out his hand towards the figure, sitting cross-legged in the straw. "And yet you have the evidence there, before your own eyes."

"His teeth are in poor condition," Lucie remarked. "Has he been ill-used in the past, do you know?"

"I shouldn't be surprised," Malkin replied, "The fellow I bought him from was an oaf. He wouldn't have been averse to giving him a thrashing on the least pretext. He had him for seven years all told, so that is plenty enough time for him to have knocked out a tooth or two. Those which remain, however, point us to the conclusion that *Homo sylvestris* is omnivorous in habit. You might like to make a note of that too, Atticus."

Atticus nodded as he began to write once more.

"And what is that book he has?" Lucie asked.

Malkin returned his thumb to his waistcoat pocket, rocked back on his heels and grinned. "Why don't you ask it yourself, Lucie Fox? I imagine you might be surprised by its reply."

Very slowly and deliberately, Lucie sank down until she was crouching in the straw, on a level with the creature's face. And although she recalled very well Joseph's warning against looking directly into its gaze, its eyes were so starkly white against the hair of its face, their irises and pupils so very dark and fathomless, that she could scarcely avoid it.

"Esau, my name is Mrs Fox." Her voice was soft, barely more than a murmur.

"I know that. Good day, Mishtresh Fox," it replied.

"Good Lord!" Atticus muttered from somewhere behind her.

"A very good day to you too, Esau. Tell me please: what is the book you have?"

The ape-man looked down at the book resting in his lap and slowly, almost reluctantly, turned it over. The sunlight streaming in through the skylight above crept across the greasy, worn leather of the binding and caught on letters, which once might have been gilt. Lucie read:

'THE NEW TESTAMENT
of our Lord and Saviour
JESUS CHRIST

"Oh, Esau, it's a Bible!"

"There now, what did I say?" Malkin said. "It would appear that even our distant evolutionary cousins possess a sense of the divine. And what is more, he can read it too."

"Can you, Esau? Can you read your Bible to me?" Lucie asked.

The animal nodded its great, shaggy head. It laid the book carefully, almost reverently, across its lap, where the cotton of its trousers was worn smooth and thin, and lifted up the cover. The pages fell open to the Gospel of St Matthew.

"And many women," he read, *"were there beholding afar off, which followed Jeshush from Galilee. Among which wash… Mary Magdalene.*

"Among which wash Mary Magdalene," it repeated softly, as if to itself, and fell into a brooding silence, staring at the page.

It glanced up at the sudden rattle of bolts being slid back.

The slender silhouette of a young woman was standing in the open doorway. The afternoon Sun shone across her elaborately-braided, reddish-blonde hair and glinted off a silver tea tray she carried in her hands.

"Mary, Mary, it'sh you!" the creature cried.

The girl squealed and shied back and the teacups on the tray began to rattle on their saucers.

"Father, that's the monster! Get it away from me. It will attack me again. It believes I'm—"

"Alice, it will not." Joseph strode towards his daughter. "You are perfectly safe. John Oates is here and, as you can see, he has his gun."

"Aye, I'm here right enough, Miss Alice."

Joseph lifted the tray from Alice's trembling hands and the cups stilled.

"Mary!" The beast was on its feet now, towering over Lucie. It pressed a hairy finger against the crumpled page of its Bible and held it up, offering it for them to see.

"Mary," it repeated, "Mary".

"But I'm not Mary," the girl stammered, "My name is Alice – Alice Victoria Malkin."

"Esau, please sit down," ordered Joseph sternly.

Esau, his finger still pressed against the page, sank back once again into his nest. If he had been human, the expression in his eyes must surely have been of confusion.

As he set the tea tray down across the broad rim of an iron drinking bowl, Joseph's own expression held something of that same, if not confusion, then most certainly puzzlement.

He said: "Esau, this is my own daughter Alice. A-lice. She told me you shouted that same name at her yesterday, when she came to see you in the freak show. Why do you call her Mary? Does she perhaps remind you of someone with that name?"

The creature lifted up its Bible once again and pointed to the same portion of the text, where the paper was stained and grimy with finger marks.

"She ish Mary Magdalene."

"Mary *Magdalene*? No, no, Esau, my daughter is most certainly not Mary Magdalene." He picked up a pair of sugar-nips and chuckled. "She lived almost two thousand years ago. That is long before either you or I were born, and she was what we would call an Israelite. That means she would have had black hair and dark eyes. My daughter, as you can see for yourself, has blonde hair and eyes of the clearest blue."

"Yet in art, St Mary Magdalene is invariably depicted as having blonde or red hair," Atticus interrupted, "Just look at Régnier, Reni, Titian, and the like."

Esau nodded excitedly. "You see, Mashter? It ish her. I shore her in chapel; I shore Mary's shtatue there."

"Hush now, calm yourself," Malkin said. "We shan't talk about it now."

"It ish her!" Esau insisted, desperation, anger even, edging his tone.

Experienced in the ways of beasts, Malkin immediately dropped his eyes to the straw and began to retreat slowly towards the door.

"John Oates," he called in a deliberately calm and matter-of-fact tone, "Would you be kind enough to come in here? The specimen is becoming agitated again."

With the tiniest of movements he beckoned the Foxes to follow him out into the yard.

It was a relief to be outside and able to take a break from the charged and tensioned atmosphere of the loose-box.

"He was becoming much too excited to observe either usefully or safely," Malkin observed. "It isn't really surprising, I suppose, with him being so soon into his new home. I think it best if we leave him with John Oates for the rest of the day, in the dark and the quiet, to calm down properly. Alice, my dear, would you be kind enough to ask Cook to send up a fresh brew of tea? Atticus and Lucie Fox and I can finish writing up our initial observations in my study."

It seemed that, like Sisyphus, Joseph Malkin performed his labours at height, and his private study was at the head of a spiral staircase that wound its way up to the very top of the house.

'I work with my head in the clouds,' he remarked more than once during their steep climb and each time he did, Atticus and Lucie chuckled dutifully in response.

A final turn brought them to a landing and a handsome teak door on which the words 'J.B. Malkin, Naturalist, Explorer & Friend', were picked out in black enamel across the polished brass of a plaque.

Malkin pulled a fob chain from his waistcoat pocket. There was a key on its end, which turned smoothly in the lock. The door swung away; the plaque glinted, and they were suddenly drenched in bright sunlight. For the second time that afternoon, Atticus and Lucie Fox had cause to gasp. For they were staring into an octagonal room, surrounded on all sides by windows and glass-topped specimen tables so that the light bounced hither and thither as if it were not a gentleman's study at all, but an enormous magic lantern. The lantern slides were nothing less than a dramatic panorama of Harrogate itself.

"I cannot deny but that it is a delightful place in which to work," Malkin said, waving them towards a pair of big Windsor arm-chairs. He pulled a captain's chair out from beneath an enormous, mahogany writing bureau and dropped heavily into it. "I may sit here at my desk and contemplate the Heavens, or equally, turn and watch the mundane world go about its own affairs. Atticus, I had quite forgotten you have never been up here before."

He leaned back comfortably in his chair, folded his hands behind his head and grinned.

"So, I seem to have bagged myself a wild-man."

"It really is quite extraordinary," Atticus agreed, "And I can still scarcely believe it. You have, at a single stroke, not only proven the truth of the theory of evolution, but solved the riddle of the wild-man legends we were speaking about just the other week: the yetis, woodwose, satyrs and the like. There'll be a Fellowship of the Royal Society[4] in this for you, Joseph, even a knighthood, I shouldn't wonder."

He glanced to his wife for her agreement, but Lucie instead stood and turned to the window. She stared out over the roofs of the little terrace of cottages, to the broad and verdant acres of the Stray beyond.

"Gerard Prêtre, my architect, will design an enclosure for him in the grounds here," Malkin said, "Something classical, I think, and very grand, as befits a modern wonder of the world. That will delight the Dame. It will have its own lecture hall and a well-stocked library for all the naturalists and scientists who will come to study it – yes, and surely marvel at it too."

"He is intelligent, Joseph," Atticus said, "Just as you said he was, but I never dreamed we should be able to converse with him in English."

"He can speak – after a fashion. His enunciation is poor, but after all's said and done, he's little higher than a monkey, so one cannot really complain."

Lucie turned back from her window. She seemed troubled and was biting her lip.

"How well would he speak if he had a full set of teeth, do you think, Mr Malkin?"

Malkin sat up straight in his chair.

"You ask a good question there, Lucie Fox, a very good question actually. How do you suppose we might find out?"

"By having a dentist make him a set of replacements," Lucie replied curtly.

"Get him a set of Waterloo teeth? Would that be safe do you think – putting the teeth of dead soldiers into what is a completely different species?"

Lucie turned back to her window.

"I really don't believe there is a great deal of difference between Esau and the people walking across the Stray down there – apart from his hair of course. I have no doubt whatever that it would be perfectly safe."

"Then the question is easily enough answered, or it would be if I could find a dentist brave enough to work inside his mouth."

Lucie did not reply immediately, and the silence that followed was filled by an inexplicable tension, a sudden discomfiture that seemed to build rather than ease.

Malkin said: "Esau's hair is much too matted to be able to groom easily. It must be very unpleasant for him. I was rather hoping you both might assist me with clipping the worst of it away. That will be tomorrow now of course, when John Oates has him pacified again."

Atticus glanced to Lucie but she was still looking out through her window, seemingly distracted. Then he too heard the faint sounds of conversation, which seemed to be coming from right outside the glass.

Malkin laughed. "You would be astonished at what carries up to me here in my eyrie: the servants' chatter;

visitors whispering about me at my door; those dreadful barrel-organ grinders. Unless I am much mistaken, that is the voice of the Dame herself."

Lucie leaned forward over a cabinet, filled with row upon row of neatly-pinned scarab beetles, and peered down into the front gardens of the house. He was right. Victoria Payne-Malkin, Joseph's large and formidable wife, was standing in the driveway in animated conversation with a small and precise-looking gentleman. She was pointing towards the house and gesticulating, and the man was nodding sagely in agreement.

"We would be delighted to help you to groom him, Joseph, of course," Lucie heard Atticus say behind her.

"I had intended to crop his head in any event to enable a proper phrenological examination of his cranium," Joseph explained. "This is the greatest opportunity to ascertain how the various organs of the brain have developed throughout the course of man's evolution. Don't you agree, Lucie Fox?"

Again Lucie did not reply immediately. Her breath pulsed on the window glass like the tongue of a serpent.

"You don't hold with phrenology then, I take it?"

The mist pulsed again. Then she said: "I do not, as it happens, Mr Malkin, but you are the naturalist, and you are the one who has paid a thousand pounds for him. You may undertake any test you please."

Malkin nodded cannily.

"Yes, that is true, of course. But I have been giving the matter no little thought and I believe that a detailed phrenological examination would be quite appropriate in this case. It all comes down, do you see, to whether or not *Homo sylvestris* possesses a soul."

Lucie turned at last from her window.

"Whether he possesses a soul, Mr Malkin?"

"Yes, Lucie Fox, a soul."

Joseph Malkin rose to his feet and began to pace slowly back and forth in front of his desk, and across the face of the great dome that dominated the view from the window behind it.

"Consider the science of phrenology and how the careful examination of a person's cranium, his skull, enables us to determine the various aspects of his character. Now the Holy Scriptures tell us, and indeed it would seem self-evident, that the very heart of a man – his character – must be contained within his soul, which, being in spirit form, cannot possess 'bumps', or organs, of Benevolence, of Wit, or of any other aspect of personality for that matter. A phrenological examination in that case would patently be of no use whatever. But a creature *without a soul* would necessarily possess such organs. It would therefore be quite reasonable to conclude that a skilled phrenologist should be able to determine a very great deal."

"That is an… interesting view," Lucie conceded.

Malkin nodded graciously. "Thank you, I knew a bluestocking[5] such as you would see the force of the argument. One should never be too swift to dismiss the old sciences just because they happen to be out of fashion. So that is all settled; I shall expect you both at ten o'clock sharp, tomorrow morning."

CHAPTER SEVEN

"Well, upon my word, what about that?" Atticus Fox was almost dancing with excitement as they made their way back towards their own house in the middle of town. "The discovery of *Homo sylvestris*, Lucie: the very intermediate link itself."

"Hmm," his wife replied.

"Joseph will go down in history for this. You mark my words. I don't suppose a Quaker would accept a knighthood, but he must receive some sort of medal for it, and at the very least, a Fellowship of the Royal Society."

Lucie did not answer him.

"Is something wrong, my dearest?"

His wife shrugged, and they walked a little further in awkward silence.

"Are you concerned about clipping the wild-man tomorrow? I'm sure Joseph and I could manage—"

"No, Atticus, I'm not concerned about clipping him."

"Then is it this business with the phrenologist? I agree with you that it's all utter bunkum, but—"

"Atticus!"

Lucie stopped by the great boundary-stone that marked the meeting of the Ripon and Leeds turnpike roads and pursed her lips. Her expression was set as hard as the grit-stone behind her.

"Atticus. Esau may very well represent a new species of humanity; I don't pretend to be a naturalist, and I really couldn't say either way. It's just that, well, it's just that he seems so very much like us. His eyes especially – he has such human eyes."

"But he *is* a human, Lucie, just as we are, and even, dare I say it, just as Victoria Malkin is."

Lucie's expression softened a little at that.

"He's a human," Atticus went on, "in precisely the same way as, let me see, a jackal and a dog are both species of *Canis*."

"And Joseph has bought him just exactly as he might buy a dog," Lucie retorted. "If Esau really is human, as you say he is, then that would make him nothing more than a slave."

Atticus scratched awkwardly at the side of his chin.

"Yes, I suppose it might at that. But our task is to help Joseph to determine just how much like us Esau really is, underneath that matted coat of his. If it transpires that he is very much more human than ape; if, as Malkin would say, he could be considered to possess a soul, then I'm certain he will do the very best for him. Joseph Malkin is not one to allow the light which science might shine on the physical, to take anything away from the moral."

They walked the rest of the way to their home in silence, as each mused on the truth of that.

As Atticus Fox took off his cap and dropped his cane with a clang into the stick-stand in the hallway, Mrs Morris, their housekeeper, was suddenly by his side, pecking at his coat-sleeve.

"Sir, ma'am, you have callers. It's the mayor, and he has a policeman with him."

"The mayor!" whispered Lucie, "Did he say what they—"

"ATTICUS FOX, IS THAT YOU JUST COME IN?"

Atticus winced. Samson Fox, the Worshipful, the Mayor of Harrogate, was generally reckoned to possess the biggest bark in Yorkshire. If Atticus had not just pushed shut their big front door, its familiar boom echoing down the stairs and along their hallway would have slammed it every bit as surely.

"ATTICUS?"

"Yes, yes, it is us, Samson. Good day to you. We shall be up directly."

Atticus straightened his waistcoat, took a long, calming breath, and made his way up the stairs to their drawing room. There, his distant cousin Samson Fox, industrialist, millionaire and thrice mayor of Harrogate, stood in front of their fireplace with its brass double-fireguard of his own design. He was standing with his feet wide apart and his great hands gripping the lapels of his jacket, somehow seeming to fill every last inch of the room with his presence. A second man, as physically large as Samson and, if anything, even stockier, seemed dwarfed in comparison. As Atticus and Lucie entered, he heaved himself out of his armchair and stood expectantly.

"Aha, Fox, there you are," Samson growled. "We were beginning to wonder if you might have gone off on another of your little pleasure-excursions. *Quo Fata vocant* and all that, eh?"

He grinned.

"And Lucie. Welcome home, m' dear. How do you do, eh?"

"Quite well, Samson, I thank you."

The mayor reached out and planted a hand on the second man's shoulder.

"This is Detective Inspector Douglas of the West Riding Constabulary, Harrogate Division. Douglas, may I introduce my cousins, Atticus and Mrs Fox."

"We have met upon a previous occasion, Your Worship. It was in the matter of the murder of Alfred Roberts, back in 1890, as I recollect. Good day to you, Mr and Mrs Fox." Douglas nodded his head curtly in greeting.

Samson lifted his hand and waved it towards a group of armchairs, set around a large and splendid, marble chess set.

"Do take a seat, everyone; I've already asked your Mrs Morris to bring tea the instant you returned. But, I'm not here for a social call, eh. Douglas and I are here on matters of the greatest importance."

"What matters would they be, Samson?" Lucie asked.

Samson Fox stood patiently in front of the fireplace and waited until they had each taken a chair before he answered.

"Why, the terrible business of this beast that walks amongst us, of course. You'll have heard about it, I expect?"

Atticus glanced across to Lucie and saw his own alarm reflected in her expression.

"We have, Samson," she replied, "but we—"

"I know, I know. Strictly speaking, this is a job for Douglas here, and his fellows at Raglan Street. I do know that, of course, but then as mayor, I also know that our town lives or dies by its visitors. The very last thing we need is a brutal murderer in our midst, eh. The woman may well have been of ill repute but that fact will serve only to sully our reputation even further."

He pushed out his great chest.

"Besides which, an attempt at murder is an attempt at murder. Isn't that so, Douglas?"

"Indeed it is, Your Worship."

For several seconds, the hiss of the fire and the steady ticking of the clock above it were the only sounds in the room.

"What woman?" Atticus asked.

"Why, the woman who was attacked last night, of course, butchered to within an inch of her life in de Medici's bath-chair yard. It couldn't have been in a worse place, smack-bang between the hotels, the pump room and the pleasure gardens. A lamplighter discovered her, close to death. He picked her up and carried her in his arms over to the Bath Hospital, but by then she wasn't in any state to tell 'em much more than her name – Hannah, I believe it was – and that she'd been attacked by some kind of a hideous beast. After that, she became insensible. I thought you said you'd heard about it, eh?"

Samson surveyed him. His heavily-creased eyebrows gave him a penetrating, quizzical air and Atticus reddened.

"I'm sorry, Samson, we were speaking about different b—, about different things entirely. Lucie and I have been up at Joseph Malkin's place for most of the day and we have heard nothing."

The mayor's eyes narrowed.

"Hmm, I see. Well, police work or not, you've both demonstrated some aptitude for turning up murderers, so I want you to work alongside Douglas and his men in finding this man and I want you to begin right away. The *Herald* comes out on Wednesday and the *Advertiser* on Saturday. I'm already hearing this man being referred to as the 'Beast of the Bogs Valley' and that's exactly the sort of name that sticks. What I do not want is for the newspapers to get hold of it and in one week destroy what has taken a hundred years to build. I will pay your account from my own purse."

Atticus opened his mouth as if to speak but was interrupted by a gentle tapping on the door.

"Come in," Samson bellowed and the brass doorknob obediently twisted.

"Ah, here is our tea, thank you, Mrs Morris, and upon my soul, dainty-cakes too."

"We accept the commission, of course, Samson," Lucie said as Mrs Morris set down the tray. She could not recollect ever having seen their housekeeper quite so flustered.

Atticus said: "As Inspector Douglas would doubtless agree, time, in any manner of investigation, is always of the essence. We shall visit the place of this attack this evening and then, depending upon what we might discover there, go up directly to the Bath Hospital."

"What have you managed to glean already, Mr Douglas?" Lucie asked.

Douglas accepted a teacup from Mrs Morris and glowered over the dainty flowers around its rim as he sipped at the scalding liquid.

"Yes, time is of the essence," he muttered into the porcelain, then: "The hospital called us by telephone last night; around ten o'clock it was, or shortly before. They had been obliged to admit a female with formidable wounds to her face and body. I say obliged, because, as you'll doubtless know already, the Royal Bath Hospital is not appointed for dealing with injuries. But she had bled a great deal and was very weak and they dared not move her further.

"The doctor bound her wounds and managed to staunch the bleeding and she was still just about conscious when I arrived with my Sergeant Hainsworth, the morphine having only just been administered. All we could get out of her was that her attacker was a monster. She kept screaming it over and over again."

He took a sip of his tea, and then another.

"Twenty years and more I've had in the constabulary, Mr and Mrs Fox, and in that time, I've seen all manner of things. But I don't mind admitting that it quite gave me the shivers to listen to the poor woman."

"Have you spoken with the lamplighter who found her?" Atticus asked him.

Douglas cast a glance towards Samson.

"No," he admitted, "We've not been able to as yet. He left the hospital directly after he dropped the woman off, anxious to get his lamps lit, so he told them. But no doubt he'll be back on duty this evening and we'll make certain to speak with him before the night's out."

"Tell 'em about this freak show, Douglas," Samson ordered, his mouth full of cake.

"Yes of course, Your Worship. There has been an itinerant freak show set-up of late, down in Low Harrogate, next to the Punch and Judy stall. You might even have seen it from your window there. We have received a large number of complaints concerning it, both from the other street entertainers and from the public. The principal exhibit, a so-called half-man-half-ape, has been inclined to attack female members of the audience. There have been no actual injuries, so far as we are aware, but that's not been for the want of it trying. Rather suspiciously, it would seem to me, the proprietor of the show, one Thomas Wilberforce, together with his horse and van, have conspired to vanish into thin air."

Atticus looked over to the window.

"The light is fast fading," he remarked.

Samson took a deep gulp of his tea and clattered the delicate cup onto its saucer.

"Indeed it is, Cousin Atticus and there is never a time like the present time, as they say, eh. Douglas, drink up, man! Take Mr and Mrs Fox to the place where this poor woman was attacked before it gets too dark to see aught. Show 'em whereabouts this freak show was too, while you're at it, and be sure to render them every assistance."

He nodded his head towards the side-table.

"And you might care to take a dainty with you. It'll be a long night for you all, I shouldn't wonder."

CHAPTER EIGHT

Detective Inspector Douglas hastened down the steep hill that dropped from Prospect Place into Low Harrogate like a fast-pacing bear. Atticus, with his long legs, kept up with him easily, but Lucie was forced to bustle.

"Mark you this, Fox," Douglas exclaimed suddenly, "If I hadn't already planned on coming down here to speak with my sergeant, I wouldn't be wasting police time on you, Samson Fox or no Samson Fox."

"It is very helpful of you," said Lucie.

"Helpful to you perhaps but not to me," Douglas retorted. His eyes were fixed straight ahead. "Speaking plainly, my time would be far better employed in effecting the capture of this Bogs Valley Beast than in pandering around after a pair of amateur detectives, rendering them *every assistance*." He hesitated for a moment, casting Atticus a sideways glance. "And I am mindful that you are a close relation of His Worship."

"A distant cousin only," Atticus cried, and a man leading a pair of donkeys along the pavement opposite stopped to stare, "Our grandfathers were brothers. And you might recollect that he is paying us from his own pocket."

"Looking to buy the mayor's chain for another year, I shouldn't wonder. Cheap at half the price. Never backwards in coming forwards isn't the great Samson Fox, when it suits his purpose."

Lucie said: "I think that is very unfair of you, Mr Douglas."

"We'll see."

Douglas slowed to cross the road at the bottom of the hill.

"Anyway, here we are. The girl was attacked over yonder, in the entrance to de Medici's bath-chair yard. I'm surprised you didn't hear her screams from your parlour."

He turned and pointed across the Stray, to where a rectangular patch of chlorotic, yellow grass was littered with empty bottles and a blackened ring of stones.

"And just over there was where this freak show, Wilberforce's Wonders of the Modern World, was parked until this morning. The biggest wonder of them all would be if the ape-man *wasn't* what did for the poor woman."

Atticus threw a furtive glance towards Lucie, but it was Douglas, shrewd as a serpent and twenty years and more a policeman, who caught it.

"What is it?" he asked. "You know something about this, don't you?"

"We know nothing for sure, Mr Douglas," Lucie replied.

"I can read faces like your husband can read Latin, Mrs Fox and something's afoot. Has this Wilberforce conveniently died before he can be brought to trial, just like the old girl who did for Alfred Roberts? Another case solved by the extraordinary A&L Fox; is that what it is?"

"It is nothing of the sort." Lucie cut across his philippic. "And bickering amongst ourselves will get us nowhere. When we do discover something, I promise that you will be the first to know. Now, please, assist us by telling us exactly what you found here."

"Very well." Douglas nodded towards the entrance to the bath-chair yard. "When old de Medici came to open up this morning, he discovered it had been turned into a charnel house. The whole of the archway was spattered in blood; up the walls, across the cobblestones, it was even running down the gully as far as the drain there."

He pointed towards one of the ornate, wrought-iron grills that covered the drain tops in this part of town.

"There was a fair lot of broken glass too, from a broken ether bottle. By his account, it took two men and a couple of dozen pails of water to wash it all away. It was the broken bottle this Bogs Valley Beast used to make his attack on the woman. A right mess he made of her too. If she does survive, and the doctors were rather doubtful on that score, well, she might be obliged to lower her rates, if you know what I mean."

Atticus grimaced and Lucie scowled.

"Did you recover any pieces of the bottle, the neck perhaps, to examine for finger-prints?" Lucie asked.

"We tried to, of course, Mrs Fox. Famous, privately-commissioned investigators are not the only people to apply science to their methods; we humble policemen do so too, when the occasion suits. There was no sign of it, so either the glass got swilled away with the blood, or else this Beast threw it away somewhere. Dr Wormald at the hospital told us the woman had a bottle of water in her pocket, so that would be in line with her being an ether addict."

He pulled a watch from his breast pocket and glanced at the face.

"Right then, that's every assistance dutifully rendered; I'm going to speak to my sergeant now, to see if he's managed to get anything out of this lamp-man. If you do happen to stumble across anything of interest, send word up to Raglan Street station for my attention. Have it marked 'Of Pressing Importance'. I wish you both a good evening."

Detective Inspector Douglas pinched the brim of his billycock hat and nodded, and left them to their wits.

Esau sits in his nest of straw, and stares up at the swarms of dust, twisting and turning in the column of light from the tiny roof-window. It is a curious feeling, to be sitting once again with a locked door before him and a chilly wall of brick at his back. Not since the workhouse has he known it, and with the cold, the memories of that place are seeping back into his blood.

His fingertips trace the broad track of flattened hair at his throat, where the iron collar no longer sits and where the restraints sat before it. Esau remembers the leather straps of the restraints, and he recalls the tramp-major.

The tramp-major was the man put in charge of the vagrants, the in-and-outs, at the workhouse. He had a cell of his own, a large and comfortable cell, with a table and a bed and a nice hot stove. By day, he would set the in-and-outs to work, breaking big stones into little stones or picking old ropes into great piles of oakum. But by night, he would choose the youngest, the least ugly tramp woman, to take to his cell, and he would keep them there until morning.

When he was minded to sport, Tramp-major would set him, Esau, running through the work sheds – a driven hare with no Fair Law[6]. He would laugh as the vagrants pelted him with newly-broken stones or lashed at him with ropes. He would laugh, and he would dance until he spat.

At other times, and always at night, when the women were too old or too ugly even for him, Tramp-major would come to his, to Esau's, cell. On those nights, the door would creak wide, and in the shadows of the corridor he would be there, wheezing and rasping. Tramp-major did not laugh on those nights, and nor did he dance. He would be breathless and staring, and he would do unspeakable things.

Atticus and Lucie Fox stood side-by-side and gazed about themselves. It was as if they were seeing these places: the Irongate Bridge Road, the Montpellier Stray, and the narrow alley that led into Mr de Medici's bath-chair yard, for the very first time instead of perhaps the thousandth. They seemed so very different tonight, somehow menacing and sinister, like bosom comrades who had betrayed them. Even the sign bearing George de Medici's name and a picture of a bath-chair was too gaudy, altogether too gay, so that it all but mocked their presence here. A second sign beneath it, this more solemn and businesslike, announced the hire rates. They were one shilling and thruppence for the first hour and four-pence for each subsequent quarter, and they were reminded harrowingly of the reason the woman would have been standing in its shadow.

Side-by-side they advanced into the arch, into the alley, with its shadow of death, sensing a newly-awakened evil within. They cast their eyes back and forth; between the cobblestones, across the bricks, searching for anything, anything at all, that might have survived Mr de Medici's deluges of water. But from the bath-chair store with the little office above, all the way to the drain-cover with its faint wisps of vapour rising from between the bars, there was nothing. Mr de Medici, solicitous, no doubt, of the celebrated pneumatic tyres of his chairs, must have taken great care to remove even the tiniest shards of glass.

"To the hospital then," said Lucie grimly.

Atticus nodded.

"Mr de Medici has left not the smallest vestige for us here, so yes, that must be where our time will best be served tonight."

He adjusted the broad strap of their investigations bag on his shoulder and turned with his wife towards the forest of fast-deepening shadows that was Harrogate's renowned Bogs Valley Pleasure Garden.

"Oh, Mr Fox, Mr Fox, wait just a minute, if ye please."

A stout, elderly lady in a white apron and poke bonnet was hobbling towards them. She was leaning on a long staff, which tapped loudly on the asphalt surface of the road.

"Good day to you, Betty," Atticus cried. "But you are out good and late this evening."

"I were just in t' pump room, getting things a-ready for the morrow, Mr Fox; you know how busy we genny get of a weekend."

"Lucie, may I introduce Mrs Betty Barber, volunteer server at the Royal Pump Room, and the present holder of the title: Queen of the Harrogate Wells. Betty, this is my wife Mrs Fox."

Betty dropped into a clumsy and awkward curtsey and hauled herself back up on her staff. Lucie noticed that the top was in the form of a large brass ladle.

"I have heard a great deal about you and I am very pleased to finally make your acquaintance, Mrs Barber," she said.

Betty grinned, her lips parting to reveal a solitary tooth on each of her gums.

"Call me Betty, Mrs Fox, everyone else does. Are y' here about poor Sarah the Dragon?"

"We are here about a lady who was attacked last night in the entrance to the bath-chair yard," Lucie replied, "We were told her name was Hannah."

Betty lifted her free shoulder in a shrug.

"Aye, well Sarah used a few different names, dependin' on how the mood took 'er – an' whether or not the rent man was due. Sarah an' Hannah an' Mary mostly. I doubt even she remembers which one she was christened wi'. Did he do for her in the end?"

"She remains at the Royal Bath Hospital, where Mr Fox and I are going now," said Lucie. "We have been told that she is still alive although very badly injured."

"Did you see or hear anything of what happened to her, Betty?" Atticus asked.

The old woman glanced around, squinting for several moments deep into the shadows of the pleasure gardens. Then she nodded. "Aye, I did an' all. It were about five-and-twenty past nine, and I were scrubbin' out t' floor o' the pump room ready for t' mornin'. I saw Sarah, or whatever you want to call her, waitin' in t' entrance o' the bath-chair yard. I took particular notice because she ain't genny there on a Thursday, with it being a mass day up at St Roberts and she a Catholic an' all."

Betty glanced again towards the wooden gates of the pleasure garden.

"And then ah heard a clappin' and a slappin' on t' road. It were just exactly like this…"

Wedging the bowl of the ladle into her armpit, she clapped her hands together, beating time like a master of ceremonies at a music hall.

"…and a gaspin' and a groanin' like someone were in right bad pain. Anyways, I straightened mysen up quicksmart and looked ower, and there was a man. He was wearing a hood and walkin' very peculiar, kicking his feet out against 'is coat and slappin' them down on t' road like he were drunk. He went straight for Sarah an' pushed her back into t' yard. I heard her screamin' fit to wake the dead, but by the time I'd managed to get out an' ower there, he had stuck her wi' her own ether bottle an' vanished back into t' gardens."

"I heard she was injured with an ether bottle," Lucie said. "Sarah is an addict then?"

Betty nodded. "Oh, aye, aye she is. Once upon a time she liked to take a drop or two o' gin, but then Father Pope up at her church started to preach agin' drunkenness and the evils o' drink. That was when Sarah first took to ether. She said it must be healthier for her because she had to take the waters with it."

"Yes, I have often noticed her waiting in line to take the waters. People were frequently rude to her. They thought she might be begging." said Atticus.

"Why would she need to take the waters?" Lucie asked.

Betty burst into a cackle of laughter. "I'm sorry to joke, Mrs Fox, but you see, she had to take water along with her ether or else when she burped, her breath might catch fire. It did once, in Hale's Inn, and a gentleman gave her half a crown for it. That's why we call her Sarah the Dragon, you see – on account o' her breathing fire."

Lucie scowled. "But she could easily have done herself a very serious injury."

Betty made another lop-sided shrug.

"Aye, I dare say she could have, but then she started with the water too. She took magnesia water mainly, to take t' sweetness off the ether. Poor Sarah, that's why she had to take to whoring: to pay for it all. Once she'd pawned every last scrap she owned, there were nowt else for her."

She sighed and shook her head.

"A lamplighter found her first, we heard," Atticus prompted.

"Aye, Mr Fox, Arthur, the leerie for the Cold Bath Road, it was. He came a-runnin' around the corner like

Donald Dinnie[7] himsen. 'We need to get t' lass to a surgeon, proper-lively,' says he. So he up and carries her off through t' pleasure gardens. Pasty white she was, as white as a ghost, under t' gaslight."

"Did you see this hooded man's face?" Lucie asked. "We were told he had the appearance of a monster."

Old Betty pursed her lips.

"Aye, an' I dare say he did too. I couldn't see his face, if truth be told, Mrs Fox but ah'll tell ye this: he were walking like nowt human that I've ever seen. And to attack a poor waif of a soul like that, whore or not, and her just come down from Evening Prayers. It's wicked. That's what it is, wicked."

CHAPTER NINE

There is a path, which extends up through the Bogs Valley Pleasure Gardens to the Bogs Field beyond, and thence to the Royal Bath Hospital. By day, this delightful walk follows a stream ornamented with pools, fountains and dramatic cascades, and by the most curious plants collected from the farthest corners of the Empire. But by night, it is a place of darkness and of deep, rustling shadow.

With this night, fingers of mist were stretching down from the heathlands beyond the hospital. They were reaching-in towards the beating heart of the town, caressing the ground and transfiguring everything they touched into ghosts and phantasms. At this late hour only Atticus and Lucie Fox were walking the pathway. Those who might frequent the gardens to indulge particularly nocturnal pleasures were inclined to seek out the private and more secluded places.

Carrying her trepidation with her like a brimming brass ladle, Lucie glanced around, peering from shadow to deepening shadow beneath the silver-lit tree tops. The Bogs Valley Beast might yet be lurking in any one of them, watching them, stalking them, preparing himself for the kill.

'Monster!' the woman had screamed, again and again, before the morphine had mercifully overwhelmed her. Could that monster be Esau? Were his tormented, ever-watchful eyes following them now, just as they had followed their every move earlier that day? But how could he be? Had not Joseph assured them that Wilberforce kept Esau collared and chained, and locked inside a van?

But the woman had shrieked, 'Monster!' And the shadows were deep.

Her husband's walking cane, with its hidden blade, sliced through the mists, again and again, tapping gently and regularly onto the asphalt beneath. Atticus Fox would not be seeing monsters – in the trees at least.

And then a cloud passed over, and the gibbous moon shone bright, and there was the Bogs Field spread out wide before them. Here, in a seemingly unremarkable swathe of sodden ground, lay the world's greatest natural laboratory, where no fewer than thirty-six mineral springs were fomented, each one of them quite different from the rest. Here was the source of Harrogate's wealth.

Atticus stopped, suddenly and unexpectedly, and Lucie's fear reared up inside her. This was no night to linger. Not here. She urged him forward, but his arm remained rigid, unmoveable, in her grip.

"What is it, Atty?"

Her husband lifted his cane towards an edifice looming up from the mists ahead, its perpendiculars and towers cast into eerie relief by the moonlight. It was the hospital – the great Royal Bath Hospital – built by the rich of Harrogate for the deserving poor of the nation.

"Atticus, what's wrong?" Lucie asked him again.

"I can't go there," he whispered.

"The woman will have been bathed and properly bandaged; you won't need to see her wounds." (Atticus Fox has a profound aversion to all things bloody or sanguinary). "Or you could wait somewhere – in the Central Square perhaps – and I'll see her alone. You do have your travelling chess set with you, don't you?"

Atticus, the moon reflecting in his eyes as two great ovals of light, nodded, slowly and mechanically, as an automaton might nod, and touched the leather of their bag hanging from his shoulder.

"It isn't what state she might be in, Lucie, it's the hospital. It…"

"It reminds you of before, doesn't it?" Lucie squeezed his arm and felt the muscle bunched, as hard as a knar, beneath his coat sleeve. "But that was a different time, and you were a very different man. Everything has changed; you are better now, and those demons have been exorcised."

She took his hand. "Come, Atticus."

Lucie's sharp pull on the doorbell was answered almost immediately by the hospital's night porter. He opened the door, just a little, just enough to peer out with his good eye and allow the light of the big gas mantles to spread into the porch and illuminate whoever – or whatever – might be out there. The woman was here still, lying upstairs in the electrifying rooms like a tethered goat, and he, for one, was taking no chances of the Beast returning to finish its work. With his own ears he had heard the things she had screamed as she had writhed and clawed at the doctor's arms and now he made sure to keep a crucifix in his pocket.

"Nursing Sister Pearson – or Mrs Fox, as I suppose I should be calling you these days – how wonderful it is to see you again, and bless my soul if it isn't Atticus Fox too."

It was an older, wearier Dr Frederick Wormald smiling down from the balcony of the Central Square courtyard than either of them remembered. His hair was a degree thinner and his long, sagacious face even more creased and lined, as if it were taking on the perpendiculars and towers of the hospital itself, but it was unmistakeably him.

"I expect you are here about the poor woman who was attacked," Wormald went on, "It's a little late for afternoon tea, after all. But come up, come up; you'll still remember the way. I had a bed put up for her in the electrifying room. We hardly use it at this time of the year."

The long years melted as Atticus Fox followed Lucie, again become Nursing Sister Pearson, along the broad ambulatory corridor of the hospital, with its columns of dread and its doors of fearful memory. He sensed again Wormald's omnipotence, and the eyes, the great, staring eyes, curious and mocking, taunting him from every corner. Here now was the stairway, where once he would sit and he would rock, back-and-forth, for hours on end.

Dr Wormald was waiting at the landing.

"What was that saying we had, Atticus?" he called down the stairs to them: "'No great mind has ever existed without a touch of madness'. So said Aristotle, and so, if you recall, said I. Well you've certainly proved your mind since then, you and Mrs Fox both."

"Yes, Doctor," said Atticus.

They came to an unusually wide door, with a brass plate that carried the words 'Galvanic Baths'. Dr Wormald chuckled as he put his hand on the porcelain doorknob.

"We never did manage to get you in here, did we, Atticus?"

"No, Doctor."

The Galvanic Room of the Royal Bath Hospital had a high, perfectly square ceiling inscribed by a circular plaster moulding, which gave it something of the air of a temple, or of a mausoleum. Between the tiled, starkly white walls, a pair of porcelain slipper baths stood gleaming side-by-side, each with a teak cabinet at its head which spewed a torrent of wires and polished copper electrodes into the tubs. Beyond those, a nurse's blue headdress and the magazine on her lap provided almost the only other colour in the room.

"How is she, Sister?" Dr Wormald asked.

In one fluid movement, the nurse slid her magazine down to her side and leaned forward to survey a cot at her knees with what might have been a corpse or a mummy lying on it. That the form wrapped from head to knee in a shroud of bandages had not yet been granted the final mercy of death became evident from the way it twitched and jerked occasionally, and by the fact that the spots peppering the swaddling were still fresh and shockingly, shockingly red.

"She's about the same, I should say, Dr Wormald, neither better nor worse. Her stitches are oozing a bit, but they've none of them burst."

She watched as the form's head lifted from its pillow in an agonised spasm.

"I thank the Lord for the morphine and the chloral hydrate though, or else I can't think what she'd be doing – clawing down the walls, more than likely."

"This is Mr and Mrs Atticus Fox," Wormald said. "Mrs Fox once wore the nurse's silver buckle for us here."

The nurse smiled in greeting and her eyes dropped to Lucie's waist, as if she might be wearing it still.

"And this is Hannah," the doctor continued, indicating the tortured form. "We've done all we can for her – of course we have – but the lamplighter would have been much better advised to have taken her up to the Cottage Hospital. They are much more used to injuries like these than we will ever be."

"What are her injuries?" Lucie asked.

"Most of them are stab wounds," Wormald replied. "Some of them are deep and not a few grievous. The ruffian who attacked her used her own bottle to do it, an ether bottle, by all accounts. The worst are on the right side of her face and across her chest and lower abdomen."

"Did he force himself upon her?"

"We believe not. The attack appears to have been exceedingly violent, but mercifully brief. All this has rather unnerved the staff though, Mrs Fox. What with the nature of her injuries, and the way she screamed so."

"And not forgetting *what* she screamed," the nurse added.

Lucie asked: "What about the other patients, Doctor; do they know about her?"

Dr Wormald turned and leaned back against one of the teak electrical boxes. Its copper tentacles began to swing gently and they had made two complete oscillations before he replied.

"Samson Fox himself came up this morning, asking me that very same question. I imagine he was concerned about the patients fleeing back to their various patrons with tales of murders and monsters, and the effect that might have upon the subscriptions. A perfectly legitimate concern of course, but he needn't have worried. The deserving poor of this country are a resilient breed and quite used to peril." He shrugged. "Besides which, we have precious few patients in, this late in the season."

"Mr Bennett, down in the east ward, believes it was Jack the Ripper did it, and that he's come up to Harrogate for the air," the nurse observed.

Atticus shook his head as he stared down at the swaddled shape laid before her. It was rigid now and trembling and a bright red blotch was growing steadily across its front, soaking the bandages in fresh, shining, arterial blood.

"No, it's not him," he managed to say. "I have read about the Whitechapel murders. They were different from this, across a number of points."

He fumbled his handkerchief from the pocket of his jacket and dabbed at his brow. The damned whiteness of this place was oppressive, and it was hot too – ridiculously hot.

"Are you quite well, Mr Fox?" The blurred face of the nurse was suddenly in front of his own.

"My husband is not at his best with traumatic injuries," Atticus heard his wife's voice saying. He felt her grip on his arm, guiding him down on to a solid, narrow something. The edge of a bath, he realised.

"Is Hannah likely to come round soon, do you think, Dr Wormald?" Lucie continued, twisting the bath tap and wetting Atticus' handkerchief in the suddenly spluttering stream.

Dr Wormald cast a quick, almost furtive glance to the nurse. He said: "We have been obliged to administer heavy, very heavy, in fact almost lethal, doses of both morphine and chloral hydrate. It was a devil of a job to put her under in the first place – the ether addiction no doubt – so it is going to be some time before she does awaken."

He hesitated.

"If, to be candid with you, she ever does at all. You must understand that we had to give her relief from her pain. Canon Pope has been over from St Robert's, to administer the Last Rites."

"We understand perfectly what you're saying." Lucie was holding the sodden handkerchief against Atticus' brow. "So it might be prudent if Mr Fox were to go home and rest. I could wait here with Sister. Then if S——, if Hannah does come out from her sedation, I shall be here."

After a somewhat embarrassed, but equally relieved, Atticus Fox was helped from the room by Dr Wormald, the nurse exhaled sharply through her nose.

"Mercy me, Sister Fox, but I thought I was for the high-jump then; reading a magazine when I'm supposed to be watching missy-harlot there. Do you blame me, though? She hasn't moved in hours, and why should I sit here, twiddling my thumbs, and on a Friday night too? You'll know as well as I that she'll never live another day. Her soul will be half way to Hell by now, I shouldn't wonder."

"Look there; she's bleeding again, Sister. Why don't we change her dressings?" said Lucie.

CHAPTER TEN

Esau the Beast picks up the pencil. It is a sharp, new pencil, and the first he has ever used that is not a chewed or broken stump, which even the workhouse children have discarded.

In his other hand he holds a writing book; a beautiful new one in green, with every single page white and unmarked. Like the pencil, it is a gift from his new master.

Turning it to the first page, as reverently as he might open a Bible, he writes: *Mary Magdalene is beloved of Esau. She is beloved above all other women. Amen.*'

CHAPTER ELEVEN

In his design for the Royal Pump Room, the renowned architect I. T. Shutt had taken care to create nothing less than a temple to the great healing powers of the Harrogate waters.

Atticus Fox, perhaps their most ardent disciple, made a pilgrimage to this place several times each day in order to take a glass of the sweet and iron-rich chalybeate water for the sake of his mind. It was, after all, the principal tool of his profession.

On this particular day, Atticus knew that he would need every last particle of the water's beneficial effect. He had slept only fitfully, and even a knight's tour[7] of chess in the small hours of the morning had been no aegis against the spinning images of the woman and her bloodied dressings and her screams of Monster! Monster! Monster! Once in the night, the fingers of his imagination had peeled away the layers of bandage to discover beneath them Lucie's face, as pale and as ghostly white as the galvanic room of the Royal Bath Hospital.

His friend, Joseph Malkin, kept a monster in his stables. He had seen it. He had taken his wife to stand before it, and together, they had felt the breath of its roar, as it had risen up in fury. And before that, it had been in a freak show, bound by a single chain, not fifty yards from George de Medici's bath-chair yard.

They should have told Samson about it, and they should have told Douglas.

They should.

So why had they not?

Atticus stared through the window of his front parlour down into Low Harrogate and a little square of yellowed grass. It was true of course, that they had no evidence to link Esau to the attack – no solid, undeniable evidence at any rate. In law, a man – any man – is considered to be innocent, unless his guilt can be proven, beyond doubt, to a jury of his peers.

But, a niggling voice kept asking him, how many monsters could there reasonably be within a single town in the West Riding of Yorkshire? And what if it should attack again? What if the monster were to rise up, and bellow, and run rampant through those gentle streets, roaring and slashing and flailing? The voice held up an image. It was the woman and then it was Lucie, lying on the bed-sheet, twitching in agony in her bloodied bandages. He pushed it away. Mr Oates kept armed watch over Esau now, and Oates was a good man. Joseph had promised he was a good man. *As cool as iron and a first rate shot*, that was what he had said. He could stop a rhinoceros. Harrogate, surely, was in no danger.

Or was it?

Even Mr Oates, the little voice reminded him, must sleep sometimes. And if the worst did happen, and Esau did break free, what then? They, A&L Fox, commissioned investigators of Harrogate, would be finished. Joseph Malkin and Samson Fox would be finished, and so indeed, the voice exulted, would Harrogate itself.

Atticus became aware of the great, long-case clock in the hall marking out the seconds.

So then, what should he, Atticus Fox, alone, and with no wise and sensible Lucie to offer him counsel, do now? Go to Samson Fox perhaps? Go to Inspector Douglas even, and lay bare their sins?

"No." Atticus spoke the solitary word aloud and his tone was emphatic. Both Samson and Douglas had suspicions as to Esau's culpability, but they were merely that – suspicions. And a man must ever be presumed innocent.

Atticus frowned. A man – *Homo sapiens*. Would that same presumption be extended now to *Homo sylvestris*? Or would it not? 'Accusing is proving, where malice and power sit judges', after all.

"Evidence," said Atticus Fox, and he was right. Whichever the case, clear, irrefutable evidence was what was needed to establish Esau's guilt or innocence. His task now must be to uncover it.

Atticus pulled out his old Wehrly pocket-watch. It was not quite seven o'clock. The leerie, Arthur, would be out there now, fluttering from streetlamp to streetlamp down the Cold Bath Road like some great species of moth, shutting off their gas. Should he hasten there, to speak with him? No. Preferable to wait for Lucie; she was always far better with people than he.

Atticus' gaze lifted across the valley, to the roofs and chimneys of the Royal Bath Hospital just visible above the treetops, and he thought again about the galvanising room there. Perhaps the woman had awoken. Perhaps, at that very moment, she was clawing frantically at the gleaming white tiles and screaming out her agony, just as the nurse had predicted she might. Perhaps, contained in one of those screams, was the name of the Beast.

The movement of the clock in the hall began to rattle, and to chime the hour of seven. The Pump Room would be opening its doors and Betty would be expecting him, ready to dispense the chalybeate water that would so soothe and fortify his brain. He was expected at Beagle House at ten o'clock, and like Lucie's, Joseph's counsel would be wise. But what could he do in between? Where might the vestiges of evidence be found?

As he stood, pondering the question, watching through the sash as little groups of the Ailing gathered and converged on the wells, an ancient and almost skeletal lady trundled past, tucked under a blanket into a de Medici bath-chair. Atticus knew then what was to be done: From the Pump Room, he would walk the short distance to the bath-chair yard and examine it all once again. He would have the Sun with him now, after all.

CHAPTER TWELVE

It was not Mr Oates but Joseph Malkin himself, who, at ten o'clock precisely, was sitting, hunched on a low, three-legged stool, beside the door to Esau's loose box. A cobbler's long, leather apron covered his day clothes.

Atticus cleared his throat and Malkin glanced up, startled, from his work. He had been engrossed in honing the blades of a sheep clippers against a sharpening-stone laid along his thigh.

"It can write, Atticus!" he gushed. "It can write quite as well as it can read, in a perfectly round, copybook hand too. The Linneans[9] will hardly believe it. And I've got some Waterloos for it. Well, they aren't strictly Waterloo teeth; they're porcelain. I found a dentist with his own vulcanising apparatus. He made me a set in the night from a clay impression I took myself. A full ten guineas it cost me but it's a quite beautiful piece of work. It fits over Esau's remaining teeth perfectly. He kept gagging on them at first but now he has become used to them he can speak quite as well as you or I."

"I look forward very much to hearing him," said Atticus.

Malkin scratched his thumb across the blades of the clippers. Evidently satisfied, he laid the sharpening-stone down onto the cobbles and picked up the stool.

"Good day to you, by-the-by, old fellow. Is Lucie Fox not with you?"

Atticus shook his head. "I am alone today, Joseph. Lucie and I had occasion to go up to the Bath Hospital last night, and she has been detained there."

"Oh!" Malkin exclaimed, "How dreadful, I'm so sorry for you both. Was it… was it our *Homo sylvestris* to blame for it?"

Atticus was completely wrong-footed by Malkin's plain-spokenness.

"That is exactly the question, Joseph. I do hope not, of course, but we shall know more if she ever regains consciousness."

"Great Scott! But that's abominable! I know women can be peculiarly sensitive to the effects of wild-men – my own Alice was frightened half out of her wits, as you know – but to be rendered unconscious…"

He set his stool back onto the floor and slumped down onto it.

"And I am so sorry for it, Atticus, insisting that she come round here and all. I thought she'd be able to help with the anatomy, you see? Poor Lucie Fox."

"No, no, Joseph, you misunderstand me; Lucie is perfectly fine. It's a woman, a prostitute woman, who is at the hospital. She was attacked and gravely injured the night before last. Lucie is sitting at her bedside."

Malkin's mouth dropped open in comprehension, and not a little relief.

"Ah, now I see. Thank the gods! Then the poor woman has my every good wish, and my prayers for a speedy recovery. Weren't both Rahab[10] and Mary Magdalene prostitutes too?"

He sat in respectful solemnity for a few moments longer and then stood and held up the shears. The Sun glinted off the newly-honed edges of the blades and threw crescents of light across his eager expression.

"So then, old fellow, what say you? Shall we discover what a wild-man looks like under his hair?"

Atticus bit his lip.

"Joseph, the woman was attacked by what she described as a monster. It was in Low Harrogate, just off the Montpellier Stray, in the entrance to the bath-chair yard."

The stool and the shears clattered onto the cobblestones and lay there, one blade of the clippers quivering gently on its spring.

"What do you mean, monster?" Malkin whispered, "What sort of monster?"

"I don't know, and neither do the police. When I left the hospital last night, the woman was still insensible under heavy doses of soporific drugs. Lucie and a hospital nurse are sitting with her, waiting, or perhaps I should say hoping, for her to awaken."

"Atticus, I passed within ten yards of de Medici's yard the night before last. It was with Thomas Wilberforce, when I drew up the arrangements to buy Esau from him."

Atticus stooped to pick up the shears and the stool. He held them out, but Joseph did not appear to notice. He was gnawing at his lip, and staring towards the stable door.

"It can't have been Esau. Do you see that, Atticus? How could it have been? He was chained-up inside the freak show all the time we left him. You say the police are involved?"

Atticus nodded. "And the mayor has asked if Lucie and I might make our own private inquiry into it too."

"Do the police know about Esau?" Malkin asked.

"They do. They know about Wilberforce and his freak show, and they know that he disappeared immediately after the attack. They've also remarked on Esau's propensity to attack women. However, they don't know yet that you bought him from Wilberforce, or that he is here."

Malkin glanced up again to the big stable doors.

"But it can't have been him. It just can't have."

"Good morning…" Esau the beast pushed a great, hairy finger into its mouth and flexed its jaw, revealing two rows of black, vulcanised gums. "Good morning, Master Fox."

"A good morning to you, Master Esau," Atticus returned. The polite formality of his tone was in complete contrast to the astonishment in his expression.

"I know, Atticus, I know." Malkin raised his arms as if to heaven. "It's a miracle. He is the first beast to speak since the serpent of Eden. Lucie was correct; with those new porcelain teeth, he sounds just like a human. I declare he looks a deal more like a human too."

Atticus could only agree. The creature's muzzle still protruded, to be sure, but not remarkably so. He looked far less ape-like and much more human than ever he had on the day previous. Indeed, Atticus mused, Joseph would be well advised to have the dentures removed before ever he presented it before the learned men of the Royal, or the Linnean Societies.

Malkin interrupted these thoughts by addressing the animal directly.

"Esau, Atticus Fox and I are going to cut some of your hair off."

He took a sharp breath and held out the clippers for the creature to sniff, were it to be so inclined. It was not.

"Now I promise you that it won't hurt, not one bit. On the contrary, you are going to feel a great deal more comfortable after we have finished. I am now going to prove my words to you. Please observe what I do."

Malkin went over to Albert and took a fistful of the freshly-groomed hair of his tail. He lifted the clippers and squeezed and a black rope of hair dropped onto the straw. "There, that is all we shall be doing. Did you see? Not even a whinny. It's as easy as nine-pence."

Esau nodded impassively. Evidently Joseph's ploy had worked because he appeared not the slightest bit concerned.

"To help you to stay calm," Joseph went on, "I have fetched a special drink for you."

He reached down into the pocket of his apron and pulled out a little silver hip flask. Esau's black eyes followed his movements, and he sniffed gently at the air as Malkin twisted a cup from the flask's bottom and filled it to the brim with a brownish liquid.

"Here it is, Esau; this is called sweet sherry. Sweet sher-ry."

With surprising care, the wild-man took the beaker in his brute, hairy fingers and lifted it to his nose. He sipped at the contents and seemed almost to consider the taste. He sipped once again; working his jaws with their new sheaths of rubber, then threw back his head and drained the whole measure in a gulp.

"There's a good man." Malkin seemed suddenly breathless and his relief was evident. He took the little three-legged stool and settled it into the straw between them.

"This is a seat for you, Esau," he explained. "It will make it more convenient for us if you were to sit upon it. Do you think you will be able to do that for me?"

Esau was indeed able. He sat down easily onto the stool, not cross-legged in his usual way, but mimicking the manner of a human, with his legs out before him and his feet in the straw. He began to wipe his finger around the beaker bottom and Atticus watched in dismay as he pushed the hairy tip into his mouth and sucked noisily at it. They must take care to remain both cautious and vigilant, Atticus reminded himself, since here, there could be no doubt that they were dealing with the most primitive form of humanity.

"Esau, I understand from Mr Malkin that you can write," Atticus ventured to ask, "And in an excellent hand too. Would you please be good enough to show me your notebook?"

Treading carefully the fine line between aggression and self-possession, Atticus allowed his eyes to meet those of the creature. In that instant, it seemed that their very souls locked, as if he had looked directly into the black abyss of Hell itself. He recoiled, flung out from those terrible depths, and as he gathered his wits, he recalled Malkin's warning of the previous day – that he should never stare, even for a second, into a wild creature's eyes.

"Atticus Fox will give it back to you directly he's looked at it," he heard Joseph say. "You may depend upon it."

Esau hesitated. Perhaps he too had been shaken by their encounter. Then, he reached down into the straw by his feet and lifted out a notebook, handsomely bound in emerald-green ray-skin.

Atticus bowed his head. "Thank you, Esau."

Taking care to use only the most measured and deliberate of movements he took the book, and, with the backs of his fingers, gently brushed the sprinkling of straw dust from the cover. Then, with exaggerated care, he opened it.

"He does have the most beautiful hand, Joseph," he said. "Esau, I see that you have written your own name, and that of Mary Magdalene, in a sort of verse from the Bible. Did you copy her name from there?"

Esau's eyes flared and Atticus glanced down, chary of another glimpse of what lay within them. He was aware, nonetheless, of the creature staring at him.

"I knew already how to write her name," it said. "I can write it in both ways."

"In both ways'?" Malkin repeated.

Esau nodded. "In the Holy Scriptures, it has the letter 'e' at the end of Magdalene, but at the leper chapel I went to, it did not. You may spell it either way; Schoolmistress said so." It was a lot of words for Esau, and indeed for any wild-man, to have spoken at one time.

"What is a leper chapel, Atticus?" Malkin asked.

"It's a hospital chapel; one built especially for lepers infected by the crusaders returning from the Holy Land. There were hundreds built across England around that time and one still stands in Ripon: the Chapel of St Mary Magdalen."

Malkin frowned. "Returning crusaders, eh? So how did a *Homo sylvestris* come to go to a leper chapel?"

"That is a very good question," Atticus replied, "Especially since the chapel in question was abandoned long ago and replaced by a modern church. Perhaps we should ask him."

"Yes, that's a capital idea. How did you come to go to the leper chapel, Esau?"

Esau did not reply to Joseph's question immediately. He stared instead into the gilt bottom of the empty beaker, intrigued, no doubt, by his own reflection, as all beasts are.

"Tramp-major took me there – every Sunday and Good Friday."

"The tramp-major took you?" Atticus repeated, "You have been in a workhouse then?"

"Tramp-major, Atticus?" Malkin interrupted.

"An employee of a workhouse, Joseph, more often than not a former tramp himself, used to supervise the vagrants."

Esau nodded. "Aye, Master Atticus Fox, I was born and raised in the Ripon workhouse. The chaplain did not want me to pray with the other inmates and Your Lordship said I must never go to the cathedral. So the schoolmistress told Tramp-major to take me to St Mary Magdalen's chapel. But Tramp-major always laughed and said she never told him which one."

"So he took you to the wrong church." Atticus finished the explanation for him. "He took you to the old, abandoned leper chapel instead of the newly-consecrated church across the lane."

Esau nodded and his eyelids suddenly drooped.

"It's working," Malkin whispered. He lifted the beaker from the creature's unresisting grasp. "I slipped a few drops of laudanum into that sherry. Keep him talking if you can, Atticus; it seems to help."

Atticus took a breath. "Why did the tramp-major take you to an empty chapel, Esau?"

Malkin's clippers scissored and a large ball of hair rolled off the creature's shoulder and dropped to the straw. Esau's eyes snapped open and Malkin froze. They watched, not daring to move, until the lids began to sink once again and the beast's head sagged.

"So he could smoke his baccy." Esau's words were slow and laboured now; the laudanum was evidently taking its effect. "And have a snifter of… gin."

"And what of you, Esau," Atticus asked, "Would you smoke and take a drink there too?"

"No," Esau's head moved from side to side like a clockwork toy. "I would sit in the pew and read my Bible and look at Mary Magdalene."

Atticus watched a second and a third clump of black, matted hair chase each other down to the floor.

"You would look at St. Mary Magdalene?"

The ape-man's eyes closed and he nodded sluggishly. Then his great, shaggy head slumped to the side.

"That's it. The laudanum has him now," Malkin murmured. "Lift his arm for me, would you? There's a good chap."

Atticus reached out tentatively for Esau's arm, and blenched as his eyelids fluttered at his touch.

"Careful now, don't drop it," Malkin cautioned, "And don't stop talking, old fellow; we need to keep him distracted."

Atticus grimaced. He dearly wished that Lucie were here; she could conjure up no end of things to say.

"Tell us about St Mary Magdalene, Esau."

"She was… in the corner… on the wall." The words were barely audible.

"What was she: a painting, or a statue or suchlike?"

"She was a statue. She was… she was beloved of me, the loveliest of all."

"It would seem that our friend has become infatuated by a church effigy," Malkin said. "That is a matter of very great interest, Atticus and we must be sure to make a note of it. You see, there are many accounts of wild men –

satyrs most especially – and even of great apes experiencing a strong physical attraction to human females, and, on occasion, even of their carrying them off."

"Then you need to be careful, Joseph. Remember that he believes your own daughter to be Mary Magdalene."

"Yes, and that's true." Malkin's mouth fell open in perturbation, as if the idea had not previously occurred to him. "Upon my word, that is very true!"

He wiped an oiled rag along the blades of his clippers and pushed it back into his apron pocket. Then he asked: "Do you miss chapel, Esau?"

Esau nodded.

"Then I'll see if I can't have a new one built for you."

In response to Atticus' raised eyebrows, he said: "I am thinking I might ask Gerard Prêtre, my architect, to replicate this leper chapel in the menagerie I'm having built for him. Gerard has designed many a fine steeple-house in his time. Yes indeed. And a number of temples too, come to that, for the Freemasons, *et cetera*. I could even ask him to have the statue of Mary Magdalene copied and mounted onto the wall for Esau to look at."

He scowled.

"That is, if I can ever get his ear."

"How so, Joseph?" Atticus asked.

"Because my dearest Victoria remains determined to make Beagle House the stateliest mansion in Harrogate. She's already asked him to design a whole new wing – and a grand rear annexe. And can you believe, she's even suggesting that I buy the entire row of cottages in front of the house, so I can have them demolished and the land made part of the Stray?"

Malkin's jaw tightened and the action of the clippers became harder and more savage.

"She has wanted us to move to the Stray-side ever since we were first married. I like it perfectly well here, Atticus, where it's quiet and out of the public view. The last thing I need when I am trying to work is the infernal din of a street organ outside my door. So now she maintains that if we cannot move to the Stray, then the Stray will have to be brought to us."

Bright sunlight washed suddenly across the stable, and Atticus and Joseph turned to see the cause of it. The top stable door had been pulled open and Lucie, red-eyed and grim, was looking in at them.

"Good morning." Her voice, in direct contrast to her bone-weary expression, or perhaps because of it, was brisk and businesslike. "I'm expecting a visitor to join us here shortly and I believe both of you need to speak with him."

She rattled back the bolt of the lower door, pulled it wide, and stepped into the stable.

"And I've brought some regrettable news with me too."

"Oh?" said Malkin curiously.

"Yes, I fear so. I have been at the Bath Hospital all night; Atticus, no doubt, has told you why. While I was waiting for the poor woman to come round, I took the liberty of discussing Esau's case with one of the doctors. That doctor – Dr Frederick Wormald – is my visitor, and he will be with us as soon as he has completed his morning rounds."

"Lucie Fox, I must say, with all the respect due to you, it was hardly your place to—"

"Perhaps not, but Dr Wormald was once attached to the Army Hospital Corps. During his time in India, he tells me he came across a case identical to Esau's – an entire family of people, just like him."

She pursed her lips.

"Mr Malkin, I am very sorry, but you have almost certainly wasted a thousand pounds of your money. Esau is a man, an otherwise ordinary man, who suffers from a very rare condition called *Hypertrichosis universalis, Hypertrichosis of the dog-man* or *dog-man syndrome*. It causes hair to grow over the entire body and Dr Wormald tells me that it is very often also associated with gum problems, just as Esau has."

"The dentist who made his teeth said his gums must be very much enlarged."

Malkin closed his eyes. Somewhere, a great boulder was beginning to roll away from him with unstoppable force.

But then he opened them and said: "Though I am not yet wholly convinced, Lucie Fox. Not because of the thousand pounds; no, no, not at all, the love of money is the root of all evil, as we know. It is because I myself am a naturalist, and my own opinion remains steadfastly that our subject is indeed of the species *Homo sylvestris*. Thomas Wilberforce, during our very first meeting, cited another gentleman-naturalist who had arrived at precisely the same conclusion as I."

He seemed to take heart from the force of his own argument and wagged his finger in gentle admonishment.

"Copernicus, Galileo, Darwin, it seems there can never be a scientific advancement without the very greatest opposition. How in all good conscience therefore, could I abandon my studies for the word of one man, who has not even taken the trouble to examine the specimen for himself?"

"He is eager to do exactly that, which is why he is coming across as soon as he is able."

Joseph Malkin stroked his nose for a moment, and then nodded sagely.

"Very well, I shan't stop him. A true man of science must welcome all opinion, *pro et contra* his own."

"Thank you, Mr Malkin" said Lucie.

"There is no need to thank me for applying good scientific method, Lucie Fox." Joseph was chuckling now. "Indeed, it may very well be I who convinces your Dr Wormald to my hypothesis. After all, who is to say that this family in India are not of that very same species as Esau?"

He held up the clippers as if it was a lecturer's pointing-stick.

"As your husband and I were discussing just the other week, the celebrated naturalist B.H. Hodgson recorded a man-like creature covered in long, black hair, on the slopes of Nepal just sixty years ago. The Old Testament, come to that, is choc-full of references to creatures it calls satyrs. No, Lucie Fox, I am quite certain that your doctor is perfectly sincere in his opinions but I cannot believe that your news is quite so regrettable as you say."

"Oh, no, Mr Malkin," said Lucie, "That isn't my news."

"Then what is?" Atticus asked.

"The woman who was attacked, I am afraid that she died. She regained her consciousness this morning, for a time anyway, but her injuries and the great loss of blood proved just too much for her."

"I'm very sorry to hear that," Atticus said, to which Joseph added, "Yes, indeed."

"Was she able to tell you anything?"

At Atticus' question, Lucie turned and leaned back against the heavy timber kicking-boards lining the stable wall. She felt all at once bone-weary and she let go of the events of the past twenty-four hours in a long and heavy sigh.

"She told us that the man who attacked her was wearing a hooded coat, like a monk's habit. When he caught hold of her and pushed her back into the archway, he pulled the hood back from his face and screamed for her to look at him. His face, Atticus, was scarcely human. It was red and bloated and covered in lumps. That's exactly what Sarah said: 'Red and bloated and covered in lumps'. Before she died, she told me that at first, she believed it was the Devil himself, come to drag her down to Hell for being a whore."

"May the Lord God have mercy on the child," said Joseph.

"But then she noticed he was weeping."

"Weeping?" Atticus glanced suddenly towards Esau. The ape-man was awake now, and staring at Lucie with his black and depthless eyes.

"That's what she told me," Lucie replied. "Tears were streaming down his face. She knew then that he couldn't be the Devil, because Satan would never cry over a fallen woman."

"Streaming down his *hairy* face?" Atticus asked.

Lucie shook her head.

"He had no hair, either on his face or on his head."

"Then it could not have been Esau, after all," Malkin exclaimed. "The police will know now that it couldn't have been him."

"And then she died, there in my arms." Lucie pressed her eyes tightly shut and a tear glistened on the skin of her cheek. Atticus went to her and took her hands in his own, and Joseph turned and began to fumble in the pocket of his apron.

"Lucie, I can't pretend to believe that she's in a better place now, but at least she's out of her pain and at peace. We've been commissioned to bring her murderer to justice, so let us make sure we do precisely that and prevent her fate befalling some other poor soul."

Lucie nodded.

"I returned to de Medici's yard this morning," Atticus went on, "and took the opportunity to lift the cover from the drain outside."

He let go of Lucie's hands to reach into his pocket and pull out a handkerchief. It had been folded and rolled into a thick sausage.

"I discovered these caught on the brickwork."

Atticus unrolled the handkerchief across the palm of his hand. He spread each of its corners in turn to reveal three small, slightly elongated balls. They were scarlet in colour with one black end, which made them look for all the world like three fat ladybirds.

"I believe them to be some species of bean."

He offered them around and Lucie and Joseph took one each and began to examine them, just as a child might an unfamiliar sweet.

"Mine has a tiny hole bored through it, as if it might have been threaded as jewellery," Lucie said. "It could be from a necklace or a bracelet. Sarah's, do you think, Atticus?"

They were interrupted by the sound of heavy boots tramping across the cobblestones outside, punctuated by the metronomic tap of a gentleman's walking cane.

"Here comes John Oates," Malkin said, "And I do believe, Lucie Fox, that he might have your satyr expert with him".

They turned to see the coachman standing outside, together with a taller, thinner man in a frockcoat and glossy top hat.

Lucie stood forward and hastily smoothed her coat.

"Mr Joseph Malkin, may I present Dr Frederick Wormald of the Royal Bath Hospital."

"Glad to meet you, I'm sure, Frederick Wormald." Joseph bowed his head politely.

Dr Wormald did not respond immediately. Instead, he ducked his head and stepped forward into the loose-box. The gloom deepened the venerable lines on his face, which were gathered into a troubled frown.

"Do take the greatest care, Mr Malkin." He lifted the pommel of his walking cane towards the bean on Malkin's palm. "That gunja is deadly."

"This, you mean? Malkin held up the bean. "What did you call it?"

"I am at your service, Mr Malkin." Dr Wormald lifted his hat and bowed too, although stiffly and a little wearily. "I called it a gunja bean. It is the fruit of the gunja plant of the tropics, and highly poisonous both to man and horse." He glanced across to Albert, dozing in the corner. "I have seen several deaths on their account in India, mainly amongst the jewellery-makers and the native doctors, who sometimes use them in their medicines.

"Now, speaking of India, this must be the patient with the *Hypertrichosis universalis.*"

He stepped up to Esau, his eyes as wide as saucers and all traces of weariness vanished.

"Sir, my name is Dr Frederick Wormald. I am a physician at the Harrogate Royal Bath Hospital. Would you oblige me by opening your mouth, as wide as you are able?"

Esau gaped obediently, and Dr Wormald reached into his mouth and lifted out, one after the other, the black rubber crescents that were his newly-made dentures.

"Do take the greatest care, Doctor," Joseph warned.

Wormald did not reply as he bent his head to peer inside the creature's maw.

He said: "Thank you, Esau," and then turned to face Joseph.

"Mr Malkin, I am of the belief that this patient is suffering from the exceedingly rare *dog-man syndrome*. The nature of the hair growth, notwithstanding the fact that much of it has been clipped away, is proof enough, but there is also the gingival enlargement, or thickening of the gums, so typical of the disorder. I have seen it before, in India.”

Joseph’s shoulders sagged, and at the doctor’s words, he seemed to visibly diminish.

“Are you quite sure?” he asked.

Wormald settled his top hat back onto his head. “There cannot be a single atom of doubt about it.”

“Then a rascally mountebank, and perhaps my own vanity, have conspired to rob me of a thousand pounds.”

Malkin stared ruminatively at Esau for several seconds, “But then again, perhaps not.”

“What do you mean, sir?” Wormald asked.

“*Nullius in verba* – take nobody’s word for it[11]. I mean that, as a man of science, I am must arrive at my own conclusions through experiment and careful observation. And I fully intend to do exactly that. Let me promise you this though, Frederick Wormald: I will conduct everything in a right-ordered way. Whilst I make my enquiries, I will put Esau into a comfortable room here at Beagle House. It will be kept locked, of course, and John Oates will stand watch over the door, but he will want for nothing.”

“Except his liberty perhaps,” Lucie retorted.

“Perhaps so, Lucie Fox, but a guarded guest-chamber here will still be a paradise compared with a draughty stall in a sixpenny freak show.”

Dr Wormald grunted.

"Very well, so long as the arrangement is a temporary one. Now, if you will excuse me, I must go and catch up on some much-needed rest. We have all been awake the entire night trying to keep that poor woman's body and soul together. May God forgive me, but in the end, I am thankful we could not.

"Mr Malkin, before I go, may I offer what small assistance I can to your examinations. Dog-man syndrome is exceedingly rare. We could have a paper published in the journals about him – a joint paper, perhaps?"

"Perhaps," Malkin replied.

Wormald bowed his head.

"Very well. Mrs Fox, would you care to walk with me as far as the hospital? You wanted to take the woman's dress back with you to your home as I recall."

Once the sound of Lucie's and Dr Wormald's footsteps had faded into the distance, Joseph snorted in annoyance.

"Joint paper indeed," he grumbled, "The very brass of the man! I declare Esau is a *Homo sylvestris,* and what is more, I'll stand up in front of the learned societies and prove it so. We must never allow ourselves to be blown off course by windbaggery such as that, Atticus. So then, old fellow, let us get back to the task in hand."

The two men worked in a somewhat discomposed silence until the stool, and the straw beneath it, were black with hair.

"That will do, I think, for the clippers," said Malkin at last. He stepped back to inspect their work. Sitting on the stool in front of them was a wretched, bedraggled creature, gazing languidly at the uneven black stubble that covered its body.

"I've a razor in my apron pocket," Malkin went on, "a Starr safety razor. I had a dozen sent over yesterday, from William's, up in Ockham. But safety or not, and sedated or not, I don't relish going near him with any kind of blade. Do you see those great lumps all over his skin? Lice and flea bites I shouldn't wonder, but I wouldn't want to knick any of them by accident. We have no way of telling how the smell of blood might affect him."

"What are we to do, then?" Atticus asked.

Here Malkin grinned. "What else, Atticus but take a lesson from the ladies – from my young parlour-maid to be exact. It would seem that those of the fairer sex are wont to use a kind of sugary paste to pull out what they politely refer to as excessive hair."

He chuckled at Atticus' obvious bemusement.

"Young Susan came to us from the Knaresborough workhouse. Whilst she was there, she had the onerous task of sugaring the matron's chin, every other Saturday. She's quite the expert at it by all accounts. As you might imagine, nothing I can say or offer will persuade her to come anywhere near Esau, but she has described the procedure in sufficient detail for us to have a fair attempt at it. It's a deal messier than the razor, but we should be able to remove the stubble from his face and hands perfectly safely and with only the tiniest discomfort. All we need is sugar and lemon, a little water, and a quantity of linen strips to apply it with."

Atticus considered.

"But why do it at all, Joseph, if you only want to be able to groom him? If you intend to present him to the scientific world as *Homo sylvestris,* then surely he will need to be as close as possible to his natural state."

Malkin nodded cannily. "That's a very good point, old fellow, but then it occurred to me that if I am to have him first examined by a phrenologist, then he should look like any other man so as not to bias his observations. Proper scientific method, if you will. If, after investigation, it turns out that he is a member of our own species after all, I shall treat him, not only like any other man, but as my own son. He will have every opportunity, Atticus. And there is also the matter of his spiritual education too. *Sapiens* or *sylvestris,* he is as much God's creature as you or I, and you heard with your own ears how much he misses chapel."

They both looked down at the creature and watched as it picked lethargically at a sore.

"Without his hair, he does look very human," Malkin conceded, "A brutish and plain-looking human to be sure, but then there are plenty of those in the Church of England."

Atticus laughed at that and Esau looked up.

"I will respect his Anglican upbringing, so I shall take him down to St Mary's in Low Harrogate."

"Isn't Christ Church the nearest?" Atticus asked.

"It is, but I'm mindful that the Dame and Alice attend the Christ Church. Just imagine what Victoria would say if I took a wild-man along to meet her great and good friends-spiritual. No, St Mary's steeple house it must be. Quaker I am, but I dare say I could stomach a sermon or two for the sake of science. And speaking of science, I shall not neglect to teach him about Darwin and Wallace, and their ideas about natural selection. How very curious it will be to be teaching him his place, perhaps his unique place, in nature.

It was just as Joseph had drawn the last of the linen strips from Esau's forehead that they once again heard the sound of boots approaching. There was something determined about the footfalls, aggressive even, and a frown passed over Malkin's face as they stood, waiting to see who it might be.

Mr Oates appeared at the door. He stared in astonishment at Esau, who was sitting, naked on the stool, with his face as pink and as raw as a fresh-peeled blood orange.

"He doesn't look half so wild now, does he, John Oates?" Malkin joked. He dropped the used linen and it shivered down onto a pile of its fellows. A wasp, maddened by the smell of sugar, flitted irritably around it. "We shall need to bathe him in a strong solution of carbolic acid and then get him into fresh clothes. You may burn his old ones; they stink to high heaven."

Oates said: "I beg your pardon, sir, but I have two gentlemen to see you. They are both policemen."

"Policemen?" Malkin's face turned the washed-out colour of the linen at his feet. "Oh, very well, I shall be along directly. Are they in the library?"

"No, Mr Joseph Malkin and the seemingly omnipresent Atticus Fox, we are right here."

Two large and burly men pushed past the coachman and into the stable.

"Detective Inspector Douglas and Detective Sergeant Hainsworth, good day to you both," said Atticus.

"Hainsworth," Douglas growled, "Truncheon and bracelets out and at the ready, if you please. It would seem that we have just apprehended our murderer."

CHAPTER THIRTEEN

In all their many years of friendship, Atticus Fox had seldom seen Joseph Malkin, third-generation Quaker, even remotely annoyed. Today, he was positively apoplectic.

"Gentlemen, I must protest, I really must. What are you thinking of?"

"This man is a vicious murderer." Douglas' reply was brusque and dismissive. "He is almost certainly responsible for a deadly assault, two nights ago, down in Low Harrogate."

"Poppycock!" Malkin retorted, "He is responsible for nothing of the sort. I saw him myself two nights ago; he was in a showman's waggon, chained at the neck."

"A showman's waggon that was pitched not twenty yards from where the woman was attacked," Douglas returned. "And how long have you known about all of this, Fox?"

"How long have I known about all of what, precisely?" Atticus felt a familiar pulse in his neck beginning to tick out its warning. He must remain composed. He really must. As likely as not, he was shortly going to be called upon to make a carefully-considered argument, not spew a vitriolic torrent of bile.

He drew a long and calming breath.

"What Mr Malkin tells you is perfectly correct, Inspector. Esau was brought here in chains, and he has been under the armed guard of Mr Oates ever since. Besides which, he bears no resemblance whatever to the woman's description of her attacker."

"Are you quite mad, Fox? Of course he does. Look at him!"

Douglas reached down and grabbed Esau's arm and hauled him to his feet.

"Be careful!" Joseph warned.

Douglas ignored him. "Red and bloated and covered in lumps; that's what the woman said, according to the doctor, anyhow."

"No, no, those are parasitic insect bites," Malkin protested. "The redness is where we have just removed his hair. Before that he was none of those things."

"You can save all of that for his trial." Douglas pushed Esau back down onto the stool. "Until then, this fellow is going under lock-and-key in Raglan Street."

"Fellow?" Malkin roared, and Albert started and swished his tail. "Fellow, you say? He is no fellow. He's not even a man in the strictest sense of the word. Let me tell you this, *Inspector.* I am a naturalist of no little renown, and my scientific opinion is that that creature is of a different species of humanity altogether. He is a wild-man, a satyr, a member of *Homo sylvaticus,* in fact."

Douglas seemed amused. "Well I am a policeman of no little renown, and my opinion is that whatever *species* of man he might be, he matches the description of our murderer. That's quite scientific enough for us, don't you think, Hainsworth? And as soon as he is decently dressed, he's coming with us."

Malkin glowered at Douglas, his hands bunched into two trembling fists. Atticus tensed, ready to hold and restrain his friend, or else bundle him away through the door. Furious or not, Joseph would be no match for Douglas.

Fortunately the inspector did not notice him; he was watching Esau examining the handcuffs that bound his wrists.

Hainsworth said: "The murdered woman also mentioned a long coat with a hood. Does your, ah, wild-man happen to possess such a thing, sir?"

Joseph closed his eyes and raised his face to the skylight, mouthing words they could not make out. He might have been appealing to a higher power. His next words were spoken calmly, and Atticus allowed himself to relax a little.

"Esau has only a single pair of raggedy trousers. But he has soiled them and they are fit only for the bonfire."

"Anything else," Douglas asked, "Leashes, muzzles or the like?"

"He has a chain, and a rather tattered and sorry-looking Bible that I know of, and I have given him a new notebook and pencil. I suppose he might have some other possessions still in the showman's waggon. I don't know; we haven't had an opportunity to look."

Detective Inspector Douglas glared from Joseph to Atticus and then turned to his sergeant, shaking his head in affected despair.

"Can you believe it, Hainsworth? The great and celebrated Atticus Fox, under a commission from no less a personage than the mayor of Harrogate himself, discovers a murderer. But does he immediately bring him to justice, as he ought? Does he even undertake a search for further evidence, to take before the learned judges of the Leeds Assizes? No, he does not. Mr Fox decides that he will assist in barbering him and helping him to change his appearance. Remind me now; what would we call that?"

Hainsworth grinned as he took up the game.

"I believe we would call that 'assisting a felon', Inspector."

Douglas nodded. "I thought so. And would that make both Mr Fox and his fine gentleman friend felons too – to wit, accessories-after-the-fact?"

"I believe it would, sir, most definitely."

"Then I shall take care to make that very point to His Worship, Mr Samson Fox, when next I see him.

"You may do exactly as you wish," said Atticus.

"You may depend upon it that I shall! Sergeant, lend me your truncheon, will you? I'll mind the prisoner. You take a look in this showman's waggon and see what you can find."

Hainsworth's departure left a silence hanging in the stable. It was a profoundly discomforting silence, oppressive even, which only the inspector himself seemed to find tolerable. Inevitably, it was Malkin who broke first.

"Your sergeant will find nothing to incriminate him," he insisted.

Douglas smirked. "That remains to be seen, Mr Malkin. If we do, he will hang; make no mistake about that. Dr Wormald, up at the Royal Bath Hospital, didn't seem to think him to be any kind of *species of wild-man*, so there'll be no defence for him on that score – any more, Fox, than there will be from McNaughton[12]."

Stung, Malkin fell into indignant sullenness, and the silence began to thicken and press down once again.

"Here, get away from that, damn you?" Douglas prodded Esau's fingers away from a suddenly-open handcuff with the nose of Hainsworth's truncheon. "How did you manage to do that, you brute?"

He reached down and snapped the cuff tight.

"There – that's got you.

"So, Mr Wild Man, while we're waiting, we may as well put the time to good use. Why did you do it then? You may as well tell us. Did she refuse you? Were you too ugly, even for an ether-sodden hedge-whore?"

"That's enough, Douglas," Atticus snapped.

Douglas glowered at him.

"I don't doubt that some mother loved him, Fox, even looking like that, but I can't imagine the Justices of Assize being so soft-bellied."

At that moment Detective Sergeant Hainsworth ducked under the lintel of the doorway. In his fist, hanging as if throttled, was a long, black, hooded cape.

CHAPTER FOURTEEN

The line of elegant town houses known as Prospect Place, like a theatre grand circle, enjoys unrivalled views over the extravaganza that is the daily life of Harrogate. Here, just below the windows, are the massed plantings of the world-famous flower beds, like so many gaily-dressed folk in the stalls. Beyond that, and a little way down the Montpellier hill, the Temperance Band gives accompaniment to the stage itself: to the mountebanks, the townsfolk and the Ailing, all playing out their lives in day-act dramas.

Atticus Fox gazed out over this scene from the window of the top floor room that served them as an investigations laboratory. The alternative was the sight of a blue cotton dress, spread over the big table in the centre, ripped and shredded and stiffened with ugly brown patches which had once been a woman's lifeblood.

"I suppose that Sarah the Dragon might have *felt* the bumps and lumps on Esau's head through his hair," Atticus reasoned aloud, "and then, in all the brouhaha, imagined that she had *seen* them too."

"That is a possibility, Atty," Lucie agreed, "but I still think it very strange that she never mentioned his hair – not once – nor his eyes, come to that; he has notably dark eyes. Red and bloated and covered in lumps, was what she said.

To describe his skin colour, especially by gaslight – and it was coal gas, not water-gas, don't forget – well, I believe she must have taken a good look at him. And Esau was definitely covered in hair two nights ago."

"Douglas' suggestion that a wild-man might be able to grow and shed his hair at will was quite preposterous," Atticus added scornfully.

"Atticus."

"Yes, what is it?"

Something in Lucie's tone made Atticus Fox turn from his window. His wife was reaching over the table with a pair of tiny brass tweezers in her fingers to peck at the air just above a stiffened fold in the dress.

"Come and look at this."

Atticus, at once both reluctant and intrigued, obeyed. There was a sweet, apothecary smell about the dress and he was glad of it. Ether was far more tolerable than the coppery stench of blood.

Lucie nodded towards the tips of the tweezers. Atticus looked, reached for their big magnifying lens, and then looked again. Gripped between the delicate jaws was a hair. It was a very long, dark hair, and through his glass, Atticus could clearly see the jagged flake of blood that had served to anchor it to the cotton. At eight or nine inches in length it was too long to be from a man and much too coarse for a woman's.

As they stood staring at it, their theories and judgements all at once collapsing around them, there was a whisper of notepaper being pushed under the door. It would be from their housekeeper, they knew. Whenever they were busy in their laboratory, (or workroom, as Lucie preferred to call it), Mrs Morris would generally communicate using little squares of paper.

Atticus, relieved as a child to leave the table, went to pick it up. This was no quickly scribbled note however, and neither was it from their housekeeper; it was an envelope, press-stamped 'Royal Bath Hospital'.

"It's from Dr Wormald," Atticus said.

He sliced it open with the blade of his pocket knife and unfolded the letter within:

Dear Mr and Mrs Fox,

The gunja beans we discussed this morning are from a plant properly called Abrus precatorius, *or more commonly, the rosary pea, which is found only in the tropics. The beans are often employed to make jewellery and in native witchcraft.*

As I recollected, Indians use them in their Ayurveda medicine, where they are used in aphrodisiacs, treatments for skin-boils and hair restoratives.

Be sure to take the greatest care as the beans, although very beautiful, are deadly poisons.

Your Servant,

Dr Frederick Wormald, M.D.

P.S.   The coroner, who is to carry out the post-mortem necropsy on the deceased woman, is anxious also to examine her dress. Please be good enough to have it sent up to the police station upon your earliest convenience.

Atticus folded the letter back into its envelope and tapped the corner of the paper on his chin as he considered this new information. The rosary peas were there, sitting in a bonbon dish on a corner of the laboratory table.

"So which is it to be, do you suppose, Lucie: jewellery, witchcraft or medicine?"

Lucie carefully coiled the hair into a second silver dish and laid her tweezers across the rim before she replied.

"We get all manner of visitors to Harrogate, Atty, including a great many from India. The beans are all threaded for jewellery, so I should imagine it will be that."

She grimaced as she stretched over the table to examine the bloodied bodice of the dress. It had been shredded into long, gaping rents.

"It is very late in the season for the Empire visitors," Atticus pointed out. "And the ones that do come are much more likely to wear gold and ivory than a string of beans."

"I suppose so," Lucie conceded, then: "I believe the Beast of the Bogs Valley is sinistral. Sarah's wounds were predominantly on the right side of her face and body, and the disposition of the gashes in her dress is entirely consistent with him being left-handed."

Atticus recalled the memory of Esau's notebook and his neat, flowing hand.

"Esau is left-handed," he said.

CHAPTER FIFTEEN

"Mr Fox, a very good morning to you. You honour our police station with your visit. I'm just very sorry I can't offer you dainty cakes."

Detective Inspector Douglas hoisted each of his boots, in turn, up onto the edge of his desk and folded his arms comfortably over his chest.

"So, I expect you've come to tell me how you've solved the case and that, even as we speak, the Beast of the Bogs Valley is captured and confessed with a noose around his neck, all ready to drop."

"I have not, Inspector," Atticus replied. He glanced disapprovingly at a crusting of mud, which had dropped from Douglas' boot-sole and crumbled onto the desktop.

"Oh, I see. Then you must have come to collect the prisoner on behalf of your *puissant* friend." Douglas shifted his hands to the back of his head and raised his eyebrows enquiringly. "Well?"

He snorted in derision at Atticus' bafflement.

"I am speaking about your wild-man, Fox. We cannot detain him any longer. Joseph Malkin has been having conversations with the senior ranks, insisting that he couldn't possibly be the murderer. No doubt you would take his side on that point too – and Mrs Fox, most likely.

Someone very senior to me has ordered that Esau be released, and God help the poor whores of Harrogate."

"I do not know for certain which side Mrs Fox and I would take, Douglas. I came here today to return the deceased woman's dress – the coroner has requested it for examination – and also to tell you that yesterday, I found several beans of a plant known as *Abrus precatorius* in the drain outside the bath-chair yard."

Douglas sat up smartly and his boots clattered onto the wooden boards of the floor.

"Did you, by god?" he growled, and then: "Hainsworth!"

The sergeant looked round from a tiny desk in the corner. "Yes, Inspector."

"The break-in at the Corporation greenhouses last night: remind me what was taken."

"It was one half-sackful of heartsease plants. They'd just been pulled up from the borders by the Town Hall, ready for the wallflowers to—"

"Yes, yes, never mind about the wallflowers. Heartsease – is that the same plant you just mentioned, Fox?"

Atticus shook his head. "They're quite different; *Abrus precatorius* is from the tropics; heartsease is native to Britain."

Douglas tugged at a drawer below his desk. He fished out a pipe and a stamped-leather tobacco box, and laid them onto his blotter.

"The mayor wants me to investigate it, would you believe, Fox? Personally. His Worship wants me, a detective inspector of more than twenty years standing, to investigate the theft of a bag of flowers, two broken greenhouse windows and a gardener with a blackened-eye. A crime is a crime, he tells me. Never mind a deuce I have this Bogs Valley Beast somewhere still at large and a dead woman not yet cold in her grave."

He began to stuff tobacco savagely into the bowl of his pipe.

"That's her dress I take it?" he said, nodding towards the brown-paper parcel on Atticus' lap. "Hainsworth, you had better get it up to the coroner. After that you can have the prisoner released. He can find his own way back to Beagle House."

He jabbed his pipe stem angrily towards Atticus' chest.

"It's you the mayor should be paying to investigate the gardener's black-eye, Fox, and leaving the murderer to us. But we know how it works, don't we, Hainsworth? Oh, yes, handshakes and favours amongst the Brethren. No doubt you'll have a square-and-compass on the back of your pocket-watch, just the same as Samson. But very well, you've delivered the dress and you've told me about your beans. Thank ye kindly. But if that is all, I'm sure you'll excuse me; Sergeant Hainsworth and I have a monster to apprehend. Good day to you."

Atticus did not move. He was aware again of the pulse ticking in his neck.

"Good day to you, Fox."

"Inspector Douglas, for one thing, I am not, and nor will I ever be, a Freemason, and for another, you must not on any account release Esau onto the streets."

Douglas thrust the bit of his pipe between his teeth and struck a Vesta.

"Why mustn't I?" He dabbed the match onto the tobacco and began sucking it into life. "I thought you believed him innocent."

"I do. But at the same time, I recognise that he might be inclined towards aggression… in certain circumstances." Atticus suddenly wished he had brought Lucie with him. She would have laid the words out properly. "And he wouldn't have the first notion of how to get back to Beagle House, even if he were disposed to go there at all."

Douglas coughed on the smoke spilling from his pipe.

"If Esau isn't to be the Beast, Fox, then he is of no further interest to me. If he does happen to make another attack, then he'll be arrested again and my superintendant will have a pretty word to say to the chief constable about his assistant. As for him getting back to his diggings, well, if you're so worried about it, you take him." He smirked through the smoke. "It would seem to me to be the perfect employment for a private enquiry agent."

"Good day, Mr Fox and good day to you, sir."

Susan, the parlour-maid, curtsied and showed her two unexpected visitors through the vestibule of Beagle House and into the broad hallway beyond. It was still morning and much too early for social calls, but she knew that Atticus Fox would be welcomed whatever the time of day. His companion seemed familiar too, strangely familiar, but in a troubling way, like Dr Fell[13] in the nursery rhyme, which made the fine hairs at the nape of her neck stand on end.

She watched this second visitor from the corner of her eye as he passed her in the hall. Strange was certainly the word for him and no mistake. He had fine trousers and shoes, but as for the cloak he was wearing. Lordy! It was old and grimy and worn quite through to the threads. A gardener wouldn't use it on a scarecrow. Her nose wrinkled at the sudden waft of carbolic that followed in his wake and she wondered if she might have done better to have sent him round the back. He might, she thought with a start, even be a burglar, with his terrier-cropped hair. And the way he was staring around at everything with those horrible, black eyes!

Atticus interrupted her thoughts. "Is Master in, Susan?"

"Oh, yes, I'm quite sure he will be, Mr Fox, but I'd better just go and see?" She curtsied and turned away along the hallway, and immediately collided with Joseph Malkin.

"Dear me, Susan, but do take care. Did I hear Atticus Fox's voice a moment ago? It seems I did, and bless my soul if it isn't Esau with him too."

"Douglas was ordered to let him go," Atticus explained when they were all comfortably seated in Beagle House's extensive library.

"Yes, I rather thought he might be." Joseph grinned sheepishly. "I had a little word with one or two folk I know. Having said that, I was rather hoping the police might have held on to him for a few more hours. You see, Atticus old fellow, I'm afraid we've hit something of a snag."

"What sort of a snag?" Atticus asked.

Joseph glanced across at Esau, who was sitting cross-legged in a tub-chair, utterly engrossed in a book.

"A snag of the most insurmountable kind. It's the Dame, you see. Victoria has taken against him. Now, with the police having been round and set the tongues of the neighbours a-wagging, she won't let me keep him here any longer, not even in the stables."

"No!" exclaimed Atticus.

"Exactly, Atticus, exactly. So I need to find somewhere to house him, and quickly. The question is: where?" He spread his hands in a gesture of helplessness. "I won't have him in a zoo, and a hotel wouldn't do at all."

Atticus pulled thoughtfully on the whiskers at his chin and regarded Esau. He was curled over a page, running his fingertips over a colourful illustration of some jackal-headed Egyptian god.

'Anubis', he thought idly. Then he said: "Have you ever heard of a Dr Roberts over in High Harrogate?"

"Dr Roberts? Michael Roberts of the Lunatic Retreat, do you mean? Yes, I have, of course. Michael Roberts comes to our Quaker Meeting House. I didn't know you were acquainted."

"Mrs Fox and I were commissioned by him back in '90, when his grandfather, old Alfred Roberts, was murdered by his aunt[14]."

"Yes, I remember it; it was the talk of the town at the time. I believe it still troubles him even now. In any event, it has led to his convincement as a Quaker. Are you suggesting his Retreat might be a suitable place for Esau?"

"I am, Joseph. It is more in the nature of a sanctuary for those who might be suffering from a troubled past than an asylum, and from what I know of it, it is comfortable, warm and quite secure. If Dr Roberts would be willing to take Esau in – and I believe he could easily be persuaded – then yes; I believe it would be perfect for him."

CHAPTER SIXTEEN

It was a curious feeling, to be standing once again before Sessrum House, Dr Michael Roberts' large and rambling mansion, set beside the Stray at High Harrogate. The last time the Foxes had been here, they had been instrumental in fetching Dr Roberts' elderly and demented aunt from the Knaresborough workhouse to what had been her childhood home. And, as was still the subject of many a scandalised whisper, she had, on her very first night there, murdered her uncle, Alfred Roberts, the great Harrogate philanthropist, with a paper-knife.

Now, rich gold letters illuminated one of the pillars of the grand front portico and glinted brightly in the midday Sun:

The Harrogate Retreat
Principal: Michael Roberts
That which we are, we are,
One equal temper of heroic hearts,
Made weak by time and fate, but strong in will
To strive, to seek, to find, and not to yield.

Beneath the words, the gilt facsimile of a pointing hand directed visitors along a path that lead away to one side of the house.

"A poignant choice of words for a retreat," Lucie remarked.

"They are from Alfred Tennyson's poem *Ulysses*," said Atticus.

As they stood, each musing on the peculiar aptness of the poet's words, the big front door of the house opened and there was Dr Roberts himself, grinning broadly from a face that had aged far more than the two years that had passed since they had last seen him.

"Atticus Fox, my dear fellow, and Lucie Fox, how delightful to see you again, and by God's grace, Joseph Malkin. You are all most welcome. I thought I recognised you walking up my carriage-drive. And who, may I ask, is the young gentleman you have with you?"

There was a beat of awkwardness as Atticus, Lucie and Joseph all glanced between themselves. Then Lucie said: "Dr Roberts, this is Esau. We have brought him here in the hope of having him admitted into your Retreat."

"Have you now?" Roberts took a pair of horn-rimmed spectacles from his pocket and hooked each arm in turn around his ears. He regarded Esau, who was standing before the pillar, running his fingertips over the golden words as a scholar might follow the hieroglyphs on a newly-found tomb.

"You had better come round to the Annexe in that case. We can discuss his case more privately there."

Dr Roberts led them past some ancient, mop-headed hydrangea bushes, and along a path that was both familiar to the Foxes, and as forbidding as the very grave. Ahead of them, the newly-gilded statue of some mythological goddess shone in the sunlight.

Esau gasped. "Mary, it is Mary Magdalene".

"Mary Magdalene again," Joseph chuckled.

"It is Freya actually," Roberts replied with a quick glance to the Foxes, "The Norse goddess of love and beauty."

"Although," Atticus added, "a great number of the ancient love deities – Freya herself; Aphrodite of the Greeks; Hathor of the Egyptians – are, in the minds of many scholars at least, analogous with St Mary Magdalene."

Esau stabbed a finger towards the glittering statue.

"A heathen idol?" he roared, "A false god! Then shall I tear it down".

His outstretched finger began to tremble, like a prophet's of old.

"Thy graven images also will I cut off, and thy standing images out of the midst of thee, and thou shalt no more worship the work of thine hands."

Freya's sightless, golden eyes stared back impassively into Esau's black ones until Lucie stepped between them. She closed her hands around Esau's. He shied and tried to pull away from her, but Lucie held firm.

"Esau, listen to me. Listen! That is called a statue. It is not an idol, and it is most certainly not to be torn down by anyone except Dr Roberts, whose property it is. No-one worships it."

"Not these days, at least," Atticus muttered.

"It is there simply as something beautiful," Lucie explained, "Just as you thought it was, until you took it for a… a graven image."

"It is no more an idol than the statue of Mary Magdalene on the wall of the leper chapel," Atticus added.

Esau's gaze dropped to Lucie's hands, still gripping his own, and he nodded.

"Atticus and Lucie Fox are quite correct, Esau," said Roberts. "But I am very sorry if my statue causes you offence. We must be sure to sit down together in order to talk about it."

With that, he beckoned them on to a second portico, a smaller twin to the grand frontage of the house. It formed the entrance to a large annexe and the newly-built stonework was clean and bright against the smoke-darkened walls around it. Carved into the tympanum above the part-open door were the words: *The Harrogate Retreat – A Sanctuary of Peace and Light.*

"I take it you have had a strict, religious upbringing, Esau?" Malkin pressed at the door and it rolled wide. He nodded to a brown-suited porter seated primly behind a reception desk and said: "Three visitors and a prospective new guest for us."

The porter, a small man with a quick, nervous manner and the jaundiced eyes of a spirit addict, ducked to one side and watched them through the bars of a bird cage, which stood at one side of his desk. Inside, a big, brown myna bird cocked its head and peered inquisitively at them too.

"Esau was raised in a workhouse," Atticus explained as they began to climb a great, stone, spiral staircase, "But for some years now, he has been the principal exhibit in a freak show."

"An exhibit in a *freak show*!" Roberts stopped short on his stair. He turned, and in a way that rather reminded them of the porter and his myna bird, peered anew at Esau.

"A travelling show," Joseph confirmed, "And by-the-by, Michael Roberts, I would advise you strongly not to look into his eyes like that."

"But why was he in a freak show, Joseph Malkin? There's nothing especially freakish about him, at least so far as I can see."

"If you had seen him just forty-eight hours ago, you would have had a very different opinion on that." Joseph replied.

"Esau suffers from an exceedingly rare condition, which causes an overgrowth of hair across his entire body," Lucie explained. "Atticus and Mr Malkin have clipped it off for the present, but it will quickly grow back."

Behind the glass of his spectacle lenses, Dr Roberts' eyes slowly closed.

"It sounds like something from one of Mr Dickens' novels," he said after a moment; "A poor, wretched boy, condemned not only to be brought up in a workhouse, but then to be displayed as a freak in a travelling show. I can only conclude that the Almighty has had a hand in directing him here, to my Retreat. Let us be thankful for that."

"Amen," murmured Joseph.

A tear had picked its way down his cheek and melted into the grey-flecked whiskers of his beard before Roberts opened his eyes and spoke again. This time he addressed Esau directly.

"I am very sorry for the events of your life until now, Master Esau and you are to be pitied for them. But what has past has past, and there is naught we can do to change it. The future, however, is a very different matter altogether. You, like all of God's creatures, deserve a just and happy life, and I affirm here today that if you agree not to fight or to cause distress to your fellow guests, you will have such a life here for as long as you may choose to remain. Come, new friend and welcome guest, come and make inspection of your new home."

He led them, briskly now, up the remaining stairs and into a large and bright day-room, whose walls were arrayed with a great number of mirrors, paintings and photographic plates.

"I imagine you will find it very different from the last time you were here, Atticus and Lucie Fox?" he said.

"The change is quite astonishing," Lucie exclaimed.

Roberts beamed.

"A great deal of thought has been employed in its arrangement, Lucie Fox. I have observed, for instance, that sunlight appears to have a beneficial effect upon our guests' mood, and so I have endeavoured to reproduce it in the lemon-yellow walls and the judicious use of mirrors. For those yet too timid to venture out, I have provided ample views of local places of interest in the paintings and photographs. Do you like it too, Esau? Nothing to say yet, I see. Well never mind, I'm sure you will, in time. You do have the most extraordinary eyes, by-the-by. Now, let us sit together over there in the corner; my little office would be much too cramped for all of us."

He shepherded them towards several chaises longues, which were grouped together beneath an array of large watercolours. Each painting depicted one of the more splendid of the Harrogate churches.

"So then," Roberts began. His eyes lingered for a moment on Esau, who was sitting, cross-legged on his seat, staring up at a church labelled St Peter's. "Welcome to my Harrogate Retreat. We are a Quaker institution. In other words, we are as a family, and we treat one another as if we might be brother and sister, each one God's creature and each one filled with the *Light Within*. Like a family, we use names and not man-made titles. I am therefore not Doctor Roberts but simply Michael Roberts and, in the same way, the nursing sister in charge during the night-time is called Mary Lovell."

He pushed up on the bridge of his spectacles and pulled a tiny notebook and pencil from his waistcoat pocket.

"So tell me, Esau; what is your surname?"

Esau looked down from his watercolour and considered the question. "Shit-face?" he suggested.

"If he was ever given one, it has long been forgotten," Malkin interjected hurriedly. "He may use mine, Malkin, for convenience."

Dr Roberts licked the point of his pencil and scribbled in the notebook.

"And the condition with which he is afflicted causes him to grow an excess of hair, did you say, Lucie Fox?"

"Yes, that is correct."

"The condition is known as *Hypertrichosis universalis,*" Atticus added.

Roberts lifted his pencil and hesitated. "Hyper… what was that again?"

"Dog man syndrome," said Lucie.

Dr Roberts smiled graciously. "Ah, thank you, that is much easier. Medical man though I am, I agree with the Venerable Inceptor[15], that the simplest in all things is generally the noblest."

Malkin said: "An alternative hypothesis, and the one to which I myself subscribe, is that Esau represents the evolutionary missing link between mankind on the one hand and the great apes on the other. That is how he was presented in the freak show and my own investigations are continuing as to its basis in fact."

Roberts scowled. He replaced his pencil in the spine of his notebook and laid it onto the cushion of the chaise longue beside him.

"Joseph Malkin, I know you to be a Friend – a brother Quaker. Now I understand very well how some of our brethren can be what we call Universalists – how they see truth in all religions as well as in Christianity. You are a Universalist yourself, I believe. Pray tell me this though: How can you believe in God, believe that we are all *Children of the Light,* and yet, at the same time, subscribe to the theories of evolution?"

"Why, with the greatest of ease, Michael Roberts," Malkin replied. He rose to his feet and tucked his thumbs into his waistcoat pockets. "Many of our brothers and sisters do exactly that. To wit: Those whose personal and direct experience of God, whose *Light Within,* has led them to a *progressive revelation* of truth. That revelation might include elements from so-called other religions, but it might just as well include modern scientific discoveries, such as that of the evolution of species."

"Oh, I see now; so you are a *Revelationist.*" Roberts unhooked the arms of his spectacles from around his ears and began to polish one of the lenses with a corner of his waistcoat. "I have often wondered about that way of thinking myself. It would certainly be an explanation of Nature's great cruelty, how it is, as the great Alfred, Lord Tennyson reminds us, so very red in tooth and claw[16]."

"Nature – the very world itself – is corrupted and ignoble, and always has been," Malkin declared.

Roberts nodded and gazed deeply into the spectacle lens, as if it might have been the great oracle of Buto itself.

"As you know, I took up Quakerism only in recent years. It was in an attempt to come to terms with events in my own life, and, in particular, with my grandfather's death. But even now, the more I see of the cruelty and injustice in the world, the more I wrestle with the whole notion of a god of love. Yet god there must be. I have heard a spiritualist medium converse with the souls of the departed with my own ears. Perhaps Nature, with ravine, shriek'd against our creed[16], is an adversary worthier than even we might imagine."

"You have heard the spirits of the dead actually speaking, Dr Roberts?" Atticus was incredulous.

Roberts smile was hollow and stopped just short of his eyes.

"Oh yes, Atticus, I have. I most definitely have. It was not long after last we met. The spirit of my grandfather was able to communicate its forgiveness of... of his murderers. One wonders whether God Himself will be so forgiving in the final accounting."

"I cannot see why He would not be," said Lucie.

Roberts' smile thinned and he glanced up to the churches, idyllic in their frames.

"You would not think so, Lucie Fox, if you heard what is preached in those steeple-houses. Therein seems to dwell a God only of Atonement."

He sighed heavily.

"Yes, perhaps Revelationism is the answer, Joseph Malkin."

"I am quite certain of it," declared Malkin. "Instead of setting folk against one another, each mired in his own dogmas, Revelationism, along with its brother, Universalism, serves to bring them all together, each a small part of a much greater whole."

"Well I am an alienist, a psychiatrist, by profession, cursed to be a seer into the mind," Roberts replied. "And I learned long ago that man is more inclined to conflict than to concord, that he is much more in Nature's image than in any loving god's." He glanced down again to his spectacles. "And I must, for shame, include myself in that."

"You have goodness, Michael Roberts," Joseph countered, "And you have godliness. It is your soul, your own spark of *The Light Within*."

Roberts shrugged.

"I do hope so. I always mean well, at any rate."

He turned to Esau.

"And what is your faith, Esau Malkin? Anglican, I expect, if you were brought up in a workhouse. Our guests are free, of course, to practice whichever religion they choose, or no religion at all if they prefer."

"Esau was brought up in the Church of England," Joseph confirmed.

"And brought up devoutly, I have no doubt," said Roberts. "He can certainly quote scripture admirably, as we heard for ourselves just a little while ago. Joseph Malkin, I'll speak plainly: he seems to me altogether too intelligent to be a half-ape."

"He is intelligent, highly intelligent, and quite capable of reading and then reciting what he has read – aping if you will – just as well as you or I. It does not, however, follow that he is the equal of *Homo sapiens* in some of the more noble endeavours: philosophy, art, literature and the like."

"Well he looks just like a regular man to my eyes, other than in this supposed overgrowth of hair, of course. They do say that what ultimately distinguishes man from the lower orders is not art or philosophy or scientific learning, but his need for the spiritual."

"Yes, the *sensus divinitatis*," said Atticus. "I am not sure I have that myself. Like you, Dr Roberts, I cannot see how a Divine Being, beneficent and all-powerful, could tolerate there being such misery in this world." He grinned. "Perhaps I should be in a zoological garden, along with Esau."

Roberts chuckled. "*Sensus divinitatis* – a sense of the Divine. It is, as Joseph has just reminded us, what we Quakers call *The Light Within,* and I declare: Esau seems to possess more of that than any of us. Perhaps we should conclude that *he* is the higher species, and that *we* are the missing link to *him.* What do you think to that possibility, Esau? Instead of a rising ape, what if you were an angel, fallen to Earth, sent to guide and judge us?"

Malkin's mouth fell open.

"What an extraordinary thought."

"Quite so," said Roberts. "But whichever it is, it matters not. Be he monkey, or be he messiah, Esau is welcome here. We generally put our guests in the large dormitory we have downstairs, but I rather fancy he should have a room of his own. Esau, you may use the gardens, and the library too, as much as you please. In fact, I believe I have my old copy of Charles Darwin's *On the Origin of Species* locked away somewhere. Joseph Malkin has convinced me sufficiently that it is not as blasphemous as I had previously believed, so you may have that to begin. Please come and go into Harrogate as you see fit; I ask only that you refrain from profanity, gambling and violence."

"Yes, Master," said Esau.

"Please call me Michael Roberts, Esau. We have no masters here."

"Yes, Michael Roberts."

"Oh, and Lucie Fox, knowing how much Atticus benefitted from your suggestion that he learn chess, we encourage all our inmate-guests to learn and play rithmomachia – the philosophers' game of numbers. Chess is altogether too warlike for a Quaker institution but I learned to play the other during my training in Germany and it serves to distract and focus the mind just as well."

CHAPTER SEVENTEEN

The Moon, just past its third quarter, reflects in the stream and runs like a million points of light. Each point is a dagger, a million daggers, such that he cries out and draws down his tattered hood. Yet he, the Beast of the Bogs Valley, must endure it. He must follow this stream of molten agony through the pleasure gardens, to the little wooden gates at its end. This time he must – this time he will – hold his fury in check.

Beyond the gates, the streets are deserted. Mercifully, there are no policemen with ironwood truncheons; no pretty temptresses driving him to madness and no gentlemen with their mocking, mocking Psalms. There is just the gentle hiss of the gas-lamps, spilling their light onto the broad, empty pavements.

The Beast of the Bogs Valley wipes his streaming eyes, renews his grasp on his hood, and steps out into the light.

He walks, awkwardly and deliberately, through the soul of the town, shutting his mind to the muffled sounds of gaiety and laughter that might drive him to rage. The hospital is close, he remembers; it is just a little farther. There! Beyond the Punch and Judy stall and up on the hill, he sees it – the hospital for incurables, incurables, incurables.

Once he would have strode up to the door, straight-backed and proud, basking in the glorious light of holiness. Now, he must creep through the shadows, through the shadows of the Valley of Death and slip in, unseen.

"Who are you? What do you want?"

He turns, and a lantern sends a shaft of agony to pierce his brain. A nurse is holding it, staring at him, blocking his way.

"Please," he whispers.

"And what the dickens do you think you're doing with that?"

The nurse steps towards him, angry and indignant.

"Porter, Dr Watson, do come quickly! There's a thief, a thief in the dispens—."

The pot, cold and heavy, cracks on her skull, and blood and streams of quicksilver, hot and ice-cold, spatter his wrists. The lantern drops and is extinguished, and it is mercifully, mercifully dark.

CHAPTER EIGHTEEN

Atticus Fox awakens.

The room is dark and still, except for the slow and steady breathing of his wife beside him, and the pounding of his heart. Something has disturbed him, something beyond the window.

Rolling back the bedclothes, he flits to the window and eases back the shutter. A tumble of cold air falls into the room and carries the sound of voices, urgent, clamant, to him. He heaves up the sash and leans out into the night. Down the Montpellier hill, lights are flooding out from the windows of a building – a building with an unmistakeable silhouette under the waning moon. It is the incurables' hospital.

A police whistle blows, clear and shrill, and Atticus knows instantly that that is what woke him. He knows in that moment too, that the Beast has struck again.

"Is she badly injured, Dr Watson?" Lucie Fox asked.

Dr Bertie Watson, Honorary Physician of the Yorkshire Hospital for Chronic and Incurable Diseases, was a tall man with a lean face that he had attempted to improve by the cultivation of a broad, walrus moustache. In so doing he had succeeded only in giving himself a permanent air of glumness. At this moment Dr Watson was kneeling on a pillow next to a bed, where lay a nurse. She was staring at the ceiling with eyes as large and as shining as porcelain eggs, whilst Dr Watson wound layer after layer of linen bandage over a thick dressing on her head.

"I don't believe so, Mrs Fox," the doctor replied. "It looks rather worse than it is. There is some evidence of cerebral concussion but the blow was a glancing one and for that we must be thankful. It has knocked a little skin off, and she will have a lump and an aching head for a day or two, but beyond that, I see no reason why she should not make a swift and full recovery."

"Her attacker struck her with a pot of mercury, you say?" Atticus asked.

"That is correct, Mr Fox. It was a large pot of elemental mercury and extremely heavy, so, as you can see by the effects on Sister Keegan here, it made for an excellent weapon. The lid came off in the melee, so the nurses will be a while in cleaning up the medicines dispensary. There are beads of the stuff everywhere. We need to recover as much as we can for the morning rounds, for the syphilitic and the impacted patients. The ruffian stole the only pot we had. I hope he over-doses on it, damn him."

"What would happen to him if he did?"

"He would die, Mr Fox, eventually anyway." Watson fished in his pocket for a surgeon's scissors. "But until that happy day, let me see now; he would begin to sweat quite profusely, portions of his skin might be shed, and he would start to lose his hair. Oh, and he would drool like a bloodhound. I doubt he'd look the sort you'd wish to share a theatre-box with."

Lucie watched as Watson cut and neatly tied-off the bandage. Then she said: "Doctor, I am a Netley-trained nurse. May I sit with Sister, until she feels able to speak? She might recollect something that could lead us to her attacker."

"I cannot see why not." Watson rose easily to his feet and smoothed his moustache. Standing upright, he really was very tall, taller even than Atticus. "We are already one nurse fewer and with the mess in the dispensary, I should struggle to spare another. I'm sure you'll take care not to overly distress her. Be warned though; it may be some hours before she can recollect clearly what happened, if indeed, she ever does."

"In which case I shall take the opportunity to examine the dispensary," said Atticus, "It was a ferocious attack and therefore almost certain to have left some clues as to this monster's identity."

Notwithstanding Dr Watson's words of caution, when Atticus Fox returned to the bedside no more than an hour later, the nurse's face had regained much of its colour. She was clinging with both hands to Lucie's arm, and, as he knocked and opened the door, she gave a violent start.

"Mercy me, Mrs Fox, I'm all a-goosey."

"As you've every reason to be, Sister Keegan." Lucie patted the nurse's hands. "You've nothing to fear from this gentleman though; this is my husband, Atticus Fox."

Atticus bowed graciously.

"Did you find anything?" Lucie asked.

"Only the lid from the mercury pot, which, unfortunately, is cork so there aren't any fingertip prints to be had from it. And there's a small army of nurses down there, with enough carbolic acid to float an ironclad. Any traces there might have been have long since been swilled away down the drain.

"What I did find of interest, however, is this: The medicines dispensary is contained in the basement of the hospital, which is a veritable rabbits' warren. So it occurred to me that either this fellow was wandering around and happened to stumble upon it, which would seem rather unlikely, or else he knew exactly what he was about."

"It was someone from the hospital, then?"

"Quite possibly so – or a visitor, or an out-patient perhaps. Has Sister been able to tell you anything?"

"Sister Keegan has shown very great fortitude tonight." Lucie squeezed the nurse's arm and beamed encouragingly at her. "She has told me that her attacker wore a long dark cloak and a hood, which he had pulled down over his face."

She looked up, conveying in a glance the awful certainty that, but for a miracle, they would now be investigating a second murder by the Beast of Harrogate's Bogs Valley.

"Did this cloaked-and-hooded man happen to speak to you, Nurse?" Atticus asked. "In particular, did he pull his hood back and insist that you look upon his face?"

Sister Keegan gathered herself.

"He did speak, Mr Fox. Well, he screamed, more like. He wanted to know if we had any Viscum. But he kept his hood up; I'm quite sure on that point. He seemed determined on keeping his face hidden."

"Viscum, you say? He asked you for *Viscum*? Well, now, how exceedingly curious."

"I asked… I asked him what he was about, ransacking the medicine shelves like that. I declare, he was throwing everything around like a madman. Anyway, he turns and he screams out: 'Please, packets of Viscum'. Those were his exact words, Mr Fox. So I lifts up my lamp, to get a proper look at him, and he shrieks like he were a rabbit a hound had gotten a-hold of." The nurse's eyes stretched wide and her fingers clawed into Lucie's sleeve. "And his eyes… his eyes were like the eyes of the Devil himself, Mrs Fox, staring and burning like that. And then he came at me with the pot of quicksilver he had in his hand…"

"Hush," cooed Lucie, "Hush. He's gone now. The doors are locked. Mr Fox and I are here, and you're quite safe."

The nurse shook her head.

"But he hasn't gone, Mrs Fox, not properly, anyhow. He'll be back. He's been here before, do you see? That monster has been here before."

"When has he been here before?" Atticus cried.

"It was just last week, Mr Fox. He stole a pail of blood."

Atticus' and Lucie's eyes met.

"Take a deep breath, Sister Keegan," said Lucie, "I would like you to tell us everything you can remember about what happened last week. To begin with, can you recall what day it was?"

"It was Wednesday," the nurse said firmly. "I know it was Wednesday because I had just come into my fortnight on nights."

"And what happened on Wednesday night?"

"Well, it was very late. One of the patients, a malarial case, was running a 'specially high fever. He'd been getting quite worked up with himself and Dr Watson left orders that if he should get any worse he was to be bled twenty ounces."

"Bled," Atticus exclaimed, "I thought we'd long-since abandoned blood-letting, on human patients at least."

"We have done, mostly anyway. Dr Watson only orders it to be done in extreme circumstances – for high fevers in the main. We don't even keep leeches these days; we have to use a syringe."

"So tell us what happened when your malaria patient was bled," said Lucie, and with a sharp glance to her husband added: "We shall try not to shout, or to interrupt you again."

"The night physician took the twenty ounces of blood from him, Mrs Fox, just as Doctor had directed, and the porter took the pail and the syringe to pour the blood directly down the drain outside. Dr Watson is very particular on that score, for reasons of hygiene. Anyway, he is no sooner out of the door when that… that creature barges him, grabs the pail, and runs away down the street with it, blood, syringe and all. Mr Chambers, the night porter, doesn't have the constitution to run after folk these days, so away he got, with a glass syringe and one of our best enamel pails."

"And twenty ounces of blood," added Atticus.

"Well yes. I really can't imagine what he must have thought when he looked to see what he had thieved and found that." The nurse made a sound somewhere between a gasp and a sob.

"Was all of this reported to the police?" Lucie asked.

The nurse shrugged against her pillow.

"I doubt the police could have done anything about it. Mr Chambers wasn't badly hurt and we've a whole cupboard full of pails."

"Would Mr Chambers be available to make a deposition, Sister?" Atticus asked. "We should very much like to ask him about it."

The porter's room at the Yorkshire Hospital for Chronic and Incurable Diseases was scarcely large enough to accommodate Mr Chambers, large and stout as he was, never mind the Foxes too. A tiny coal fire served to render it oppressively hot, so Atticus was very pleased to stand in the cool draught at the doorway as the night porter described in great and dramatic detail, his encounter with the Beast of the Bogs Valley. For the Beast it surely had been; the cloak, the hood, the curious, high-stepping gait left no room for any doubt at all on that score.

CHAPTER NINETEEN

On the northern outskirts of Harrogate, a little further out than the very smartest parts of the town, was a shop.

It was a curious shop, one which caused passing ladies to turn away their heads or even to cross the street entirely, to avoid having to look at it. In equal measure, it drew fascination from the local schoolchildren, who would gather at its little, latticed window and stare through the grime and the dust at the single item exhibited there. It was a skull, a human skull, from a murderer it was said, which had been divided neatly, in long-faded ink, into two- or three-dozen sections. A curled and yellowed card propped against the jawbone advised that the shop was, in fact, a phrenologist's parlour, the proprietor being one Professor E.P. Ryan, a fellow of the Wakefield Phrenological Society and a skilled practitioner of the celebrated Combe system. It was to Professor Ryan's parlour that Joseph Malkin brought Esau.

As the pair entered, a bell tinkled above their heads and there was Professor Ryan himself, standing just inside the doorway. He greeted them with a low and sweeping bow, and a smile not unlike Mr Wilberforce's.

"A pleasant morning to you, Mr Malkin," he purred, regarding the wild-man at Joseph's side with evident curiosity. "It is always a great honour to receive you into my humble parlour. And might this be the young gentleman you made reference to in your telegram?"

"It is indeed, Ernest Ryan. This is Esau… Malkin and I should like you to undertake a full phrenological examination of his cranium for me."

"Of course, Mr Malkin, of course; I should be delighted to."

Professor Ryan drew Esau forward into the parlour and began to slowly circumambulate him, now and again darting forward to peer closely at his head, as a hummingbird might inspect a freshly-opened blossom.

"And would you be interested in any of Mr Esau's phrenological organs in particular, by which of course I mean his faculties?"

Malkin bit his lip.

"Perhaps those which might be considered to separate man's character from that of other… creatures."

"Ah, yes." The professor lifted one of a line of chipped and battered wall chairs into the middle of the room and made a show of dusting off the seat-pad. "You are referring, of course, to the second phrenological Genus and to the second group of Sentiments: the *Sentiments Proper to Man*. I shall take care to pay particular note to those.

"Now if the young gentleman would be good enough to sit in this chair and remove his hat, I will begin my examinations directly."

CHAPTER TWENTY

Atticus Fox stood once again by the window of their laboratory workroom, to stare out across Low Harrogate towards the Royal Bath Hospital. Beyond it, and high on Harlow Hill, the stub of an observation tower rose tall above the treetops and Atticus was reminded of the Harrogate Corporation's nursery garden, which lay in its shadow.

Why, he pondered over the muted sounds of the Temperance Band carrying up to the window from the bandstand below, would anyone wish to steal a sack of half-dead border plants? For the seeds, perhaps? That would have been why the gardeners had kept them instead of tossing them unceremoniously onto the compost heap. But if that were the case, why not wait for the seeds to dry and be collected, and take them then?

It was exceedingly curious, just as curious in its own way as someone stealing a bucket of blood, and that in itself connected it to this oddly perplexing case of the Beast. Whoever had taken the bucket, and whoever had stolen the plants, had wanted them badly enough to risk both discovery and injury. And, of course, the hospital and the greenhouses lay at opposite ends of the same Bogs Valley.

He gazed at the tower and pulled thoughtfully at the hairs of his chin. It really was all very puzzling.

"Atticus!"

He turned sharply from his reverie to see Lucie standing by the table, their big investigations bag swinging gently from her shoulder. She had returned from a second visit to the incurables' hospital and was regarding him now with an expression somewhere between exasperation and amusement. He realised all at once that she must have been speaking to him.

"I'm so sorry, Lucie, I was just thinking about the greenhouse theft."

"And I was just saying that I've checked the incurables' dispensary with the big magnifying lens and you were right; there are no workable finger-prints of any kind that haven't been left by the porter or the night nurses – only a badly smeared thumb-print on the dispensary door-knob that I couldn't be sure of. Everything else has been wiped clean."

Atticus nodded.

"It's a pity, but not altogether unexpected."

He turned back to his window and its light spread across his face, pensive and grave. Then he said: "Lucie, I believe this case may be to do with medicines."

Lucie lifted their bag onto the work table and turned to perch on its edge.

"But we know that already, Atticus. The Beast was rifling through the hospital dispensary, after all."

"No, I mean the whole case – all of the attacks; they are all strongly suggestive of medicines."

He nodded towards the tabletop by Lucie's leg, where Dr Wormald's letter was folded under the green glass dome of a paper-weight.

"The beans of *Abrus precatorius* I found in the drain; Dr Wormald told us they are used in Indian medicine, and specifically to treat boils. The heartsease taken from the Corporation greenhouses was once used in magical love potions, but I'm sure it can be used in medicine too. You're the nurse, Lucie, do you recollect?"

"I know it was used in folk-medicine," Lucie replied, "For the treatment of lung disease and skin complaints: eczema, psoriasis, syphilitic rashes and the like."

Atticus pressed a finger against the window, towards the incurables' hospital.

"And then we have this latest attack. The Beast took a medical syringe and an enamel bucket containing twenty ounces of human blood. He returned, presumably with the intention of stealing a pot of mercury – at least that is what he had in his hand when Sister Keegan surprised him – and Viscum. I imagine that would be an extraction of *Viscum album,* or as it is more commonly known, mistletoe. Mercury, we know from Dr Watson, is used for syphilis and impaction."

"And for skin conditions," Lucie added. "And extract-of-mistletoe is used in the treatment of tumours."

"Of skin tumours?"

Lucie nodded. "Very often, yes. Red and bloated and covered in lumps; that is how Sarah the Dragon described her murderer. Could she have meant tumours and boils, I wonder?"

"Quite possibly so," Atticus agreed. "But then we still have the theft of the bucket to consider. I cannot for a moment believe it was a random act. Our beast was clearly waiting for his opportunity to take it, but why? Why risk discovery for the sake of a two-shilling bucket?"

"Perhaps it was the hypodermic syringe he was after?" Lucie suggested. "They are much more difficult to obtain and if he has skin tumours, it would be far better to administer the drug directly into the tissue."

Atticus grimaced. That image was not one he particularly cared for.

"Then we may, at long last, be getting somewhere with this wretched puzzle. And, Lucie, I was also wondering whether you might be good enough to pay a visit to the municipal library."

CHAPTER TWENTY-ONE

In his parlour, Professor Ernest Ryan FWPS coughed, very gently and politely, and waited. After a moment or two, Joseph Malkin glanced up enquiringly from his *Daily Chronicle* and the professor bowed.

"I have now concluded my phrenological examinations, Mr Malkin. Your son—"

"My adoptive son," Malkin corrected him, folding the newspaper and tucking it through the seat-back of the chair adjacent.

"Yes, yes of course, please forgive me; your *adoptive* son is a most… intriguing subject." Ryan rubbed his palms together and glanced back towards Esau. "His cranium is fascinating, quite fascinating, and may I say now, that were Master Malkin ever to be unfortunate enough to suffer some kind of a misadventure, you should certainly consider donating his skull to medical science – as a gift, of course. I myself would be very pleased to receive it."

"Thank you, I will bear it in mind, but until then?"

"Yes, yes, until then." Ryan coughed, and tapped his boot-toe nervously on a frayed rent in the oilcloth. "Mr Malkin, if I may speak frankly?"

Joseph nodded. "Please do. We are all exhorted to plainness of speech, are we not?"

"We are indeed, Mr Malkin, that is quite so."

"Well, then?"

The professor pursed his lips.

"Mr Malkin, I observe that your adoptive son has a singularly large brain, with a prominent frontal development which bespeaks a fine intellectual capacity. Indeed, I have rarely, if ever, seen such intelligence contained within a single skull. The cranial organs are all properly moderate in size… with the notable exceptions of the following: *The Propensities to Destructiveness and Combativeness*, and the *Faculty of Comparison*.

"Mr Malkin, if I might take the liberty of giving you some professional words of warning: Do please be cautious. If, even at this late stage, there is the slightest possibility of sending your adoptive son back from whence he came, it is my sincere and scholarly opinion that you would be well advised to do so."

Esau, standing by the window, turned, and although the little panes were almost opaque with grime, and his eyes were so terribly black, they seemed to blaze in the sunlight.

"There isn't the remotest chance of that," snorted Malkin. He stood and rapped his cane on the floor. "In any event, although you, Ernest Ryan may examine the mind, it is only God who may make a judgement upon the heart and the soul."

CHAPTER TWENTY-TWO

The public library in Raglan Street seemed rather busier than usual, and an old man curled over a copy of the *Harrogate Advertiser* reminded Lucie sharply of the pressing urgency of her errand. There was only so long even Samson Fox could keep all of this quiet. Sooner or later, Mssrs Breare and Ackrill, the sedulous editors of the town's newspapers, would run out of patience and take the story to press. Once that news broke, the town would be teeming with journalists and day-trip ghoul-seekers and inevitably, many of those would end up on the doorstep of Atticus and Lucie Fox.

"Good morning to you, Mrs Fox." Mr Varley waved cheerily from the very top of his stepladders. The young second librarian delighted in balancing on the topmost rung to elicit gasps and, on occasion, even screams of horror from the readers below.

"It was a terrible business at the incurables' hospital last night."

"Yes it was," Lucie agreed. She sensed several pairs of eyes turning inquisitively in their direction. "We must be thankful the nurse has suffered no lasting harm.

"I am looking, Mr Varley, for a book concerning the medicinal uses of herbs and plants."

The librarian flitted down his ladders, straight-backed and with a book in each hand. It made even Lucie cringe to watch him.

"There's one on the desk there that should do you very nicely: *Magical and Medicinal Herbs of England.* It'll be its second outing in a week; I haven't even had opportunity to put it away yet."

"Its second outing," Lucie repeated, "How so?"

The librarian laughed good-naturedly as he laid his books onto a big sheet of brown paper and squared them, ready for wrapping.

"I had the most peculiar fellow in here last Thursday – a vagrant of sorts. We get them wandering in now and again, looking for shelter. This one stank like a wet goat. I'll give him his due though; he really was looking for a book, the same one as you, although I insisted he washed his hands before I even let him lay a finger on the cover. He couldn't have been in here for more than five-and-forty minutes before he dropped the book on the floor, just exactly where you're standing now, and left, quite as bold as you please."

"What did he look like, Mr Varley – his face, his hair, the way he walked?"

Varley spread his hands. "I could see neither his face nor his hair, Mrs F. He was wearing a kind of a long coat, very dirty and very tattered, with a hood. He kept that pulled down over his face the entire time, even when he was speaking to me. I did say he was peculiar! As for the way he walked, well it's curious you should ask that, because it was very odd. It was awkward, as if he might have been in drink." He frowned. "Although when he spoke, he sounded as sober as a Methodist. He warned me to beware the sins of lust as he left – not that there is great opportunity for lust in a public library in Harrogate, you understand. Do you think he might have been the one who broke into the hospital?"

Lucie nodded gravely. "From your description, I do. I also think it might be prudent to have the police send you over a whistle – to summon them if he should return here. Mercy me, Mr Varley, but this news is alarming. Until now, we believed the Bea—, that this fellow was keeping to Low Harrogate and the cover of darkness. Now it would appear he's been coming right into the middle of town, and in broad daylight too."

The young librarian paled, his parcel, for the moment, forgotten. He said: "If it might help you, Mrs Fox, there was another thing about him that struck me as being strange too."

"And what was that?"

"It was that he kept one hand in the pocket of his coat all the time he was in here, as if it might be injured or deformed or something. He really was the most peculiar fellow."

"His right or his left hand?"

Varley considered.

"His right, but he was working his fingers the whole time; I could see them moving, through the cloth."

Lucie smiled at him. "Thank you, Mr Varley; that is very helpful. I must say, you really would make a first-rate detective yourself."

Lucie Fox sat in her armchair beside their parlour fire, the borrowed library book open across a cushion on her lap.

"It's such a great pity Mr Varley made the Beast wash his hands before touching the book, Atticus," she remarked as she read, "or we might have had a perfect set of finger-prints."

"Yes it is." Atticus glanced up from his chess game. The firelight was throwing dancing shadows across his wife's face and he watched them for a few moments. "And we could have seen exactly which parts of the book were of interest to him too. Notwithstanding that, at least we know now that he requested that book from the library, and consequently, our eduction as to his interest in medicines is correct."

"But if he needs medicines so badly that he is prepared to kill for them, why doesn't he simply go to a workhouse and seek relief? They have good infirmaries and properly trained medical officers, and he could always discharge himself once he's cured."

Atticus picked up a chess pawn and stared at it as he considered Lucie's question, which was an excellent one. "So what is stopping him doing precisely that, do you suppose?" he mused aloud.

"Pride or shame," Lucie replied curtly. "It has to be. How did you get on at the nursery-garden, by-the-by?"

"It was most definitely the work of our Beast, just as we suspected it would be. Old Bradley, the nurseryman, told me that he saw something moving about inside one of the greenhouses from his scullery window. When he went out to investigate, a hooded figure ran at him and barged him to the ground. He hit his head on a potting bench and got a nasty gash and a blackened eye for his trouble. I have cautioned him about the possibility of tetanus. It seems the Beast got away with half a sack of plants that Bradley had intended to hang up for seed. He told me he stumbled off into the pinewoods with it over his shoulder."

"Stumbled off with it?"

Atticus nodded.

"That's how he described it. Like your Mr Varley, Bradley believed he was drunk."

CHAPTER TWENTY-THREE

The big brown myna bird dropped its head to one side and watched through the bars of its cage. Beside it, the porter of the Harrogate Retreat also inclined his head and darted glance after glance towards the part-open doorway and the patter of approaching footsteps.

"Aye, I know, Mr Disraeli; I can 'ear 'im too," he muttered through tightly clenched teeth. "He's come back, just like you was worried about. An' you was quite correct about 'im, just like you always is. There's summat o' the devil about that one, there is. Oh yes. Just the same as that man as was asking about him not one hour since, the one with the crooked fingers what wouldn't tell us 'is name."

The porter ducked down to study the columns of entries in his day book as Esau passed and did not look up again or even take a breath until he heard the door to the day room click shut high above them at the head of the stairs.

"Anyways, Mr Disraeli, we'd better mark 'im down in our book, just like we're supposed to. There: Esau Malkin has returned to the Harrogate Retreat at..." He turned and threw a glance at a clock mounted on the wall behind his desk, "...eight-and-twenty minutes past six o'clock. Just in time for supper. You be keepin' an eye on that one, Mr

Disraeli, now you've got the measure on 'im. You be a-watching him close."

Although a hearty and nutritious supper was indeed about to be served in the little refectory of the Harrogate Retreat, eating was the very last thing on Esau's mind. He was perfectly used to hunger. Of much greater interest to him was a pair of books he recalled having seen in the Retreat's extensively-stocked library.

CHAPTER TWENTY-FOUR

Esau sits, cross-legged, in his nest of pillows and blankets, and gazes around his room. For it is a room, a proper bedroom, and not a cell. And as he looks from the great carved fireplace, with its marble cherubs cavorting under the mantelshelf, to the ornate, corniced ceiling, he thinks that it is a room far nicer than the tramp-major's or the schoolmistress' at the workhouse. He thinks it is grander than even the master's itself.

Michael Roberts has said, just as His Lordship once said, that he should not sleep in a ward but that he should have a room of his own. Michael Roberts has said that never again should he be fearful of people ridiculing him for his hair, and that if ever he should like to have it clipped away, then Mary Lovell, the elderly nurse who took charge of the Retreat at night, would be very pleased to arrange it.

Esau sits, cross-legged, in his nest of pillows and blankets and thinks he should like that very much.

Michael Roberts has said that he may have his own Aunt Elizabeth's bedroom because she had died in her sleep more than two years ago and it was a sinful waste, it lying empty any longer. It occurs to Esau that Aunt Elizabeth must have been a very fortunate woman indeed to have slept in a room like this.

And as Esau sits on his bed in his nest of pillows and blankets, he looks down to the Bible lying open across his lap. Michael Roberts has said that he can quote scripture admirably. And so he can. He can quote it better than the chaplain at the workhouse and better than any of the apocalypticists he sometimes heard through the freak show walls, standing on their boxes and preaching about the Millennium and the Second Coming of the Messiah.

And as he sits, he begins to rock very gently to-and-fro and he remembers the apocalypticists, and he remembers those very particular scriptures concerning the Coming of the Messiah. Perhaps his movements are not the self-soothing motions of a caged beast or of a lunatic, after all. Perhaps they are simply the result of his being buffeted by wave after wave of marvellous, marvellous epiphany. Because it has occurred to him that, like the first messiah before him, he, Esau, was born of a virgin. At least he has never heard that he ever had a father. Jesus had been born, humbly, in a stable and he, Esau, had been born in a workhouse. But then he had been taken to live in a stable by Joseph.

Dear God, he had.

Both Jesus and he had a step-father named Joseph and it was said of each how all that heard them were astonished at their understanding of scripture.

There is another book lying open in his nest of pillows and blankets. It has been given to him by Michael Roberts and it is called: *On the Origin of Species by Means of Natural Selection, or, The Preservation of Favoured Races in the*

Struggle for Life. That is a very long name for any book to have.

The man who had written the book seems to have been a very clever man indeed. Like Joseph Malkin and like Michael Roberts, Charles Darwin was a scientist, and he had written in his book the most astonishing thing. Esau turns his head and looks at it, and once again, the printed words seem to leap at him from the page:

'I entertain no doubt... that the view which most naturalists entertain, and which I formerly entertained – namely, that each species has been independently created – is erroneous'.

Esau has read Mr Darwin's book from the first page to the last and now he too can entertain no doubt whatever but that he was right. The myriad species of animals, and indeed, man himself, could only have arisen through the marvellous processes of Natural Selection.

And as he sits, cross-legged, in his nest of pillows and blankets and rocks to-and-fro, the buffeting waves of realisation become edged with the boiling foam of anger. He has never in all his twenty-one years of life been allowed any book of learning, save for the Bible and a child's copybook. Until now, he has never been allowed this book, this wondrous book of truth. Instead he has been cloaked and hooded and sent like a leper – like a shit-faced monkey – to sit in cubby-holes and abandoned chapels. All his life, ever since His Lordship first ordered it, he has been instructed to believe on the Lord with all his might and with all his soul.

But now he knows.

Now he knows that everyone: he, Charles Darwin, even His Lordship himself, are all descendants of shit-faced monkeys.

And, as he rocks, to-and-fro and to-and-fro, his revelation progresses yet further.

Had not Michael Roberts announced within minutes of their meeting that he, Esau, might be the superior species – that he might even be an angel? And straightaway, Joseph Malkin had agreed with him. Joseph Malkin had gasped and called it 'an extraordinary thought'. It must be so. It really, really must! He, Esau, was the cleverest scholar at the workhouse. He, Esau, was the one every man, and every woman, feared. And he, Esau, alone had grown hair against the cold.

He stares at his Bible and feels a spark of hatred flutter in his soul – no, not in his soul, in his breast – a spark that takes hold and burns bright and strong, and erupts into a raging conflagration.

The two carved cherubs cavorting under the mantelshelf pause and watch, smirking, waiting for the wrath of the Lord to surely descent upon him for his blasphemous thoughts. Esau waits too, his muscles taught, the skin at his hackles itching and prickling, just as it did when he was sent careering through the workhouse yard, when the stones and the ropes would sting. But as the moments stretch out into seconds and the seconds into minutes, there is nothing.

Esau Malkin lifts his *On the Origin of Species* from its pillow and lays it gently on top of his Bible. He turns to the back, to Charles Darwin's concluding words, and follows them once again with his trembling, naked finger.

'There is grandeur in this view of life, with its several powers, having been originally breathed into a few forms or into one… From so simple a beginning endless forms most beautiful and most wonderful have been, and are being, evolved.'

So that was it! As Joseph –as his step-father – had said, and as Charles Darwin had written: from that original holy breath, so all things had evolved. He, Esau, had evolved too. He had evolved further than anyone else, which clearly meant that he, Esau, must be the very form – most beautiful and wonderful – that Charles Darwin was writing about.

As John the Baptist had prepared the way for God, so Charles Darwin and so too, perhaps, the apocalypticists have prepared the way for him. He, Esau is the higher species. He, Esau is the favoured race, and he, Esau, is neither dirty monkey, nor shit-face, nor freak. He is an angel; he is the Second Coming of the Messiah.

He is a god.

As he sits in his nest of pillows, as warm and as soft as a cloud, no longer rocking to-and-fro, a soft pattering sound catches his attention.

There, again! Someone is throwing pebbles against his window.

CHAPTER TWENTY-FIVE

Police Constable Lawson leans against a pilaster of the Royal Pump Room and feels the stone, chill as the tomb and brutally hard, pressing against his shoulder. The wind is bitter and he curses the superintendent and the Beast, who together mean that he must stand here and spend this night staring across the road into the blackness of the Bogs Valley gardens. The town is hushed – out of the wind at least – and the streets eerily deserted, but he stands with his truncheon drawn, hanging from his wrist by its double leather thong, and ready.

Just let him appear; this animal, who preys on women and old men. He sets his jaw, and his fingers curl around the familiar, smooth-worn handle at the thought of it. Just let him come through those gates. Then he'll learn what a full 12 ounces of constabulary ironwood feels like.

Lawson grunts at the thought, and shifts and nestles his whole weight against the column. It is going to be a long night and no mistake. Maybe he can scrounge an early-purl from the hotel opposite when it wakes in the morning. He'll be ready for one by then. Lordy, won't he just! The sergeant would smell the potent mix of gin and beer on his breath, but he won't say anything – not a word. Lawson smiles wryly to himself. No, the sergeant has had too many freezing nights himself for that, staring for hours into shadows.

He laughs bitterly, but then he stops and glances about. The sound has unnerved him. Best to keep quiet this night.

At least he isn't alone. All across Low Harrogate, constables are standing and watching and waiting. Mayor Fox will be pleased, God bless him. He can sleep all the sounder in his nice warm bed.

A scream rends the silence.

"What in damnation?"

Lawson is on his feet, turning around and around, peering this way and that. A whistle – a police whistle – shrills, and then a shout, and another.

There!

Over the way, by the cab-stand, a policeman is down, writhing, struggling against something that is dragging him away inexorably into the darkness.

Lawson is set running, and as he does, he fumbles his own whistle free and its blast is long and strident.

In an instant he is there and the shadows have fled.

"Billy?"

It is Billy, his face ghostly white in the gaslight, his hair glossy with blood. His body lies limp across the pavement but he's breathing. Thank God he's breathing. Thank God he's alive.

Lawson stands over him, wielding his truncheon high and snarling and glaring about – a bear with its own. All around the valley, whistles are shrieking, windows are lifting and night-capped heads are peering out.

A tall, hatless gentleman is running down the road, the tails of a nightshirt fluttering below his frock-coat. He has an unusually thick walking cane held tightly in his fist.

"What is it? What has happened here?" he calls.

"Oh, it's you, Mr Fox. Thank god. It's my mate Billy. He's been injured. I believe…" He sobs at the sudden realisation. "…I believe it might have been this Beast of the Bogs Valley."

Heavy boots pound on the pavements and constables pour in from every direction. People too, from the hotels and the private houses are milling around, by turns curious, alarmed and aghast.

"Everybody back now. Step away, if you please. Give him some air." A sergeant is there and taking charge, the big chevrons on his cuffs flashing in the light, and instantly, the clamour is throttled.

The injured constable rolls his head and groans and vomits into the gutter.

"Sergeant, my home is just up the hill, at Prospect Place," Atticus says, "Bring him up. My wife is a Netley-trained nurse."

"Thank you, sir." The sergeant dabs Lawson's shoulder and another constable's, and obediently they reach under Billy's arms and hoist him to his feet.

"Bring him in here, constables, into the parlour, where it's warm."

Lucie Fox ran to the fireplace and drew the poker and began to stab new life into the embers of the previous night's fire.

"Quickly, Mrs Morris, brandy and blankets if you please, and then you can load fresh coals. We need to keep him warm."

The constables lowered their comrade into Atticus' big armchair and Lucie fumbled open the buttons of his high collar.

"We'll find this beast for you, Billy." Lawson lifted off his own helmet and kneeled down in front of him. "Me and the lads won't rest 'til he's under lock-and-key up in Raglan Street. And when he is, you mark my words, we're going to give him such a seeing-to as he won't forget in a month o' Sundays."

Billy managed a weak smile. As feeble as the fire yet was, his face already looked stronger, more vital, in its light.

Lucie was wearing one of her very purposeful expressions. The constables' concern for their comrade was touching, to be sure, but now they were in her way.

"Thank you, gentlemen," she said brusquely, "Mr Fox and I will look after him now. Would one of you kindly let Detective Inspector Douglas know that Constable…?"

"Watts, Ma'am, Billy Watts," Lawson replied, "He joined the force the very same day as I did."

"Very well, please tell him that Constable Watts is here. Rouse him at home if you must. He will want to know."

Mrs Morris was suddenly at her shoulder, hugging their thick winter travelling-rug against her apron-front. She passed it to Lucie and then a small glass decanter. It had a silver label marked 'Cognac' swinging from its neck.

"I'll see these gentlemen out," the housekeeper said.

Constable Watts' gaze had been drawn into the glowing coals in the fireplace, and he barely seemed to notice when Lucie pressed the rug around him. It was only when Mrs Morris came to kneel by the hearthside, blocking his brown study with her heavy woollen night-coat, that he glanced up.

"What happened, Billy?" Lucie asked him.

Watts frowned, furrowing his brow as he watched Mrs Morris carefully placing new coals onto the orange embers with tongs. Smoke began to pour thick and fast up the chimney.

"I can't recall, Ma'am."

"Please call me Mrs Fox."

"Thank ye, Mrs Fox. I can't remember exactly what happened, and that's the truth and the whole truth of it. One minute I was sitting in the cab shelter and all was quiet; the next I was on my back with something pulling at my arm, trying to drag me away onto the Stray."

He shuddered under the blanket.

"Here, drink a little of this." Lucie held a brandy glass against his lips and allowed the brown liquid to brush up against them. "You've been very lucky. You've had a bang on the head but that's all. It's nothing too serious."

Watts fumbled against the rug and his hand appeared like a trembling white claw. He took the glass.

"But it never got me in the end. It's Peter Lawson I've to thank for that. He's the one as scared it off."

"Mercy me, Billy! That does look sore." Lucie pointed to an angry red stripe on the skin of his wrist, where a short, black truncheon was still attached by its leather lanyard. "Atticus, would you get this off, as gently as you're able, whilst I go to fetch some cold cream?"

"Of course." Atticus reached across to very gingerly peel the strap away from the weal. He lifted it free.

"Upon my word, but this has got some weight to it." He hefted the truncheon in his hand. "If you'd managed to land a blow from this, the Beast's game would have been up in an instant."

Watts took a sip of brandy and winced.

"Aye, Mr Fox, that it would. I did try, but he grabbed a-hold of my arm. If he'd managed to drag me back to his den though, it would have been me whose game was up."

"Did you manage to see anything of him?" Atticus asked. "Think now, as hard as you're able."

The shoulders under the blanket lifted in a shrug.

"I'm sorry, Mr Fox but no, not much. It all happened so quickly, you see? He had his back to me, and I think he was wearing a hood. Yes he definitely was. And I can remember his hands seemed very white, even in the gaslight. Oh, and he stank too; he stank to high heaven."

Atticus swept up a wall chair and settled it next to the armchair. He sat perfectly upright, closed his eyes and folded his hands together in his lap.

"I am going to recreate the scene of your attack as a picture in my mind, Constable Watts. So then, I have you on your back, by the shelter, just as you say you found yourself the instant after the Beast attacked. He had your right arm, which I can clearly see is your truncheon arm, in his grip. Do you recollect how he was holding you? It wasn't with his teeth because there are no marks in your skin. So was it with his peculiarly white hands? With his left perhaps, or his right, or with both of them?"

"Let me think on it a minute. He had my arm in his left hand. Yes, I'm sure of it."

Atticus nodded. "And you believe he was trying to drag you away?"

"Aye. He was pulling on me like a plough-hoss, and gasping and grunting like one too. If I hadn't managed to get to my whistle, I can't think what might have happened. I'd be lying on a slab like poor Sarah the Dragon, I shouldn't wonder, instead of sitting here sipping brandy in your front parlour."

"Ironwood!"

Atticus opened his eyes to stare down at the truncheon still lying by his feet. He reached down and lifted it up to the light from the gas mantle.

"And that is a stroke of luck," he murmured. "It would seem that the Beast of the Bogs Valley does give up his fingertip prints, after all."

Detective Inspector Douglas gulped down his coffee in one extravagant scoop of his arm and passed the empty cup to Mrs Morris.

"Thank you, I'm glad of that," said Douglas, ignoring her sniff of disapproval, "It's been a long and difficult few hours and no mistake. And it was very good of you to tend to my constable last night, Mrs Fox, I don't mind admitting, and to have the presence of mind to send word."

Lucie nodded graciously. "We both desire the same outcome when all is said and done, Mr Douglas."

With its splendid views across Low Harrogate, Lucie had insisted on appointing the front room on the first floor of their house as their drawing room. Douglas was standing by its window now, staring out over the town, with his broad back to them.

"The searching-party found nothing," he growled to the glass, "Not so much as a footprint in the earth."

"What with the cab shelter and the mountebanks, the ground is trodden so hard around there that we didn't have a prayer at footprints," Sergeant Hainsworth explained.

"Mrs Fox and I have been somewhat more fortunate," said Atticus.

Douglas glanced curiously from his window and Atticus held up the truncheon he had taken from Constable Watts' wrist.

"Firstly, the Beast has obliged us by leaving his fingertip prints on your constable's truncheon. Mrs Fox has been busy with her powder and ostrich-feathers, and if you examine the area by the Queen's cipher, you will notice two whole fingertip prints and one fragment, which she believes might come from a thumb."

"I should say that all three are from his right hand," Lucie added, "Which is queer, because the girl's injuries led us to believe he is left-handed."

Douglas drew a small, but very handsome, ivory-handled magnifying glass from the pocket of his jacket and, in the convenient light of the window, spent some time in examining the faint deposits of grey powder beside the royal warrant painted on the shaft.

Lucie said: "Do you see how the minutiae of the thumb fragment and what I believe is the forefinger have been worn almost smooth?"

Douglas peered again through his glass and nodded. "Yes, I see it."

"They make his prints very distinctive. If we find the man, I could identify or eliminate him in an instant."

"And secondly," Atticus went on, lifting a silver bonbon dish from a side table, "Mrs Fox found this hair on the first victim's dress."

"It was trapped in the surface of a bloodstain," Lucie explained, "Which means it could not have been present before the attack."

"Ye gods, Hainsworth," Douglas murmured, "Look at the length of it. The woman was blonde, so it wasn't hers. This can only mean one thing; it was Joseph Malkin's wild-man after all."

He threw an accusing scowl at Atticus and then turned to his sergeant. "Do we have Esau's finger-prints, to compare these with?"

Hainsworth shook his head. "We already had the man, or whatever he is, in custody, so there was no need to take any. The finger-prints on that truncheon are the first ones we've seen. If you recall, we weren't even certain at the time that a wild-man would have finger-prints."

Douglas coloured. "Yes, yes, I dare say, but at least we can be certain now that he does. Mrs Fox, would you be obliging enough—"

At that moment, the door burst open and Mrs Morris charged into the room. She had a tea towel gripped in her hands and she was twisting the fine linen as if she might be trying to wring the very embroidery from it.

"I do beg pardon, ma'am and sirs, but I have just heard the news. St Peter's church has been broken into. It was sometime in the night. It's been broken into and completely ransacked. Canon Foote came in to prepare for prayers this morning and he found the windows put-through and the holy cross itself smashed to pieces all over the floor."

CHAPTER TWENTY-SIX

"God moves in a mysterious way, His wonders to perform."[(17)]

The almost universally adored Canon Lundy Foote, tall, independently wealthy and strikingly handsome, was leaning against the stencilled wall of his church, watching as two curates deftly worked their sweeping brushes between the long rows of pews.

He tilted his head towards them and smiled wryly.

"Wondrous indeed that He has succeeded in getting Mr and Mrs Atticus Fox into His house, together with no fewer than two of their acquaintances."

Douglas bristled.

"I am Detective Inspector Douglas of the West Riding Constabulary, Reverend and this is my sergeant Mr Hainsworth. We have been given to understand you've had a breaking-into?"

"Indeed we have, Detective Inspector Douglas. We have had the very thief of Joel among us, although nothing appears to have actually been stolen. Nevertheless, we have been obliged to hold Morning Payers amidst the desolation of glass shards and splinters of wood, petitioning Our Lord for the soul of one so debauched and so low that he would stoop to desecrate a church. There, see for yourselves."

He inclined his head towards the farthest side of the church, where the rich, mellow glow of a stained glass window was ruptured by coarse, ordinary sunlight, and by cames of lead, twisted and bent like so many broken teeth.

"I myself will arrange for repairs to be made this very day. Autumn is not the season for any congregation to be waiting upon church trust committees, and in any event, I shall be setting off to winter in France ere long, and St Peter's must be made whole again before I leave."

Canon Foote lifted himself from the wall and spread his palm towards a pair of gilded-iron gates, which stretched across the church between the nave and the choir.

"Our eagle lectern was tumbled-over too, but by some good fortune appears to be undamaged. Alas, the same cannot be said of the altar cross however. It is the very greatest outrage. Do you see there?"

A large and slender, wooden cross was leaning against the golden bars of the gates, one of the arms broken off to a jagged stump.

"I should not have believed it possible for mortal man to have broken that cross. It is made from the wood of the tree of life, and it's as hard as iron."

Hainsworth made the sign of a cross over his tunic.

"Moreover," Canon Foote continued, glancing at the movement, "It was left standing upon its head, and that seems to me to be a blasphemy in itself."

Douglas said: "I dare say it does, Reverend, but I'm afraid I shall have to leave my sergeant to attend to you today. Mr and Mrs Fox and I have a murderer to apprehend and the mayor is insistent upon hourly reports."

The vicar spread his hands.

"A murderer, you say? Then the poor child has passed away. My friend and adversary in faith, Canon Pope, told me about poor Hannah and her salamander-like proclivities. I understand that her death was expected, hoped for even? Yes? Well, it should be lamented none the less for that. Even though she was Catholic, no doubt even that will be forgiven her and she will be in a far better place in death than ever she was in life. After all, the Lord's embrace is much to be preferred to a tuppenny clinch in a bath-chair yard, begging your pardon, Mrs Fox."

He regarded Douglas for a moment.

"You must render unto Caesar what is Caesar's, of course, Inspector. However, let me remind you that this act of violence has been committed against a power greater even than Samson Fox, and that you are rendering reports unto Him, continually."

Douglas swallowed. "I suppose, now I come to think on it, we could spare a little time to take a look, Canon Foote. Of course we could. What do you think about it all, Mr and Mrs Fox?"

Atticus pointed towards a massive casting in brass, standing opposite the pulpit.

"That is the lectern you spoke about?"

"That is the very one, Mr Fox," Foote replied, "Come, let me show you."

He led them through the nave, processing under the ever-watchful eyes of the great Lords Spiritual, whose pietistic disdain had been carved forever into the high vault of the roof, to the gates.

The lectern of St Peter's Church was fashioned in the shape of an eagle, with wings outstretched to receive the Holy Scriptures and its talons gripping a substantial brass pedestal. It was staring out across the church with an expression not unlike that of Canon Foote himself.

"The Gospel of St John is read from this lectern each Christmastide," Canon Foote explained. "When I arrived this morning, it had been thrown over, and was obliged to remain so until the curates came in. It required fully the strength of all three of us to right it again."

Atticus stepped forward and stooped to examine it. He said: "The eagle is the symbol of St John, I believe."

"It would seem you are not wholly ignorant of the gospels, after all, Mr Fox. You are quite correct; the eagle is figurative of the heights to which St John rises in the first chapter of his gospel." A flicker of amusement passed suddenly over Canon Foote's craggy features. "Although he seems to have been brought down with something of a crash last night."

"Knowing about a thing and believing in it are two entirely separate things," Atticus returned and Douglas smirked. "And the eagle is symbolic of a great many things outside of Christendom too, as is St John."

"Its beak is bent," Lucie said.

They all looked. She was quite correct; the metal of the eagle's beak had been fractured and pushed back, so that it was bent almost double.

"Upon my soul, so it is," Canon Foote exclaimed, throwing up his hands. "My dear lady, you must have the very eyes of an eagle yourself."

"Yet the floor tiles around it are intact and unbroken," Atticus observed, "So something must have broken its fall. Do you suppose this lectern could have been used to break the wood of the cross?"

"It's certainly looks heavy enough," said Douglas.

"But why, Mr Fox?" Canon Foote interrupted, "Why should someone wish to break a holy cross, and then leave it topsy-turvy against these gates. That is the question which vexes me."

"Do you have the missing piece, Canon?" Atticus asked.

Lundy Foote frowned. "I don't recollect ever seeing any pieces, now you ask me."

"That's right, Your Reverence," one of the curates called over. "There's no sign of the missing bit anywhere. I thought it was queer. I've been keeping an eye out for it, in case we could set it back in with glue."

"Good Heavens, no!" The canon was aghast. "There can be no jury repairs to the living cross. What would our dear Lord think of us? No, I forbid it. It will need to be replaced anew. I myself will arrange it."

Atticus straightened and rose to his feet.

"In which case, it would seem that your thief of Joel was exactly that, Canon, a thief. He must have taken the missing arm with him."

"But again I ask you: To what purpose?"

"For a holy relic, perhaps?" Hainsworth suggested.

Canon Foote shook his head. "You are a Catholic then, I take it, Mr Hainsworth? But no, I cannot think it would be for that. The church is a modern one and our cross is not yet twenty years old."

Douglas said: "So what do our great and celebrated private enquiry agents think of it? Is this the work of the wild-man too?"

"The work of a wild-man?" exclaimed Canon Foote.

"I think that proper method is proper method, and before we can say anything for certain, we will need to conduct a thorough examination," Atticus said firmly.

Douglas snorted.

"You've no more idea then we have. Very well, Mr Fox, make your examination if you must, but look lively about it, and then go and take this Esau fellow's finger-prints. Hainsworth, you can go with them. Take Watts' truncheon with you so you can compare them directly. Upon my word! What with murders and brainings and the desecration of churches, this town is being swamped with wickedness. Until we have got this man safely under lock-and-key, every constable we have is going onto searching duties – and reinforcements from Knaresborough and Ripon too, if I can get 'em. At least then I'll have something positive to mollify His Worship."

CHAPTER TWENTY-SEVEN

"I am very sorry, Atticus but Esau Malkin is no longer a guest here. He left our retreat sometime during the course of last night and we have seen neither hide nor hair of him since."

"Hide nor hair sounds about right," Sergeant Hainsworth muttered into his cheek. Then he said: "Might you know where he has gone, Dr Roberts?"

"I am sorry, I do not. You must understand that we are a retreat and not a prison. Our door is kept open at all times and in all weathers. Speaking frankly however, even if Esau were to return, I should think twice before admitting him again. When I knocked on his door this morning, I received no response. I entered to find his room deserted and his bible burned almost to ashes in the grate. As I told Atticus and Lucie Fox, and indeed Esau Malkin himself, our guests may follow whichever religion they please. But I will not have God's Holy Scriptures desecrated. His other belongings, few though they were, were gone."

"Esau burned his Bible?" Lucie enunciated each word in turn, as if she could scarcely believe what she was saying. "But why would he do that? He's as devout as a bishop."

"I have not the slightest notion, Lucie Fox. Mary Lovell, our night superintendent, saw him take a pair of books into his room around suppertime, and that is the last anyone here has seen of him. He has taken my *On the Origin of Species* with him too, and whichever books they were he fetched up from the library – two large, red ones was all that Mary could tell me."

"Might they have been Combe's *System of Phrenology*?" Lucie ventured.

Michael Roberts stared at her in astonishment. "Why yes, now I come to think about it, they must have been. How could you know that?"

"Because I picked one of them up two years ago, whilst we happened to be waiting for you in your library. I remember them particularly because I was surprised that a Charité-trained psychiatrist such as you would entertain books about phrenology."

"Yes, well one can have knowledge of a thing without necessarily believing in it."

"We should check at Beagle House," Atticus interjected, "It is very possible he has gone back to Joseph Malkin's."

Roberts bowed his head, rather more curtly than was his custom.

"In which case, I will wish you all a good day. You must excuse me; one of our guest-inmates, whom we also employ as the porter at the front desk, is quite beyond grief this morning. Sometime in the night, his pet myna bird somehow contrived to break its own neck.

CHAPTER TWENTY-EIGHT

As it transpired, Joseph Malkin had seen Esau no more recently than had Michael Roberts.

"The last I saw of him was when I took him to see my phrenologist," he explained as they sat around the grand drawing room of Beagle House, "I… I had intended to take him on a railway train today… to Ripon perhaps."

"Why you bother with him at all, I cannot imagine." Victoria Malkin's pudgy head was framed by an elaborate hairpiece of curls and ringlets, and she shook it in exasperation. "This Esau – half-monkey or diseased and most certainly nothing more – is still a freak, and wholly beneath the company of a gentleman banker of Harrogate. If he has taken it upon himself to disappear, then good riddance of bad rubbish I say. This is the second occasion upon which he has brought the police to our door – no offence to you, Sergeant Hainsworth."

Hainsworth sniffed. "None taken, I'm sure, Ma'am."

"May I ask why you want him?" Malkin asked.

It was Lucie who answered him.

"Two very serious crimes were committed in the town last night. I have managed to obtain finger-prints from both, and there can be no doubt but that they were left by the same person. Inspector Douglas has requested that we compare them with Esau's."

"I really cannot imagine why you should wish to conduct your life as you do, Mrs Fox," Victoria interrupted. "I mean, I ask you: what is a respectable lady to do with crimes and finger-prints and the like?"

She waved her hand dismissively.

"You only have a housekeeper for staff, I believe? Yes? Well I know that yours is not the very *grandest* of houses, but surely you must still have more than enough to do at home without getting caught up in all of that. And you, Mr Fox, you should be ashamed of yourself for allowing her to."

Joseph was gazing out through the window. When his wife finished speaking, he said: "I did hear about the poor policeman being attacked on Montpellier, and also that the holy eagle lectern at St Peter's had been vandalised. I cannot believe for one minute that Esau could have done that."

"Finger-prints will prove beyond doubt his innocence or his guilt," Lucie said firmly. "And for that, I don't actually need him in person; I can lift his prints from anything of his that might still be around – anything at all with a smooth, hard surface."

"Might there be anything still in Wilberforce's caravan?" Atticus suggested.

Joseph scowled and turned back to his window. "Victoria had Oates burn the van, along with everything that was in it."

"I should think so too," Victoria declared, "The thing was an eye-sore. This is a great house next-the-Stray; it is not some rag-and-bone yard."

"The horse's harness then?" said Lucie.

"The poor beast has been sent to the slaughter-house, Lucie Fox, horse, harness and all. Albert will be little more than dog meat and glue by now."

"No!" Atticus cried.

"And just what do you mean by that, Mr Fox? You weren't the one faced with the expense of feeding and stabling a broken-down old nag, even if you had a stable in the first place," Victoria simpered scornfully, "Which, of course, you do not. And what if it were seen here? What would people think of us? We have a certain respectability to maintain. Joseph is a banker and a pillar of society, and I myself am from a *very* old and venerable family. Anyway, this is my home and I may do exactly as I please here, thank you all the same."

"I had thought to use it for pony rides, for the poor and ragged children," Joseph said ruefully.

"And encourage them to hang around outside our gates?" Victoria's jowls and ringlets quivered in unison. "Absolutely not, Joseph; I should have forbidden it. As I was saying to *dear* Monsieur Prêtre just the other day: first you would get the children, and next you would get their feckless and wretched parents, begging and loitering, and stealing from you whenever your back was turned."

"Perhaps it is for the best that Esau did not return here, after all," Lucie said.

Victoria smiled sweetly. "That, Mrs Fox, is finally something we can agree on."

Lucie looked out through the enormous bay window and took a long and very deep breath.

"Will Esau come to any harm out there, Mr Malkin?" she asked.

Joseph followed her gaze, concern, or perhaps the flat light of the Sun, furrowing his brow. "On the contrary, Lucie, I'm sure he will be perfectly fine. He is a quite extraordinary fellow."

"The police are searching for him, sir," Sergeant Hainsworth assured him. "Shifts have been doubled and we have requested more men from neighbouring stations. It'll just be a matter of time before we find him."

Malkin smiled. He said: "St Peter's altar-cross was stolen too, I heard?"

"Not quite the whole cross," Atticus replied, "The intruder used the weight of the lectern to break it, and he took away just a part of the cross-piece."

Victoria threw up her hands. "Oh, poor, poor Lundy Foote," she lamented. "One might have supposed that in taking up a ministry in Harrogate, one would be spared such wickedness as that. Have the other churches been warned? What about the Christ Church?"

Joseph said: "Why ever should someone want to steal a part of a cross? There was nothing particularly remarkable about it, was there?"

"I believe it was stolen for its wood," said Atticus.

"Do you indeed?" Hainsworth's eyebrows lifted. "Why didn't you say that to the Inspector, when he asked you that question directly?"

"Because he scarcely gave me chance to. But the longer I think about it, the more convinced I am that it must be the case. The cross, as Canon Foote remarked, was made from the tree of life, otherwise known as *Lignum vitae*, a very hard and immensely heavy wood from the West Indies. The constable who was assaulted last night believed he was being dragged away to his death. Mrs Fox and I, however, think otherwise. Based on the pattern of fingertip prints and the constable's own account, we believe that the Beast was actually trying to wrestle his truncheon away from him, nothing more. That truncheon was made from ironwood – another name for the very same *Lignum vitae*."

"Is this ironwood valuable?" Victoria asked.

"Not especially so, but it does possess many admirable qualities notwithstanding."

"What qualities, Atticus?" Joseph leaned forward in his chair.

"Joseph Malkin – ever the naturalist." Atticus allowed himself the briefest of smiles. "Lignum is a quite extraordinary material in several ways. *Exempli gratia*, for example, Mrs Fox and I use a solution of it to reveal vestigial traces of blood. But what we believe attracted our man to it are its medicinal qualities."

"Which are what?" Malkin asked.

"Many and varied," replied Atticus. "According to a book Mrs Fox obtained from the municipal library, it has been used to treat everything from gout to syphilis, to skin diseases. There is a common link to everything the Beast has taken, or has tried to take, which is that they can all be used to treat disorders of the skin."

"You believe he is simply trying to find some sort of cure then?" Hainsworth asked.

Atticus nodded and Lucie said: "We do. And remember that this so-called Beast of the Bogs Valley has actually killed no one, with the exception of Hannah the prostitute woman. Every one of his other victims has been attacked, but only, we believe, in the course of him seeking these supposed cures."

Atticus took up the baton again.

"Our Beast may have been angry, desperate perhaps, and brimming with rage, but he has not gone forearmed with malice. On each occasion, the attack was made using whatever happened to be at hand, and yes, I do include your Constable Watts, Mr Hainsworth. Mrs Fox swabbed moss and dirt from his head-injury, suggestive of a blow from a lump of common tree branch."

"It was very blustery last night, if you recall," Lucie said, "There were fallen branches lying around everywhere."

"Should we be calling this poor fellow a Beast at all then?" Malkin asked, glancing around from face to face, "Or is he more to be pitied?"

Victoria pouted and rolled her eyes and Hainsworth said: "A beast is what he'll be to the newspapers, Mr Malkin, and a beast is what he'll be to me. To my way of thinking, it's the girl lying cold and white in the dead-house, and the four folk gravely injured that should be pitied. Call him what you like, but the fact is, the sooner he's caught and put in irons, the better it'll be for all concerned."

CHAPTER TWENTY-NINE

It was seldom these days that the little bell above the door of Professor Ryan's phrenology practice would tinkle on two consecutive days, and rarer yet for it to ring out the presence of not just one, but fully two new customers.

"Good afternoon to you, gentlemen," said Professor Ryan, welcoming them with his deep and sweeping bow. "May I say what a singular honour it is to welcome you both into my humble parlour."

The men strode past him without replying. In his younger days as a newly-elected Fellow of the Wakefield Society he might have been affronted by this, but no longer. These days, he found that fashionable coat-tails and fine woollen trousers could excuse a very great deal of impoliteness. The Gladstone bag each man carried suggested they might perhaps be businessmen. That would be fortunate. After all, wealthy clients invariably had wealthy acquaintances, and he could ill afford to advertise.

"Close your shop, Ryan," one of the men ordered. The professor, a little taken aback but still obliging, obediently turned the grubby sign in the door to show 'Closed'.

"Lock it now."

Ryan turned the key. Even before he began this examination, he knew already what it would reveal: a large *Propensity to Destructiveness*. He had rarely met a more impertinent fellow.

He affected a cordial expression and turned back to them.

"I believe I am to undertake two full phrenological examinations today?"

Mr Impertinence glared at him. "That is the arrangement." Despite his fine clothes and obvious wealth, he had hard, almost cruel, features and a thick, nasal intonation. Ryan tried to place the accent: The industrial West Riding, he supposed, Bradford or Halifax perhaps, and most probably a mill owner. His companion was dressed identically to him in a black tailcoat and grey, striped trousers, but instead of a glossy silk top-hat, he wore the billycock of a manager, or possibly servant.

"Please take a seat, gentlemen and be good enough to remove your hats. See, I've put two chairs out ready for you. Then you must decide which of you is to be first."

"It isn't us who are to be examined, Ryan," Billycock said, "It's these."

He lifted the Gladstone bag he was carrying and tapped its side, where the device of a six-pointed star was stamped into the fine, polished leather. The professor noticed then that the third finger of his hand was curled back rather oddly against his palm.

"Ah, then you have brought the crania with you. Skulls or plaster casts, perhaps? That should present no problem—"

Impertinence cut across him.

"Listen to me, Ryan; I must give you a warning. You would do well to heed it to the letter. It is this: Should you breathe a single word of what you are about to see to anyone, your throat will be cut from ear to ear; your tongue will be torn from its roots; you will be decollated and your head laid out for all to witness. Your heart will be given to the fiends, and your body in three parts to the birds of the air, the beasts of the field and the fish of the sea."

Ryan stared at him. The matter-of-fact way in which the man had spoken the threats was almost as chilling as the penetrating, washed-out blue of his eyes.

"I…" said Ryan, "I am not at all certain about this, gentlemen. Perhaps we should reconsider the whole matter. Yes, that would be for the best. I confess in myself a shamefully small *Propensity to Secretiveness*; I have noticed it many times. Please, sirs, let us reconsider."

Impertinence ignored him. With care bordering on reverence, he placed his own Gladstone onto the seat of one of the chairs. It too carried the motif of a star, such as the Jews are wont to use, but unlike Billycock's this was picked out in fine, gold leaf.

"Take care to show proper respect, Ryan," he said, "For you are about to behold the Divine."

Ernest Ryan wrinkled his nose. Then, overcome by curiosity, he stepped forward and eased open the bag.

It was unfortunate for him that he had locked his door.

CHAPTER THIRTY

Mercifully, it seemed that the Beast of the Bogs Valley did not visit the town that night. Maybe he had found his cure, or perhaps he had been driven to the shelter of his lair by the sharp and penetrating frost.

The pavements of Harrogate were still glistening white in the long shadows of the dawn when Atticus Fox pulled his big front door shut behind him and felt the chill nipping at his skin.

Mr Boynton, the tobacconist and stationer, had the door to his shop closed for the first time since spring and the little bell that bounced and jangled overhead as he pushed it open served to shake Atticus from his ponderings.

"One *Herald*, Mr Fox, thanking you kindly," Mr Boynton said, beaming. He was always unnaturally cheery in the early mornings. "But I see there's not a single word on the peculiar business that's been going on all week – barring what happened to St Peter's of course. You'll have heard about that, no doubt, with you living just around the corner and all. Oh, and the maps you asked me to order for you have come-in: First Edition, Harrogate West. I should have thought you'd have known your way around town by now." He chuckled merrily at his own joke.

"I do, Mr Boynton, I know it very well, thank you. I simply wish to get a feeling for the movements of whoever is behind this peculiar business, as you so correctly call it. There is no need to have them sent round; if you'd be so kind as to wrap them up, I'll take them with me now."

The clinging, tobacco smell of Mr Boynton's shop seemed to have transferred itself to the second floor laboratory-workroom of Number 16, Prospect Place, and despite the lingering chill, Lucie had already lifted both window sashes high when Atticus returned from their study bearing a fistful of coloured pencils.

She had the maps spread open across the table and weighted flat with a number of heavy dump paperweights. The green-glass mounds and the fossils they contained threw strange shadows and shafts of light across the paper.

Some months earlier, Atticus and Lucie had been to a matinee performance of a Projection Praxinoscope at the hotel next door. This ingenious device caused a series of painted images to be projected onto a screen, with the effect that they appeared actually to move. Atticus in particular had been fascinated by the invention and he was reminded of it here. By reproducing the movements of the Beast, one after another, onto the maps, his hope was to animate him on the paper and, in effect, bring him to life.

He carefully laid each pencil, side-by-side, onto the tabletop and regarded the maps.

"Red pencil to begin," he said. He reached over and drew a cross by the little black rectangle marked 'Bath-Chair

Yard'. Then he wrote: 'No. 1, Sunday. Attack on Sarah, alias Hannah. *Abrus precatorius*'.

Putting down the pencil, he picked up the next. It was blue. "And now the breaking-in at the nursery-gardens and the theft of the *Viola tricolor*."

Lucie exhaled sharply.

"Atticus Fox, your handwriting is like a drunken spider that has crawled out of the inkwell, onto the map, and suffered some kind of a fit. If we're to have any hope of making sense of this afterwards, I really think it is I who should be making the notes." She pulled the pencil from his unresisting fingers. "And it's rosary pea and heartsease, if you please. The simplest is generally the noblest, as Dr Roberts said, and this is all puzzling enough without you complicating it further with Latin names."

Atticus shrugged and retired to the sanctuary of the window. He looked through the glass to the world beyond, to where the ink-and-paper sheets became grass and trees, and the strokes of Lucie's pencil the tracks of a monster.

Through the open sash came the sounds of that world: the chatter, the cabmen's laughter, the music from the bandstand. They were the sounds of innocence, and with them, the words of Thomas Gray came, unbidden, into his thoughts: 'Where ignorance is bliss, 'tis folly to be wise.'

It seemed no time at all before Lucie stood back from her table.

"Here we are, Atticus: Six attacks, all plotted and labelled, and I've added-in the municipal library too, because we know he was there."

She reached forward and traced a sweeping line across the middle of the map with her pencil.

"Do you see? The major link in all of this is the valley – the pleasure gardens themselves and the Bogs Field. The Beast lives up on the moors, there's no doubt of it, somewhere around the moors of Harlow Hill, and the Bogs Valley is his way into Harrogate."

They gazed together through the window, towards the observatory tower and the high ground above the town.

"So we know the *where*, Atticus – roughly, anyway. The vexing questions for us now must be *who* is he, and *what* is he, and where exactly does he sleep?"

Atticus nodded as he stared out across their town. "He is out there, Lucie, somewhere beyond those trees. As to where he sleeps, and whether, creature of the darkness that he is, he sleeps at all, well, as you say, that is for us to find out."

Sitting in their little study, Lucie drew a sheet of writing paper from the drawer of their bureau and fed it carefully between the waiting jaws of an address stamp. She pressed down heavily, perhaps rather more heavily than was strictly necessary, onto the handle of the lever, so that when she pulled out the paper and laid it onto the leather of the writing slope, it held the faint oblong shadow of the printing block, as well as their address.

Taking a pen, she dipped it, and wrote in a large, round hand: 'For the Attention of Detective Inspector Douglas, Harrogate Police Station,' and then, after a moment's hesitation, 'Of Pressing Importance'.

There was a sergeant standing in front of the big front tower of Raglan Street Police Station, wrestling with the buttons of his collar. As they approached, Lucie joked, that with his lanky frame and tall helmet, he looked for all the world like the tower's miniature twin.

"Halloa, Mr and Mrs Fox." The sergeant caught sight of them and saluted smartly. "I expect you'll be here to see the inspector. He's just inside, at the front desk." He threw a furtive glance towards the station's arched doorway. "I'll warn you though, he's in a proper foul one this morning."

He was correct on both counts. Douglas glowered up from the front desk as they entered and jerked his head petulantly in greeting.

"Well, have you found him yet?"

"Good day, Douglas," Atticus tucked the roll of maps under his arm and turned unhurriedly to close the door behind them. "No, we haven't as yet. We may, however, have educed where he might be found."

Lucie posited her letter on top of the fan of papers spread across the desk.

"Well this is something at least," Douglas said, his eyes skittering down the page. "His Worship is taking no excuses – none at all – for our lack of progress so far." Douglas laid a particular emphasis on the word 'our'. "He tore a strip off me good and proper yesterday, right in front of his servants too. I trust he'll repeat the favour for you, whenever you see him next. So, go ahead then; aren't you going to tell me what you've found?"

Atticus rolled out the maps across the desktop and Douglas laid an armful of truncheons, one by one, around their edges, as if by doing so he might be somehow imprisoning the monster within.

"This is where we believe he must be, Mr Douglas." The pencil in Lucie's hand conjured a broad ellipse just beyond the western fringe of the town. "Around the Harlow or Rossett moors." She drew a second, smaller ring inside it and said: "And most probably somewhere here, between this old chantry chapel in the south, and the Oak Beck in the north."

Douglas bit his lip. Perhaps he bit his tongue too.

"It is still a large area, Mrs Fox and that ground isn't easy. To be candid, I was hoping for something a little tighter than this."

"Then may I suggest that we begin with the area closest to the town?" Atticus said. "By every account this man has difficulties in walking."

Douglas nodded thoughtfully. "That makes some sense, I suppose. Very well, I'll organise the searching parties accordingly. We'll begin at the Harlow Hill Tower and work out from there."

Atticus pointed to a large black rectangle at the town's edge. The tiny, printed script next to it read, 'Harlow Manor Hydropathic'.

"You might want to pay particular attention to this, Douglas. The Harlow waters are reckoned to be especially beneficial for skin conditions, and based on his history, he may very well strike there."

"The deuce he will!" Douglas was aghast. "What if he were to attack a visitor? Just imagine what His Worship would say to that! Mr Fenn is the manager there, I believe. I'll have him warned directly, and maybe have a constable posted to watch the gates."

"There is also the tea garden at Birk Crag," Lucie reminded him, "And the granges, the inn, the All Saints chapel-of-ease and any number of farms and cottages. Is there still a priest at the chantry?"

"Good day, Mr and Mrs Fox," interrupted a voice behind them. It was Hainsworth. "Sergeant Butterworth said you were here."

He stepped forward, unfastening the buttons of his heavy greatcoat as he came, and glanced down at the maps. For a while he stood, his eyes darting along the line of Lucie's annotations, following the stumbling, raging steps of the Beast. Then, in reply to her question, he said: "That chantry chapel hasn't been used in years, Mrs Fox, for services at least. An old hermit lives there now."

He tapped his finger inside the pencilled ring. "So this is where folk need to be warned, is it?"

Douglas had had enough.

"Everyone, hold hard exactly where you are. I'm the one to decide who's to be warned. The mayor has ordered that we be discreet, so what we are not going to do is to tell all and sundry and cause a damned uproar. The police are the guardians of the peace, and therefore it is for the police to remedy this, not the folk of the town."

He glared at them to reinforce his point. Then he said: "We've a large area to search, as I've remarked already, but on the other hand, we can put a lot of men into it. On top of our own searching-parties, we've a full waggonette of reinforcements from Knaresborough. Ripon couldn't help us, not even to spare a single man, but on this occasion I can forgive them. It seems that they've problems of their own up there – in the form of their own murder, as it happens."

He paused for a moment to allow his bombshell to take full effect.

"Their own murder?" Atticus repeated.

Douglas nodded. "The night before last, in the union workhouse, someone – a vagrant most likely – did for the tramp-major. Stoned him to death and decapitated him afterwards, as I heard it. It makes our fellow seem like a lady's maid."

Douglas waited another few moments as Hainsworth and the Foxes stood and stared at him in open-mouthed horror before he added: "And they still haven't found his head."

Atticus and Lucie leaned their bicycles into a hedgerow by a police waggonette and looked out across the rolling miles of gorse and heather moor, punctuated only by the occasional grey farmstead. It struck them that Detective Inspector Douglas had not exaggerated one degree in his assessment of Harlow Hill; it was a truly vast area to search. Impossibly small numbers of blue-coated figures were beginning to creep out in all directions.

A few yards ahead of them, Sergeant Hainsworth and the waggonette driver were deep in murmured conversation, whilst the big horse beside them nodded its exaggerated agreement.

"I still believe we should warn these people," Lucie whispered to her husband, "And anyway, who's to say any one of them mightn't be the Beast, or, at the very least, be able to tell us something that will help us bring him to justice."

"Samson wouldn't thank us for it," Atticus cautioned, "Douglas was exactly right about that". He pulled a face. "But I agree with you; we ought to tell them and hang what Samson wants. What if one of them was attacked, or even killed?"

"Then we're agreed on it."

Lucie stretched across him and rang her bicycle bell.

"Sergeant Hainsworth."

"Yes, what is it, Mrs Fox?"

"Mr Fox and I are going to ask around the cottages after all. Someone might know something of interest to us. If they happen to take a warning from what we say to them, well then, so be it."

Hainsworth inhaled sharply.

"I suppose I can't order you not to." He darted a glance at the waggonette driver, who was flexing his fingers with a pained expression on his face. "But then, if the cat's to come out of the bag anyway, I'll go over to All Saints chapel and then across to the chantry. I've heard the hermit there shuns visitors, but you never know, I'm Catholic myself so he might be agreeable to seeing me."

In the event, neither the inns nor the farms, nor even the tiny community that clawed a living from the stone quarry at Birk Crag, could add anything to the investigation. The quarrymen in particular seemed oblivious to events beyond the gritstone walls of their own toilsome world but, as Lucie later remarked, at least they had been warned.

The broad moorlands of Harlow and Rossett, usually so bracing and dramatic, had been distinctly discomforting this day. Lucie relaxed with an audible sigh as the sanded paths of the heath gave way to smooth asphalt and they came to the first of the large villas which marked the outskirts of the town proper. Here they stopped, arrested by the sight of the towering, stone-built sentinel that was the Harlow Hill Observation Tower. As they stood, staring up at it, the sunlight glinted on the lens of one of the big telescopes on the viewing platform and an idea occurred to Atticus.

"Close to the Sun in lonely lands, Ring'd with the azure world, he stands. The wrinkled sea beneath him crawls; He watches from his mountain walls. Those are lines from Tennyson's *The Eagle*. Lucie, what if we were to watch too, just like an eagle,*"* He raised his cane high, towards the tower's top, "From up there!"

His wife appeared not to have heard him.

"Lucie?"

A pair of ornate gates lay across a driveway, which curved away towards a large villa, partially hidden behind several enormous alder trees. They were splendid wrought-iron gates in the fashionable sunburst design and painted in bright, verdigris green.

"I don't recall there being a hospital here," Lucie said.

"No," Atticus replied, staring intently at the face of one of the gateposts. There, just below the finial-head, was fixed a staff. It was a curious staff, carved in a strange, mottled wood, and somewhat similar to the *Rod of Asclepius*; that symbol of the Greek God of Healing and Medicine, which has been so taken up by the medical profession. It was very much akin to it other than here, two serpents were entwined around the shaft rather than one and it had two spreading wings at its head.

"It's called Sun Villa." Lucie pointed to the name carved into the stone of the opposing gatepost and Atticus glanced across. "The name means nothing to me and I thought I knew all of the hospitals around Harrogate. I wonder whose it is."

"If indeed, it is a hospital at all," Atticus replied. "Your question is actually more intriguing than you might imagine, but one, I think, for another time." He raised his cane once again towards the tower. "Today, we have a murderer to catch."

CHAPTER THIRTY-ONE

It is a widely acknowledged fact that, size for size, no town in England has more ample facilities in respect of schooling than Harrogate. Most of these schools are private and many spiritual, with the various sects of the church vying with one another to provide the very best of an English education.

The school run by the Catholic sisters of the Society of the Blessed Child was one such establishment. It benefitted especially from its position in Low Harrogate, being very close both to the botanical delights of the pleasure gardens, and to the invigorating air of the moorlands beyond. Every Thursday, and three times each Sunday, the nuns and the girls of the school would walk through the town, two-by-two, to Mass. Then, returned, contrite and spiritually refreshed, the girls would be allowed one full hour of free time before prayers and lights-out.

On this particular Thursday, it was Sister Agnes who had been sent out into the extensive grounds in order to fetch-in the girls who had not yet returned. She knew where they would be, of course. She knew precisely where they would be: sitting on the wall like so many vultures, watching the fine ladies and – may the good Lord forgive them – the gentlemen and the boys returning from their own churches and chapels.

Sister Agnes shook her head in righteous despair. Silly-headed girls! That way led only to temptation and mortal sin, and she rehearsed in her mind some stinging words of rebuke for them. So engrossed was she in this that she neither saw nor sensed the phantom drifting towards her.

Something – a sound, a shadow, a stench perhaps – at last made her turn.

"You were sent to heal the contrite," a voice hissed from the night, "Lord, have mercy."

"Lord, have mercy," Agnes mouthed in return.

And the phantom became flesh.

CHAPTER THIRTY-TWO

It is said that on a clear day, a keen-sighted observer may discern seventeen castles from the viewing platform of the Harlow Hill Observation Tower, together with no fewer than seventy gentleman's seats. It is fully ninety feet above the high ground of Harlow Hill and equipped with several very well-made telescopes.

But this was not day, clear or otherwise; this was night, and Lucie Fox's attention was fixed, not on some far-distant horizon, but on the town of Harrogate itself.

Through the lens of the telescope, dark figures in capes and helmets were flitting through the spheres of gaslight like moths. Her fingertips tightened on the focussing-wheel as she adjusted the eyepiece by the tiniest degree. With this seventy-five times magnification, she felt almost as if she could reach out and tug on their sleeves.

"Atty," she whispered, then louder, "Atticus."

"Yes... what is it?" Her husband peered up from his pannikin of cocoa.

"Something's happening down in the town. The police are everywhere. They seem to be running towards the Pump Room. Here, take a look for yourself."

The old leather strapping of his campaign-chair creaked and Atticus hauled himself, a little stiffly, to his feet.

Tall as he was, he did not need the upturned orange crate Lucie was using as a platform and he nudged it away with the toe of his boot. He squinted down through the eyepiece. In the crisp air, the brass was warm against his eye.

"Yes, I see them," he said, "dozens of them. But they're not stopping at the Pump Room, Lucie; they're running-on right past it."

Atticus pushed the eyepiece away and turned to her. In the moonlight, his face looked craggy and grim.

"Something must be drawing them," he said. "We had better get down there."

Like thunderbolts, Atticus and Lucie descended the stairway of the tower, two spiralling, diving raptors. Barely stopping to lock fast the door, they grabbed the handlebars of their bicycles and kicked away. Fear and foreboding took their wheels in equal measure and it was fortunate indeed that the broad streets were both smooth and empty.

By the time Atticus and Lucie swept up to its gates, a line of policemen was already stretching, anaconda-like, along the walls of the convent school of the Society of the Blessed Child. The sergeant Hainsworth had called Butterworth had taken charge, his speaking-trumpet up like a bugler, sounding orders into the night.

"Stay in sight, my lads. Mind your mates. Keep your nightsticks out, and give a hearty blast on your whistle, should you see aught."

He caught sight of the Foxes and pinched the peak of his helmet.

"Go straight in, Mr and Mrs Fox. Sergeant Hainsworth is already in there." His voice sounded strangely soft without the trumpet.

"What has happened?" Atticus called back.

"There's been an attack on a nun, not more than five-and forty minutes ago. We're surrounding the grounds. If he's still here, we'll 'ave him for sure."

Lights were burning behind many of the windows of the convent building and the constable standing at the porch made no attempt to challenge them as they bustled inside.

There they were halted by the steely glare of a nun.

"Dear Lord!" she exclaimed, "First the police-men crawling all over this place of God, and now we have sightseers too. How on eart' did you get in here?"

The words, as louring as the face which spoke them, were softened not at all by the lilting Irish twang in her voice.

"We are not sightseers, ma'am; we are Mr and Mrs Atticus Fox, privately-commissioned detectives," Atticus replied.

"And we are presently assisting the police, at the mayor's own request." Lucie's voice was firm, but both affable and cordial in a way which, try as he might, Atticus could never quite achieve.

"That's as may be, but I am Sister Anne, the prioress of this holy convent, and I am seeing no need for yet more folk to be wandering around, after lights-out are ye minding, upsetting the sisters even more than they are a'ready and frightening the girls. There are plenty of policemen here already, as you can see for yourselves, and Sister Agnes, may the Lord have mercy on her immortal soul, is already wit' them and the Mother Abbess."

"What happ…" Atticus began.

"How is Sister Agnes?" Lucie cut across him.

"Sister Agnes has shown the good grace to forgive her attacker and will be spending time in praying for him. Her body, *Deo volente*,[18] will heal; her immortal soul, well the Mother Abbess has affirmed that she has committed no sin. She may stay wit'in her vows and remain here. If she happens to fall wit' child, then for the sake of the girls, it might be for the better if she leaves us for a wee while."

"And her attacker?" Lucie asked.

"Will undoubtedly burn for all eternity in the fires of Hell. He has ravished a woman of the Lord. I cannot see how that could be forgiven him. Can you?"

"Has Sister Agnes been able to provide a description of him?"

Sister Anne reached down and touched a large silver cross hanging at her waist.

"Aye, she has, Mrs Fox."

"And what did she say?"

"She said, Mrs Fox… She said that his countenance was quite ghastly to behold."

In the chill night air of the hall, time itself seemed to freeze.

"How so, Sister?" Atticus asked her.

"When we finally managed to get her calm again, Agnes told us that this man's face was fearfully ugly. She said it was horned, just as Moses' was when he came down from the Mount, although to my mind, the two can hardly be compared."

The Prioress shook her head and tut-tutted pharisaically.

"Moses, if you please. I ask you! The Devil, more like – and that's what I told her. Now, if you'll please be excusing me, I'm needing to fetch another rosary for the girl. She lost her own in the misfortune. Well, more likely *before* the misfortune, I should say. To my own way of t'inking, that would be why she lost the good Lord's protection in the first place. It's contrary to the Canon to lose a sacramental it is, quite contrary to it."

"What was Sister Agnes' rosary made from?" Atticus asked.

"Why, I believe it was a beautiful silver one, given to her by her parents when she first came here. Why ever should you be asking me that? Now, if you don't mind, I really must be getting on."

Sister Anne pressed her fingertips together, and glided through a side-arch and into the depths of the convent like a figure on some enormous automaton-clock.

"A face that was horned like Moses'; what in the world did she mean by that?" Lucie whispered when they could no longer hear her footsteps.

"It's from the Bible, the book of Exodus," Atticus replied. "When Moses came down from Mount Sinai after he had been given the Tablets of the Testimony, his face was supposedly left with horns from his being in company with God."

"Oh. Atticus, do you suppose that what she took for horns might really have been the lumps Sarah told me about? Do you think she might have been another victim of the Beast?"

"I believe she almost certainly was, and on this occasion he has been inclined towards the greatest outrage. I wonder why he took Sister Agnes' rosary though. Can we take anything from the fact it was silver?"

"What, as a medicine, do you mean? I think this goes far beyond medicines, Atticus."

A latch behind them clicked, and a great, oak-planked door creaked ajar. They could hear a murmured conversation and although it was too muffled to make out the words, one of the voices was very familiar.

"When a door of opportunity is closed, another will surely open," Atticus whispered, and as if to his command, the heavy door swung wide. Detective Sergeant Hainsworth, notebook in hand, stopped short.

"Mr and Mrs Fox!" he exclaimed, "I thought you were up at the Harlow Tower."

An elderly nun appeared at his shoulder. A large cross hanging at her breast identified her as an abbess.

"These people are with you?" she asked, peering at them with a penetrating gaze. Her eyes, rimmed with pink, were startlingly blue against her lined and sagging skin and crisp, white wimple.

"Yes, yes, I suppose they are, Reverend Mother. I should like to introduce Mr and Mrs Atticus Fox of Prospect Place."

Atticus bowed and said, "Reverend Mother Abbess," and Lucie curtsied.

"Mr and Mrs Fox, I am delighted to meet you at last. Naturally, I am aware of you both, and Mrs Fox, I am especially admiring of you and your derring-do." The old Abbess chuckled and then whispered conspiratorially: "Between you and me, I sometimes make reference to you, when speaking privately to our girls."

"You are very kind, Reverend Mother, thank you." Lucie curtsied again.

The Mother Abbess smiled and laid her hand on Hainsworth's sleeve. "It is gratifying to see that even heretics sometimes have proper manners. Whoever could have believed it?"

"Whoever indeed, Reverend Mother. His Worship, the mayor has asked Mr and Mrs Fox to assist us with this case. As I said to you, the culprit may also have been behind a number of other serious crimes over recent days."

"Yes, I had heard about the breaking-in at the English church up yonder, and about the poor harlot woman. She was Catholic, I believe – a poor lost sheep whom Father Pope was endeavouring to bring back into the fold. We have prayed for her soul more than once this week. As you know, St Mary Magdalene was once a harlot too, though repented."

"She was, Reverend Mother," said Hainsworth, "I mean they both were."

"Come, Mr and Mrs Fox," the Abbess said, "Sister Agnes is in solitary contemplation at present and cannot be disturbed. I have promised to pray with her in a wee while but until then, if you wish it, we may talk in the locutory[19]."

Lucie smiled. "That would be very kind, Reverend Mother."

The convent locutory of the Society of the Blessed Child in Harrogate was a lofty and spacious room but furnished simply. A Madonna-and-Child smiled down benignantly upon a table and pair of wooden forms, which had been softened with richly embroidered cushions. Through the Gothic arches of the windows, the lights of bulls-eye lanterns crept back and forth like fireflies as the sergeant and his men scoured the grounds.

"This is where we bring the parents of our girls," the abbess explained. "They appreciate the austerity of the place, do you see? We find it allays any lingering fears they may harbour as to the dissoluteness of the town itself."

"It really is rather nice," said Lucie, glancing up at the Madonna.

The abbess cackled with gentle laughter. "Oh dear, if our visitors are finding it 'rather nice', then perhaps we have failed after all. Mrs Fox, perhaps you should sit down before I am minded to take away your cushions."

Once they were seated Atticus said: "Your prioress told us that Sister Agnes' attacker might have had a horned face, like Moses'."

The old abbess' mouth curled into a thin and rueful smile.

"Straight to the matter in hand I see, Mr Fox. It is true; Agnes did say that. But then Sister Anne helped her to recollect that Moses was a righteous man, for the most part anyway. By the time she spoke with your Mr Hainsworth, he still possessed horns, but at least they had become more like the Devil's, which seems much more fitting."

"Oh," said Atticus.

The abbess regarded him steadily for a while.

"Do you know what it is to be a Catholic, Mr and Mrs Fox?"

"I know the creed and the basic tenets of the faith, of course," Atticus replied.

"Yes, I'm sure you do." The Abbess touched her fingertip to a dark liver spot at her temple. "You may well know something of them up here, Mr Fox. They say you know something about a great many things. But do you know what it *feels* like, here, in your stomach, or in your deepest heart? Do you, Mrs Fox?"

Both Atticus and Lucie shook their heads.

"I am blessed to be into my eightieth year. But when I was a girl, not so much younger than Sister Agnes is now, Catholics were a *gens lucifuga* – a people fearful of the light. We and our chapels were to be found in backstreets and cellars and in secret rooms, or else in the quiet recesses of the country. Do not forget, it was just a little over sixty years ago that we were emancipated in this country, that, like Moses, we were finally brought in from the wilderness."

"The Catholic Emancipation Act of 1829," said Atticus.

"Exactly so, Mr Fox: Eighteen hundred and twenty-nine, which seems almost like yesterday. Now please do not misunderstand me; some of our faith do still prefer to live in seclusion and away from the light. Father Cado up at the chantry, for example, and Brother Justin at St Robert's cave both live a life of solitary contemplation as hermits. But at least that is their choice. They need not live in fear."

The abbess reached up and twisted a gnarled finger around the black silk cord of her pectoral cross.

"Yet they do, Mr and Mrs Fox; all we Catholics do. We live in fear of sin. We exist in perpetual penitence, always failing to live up to the standards set by our blessed Lord. We confess daily our sins; we are obliged to remind each other continually of our shortcomings, and we live always in fear of the Devil. So if a poor sister of our order chooses to remember her attacker as having the appearance of pure evil, then who can blame her for that?"

"You are saying then that her description might not be the literal truth of it?" said Lucie.

"I raise the possibility of it – nothing more than that. Agnes has suffered the very greatest ignominy this night. The skin of her belly has been rubbed as raw as fresh meat where this man forced his attentions upon her. Now while her skin will swiftly restore itself, it is her mind that has been most grievously injured, and the healing of that will take a great deal longer."

The abbess glanced up to the figure of the Virgin Mary, resplendent in rich blue robes.

"We shall be petitioning Her aid in that. Several weeks in prayerful seclusion here in the convent should help, and perhaps a pilgrimage to Rome, to visit the holy relics of her blessed namesake[20]. Part of Sister Agnes' ministry was to distribute alms to the poor of the town. We will need to pass that duty over to another now, perhaps to one or two of the girls, to teach them at firsthand about the poor and the destitute. Yes, that might work very well; it may even be for the best. The ways of our Lord can oft' be mysterious."

"Was Sister Agnes carrying anything at the time of her attack; alms or… or medicines for instance?" Atticus asked.

"She was not carrying anything at all, so far as I am aware, other than her rosary, which she dropped during the course of her ordeal. She had been sent to summon-in the girls to evening prayers."

The old abbess' face convulsed suddenly into an expression of the most profound anguish and she clasped her hands together.

"But what if one of the girls had been attacked?"

"It would have been unthinkable," Lucie agreed. "But they were not, and Mr Fox and I intend to catch this man before he can attack anyone else. Do we know anything of what he was wearing?"

The nun wrung her hands and nodded.

"As Agnes explained to Mr Hainsworth, it was dark and all something of a haze. The man was dressed, to the best of her recollection anyhow, in a dark and tattered robe – something like a cassock. What she does remember very clearly though, is what he was wearing underneath. It was a coarse undergarment, very rough and scratching, and it stank terribly. That I can believe because she still had the smell of it on her when she came in. We were obliged to light an incense burner. "

Atticus and Lucie exchanged a sharp and pointed glance. Lucie said: "And did he speak?"

"She remembers only that he greeted her with the *Kyrie, eleison* and that he dismissed her afterwards."

Atticus was startled.

"The *Kyrie, eleison*, the phrase 'Lord have mercy'? So her attacker was a pious man?"

"*They profess that they know God but in their works they deny him.* As St Titus reminds us, anyone can *declare* piety, Mr Fox." The Abbess lowered her head and peered at him with her pink-rimmed eyes. "This man has committed the sin of physical outrage, which is an injury to justice and to charity. Sister Agnes was – Sister Agnes remains – a wife of Christ, so it is an abomination for which he will no doubt be given over to the Devil. As will I, if I do not fulfil my pastoral duty to pray with her. You must both please excuse me now, for the present at least."

The Reverend Mother struggled to her feet.

Lucie stood too, followed quickly by Atticus.

"We will do our very best to catch this man; you can be quite assured of that," said Lucie.

"I am sure you will, Mrs Fox, and we, for our part, will pray hourly for your success. *Pax vobiscum.*"

"Thank you," said Atticus, "Peace be with you too."

CHAPTER THIRTY-THREE

When Lucie and Atticus Fox paused to lock the visitors' door of Harlow Hill Tower for what was the second time that night, the first light of day was just beginning to pick its way across the town. They coasted, exhausted, enervated, and scarcely able even to pedal their bicycles, through the awakening streets and drew up finally to Number 16, Prospect Place to find they had just missed a constable. He had, however, left a letter for them. It was from Detective Inspector Douglas and headed with the words 'Of Pressing Urgency' written large. Atticus pointed to the places where Douglas' pen nib had twice pierced the paper, and he clearly had had no time to rewrite it.

It seemed that a labourer, about to begin his day's work on the Harrogate to Ripon railway line, had seen something break the surface of the River Nidd. It had caught almost immediately against the half-submerged trunk of a fallen tree and the curious labourer had picked his way across to it to see what it might be. It was only when he had tugged at the bloated and distended mass and it had rolled obediently towards him that he realised it was a human corpse, and one conspicuously missing its head.

The Nidd Viaduct, a magnificent bridge of seven tall arches built massively in gritstone, carried the freight and passengers of the Harrogate to Ripon railway line over the deep gorge cut by the river just north of the town. It was in its vast shadow that the labourer still sat, a little way apart from the milling policemen, with his head buried deep in his hands.

"Upon my soul," Atticus exclaimed from the top of the riverbank, steep and rock-strewn at this point, and a pair of constables turned at the sound. Below them, Douglas and Hainsworth were crouching at the waterside, conversing in low tones across a grotesque mound of something that once had been human.

"You speak to the railwayman, Atticus and I'll see to the cadaver," said Lucie.

Atticus nodded gratefully.

"Good morning, Mr Douglas, Mr Hainsworth," Lucie called down. "Thank you for your letter. We came over directly we got it."

She picked her way down the treacherous slope and crouched beside the large, grey gob of flesh, regarding it with interest.

"Do we know who he is?" she asked.

"Who he was, more like," Douglas retorted. "No, we do not, Mrs Fox. As I said in my memorandum, he's only just floated up, and in the absence of his head or his clothes or anyone reported as missing, it's well nigh impossible to say."

"So there's been no sign of his head?"

Douglas shrugged. "We've had constables looking along the river banks but no, not yet. No doubt it'll turn up eventually."

Lucie squinted up into the great stone arch curving high above them.

"Has anyone looked up on the viaduct?"

"What on earth would it be doing up there?" Douglas' tone was rising again. "Didn't you read my note at all, Mrs Fox? The navvy told us he saw the body come up just there." He pointed to where a good-sized tree trunk jutted out into the river, a ridge of dirty, yellowish foam banked up against one side. "And look at the state of him. He's patently been under for some days, so it stands to reason he must have gone in much further upstream. The Oak Beck comes down from Harlow and it flows into the Nidd just up there." He jerked his head upstream. "And that, I'm obliged to admit, would fit neatly with your own suppositions as to where the Beast lives."

Lucie regarded the corpse. She said: "I estimate the body has been in the water for around three or four days. The water will still be quite warm at this time of year and there's nothing that would serve to weigh him down. When a corpse is fully submerged in a river not in spate, Inspector Douglas, it rarely moves very far from the point of immersion. The fish have been busy to be sure, but there is little actual abrasion to the skin. I should be very surprised if he didn't enter the water very near to here."

Douglas rubbed irritably at the back of his neck.

"Mrs Fox, you are perfectly free to look up on the railway line, or wherever else you choose, but I say that

'Headless Harry' here was most likely carried down by the Oak Beck. Otherwise how do you explain the connection with the other attacks?"

"But there may not be any connection with the other attacks."

Hainsworth peered up at the viaduct.

"So what are you suggesting, Mrs Fox; that it was an accident? That he was hit by a train, decapitated, and his body pitched down into the river by the force of the collision?"

"That is a possibility, I would say, but not a likely one. To my mind, the fact that he is naked would be more suggestive of foul play. And do you see how the head appears to have been cut off cleanly? That is indicative of a knife. If he was decapitated by a train, then he must have been caught by a wheel flange or some other sharp edge, in which case there should still be some sign of it on the track bed – his head, for example." She grimaced. "Alternatively, he might have been murdered elsewhere and his corpse thrown into the river."

"Thrown down from the bridge?" Hainsworth asked.

"Quite possibly so." Lucie pulled off a glove and pushed her fingertips deep into the bloated skin of the cadaver's chest. It felt cold and clammy to her touch. "It is difficult to be sure with the corpus in this condition, but if the coroner finds a broken rib or two, or a fractured sternum, then it might be suggestive of that. It's a good hundred foot drop from the parapet."

"So if there *was* foul play," Douglas interrupted, "but there *isn't* to be a connection with the Bogs Valley Beast, then what you're saying is that there must be two murderers at work in the town?"

"What I'm saying is that we shouldn't altogether discount that possibility, Inspector."

"But how could that be poss…"

A contemptuous sneer curled Douglas' lip.

"Oh, I see. Yes, I see perfectly well. Two murderers at large would mean two commissions from His Worship, and two favourable reports in the *Advertiser* and the *Herald*. Ye Gods, Mrs Fox, this is Harrogate; it isn't some novel of… of Arthur Conan Doyle with a murderer lurking behind every lamp-post. Is it, Hainsworth?"

"That dreadful man," Lucie cribbed as she and Atticus leaned together over the fine ashlar parapet of the viaduct. They were watching the now-distant figures of the constables picking their way along the waterside, combing the reeds and the trailing fingers of the willow trees for Harry's still-missing head. "That dreadful, dreadful man; how dare he suggest I was inventing a second murderer just for the… notoriety of it."

"He doesn't like you telling him his job in front of Hainsworth, that's all."

Atticus brushed some stray pebbles of ballast from the parapet top and they watched as they took an age to fall and patter into the water slipping past far below. "And he's stretched thinly enough as it is, with just one murderer to find."

"But he must see how unlikely it would be that a corpse can drift all the way through the outskirts of Harrogate, along a shallow beck, without being spied. There was hardly any abrasion to the skin. You wonder if he's ever seen a floater before."

Atticus could not help but to agree. It did seem inconceivable, more so even than the notion that two murderers might be at large in their town at one and the same time.

"Headless Harry's corpse had been stripped, you say?"

Lucie nodded.

"But none of the other victims of the Beast had been, and nor were they decapitated."

The distant double-hoot of a steam locomotive signalled that a train was leaving Bilton Junction and Atticus and Lucie began to make their way back along the tracks to safety.

Lucie said: "The tramp-major at Ripon workhouse was decapitated, Atticus, and they haven't found his head either."

"That is exactly so." Atticus tapped the horn tip of his cane onto the silver-topped rail by their boots. It was already beginning to sing with the approach of the train. "And that line leads directly to Ripon."

The train came into sight just as they reached the end of the parapet. Lucie stepped onto the turf at the trackside and a handful of ballast skittered down in her wake.

"Did you find out anything from the poor man who found him?" she asked.

Atticus stepped down after her.

"Nothing we don't already know. He was just about to begin his day's work, repairing the bridge masonry, when a flock of ducks suddenly took off making a fearful din. He looked across to see the corpse bobbing up. He didn't know what it was at first and wondered if it might be valuable, so he clambered along that fallen tree and pulled at it. When he saw exactly what it was, he jumped back, lost his footing and fell into the r—"

Atticus' words were drowned out by a long, shrill blast from the locomotive's whistle. It was close now, a great, green leviathan roaring and spitting steam from its maw. Was the whistle a warning of its approach, or was it the machine exulting at the place of its kill?

Atticus raised his cane in salute and seventy tons of thundering steel howled past them. It was a Fletcher 1440, he could see, with four great driving wheels coupled by rods that bit down with every pant of the engine. Any one of them would crush mere flesh and blood in an instant. Yet Atticus and Lucie knew they had not, and that the behemoth had bellowed in vain. There had been no sign of an engine-strike anywhere on the bridge and this new link to Ripon was too strong, too significant, to be mere coincidence.

Lucie Fox, a trained nurse, was a firm believer in taking the correct and prescribed amount of sleep. She generally insisted upon it. So while her husband was impatient to travel the dozen or so miles to Ripon immediately in the hope of gleaning any information they could regarding the murder in its workhouse, Lucie would not hear of it.

"Slow but steady wins the race," she said firmly. "We have lost quite enough sleep as it is, up in the observation tower. The Beast will be caught all the sooner by minds that are properly refreshed and Harry and the tramp-major will be just as dead for the sake of another few hours."

For Atticus Fox however, sleep was easier said than managed and he had only just dropped into slumber when Mrs Morris made her pre-arranged knock on the door.

Little more than an hour later, they were peering down from their own train window as it whistled and thundered over the very same viaduct. They glimpsed a dozen or so constables fanned across the riverbank, beating their way through the yellowing willow-herbs and throwing up plumes of fluffy seeds like so much smoke. And then they were gone, replaced in an instant by the open fields and hedgerows of the Vale of York.

CHAPTER THIRTY-FOUR

The old city of Ripon was just a few miles to the north of Harrogate in the very same West Riding of Yorkshire, but for all that, it might as well have been on the Moon. It was a city only by virtue of its magnificent cathedral church and most certainly not by its size, which was more akin to a market town. Its people too seemed different; suspicious, aloof, taciturn even, unwilling to exchange more than the gruffest of 'good days' as the Foxes made their way from the railway station into its labyrinth of narrow streets.

Almost five hundred years before William Slingsby discovered spa waters at Harrogate, this city was already founding hospital orders for the poor. One of these was the Hospital of St Mary Magdalen and by coincidence, Atticus and Lucie's route took them past its ancient chapel, built to provide for the needs spiritual of the leprous and the blind.

But as *La Belle Époque* had gilded the world, and the hem of Victoria's robe brushed across even the lowliest of chapels, the swelling congregation had built a new and modern church just across the way. The old leper house was abandoned, and left to the mice and the tramps, and to the shit-faced satyrs.

Atticus Fox glanced between these chapels, the ancient and the modern, and it was the former, with its bell gable, its rude, simple stonework and its oversized buttresses that captured his attention.

"That is the chapel with Esau's statue of Mary Magdalene inside it, Lucie. Do you think it would harm to take a look inside, for the sake of our inquiry?"

"Look if you must, Atty but don't be too long. I'll wait out here. I should get filthy in an instant in there."

Unlike old horses, church buildings past their use are seldom rendered down. The old chapel stood, set to grass in a pleasant riverside meadow, and it opened willingly to Atticus' hand.

On another day, Atticus Fox might have been intrigued, fascinated even, by this place, with its oaken screen, its ancient piscina and font, and by its low-set lepers' window through which those so afflicted might receive Communion. He did tarry for a while before the great Norman altar-stone, cracked by the Puritan mells of Cromwell, and stoop low. But this was no act of obeisance; Atticus had bent only to brush aside some rubble from the floor, where the bricks gave way to a mosaic – a medallion. It was Roman, he was sure, with a cross of palm fronds the founders had thought holy. And so it was, in its way, but not to any Christian god. To the Romans, the palm symbolised victory: victory over the fierce Brigante tribes of this land; victory over its damp and gnawing cold; victory of the spirit over the weak and fleshly body.

Atticus Fox inspected it with a wry smile. Such symbolism in a holy place. The alchemists, the Gnostics, the Hermeticists had all used the same. Indeed, the thought suddenly came to him, in these times of esoteric revivalism, they almost certainly still did.

He rose to his feet. There, on the wall, in the corner of the Sanctuary, was his reason for coming here. The figure of a woman, robed, penitent, utterly bewitching, stood cradling a cross. It was the figure of St Mary Magdalene, her reddish-blonde hair falling across her shoulders, her beneficent smile lighting the chapel as much as ever did the great Gothic window behind the altar.

Entranced by her countenance, Atticus was struck, as few could be, by the wisdom of the long-dead Archbishop Thurstan in choosing her to be patron of this chapel. Christ, he recalled, had supposedly cast seven devils out of Mary Magdalene, and theological scholars were of the firm opinion that she had previously been a madwoman.

Seven devils.

Ferociously agnostic though he was, Atticus' head dropped a degree, if not in adoration, then most certainly in the deep respect we accord those of shared tribulation. Mary's head was inclined to the side, carven in compassionate regard. Whilst she did bear an uncanny resemblance to Alice Malkin, Atticus was reminded much more of his wife. Upon occasion, Lucie's head would incline in that very same way. In the early days, in those very darkest of days, those occasions were frequent.

Atticus Fox stood with bowed head and recalled also his mother, after firstly the absinthe, and then later the gin, had taken hold of her. He recalled her frenzied hands, slapping him, punching him, and her very last words to him, snarled in spit.

"You've a devil in you, Atticus Fox. You've a devil in that head of yours. Leave me, can't you! Let me be! Why don't you ever just let me be?"

Seven devils!

"Mary!" Atticus whispered.

They found the Ripon union workhouse just before the market place and only a short walk beyond the two chapels of St Mary Magdalen. It was built to the plans of Mssrs Perkin and Backhouse, the architectural partners from Leeds, who were justly celebrated for their design of Armley Gaol. The interiors of these buildings were strikingly similar in many respects, but whereas the gaol was faced brutally in stone, here the city's paupers were adorned in rich, red brick and imprisoned only by a low iron railing, and by the depths of their despair.

Atticus, staring at the frontage, might have been reminded of Tisiphone, she of the Furies, who stands in a bloody red dress and guards the gates of Tartarus. And like Tartarus, that lowest abyss, that place of abasement and the very personification of darkness, there was a portal, a great stone archway, from which so few returned.

Atticus and Lucie paused to gather themselves, just as everyone hesitates before they enter a workhouse, and then reached for the gate.

A porter was watching them as they walked up to the reception building, as suspiciously as Tisiphone herself. They were not of the Board of Guardians as he knew full well; nor clearly were they here for relief. But then neither were a gentleman and a lady together likely to be commercial travellers.

"Now then," he called out, weary of his guessing-game.

Atticus pinched the brim of his hat and with his other hand proffered one of their beautifully embossed calling cards. One of the corners had already been carefully folded over and the word *Affaires* – matters – written neatly on the little white triangle it formed.

"We are Atticus and Mrs Fox of Harrogate and we would very much like to speak with the master, or the matron or their deputies if he is not available."

The porter held their card out and studied it. He was thrasonically not one for book-learning and the words quickly defeated him.

"Who did ye say ye were?" he enquired at length.

"A & L Fox, commissioned investigators," Atticus replied curtly, "and we are here on behalf of His Worship, the mayor of Harrogate, on a matter of the very gravest importance."

"Are thee now?" the porter exclaimed, "Gravest importance, from the mayor of Harrogate. Well, t' master is at his 'ouse. Go and sit thee both in t' waitin' room ower yonder, and ah'll go and seek 'im for ye."

He retreated back into his room and shut the door firmly behind him.

"I presume he means in there, Atticus." Lucie pointed across the archway towards an open door. The orange glow of a lit hearth was reflected in its glossy panels, and as the day was a chilly one, the Foxes were grateful that the guardians had felt inclined to provide such comfort to their visitors – at least until they might identify them as prospective inmates. That comfort proved veneer-thin, however, as the daily business of the place: the stench of carbolic, the curses, the cries, the cracking of stones, began to seep in through the walls.

They sat, side-by-side, in silence, staring into the glowing coals of the hearth for what seemed like an age. Perhaps the master was busy. Perhaps time itself ran more slowly in a city as ancient as this one. Whatever the reason, they had quite lost track of the hour by the time the porter reappeared, followed by a neat, almost dapper, gentleman in a high top hat. He removed this hat and bowed. Bare-headed, he really was very short.

"Mr and Mrs Fox, my name is Greenwood and I have the honour to be master of this workhouse."

He held up their calling card and made a great show of reading it before nodding gravely.

"Yes, yes, I have heard of you of course, from the newspapers and suchlike. Please do come over to my private living quarters and we can discuss whatever *affaires* they are that have brought you all the way up from Harrogate."

Mr Greenwood led them without further word to a much larger building, which rose up behind the entrance block. It was constructed in the same red brick as the frontage, with the same grand Dutch gabling, but this was the workhouse proper and the austerity and the brooding menace of the place could not so easily be hidden.

The master's quarters were contained in the front portion of this block, easily discernible by the fussy curtains and by the vases of late begonias in the windows.

The sharp odour of carbolic hit Atticus and Lucie like a physical blow as they entered the apartment and clung to them as they followed Mr Greenwood into a tiny dining room. This appeared to serve also as a private office, and a lady in a green satin gown glanced up sharply from a ledger as they entered.

"Mr and Mrs Fox, may I present our matron," the master announced, "Mrs Greenwood is also my own wife, just as I am her own husband."

He reached out their visiting card to her.

"Mr and Mrs Fox have come up from Harrogate to see us, Mrs G. – at the personal request of Mr Samson Fox."

"Samson Fox the millionaire!"

Mrs Greenwood stood and smoothed her front. "Well now, that is… very agreeable, I do declare. You are called Fox too, I see. Might you be… relations of his?"

"A cousin," Atticus replied.

Mrs Greenwood smiled sweetly, revealing two rows of stained porcelain teeth, and lifted her hand towards Atticus in a way that put Lucie in mind of a lamed puppy. Atticus, ever polite, bowed and grasped her fingers and stared for several seconds at the mottled skin hanging loosely around the lines of tendons and veins.

"Do both of you sit down. I shall go straightaway and ask the kitchens to have some fresh tea brewed up," said Mrs Greenwood, "Mercy-me! Where did I put the key to the good caddy? Relations of Samson Fox come to visit us. Here in our own workhouse. Who could have thought it?" She seemed suddenly flushed.

After the door clicked shut behind her, the master pulled a pair of steel-rimmed pince-nez from his waistcoat pocket and laid them carefully onto the polished surface of the table.

He said: "So, you are here at the behest of your cousin? He is as rich as Croesus, I hear."

Atticus nodded. "He has a large forge in Leeds. It is doing very well by all accounts."

"I admire Samson Fox, Mr and Mrs Fox; I admire him very much, and so does Mrs G." Greenwood lifted off his stovepipe hat and placed it next to his pince-nez. "Although I'll admit, I am one of the very few in Ripon who does."

"But why is that, Mr Greenwood?" Lucie asked, "Samson Fox is a first-rate mayor, and a great benefactor to the poor and needy."

"And I dare say he is, Mrs Fox and that's all very laudable, I'm sure. But Ripon is an old city and it much prefers what we might call old money. Gentry, farmers and landowners, they are more to our taste. Parvenus, like Samson Fox, might be regarded as being rather too much like Harrogate itself." Greenwood smiled to disarm his words. "Newly rich, newly celebrated and if you'll forgive me, because it is neither my own view nor yet Mrs G's, something of an upstart.

"And if," he continued as Atticus opened his mouth to protest, "And if Mr Samson Fox is so well-regarding of the poor and the needy, then why does he not have a workhouse built in Harrogate itself, instead of hiding it away in a neighbouring town? In Ripon, as you can see, we allow our paupers and our vagrants into our very midst. We do not deny our workhouse lest our well-to-do visitors should happen to look upon it and think the worse of us. Perhaps Mayor Fox might consider that point before he finally passes on his chain of office."

The door opened and Mrs Greenwood reappeared. A billowing waft of carbolic and boiled cabbage rolled in after her and Atticus stood and waited dutifully until she had sat, prim and upright, by her husband.

"I was just explaining to Mr and Mrs Fox how their cousin isn't the great philanthropist everyone believes him to be, Mrs Greenwood," explained the master, "Or else he would have made certain that Harrogate had its own workhouse."

"Oh, yes, that is quite true. For our own part, Mr G. and I have chosen to forsake earthly riches in order to live amongst the poor, disciplining them and seeking to improve them. Doubtless we shall reap our just reward in Heaven some day. Indeed, one of the vagrant-women was remarking on that very point just the other day."

"It is about vagrants that we have come today," Lucie said.

"Indeed, Mrs Fox, and to what end?" asked Mr Greenwood.

Lucie hesitated. "There have been two murderous attacks in Harrogate over the course of recent days and a number of other acts of violence. My husband and I are here to ascertain whether or not the recent murder of your own tramp-major might in some way be connected to them."

Mrs Greenwood gasped. "I've heard nothing of any murders in Harrogate. Have you, Mr Greenwood?"

"Not a thing," the master exclaimed, rather too loudly for the tiny room.

"The most recent of the murders was three or four days ago," Lucie went on, "but the corpse was discovered only this morning. It was found in the River Nidd, directly beneath the Ripon to Harrogate railway viaduct."

"Three or four days ago would be, let me see now, Monday or Tuesday last," Greenwood said.

The matron's hands flew to her face. "Poor Mr Firth was murdered on Monday night."

"We heard as much," said Lucie, "And we should like to know exactly how that murder was committed."

Greenwood gave her an uncomfortable glance. "Perhaps it might be for the best if Mr Fox and I were to take a walk in the grounds and I told him privately, Mrs Fox. Mr Firth, our tramp-major, was murdered in quite brutal circumstances and I shouldn't wish to cause you any undue distress with the details of it."

Atticus coughed.

"Mrs Fox is quite used to this sort of thing, Master; I should say far more used to it than I. It is probably a better idea yet if we were both to take your walk."

Mr Greenwood regarded him dubiously. "Are you sure, Mr Fox?"

It was perhaps rather fortunate that the tea tray was delivered at that moment, that the tea was fresh and hot, and that Lucie's blood had ample opportunity to cool along with it.

"We house our vagrant inmates within the front buildings – in the wing behind the porter's office," Mr Greenwood explained as the Foxes strolled beside him in the shadow of a high brick wall. "I'm told they regard Ripon as one of the better spikes, although for the very life of me, I cannot understand why."

He glanced sideways to Lucie and his eyes slid down her figure, slender as it was in the 'rational' clothing she favoured.

"Mrs Fox, I expect our porter will have already begun to admit some of today's casuals by now. Should you be unfortunate enough to come into contact with any of them, I strongly advise you to avoid engaging in conversation. Oh, and another word of caution if I may: Never, ever, look any of them in the eye."

"Thank you, Mr Greenwood, I shall take careful note of your advice," said Lucie.

"We admit them for two nights at a time," Greenwood continued, "And if they have the capacity for it, we expect three hours of good hard labour in return. That is stone-breaking for the males and oakum-picking for the frail, the females and the children."

He led them in procession through the porter's office and then into the heat and steam of a boiler room.

Against one wall, a great, shining copper geyser hissed and spat into a pauper's waiting water-pail.

"Come in here, my lush; there's plenty o' room for another," a voice cackled from a side-room. They turned to glimpse a grimy, terrier-cropped head leering up at them from a bath.

Greenwood slammed the door.

"Half measures at supper, and the same at breakfast tomorrow morning for that one, Porter," he barked through the door, "Make a note accordingly, if you please."

"Very good, Master," came the muffled reply.

Mr Greenwood spread his hands in vexed apology and beckoned them through to a corridor. It was quiet and cool after the oppressive humidity of the boiler-room.

"Please forgive us for that oaf, Mrs Fox," he said. "We are obliged to accommodate such folk here. You may take comfort from my promise that he will go to bed hungry tonight. We shall endeavour to teach him his manners; whether we shall succeed or not, only the Lord can say."

"Those are the vagrants' cells?" Atticus asked, lifting up his cane towards a line of heavy black doors, set one after another down the length of the corridor, where Mssrs. Perkin and Backhouse had clearly been intent on replicating their Armley triumph.

"They are. We have thirteen in total, and a four-bedded ward for overflows. That isn't counting the tramp-major's own cell, of course. The police are of the opinion that he was first overwhelmed there by the use of ether, and then dragged out here, to be murdered in our refractory cell."

"Why do they believe so?" Atticus asked.

"Because we found a silk pocket handkerchief in his quarters that smelled strongly of ether, and an earthenware pot, which had been broken in the struggle."

"A tramp-major would not normally carry a silk handkerchief, I imagine?"

Greenwood shook his head. "No, although he had a chest-complaint that meant Mrs G. and I often wished he had."

Atticus nodded. "What about this earthenware pot?"

The master spread his hands. "It was just a regular pot, unglazed, around the size of a flour-jar. It had been painted with all manner of stars and crosses, together with his name: William Firth."

"What was in it?" Lucie asked.

"It was empty, Mrs Fox, by which I mean there was nothing to be found amongst the shards. Someone must have hurled it with considerable force against the fireplace because three of the hearth tiles were shattered and two more cracked beyond repair. All five will require replacement."

"May we see the fragments of the pot?"

"Alas, you are too late. We had the cells cleaned and scrubbed directly the police finished their examinations. They went off in a cartload of road stone this very morning."

Atticus made a moue of disappointment.

"So where is this refractory cell you mentioned, Master?"

"It is cell number three; that one, just there." Greenwood lifted his arm and pointed to one of the heavy doors immediately in front of them. It bore the numeral three painted neatly in white. "That is where poor Mr Firth, God rest his soul, was murdered."

He lifted off his hat and whispered the word again. "Murdered – here in my workhouse." With his tall top hat cradled under his arm the master seemed once again to be diminished. He stepped forward and leaned on the door. It sighed softly as it yielded to his touch, and obediently swung wide.

Cell number three, the refractory cell, where transgressions against the myriad rules that governed the workhouse were punished, was narrow, tenebrous and cramped, with just a single, iron-grilled window, set high in the wall opposite, for light. A lattice of shadows chequered the back and seat of a heavy wooden chair and threw into silhouette a tangle of leather straps, which hung down over it like the dangling legs of a long-dead spider.

"Are you quite well, Mr Fox?" Greenwood asked.

Atticus nodded, too quickly perhaps to be entirely convincing. "I am… quite well, thank you, Master. I've come across something similar before, that is all."

Greenwood made as if to step over the threshold of the cell, but hesitated.

"Yes, I understand that pattern of restraint is very commonly used, especially by the poor-laws[21] and the insane asylums. It renders the inmate practically immobile. I am assured it is very disagreeable indeed."

"Yes," said Atticus.

Lucie said: "So your tramp-major, quieted or insensible from ether inhalation, met his death in this cell?"

Greenwood nodded.

"In the chair?"

By dint of sheer force of will, Greenwood advanced into the cell. He rested his hand on the seat's arm, where the bare timber was covered in curious marks, as if a cat might have been scratching at it.

"Mr Firth was stripped naked, buckled into the restraints and then beaten with stones, Mrs Fox. We always keep a good store of rocks in the work yard for the casuals to break up into road-stone. Then he was throttled with a length of old rope – from the pile we have for picking out into oakum."

"Dear lord!" Lucie exclaimed, "And I suppose that strapped in there and gagged, there could be no question of him crying out for assistance."

"None at all. Not one of the vagrants heard a thing, except for a brief scuffle during the small hours. In the casuals' wing of a union workhouse, you will understand that scuffles are not at all uncommon. And we do need to have a gag on the restraints, otherwise anyone we put in here would scream all night long and keep half the West Riding awake."

Greenwood stared down at the chair.

"And had he been able to, poor Mr Firth undoubtedly would have screamed. By the time this monster had finished, all we could recognise of him was his tattoo."

"Is there anyone you know who could have hated him enough to do such a thing?" Lucie asked.

"Not at all." The master shook his head. "I cannot imagine anyone hating William Firth. I'll admit he was a little too fond of his pipe and his gin flask for either my own or Mrs Greenwood's tastes, but he was a genial enough fellow for that."

"Which rather puts me in mind of another question we have for you," Atticus said. "Tell me, Master: do you have any recollection of a child-inmate here by the name of Esau? It would have been around fifteen or twenty years ago."

Greenwood seemed to reel on his feet, stunned, as if Atticus' words had been formed of the very same rocks that were used to beat the life out of William Firth.

"The monkey-faced boy?" he whispered.

"Tell us about him," Lucie invited. "How did he come to be here? What was he like? Where did he go to when he left?"

The master of Ripon workhouse turned and collapsed into his own refractory chair.

"Those are a great many questions, Mrs Fox." He swatted the gently swinging straps of the head restraints away from his face, "A great many questions about a child who left us so many years ago."

Lucie smiled. "Our train doesn't leave for some time yet."

Greenwood shrugged.

"I had hoped, after we finally managed to apprentice him out, that we would never hear of Esau again. Lord Ripon, the chairman of our Board of Guardians at the time, did warn us that we were unlikely not to, and it seems now he was right.

"How did he come to be with us, you ask? The answer is quite simply that he was born here, in our own lying-in room. His mother came, late one night, seeking relief. She was desperate, heavy with child, already begun in labour as I recollect – which I do, very distinctly. We sent her directly to the infirmary and by morning she had given birth. The infant was as hairy as an ape and so the nurses named him Esau. He was not expected to live for long."

"What happened to the mother?" Lucie asked.

Greenwood glanced up and regarded her steadily for several seconds.

"She drowned herself, Mrs Fox; it's as plain as that. When the midwife laid the child onto her breast, she screamed fit to wake the dead, and, God forgive me, but I cannot say I blamed her. They had to take it from her in the end. She was called Maryam, or Mary, or something like that; it was difficult to tell exactly on account of her foreign accent, and she kept herself wrapped up in a sort of veil like the Arabian or Indian women do. As soon as she was able to stand, she went and threw herself into the River Ure. Her body was recovered from the water a little way downstream and… and burned. She was hairy too, you see, and the farmers who found her – well they were simple folk and they weren't for taking any chances. They believed she was a devil."

His sudden laughter peeled around the tiny cell.

"On Lord Ripon's instructions – this was before he went to become the Viceroy of India, you understand – we kept the boy segregated from the inmates and he grew up perfectly well here in the vagrants' block. He always seemed very wise for his years, I remember. Mrs G. used to remark that he saw all, heard all, but said nothing. Mr Firth kept him in cell number one, so he could keep a close eye on him. When Esau was around twelve years of age, one of the casuals thought of setting himself up as a hawker of small ware and he took him away with him, as an apprentice."

"Would that have been a man by the name of Thomas Wilberforce?" Atticus asked.

"The hawker, you mean?" Greenwood shook his head. "No, it was a scoundrel by the name of Furze. It transpired later that he was a common housebreaker, who used his hawking as a way to peddle the goods he had thieved. He believed that Esau, being a monkey, would be useful in helping him gain entry to houses. Furze was sent to gaol a couple of years later but no one knew what had become of Esau. Why do you ask about him now?"

"Because," Lucie explained, "the Harrogate police suspect he may have some connection with the murders."

"Esau? No, I can't imagine for a second he could be a murderer. He was always too quiet and god-fearing for that."

Greenwood sniffed, and gave them a sly glance.

"Unless Harrogate has corrupted him, of course."

Despite any personal reservations Mr Greenwood might, after all, have held about Samson Fox and the decadence of Harrogate, the Foxes could not dispute that he had been most generous with his time. He had taken them into the tramp-major's cell and allowed them to examine it at length for any vestiges of evidence the Ripon police might have overlooked. Finger-print evidence is seldom of any great use in a vagrants' ward and with such an abundance of labour as is available to the master of a workhouse, what other traces there might once have been had long since been scrubbed and sluiced away.

Greenwood had been obliging too with his own copy of William Firth's necropsy report. Its grey smudges of carbon and faint lines of script were not easy to read, so he had acceded readily to Lucie's request that they take the report away with them to study on their short journey back to Harrogate.

In the event, the beating of the carriage wheels and the scream of the locomotive were perfect accompaniments to Lucie's reading of the monstrous findings of the Ripon coroner.

It seemed that Mr Firth, long time tramp-major of the Ripon union workhouse, had been strangled. The marks on what remained of his throat and the pattern of blood under the skin indicated the use of a very particular type of double-loop garrotte. The French *Légion Étrangère*, as Atticus had interrupted her to remark, referred to it as *la loupe,* whereby a double coil of rope is dropped around the victim's neck and drawn tight. Even if the unfortunate Mr Firth should have managed to get a hand onto one of the coils in a desperate attempt to save himself, he would have succeeded only in tightening the other.

The coroner was also of the opinion that Mr Firth had still been alive when he was taken from his quarters into the refractory cell, strapped into the chair and gagged. He remained undecided, however, as to whether the stones brought in from the work yard were then used to beat him, or to pelt him with, although, he conceded, that distinction ultimately mattered very little.

Before he had been restrained, Mr Firth had also suffered the indignity, and almost certainly the excruciating pain, of having a jagged, broken rock inserted into the fundament of his body. The coroner could only speculate as to the motive for this. Most probably, as he had suggested in his notes, the assailant had intended to sink the corpse into a body of water. But whatever the reason, it would have been merciful indeed when Mr Firth's attacker had finally pulled on *la loupe* and trepanned off his head.

It was as the fields dropped abruptly into the Nidd gorge once more that Atticus Fox reached up and pulled firmly on their carriage's communication cord.

Lucie jumped to her feet too.

"What is it, Atticus? What's wrong?" she demanded. But then her seat scooped her legs from under her as the train's brakes bit hard and the steel tyres squealed.

Atticus, wide eyed, stood hanging from the cord. The wheels were silent now, and the train stopped.

"It isn't medicine," he said.

Doors began slamming up and down the train, and there were little rushes of gravel as passengers jumped down to the trackside. Indignant shouts punctuated a crescendo of murmur.

"Who was it?"

"Who pulled the cord?"

"Someone in first class, I hear."

Their own door burst open and there was the guard, staring up into the compartment at Atticus, whose bunched fist was still gripping the communication cord.

"Sir, what's wrong? Are you in danger?"

Atticus' eyes focussed down onto the guard and he nodded. "I fear we are all in danger," he said.

"From what; what is it, sir?" The guard glanced in alarm to Lucie and then back to Atticus.

"Witchcraft," said Atticus Fox.

CHAPTER THIRTY-FIVE

"I'm so very sorry for it," said Atticus Fox for perhaps the dozenth time as he and Lucie made their way through the northern outskirts of Harrogate. "You must have been horrified. But at least you had the presence of mind to tell him we were on police business."

Lucie giggled. "Yes, I suppose I did. It saved you from a forty shilling fine, most likely, and from having the station master tear a strip off you."

"That's very true," Atticus agreed ruefully.

"Not to mention the other passengers. That old gentleman in green seemed almost ready to murder you."

"He said I'd caused him to spill his whisky, and ruin his best trousers. Well, he shouted it, actually. But I'm sorry we had to get off at Bilton Junction, and now we've to walk home with all these filthy steam waggons thundering past us every few minutes."

They stepped down into the road to avoid a group of boys clustered around what appeared to be a phrenologist's shop window and followed a line of broken cobbles, where the great iron wheels of the steam waggons had crushed the surface of the road to rubble.

"And Samson will be furious with me."

"Possibly so, but only if he hears about it."

Lucie giggled again.

"Oh, Atticus, the look on that guard's face when you cried 'witchcraft!' I declare, it was a picture."

"It was the River Nidd that made me think of it," Atticus explained. "You see, there's a plunge-pool up at Knaresborough, where people suspected of being witches were once thrown. If, as was usually the case, they drowned, they were pronounced innocent. But if they survived, then it was assumed that they must have been guilty because to have done so, they must have been in league with the Devil."

The boys behind them began to laugh raucously at some joke or other and Atticus glanced round.

"So what has that to do with our case?" Lucie asked him.

"It has this, Lucie: Consider that in those days, there was very little difference between witchcraft and healing. Potions were used as folk-medicines, and herbs and wild plants were used in both. The book you fetched from the library: *Magical and Medicinal Herbs of England*, our Beast looked at too. We have assumed it was for the medicinal, but it might just as well have been for the magical."

He stopped short.

"And, Lucie, the symbol we saw on the gatepost up by the tower, do you remember it?"

Lucie nodded. "At Sun Villa, do you mean? The Rod of Asclepius?"

"No, that's just it, it wasn't the Rod of Asclepius at all; it was a Caduceus."

They began to walk forward once again and Atticus explained: "The Rod of Asclepius is a staff with a single serpent entwined around it, named for the Greek God of Healing and Medicine. That is why it is so often used as a symbol by the medical profession. The Caduceus is different, entirely different, although I admit the two are often confused. It is winged, with two snakes, not one, twined about its shaft. It was carried by the god Hermes, the mediator between the gods and man, the God of Wisdom and Magic, who was to the Greeks what Mercury was to the Romans, and Thoth to the Egyptians."

He glanced about himself and lowered his voice to a whisper.

"Hermes was central to the study of alchemical transformations, Lucie. And mercury is used in alchemy."

Atticus could feel Lucie's eyes searching his face as they walked. She said: "So this cloak and hood the victims describe the Beast as wearing; you think they might be the robes of an alchemist?"

"I think they might be the robes of a *Hermetic*, Lucie. The Caduceus is the symbol of Hermes. It is also, therefore, a symbol of the Hermetic Societies which seem to be springing up everywhere. Hermeticists are disciples of an ancient figure called *Hermes Trismegistus,* or Hermes the Thrice-Great. They believe him to be the embodied manifestation of Hermes-Mercury-Thoth. His writings, the *Corpus Hermeticum,* or the *Hermetica,* are considered to be of immense antiquity and concern principally the three great wisdoms of astrology, alchemy and theurgy. That is why he is revered as Thrice-Great."

"What is theurgy, Atticus?" Lucie asked.

Atticus turned to look down at her and drew a long and very deep breath.

"Theurgy, Lucie, concerns the summoning-up and control of supernatural forces. It is what you or I might call magic."

CHAPTER THIRTY-SIX

That evening, the daytime seemed to drop steeply into night. At Lucie's insistence, they had taken up their position on the observation platform of Harlow Tower well before nightfall, and securely closed, and bolted, the entrance hatch. But neither the locks of the tower's doors, nor the constables far below, nor even Atticus' walking cane, its hidden blade naked and drawn, could take away the hanging menace of the word 'witchcraft'.

The moon was waxing crescent and beyond the reach of their dimmed lantern the land was cloaked in a darkness that not even the power of the telescopes could penetrate. Within the body of the tower, the great pendulum of Foucault was oscillating to-and-fro, as if the world itself was turning about their high, stone eerie.

"We are wasting our time here," Atticus said suddenly, peering in vain into the eyepiece of his telescope.

Lucie did not reply immediately, but when she did, her tone was emphatic.

"We must wait for the police, Atticus; I'm sorry but we really must. If you are right in what you say, then there is no telling what forces we might be up against."

"Fox?"

Atticus started, and his telescope jerked from his grip. The voice was clear, as if some phantom had spoken from the air beside him.

"Fox, are you up there? Answer me, won't you."

Lucie was leaning out, peering down the tower's side.

"He'll be down directly to let you in," she called.

"Smartly, if he would." It was Douglas' voice and it sounded anxious, fearful even.

"Yes, of course." Atticus twisted up the lantern flame, snatched up his swordstick and began furiously to wind the little hydraulic motor that drew open the hatch.

Soon, there was a gap wide enough for him to climb through onto the iron ladder below. He clattered down it, wordlessly counting the rungs as he went – eight, like the eight ranks of a chessboard – then down the stairway proper. He seemed to be nothing more than shadows and lantern-light, leaping from wall to wall, spiralling ever lower towards the latch on the door below as it rattled and shook.

Ninety-two steps – eleven eights and four left hanging – and he reached the door and twisted the key. The door burst open, a turnstile cranked and there was Douglas, catching his breath, a big black revolver glinting in his hand. Beside him, Atticus' lantern beam caught also on a pendulum bob as it oscillated and precessed.

"What on the Lord's earth is that?" Douglas lifted his own lantern high and its light illuminated the great brass weight and a cord that disappeared up into the black void above them.

"It's an example of Foucault's pendulum," Atticus replied, "Ninety feet long. It demonstrates and measures the rotation of the earth; one degree of rotation approximately every five minutes at Harrogate's latitude."

"Right," said Douglas. "I thought for a minute it might be some contraption you'd rigged up to help us catch this beast. Or at least ward it off."

He held up his handgun, his eyes fierce and grim.

"I've read your note, Fox, though I can scarcely believe it. It seems we're investigating the preternatural now. Perhaps I should have loaded this with silver bullets, eh?"

"Not at all, Douglas; the use of silver bullets has no basis in science. It arose from the association of silver with the Moon in folklore," Atticus frowned, "and in alchemy."

Inspector Douglas stared out over the lead-sheathed parapet of the observation platform in the direction of Atticus' raised cane. He had been breathing heavily when he first clambered out from the hatchway, most probably from the length and steepness of the climb, but he seemed now to have regained at least some of his composure.

"So you really do believe this fellow to be some kind of wizard then, Fox?"

"I believe he may be an adept, Inspector, which is something altogether more than a wizard. It means that he will be a practitioner, not only of the magical arts, but of alchemy and astrology too."

"And by alchemy, you mean the turning of ordinary metals into gold?"

Atticus Fox turned and settled his back against the stone and considered how best he might explain this, the very deepest of philosophies, to Douglas.

"Part of alchemy does seek *chrysopoeia,* or the transformation of base metals – the lead beneath our feet, for example – into gold. But it is more than that, Douglas; it is vastly more. Hermes is well known as being the messenger of the gods. He may, therefore, be considered as being the conjunction between the Earthly and the Divine, the *microcosm* and the *macrocosm*, that which is Below and that which is Above. In short, the true meaning of alchemy is to do with Enlightenment – the transformation of the base human body into spirit."

"Clear as mud! But doesn't all of this belong with the Dark Ages? Surely no one believes in all of that bunkum these days?"

"You might be surprised," Atticus returned. "Alchemy may have had its origins in ancient Egypt, but we may easily trace its thread through Greece, Arabia and India, through our own Age of Enlightenment and into the modern age. Some of our most celebrated scientists – Newton, Boyle and Bacon, for example – were, in reality, also alchemists. We find their like today in the esoteric revivalists and the Hermetic societies we mentioned in our note to you."

"Where you said there might be a link between the attacks and this society of… of adepts," said Douglas.

"Of Hermeticists," Atticus corrected him. "Our murderer may not yet have reached the level of adept. But yes, I believe there may well be a connection. Consider that all of the items stolen relate in some way or another to Hermetic beliefs. Heartsease, mistletoe and the wood of *Lignum vitae* are all used in theurgic magic. *Abrus* peas are used not only in magic but also in Ayurveda medicine, which is itself associated with Indian alchemy. And mercury is well known as being the most important element of all those used in alchemical transformations."

"This is all too peculiar by half." Douglas stared into the darkness swarming around them, slowly shaking his head in incredulity. "What about Headless Harry and the attack on the nun?"

"And the tramp-major at Ripon," Lucie added, "Atticus believes that to be connected too."

"Yes, I do," said Atticus. "You see, Douglas, human heads were used in Hermetic ceremonies both in Egypt and in India in ancient times. It is possible, even likely I would say, that they might be used in the same way today."

"Ye gods! Do you realise what you're saying? And why is this all happening now? I've served as a policeman for over twenty years and seen all manner of things, but I declare, Mr and Mrs Fox, I've known nothing like this."

"It is the current revival of interest in the mystical," Atticus explained, "Spiritualism, Gnosticism, Hermeticism and their like. And now is the time of the autumn equinox. To Hermetic theurgists, that is the time when the darkness catches up with the Sun and causes it to wither and fail. This year, it fell on September the twenty-second."

"That was the night the nun was outraged."

Atticus nodded. "That is correct. And by tradition, it is the time when the re-birth of the Sun is invoked. One way that is done is with certain rites of fertility – of sex." Atticus felt his face suddenly flushing and, for a moment, he was glad of the darkness. "The Catholic sister was a virgin and that must be significant in this. And be aware also that the Hermetic Societies are closely associated with the Rosicrucians and with the very highest degrees of Freemasonry, both of whom despise the Catholic Church."

"I know the Masons do; half the folk at Raglan Street are Freemasons, but who are these Rosicrucian fellows you mention?"

"The Rosicrucian fellowship is the inner order of Hermeticism, Douglas. Its disciples are *Gnostics,* seekers of *Gnosis,* a secret wisdom said to have been handed down from ancient times. They believe that our souls are sparks of the Divine, which have become imprisoned within this base physical world. The progressive attainment of Enlightenment allows a Gnostic's soul to ascend, and eventually to return, to the higher, spiritual world and the transcendent god who is the ultimate source of life."

"I'm sorry I asked," Douglas rejoined.

"And another thing which strikes me as being particularly suggestive," Atticus went on, "is this: The re-birth of the Sun was also invoked using particular rites of healing. In Egyptian times, these involved the ritual bathing of the priests in blood. Recall that a bucket of blood was taken from the Incurables Hospital on the night of the fourteenth of September."

"So if all of this happens around the equinox, Fox, and if we can say we're safely past that now, can we believe there'll be no more murders?" There was something almost pleading in Douglas' tone. "After all, there was nothing last night – so far as we know."

Atticus shrugged. "That, I cannot say."

Douglas took a breath. "Very well. Has anyone left this villa tonight?"

"That we don't know either, Mr Douglas," said Lucie. "It is much too dark to see anything, even with the telescopes. And in any event, the house backs directly onto the pine-tree plantations. It would be very easy for anyone to slip out; they could get as far as the Pump Room without being seen by a soul."

Douglas set his jaw. He had quite plainly come to a decision.

"Well, it's dark," he said, "but it isn't yet late. What would you say to our paying these Hermeticists a visit – in an official capacity?"

Whilst the professors and fellows of the phrenological societies were working tirelessly to push back the boundaries of their own field of knowledge, a certain Dr William Carpenter was turning his attention to the deepest mysteries of all: to those held within the subconscious mind. Dr Carpenter had considered the theories of Wallace and Darwin and sought to apply them in the curious matter of unconscious perception. He for one would not have been surprised that a detective inspector of the West Riding Constabulary, who would have laughed long and mockingly at the very idea of witchcraft in the gas-lit safety of a busy police station, might perhaps find that very same notion entirely plausible, terrifying even, in the dense stillness of the night.

"Eerie place this, Fox."

Detective Inspector Douglas was crouching by the gatepost of the forbidding Sun Villa, his one hand resting on its great pyramidal pier-head, his other lifting his lantern up to the smooth, mottled surface of the Caduceus fixed below.

"And it's a queer wood this thing is made from too."

"It's olive wood," Atticus muttered in reply. "By tradition, Hermes' staff is always fashioned from an olive tree."

"Well, Hermes himself ain't above the law, any more than you or I or anybody else. If he's at home, and if I can see he's had anything to do with these attacks, then he'll be arrested just the same. Keep your swordstick handy, Fox and we'll go in smartly – before he has a chance to rumble us. The drive is gravelled so mind you both keep to the lawn."

At his signal, the three of them advanced towards the house, creeping beneath the great alder trees, whose branches seemed to be curling over them like eager, spreading fingers. In an upstairs casement a gasolier burst into life. Its brilliant light swelled and washed out over the lawn, engulfing them like so many mice caught by a rat-catcher's lantern. The long, dark silhouette of a man was standing motionless in the window, watching them.

"So much for us not being rumbled," said Lucie.

"Damn him!" Douglas growled. "But he can stare all he pleases; we're here under the Queen's warrant."

He stood tall and led them in dignified procession across the remainder of the lawn, to where the stone roof of a porch gathered them into its welcome shadow.

"And at least he can't pretend he's not at home."

Douglas reached up to the knocking iron of the door.

"What the deuce?"

He jumped back, as if the big metal ring was somehow electrified.

"I thought… I thought there was a snake hanging there for a moment."

Neither Atticus nor Lucie laughed. In the moving light of their lanterns, the iron, cast in the form of a serpent devouring its own tail, seemed alive.

"It is of interest to us though, Douglas," said Atticus softly. "That is a very ancient symbol of eternity and renewal, also considered to represent the alchemical action of mercury. It is called an *ouroboros*."

At his words, as if they might have been an *iftaḥ yā simsim*, the broad swinging shadows on the door began to move. They slid and spilled off and the door opened wide to reveal the figure of the man from the window. He was a tall man and clean-shaven, with the close-cropped hair of a convict or workhouse inmate. Like his silhouette, he was dressed entirely in black, and like it too, he stood and regarded them coldly and without expression.

"I am very sorry to disturb you at this late hour, sir." Douglas' voice sounded slightly false, like the insincerity of his words. "I am Detective Inspector Douglas of the Harrogate police and these are my associates, Mr and Mrs Fox."

As Douglas spoke, the man's eyes shifted to Atticus, lingered for a moment on Lucie and then dropped back to Douglas.

"May we come inside, where we might talk more freely?" Douglas' hand crept into the pocket of his jacket, where they knew he had his revolver.

"Of course." The man's tone was disdainful, haughty even, and as devoid of humanity as his expression. "Leave your lanterns here in the porch and come this way, although I ask that you scrape your boots before you do so. I observed you walking across my lawn and there are worm-casts at this time of the season."

He turned away and beckoned them to follow.

"May I ask what your name is, sir?" Douglas spoke as if by rote. His attention, like that of the Foxes, was taken up by the curved, decorated plasterwork of the hallway ceiling, where the heads of animals: birds, baboons and crocodiles, were carved so vividly in sunken-relief that they had to resist the urge to duck as they passed beneath.

The man stopped in the shadow of a huge figure, which was standing with its back pressed against the wall like some great brooding sentinel.

"You may address me as Gaspar."

Douglas stared up at the figure and murmured: "Very well; thank you, Mr Gaspar."

Atticus was staring up too but with an expression very different to Douglas'.

"Is that a mummy case, Mr Gaspar? Is it genuine?"

Gaspar reached across to turn up a gas mantle. The jets hissed, and the shadows around the form shifted and petrified into roughly human shape and into colours so intense that they seemed to leach out into the very air around it.

"Yes, it is both, Atticus Fox, the son, I believe, of Joseph Fox. This is the mummy case of a high priest, who almost three millennia ago was honoured to serve the wise and mighty Thoth."

"Three thousand years ago," Atticus breathed. He appeared unsurprised that Gaspar knew the name of his dead father. "Yet it looks as if it were painted only yesterday."

Gaspar's lips tightened into the thinnest of smiles. He stepped forward to push open a door at the end of the passageway and then waited, head bowed, as they filed past him into what appeared at first glance to be a large drawing room.

It was a very comfortable room, rich to the point of sumptuousness, with papered walls, a rich carpet and several large, buttoned-leather sofas. A pair of French doors cast their pallid, staring reflections across an obsidian lawn and a domed shadow beyond, surrounded by swaying black pine trees. But they noticed none of these. Rather, their attention was drawn to the chimney breast, and in particular, to a mirror hung above its magnificent marble fireplace.

It was a most curious mirror for any gentleman's drawing room: Firstly, because it was fashioned, without frame, in the form of a triangle with its apex uppermost.

And secondly, and most disturbingly, because within this triangle was reproduced the stylised image of a single human eye. As they stared into the depths of its pupil, so their own images, startled and hagridden, gaped back out."

Gaspar must have been watching for their reactions. He said: "It seems strange that detectives and… investigators, who have dedicated their lives to the seeking out of knowledge and understanding, should be so fearful of that which is all-seeing and through which we might receive the light of wisdom."

"It is the Eye of Horus," said Atticus.

Gaspar's eyebrows rose sharply and pushed his forehead into several deep folds against the shorn stubble of his hairline.

"You are not only correct but you have also rather surprised me, Mr Fox. Most people, even common Freemasons such as your father was, would have called it the 'Eye of Providence', by which they mean the omnipresent eye of God – of their Christian god. Tell me then: What do you see in the triangle which surrounds it?"

Atticus stepped forward and stood squarely before the mirror.

"The silver of the mirror is the Moon," he began. "As for the three sides of the triangle, they are generally said to represent the three faces of God – the Holy Trinity. I rather suspect that isn't the case here, however. From the Caduceus at your gate and the ouroboros on your door, I fancy it is an expression of the three Greatnesses of Hermes."

Gaspar's eyes narrowed.

"Correct again, on both counts. So now I must ask you directly, Mr Fox: Are you one who flies as the eagle?"

Atticus considered the question. What precisely could Gaspar mean? How exactly could one fly as an eagle? An image, bright as a magic lantern slide, came into his mind. It was the shining lectern at St Peter's church and Canon Foote, standing by it, informing them how the eagle was figurative of the heights to which St John the Apostle was said to have risen in his gospel. Possibly so, but both St John and his namesake, St John the Baptist, were important in Freemasonry too. And, as Atticus had reminded him at the time, the eagle had other, rather more occult, associations. The question was: what would an eagle be to a Hermetic adept?

"The eagle may fly close to the sun," he reasoned aloud, "And famously look directly into its rays. You are asking if I seek the light."

"And do you?" Gaspar pressed, "Do you seek Enlightenment?"

"The answer is no, Gaspar. Neither Mrs Fox nor I have any great belief in the preternatural, be that Christian or Hermetic."

Gaspar jerked his head in contempt and bared two lines of very white, very even teeth.

"Then you condemn yourselves to the darkness of the base, material world. That is regrettable. You could see so much more. The path to Enlightenment is open to all those who might choose to unclose their mind."

"In that case, Gaspar, perhaps you might be good enough to enlighten us on a few things," Douglas interjected.

"If you so wish, Inspector." Gaspar's expression twisted into a scornful lour. "Please, won't you all take a seat?"

They sat together, perched in a line on the edge of a settee. Gaspar, in his turn, pulled out a wall chair and settled it in front of them. He rested his chin on his steepled fingers and said: "Well then, *Detective Inspector* Douglas of the Harrogate police?"

Douglas glared up into the sapphire blue of Gaspar's gaze. He would stare this impudent freak down — or he would, if it wasn't for that damnably disconcerting mirror at his back.

"Right, well first off, are you a hermit?"

"Hermetic," Atticus corrected him.

"Hermetic, then."

Gaspar's face relaxed into a thin and enigmatic smile.

"Am I a disciple of the Hermetic Way, you ask? That answer must depend very much upon what you consider to be a Hermeticist, and at what point the disciple becomes the adept. Does the adept remain always a disciple?" He spread his hands wide. "I have long walked upon the Qabalah to Enlightenment, if that answers your question."

Douglas snorted.

"Scarcely, sir! Let me ask it a different way then. Mr Fox here tells me that alchemy is a big part of this

Hermeticism. Will you admit that you are attempting to make gold from ordinary metal? In short, Gaspar, are you an alchemist?"

Gaspar regarded Douglas for a time. "I believe I have already answered that question, Inspector."

"Well then please oblige me by answering it again."

Atticus raised his hand. "What Gaspar means, Douglas, is that by following what he refers to as the Qabalah, or the Hermetic path to Enlightenment, he is seeking, through alchemy, to purify not base metals into gold but his own base self into something more pure and spiritual."

"Mr Fox has explained it sufficiently well," said Gaspar. "The gold the true Hermeticist seeks is not the vulgar gold of man."

"So, if you admit to being an alchemist," Douglas pressed, "then you must admit also to making extensive use of mercury?"

Gaspar nodded. "That is self-evidently true, Inspector. Mercury, of course, is Hermes, who is Thoth, the medium of the conjunction."

"I see," said Douglas. He glanced uncertainly towards Atticus, who nodded his confirmation.

"So, what were you doing on the nights of Sunday last and last Wednesday week? I will have a straightforward reply from you this time, if you please, Gaspar."

"I take it that you suspect me of the intrusion into the hospital for incurables? Then so too must you of the murder of the whore, and of the violation at the convent of Babylon."

"I am the one asking the questions tonight, thank you all the same."

Gaspar appeared suddenly amused. He said: "Very well; Wednesday, in the Latin, is *dies Mercurii*, the day of Mercury, and Sunday – *dies Sōlis* – is the day of the Sun. Both days are sacred to me and to my fraternity and we generally spend them in worship in my temple."

"This temple being?"

"My own, built in the grounds of this house so that the Sun god Ra's rising might be observed and He properly venerated."

"Then I must insist on looking at it. Show us, Gaspar, directly, if you please."

"No, I most assuredly do not please. You think that because you are a policeman – one of no great consequence, I add – you may intrude into the sacred places of the Qabalah as if they were some kind of pleasure garden?"

Gaspar reached back his arm and extended a trembling forefinger towards the strange mirror.

"Make no mistake about it, Inspector Douglas; there are officers far senior to you in the West Riding Constabulary who tread the pathways of the Qabalah. By your actions today, you may find them to be powerful allies or else deadly enemies. Beware!"

"I do my duty, Gaspar, without fear or favour, as I have these twenty years."

"Hah!" Gaspar bared his teeth contemptuously.

Lucie said: "Mr Gaspar, I was given to understand that you worshipped Hermes. Why are you now talking about Ra?"

"Because the two are inextricably linked, Mrs Fox, Hermes, also called Thoth, also called Mercury, is Hermes Trismegistus, the wise, the messenger and the voice of Ra. He is the means to God himself, just as your own John the Baptist was the means and the way to your Christian god."

"How intriguing," Lucie exclaimed. "Mr Fox and I would regard it as a singular honour to be allowed to see your temple to them."

Gaspar regarded her from the superior height of his wall-chair, rather as an eagle might look down on a new-born lamb.

"Very well, Mrs Fox, then I will be singularly honoured to show you. Women are allowed into the Hermetic orders just as freely as men, and should you wish to become better acquainted with our rites, you may well find the, ah, physical aspects of them, to be very intriguing indeed."

The Hermetic Temple of the Golden Light in Harrogate was a small but quite magnificent building, built, as Gaspar had told them, in the extensive rear gardens of the villa. It was constructed in the classical style, strikingly similar to the Royal Pump Room itself, with ornate pilaster columns and a high, domed roof. This dome was of copper and by day most likely of the same mellow verdigris as its counterpart down in the valley. But now, by night, it was black and full of menace, like the body of some great spider that had come down from the pine forests to feed.

Gaspar led them with a staff and the light of an oil lamp across a broad, paved terrace and then along a pathway to the furthermost, what must be the eastern side of the temple. Here, framed by two pilasters, was a pair of heavy, carven doors, each bearing a handle in the form of a double-headed eagle. Set in the wall above them was an oculus, just visible as a circle of soft light.

"Welcome," said Gaspar.

There is a part of the human condition that is roused to passion by sacred places. It is an ancient part, one which evolved before any notion of agnosticism or denial, and a part over which we have no conscious control.

So it was with awe that Atticus, Lucie and even Inspector Douglas regarded the interior of the Temple of the Golden Light. It was every bit as numinous as the exterior and their imaginings promised it might be. Here, inevitably, the square and the circle – the Earthly and Divine – were reconciled. The floor beneath the dome lay foursquare, and from the farthest side, the light from the candles of two large lamp-stands reflected around an interior of pure white and gold. Between these lamp-stands, and draped over what they took to be an altar table, was a large emerald-green cloth, silken and shimmering in the light of the twenty-two candles. Where this hung down in the manner of an antependium were embroidered four symbols: a representation of a red rose, a compass over a mason's square, a caduceus and one other. Three golden figurines stood on the altar-top next to a small heap of coins and on the wall above all of these was a large, green-painted reredos bearing the image of a triangle surmounted by a colourful and intricate cross.

"Thank the lord there's a cross in here, at least," Douglas muttered under his breath.

"Just look at it though!" Lucie whispered, and she was right. The body of the cross was inscribed with all manner of strange and outlandish symbols with the arms, left, right and above, picked out respectively in colours of red, blue and yellow.

Atticus stepped forward, his heavy boots tapping noisily across the white marble slabs of the floor, and bent forward to examine the figurines.

"Exquisite, are they not?" said Gaspar and Atticus nodded. They were beautifully cast, not in brass or ormolu or even silver-gilt, but in what appeared to be pure gold.

The first was clearly Egyptian in style. It had the body of a man but the head of a bird, whose beak curved down like the crescent moon, which at that moment hung above them in the sky outside.

"Thoth," said Atticus glancing round and Gaspar nodded.

The second was also of a man, an athletic young man, completely naked, other than for the short, winged staff he carried in one of his hands.

"Hermes, of course," said Atticus and Gaspar nodded once again.

"And the third?" Gaspar asked. He padded forward noiselessly in his sandals to stand at Atticus' side.

The third statuette was somewhat similar to the first and again clearly Egyptian in form and stance. But instead of a bird's – an ibis' – head, however, this one possessed the unmistakable head of an ape.

Atticus stared at it as he recalled the things he had read of Egyptian mythology.

"It is Astennu, the dog-headed ape – the Ape of Thoth!"

Gaspar inclined his head and regarded Atticus curiously, as a myna bird once had before it was plucked from its perch.

"It is indeed the Ape of Thoth; my Lord Astennu, who is the further, and indeed the present, manifestation of Hermes Trismegistus, knower and scrivener of the three great wisdoms of astrology, alchemy and theurgy."

"All of which appear to have been involved in a recent series of crimes in the town," Douglas interjected. He nodded towards a large apothecary's rack standing against the side wall of the square, filled with row upon row of all kinds of jars and bottles. Below it was a broad marble shelf on which rested two large and horned headdresses such as might be worn at the most daring *Ridotto* ball.

"And I should very much like to know what you keep in those bottles, too."

"And what do you suppose might be kept in them?" Gaspar twisted his head towards Douglas and his conspicuous Adam's apple bulged.

"At the very least I should say mercury, human blood, heartsease and mistletoe, not to mention… what was the other thing that was taken, Fox?"

"*Abrus precatorius*, Inspector, the rosary pea. It may already have been made into a preparation by now, of course."

Gaspar scowled.

"Rosary pea? *Rosary* pea! What use would I have for *rosaries?* The Catholic Church has persecuted my brothers for almost seven hundred years. I despise everything there is to do with it." He jabbed the tip of his big staff towards Douglas. "Whatever else there might be in those vessels, you may rest assured there is nothing that bears the foul stench of Catholicism."

"That's for us to determine for ourselves, thank you very much, and until we have, I am taking you down to Raglan Street. It's a chilly night and we don't have a waggon with us, so you may fetch a hat and coat, if you wish."

Douglas turned to the Foxes. "I'll ask you both to sort through the contents of those racks. See what there is and report back directly on anything of interest you might find."

"Of course," said Atticus.

"Will you be safe here, until I can send an officer to wait with you?"

"Perfectly safe, thank you."

"Are you quite certain of that?" Gaspar lifted his staff high, like a prophet of old, and brandished it towards the doorway: "Do you see there?"

As one they looked.

Above the doors, the oculus they had noticed earlier cut a dark circle in the white marble face of the wall. And, as they stared, the faint moonlight outside began to colour it with shapes and colours into a now-familiar symbol.

"It's the Eye of Horus again," gasped Lucie.

"Exactly so, Mrs Fox. The great Eye of Horus, which watches you always. I give you all this warning: Take

great care in this secret and holy place, lest perhaps it
should… swallow you up.”

CHAPTER THIRTY-SEVEN

As the doors to the temple swept shut, they pushed a breath of wind through the place that sent the twenty-two candles of the lamp-stands spluttering and dancing.

Atticus Fox turned again to the altar and under the watchful Eye of Horus, stooped once more before it. He reached out to the green silk overhang, running his fingertips over the rich embroidery of the symbols it carried and murmuring, as if as incantation:

> *"For what we do presage is not in grosse,*
> *For we are brethren of the Rosie Crosse;*
> *We have the Mason Word and second sight,*
> *Things for to come we foretell aright."*

The last of the four symbols seemed oddly to repulse him. Certainly he appeared reluctant to touch it as he had its fellows and instead leaned close, to examine it by sight only. There, worked in rich silver threads, was a creature, an abhorrent and palpably ancient creature, sitting cross-legged like an ape. Paradoxically, it had the genitals of a man yet a woman's breasts, its right arm held upward but its left down, and across its chest a cross. The most disturbing parts to it however, even to Atticus Fox, were its head, which was like a goat's or a satyr's, and the great spreading wings at its back. Its identity he already knew; he had no need of the words – *SECRETUM TEMPLI* – woven around the symbol's edge, although they chilled him to his bones.

He rose to his feet.

"We must make haste, Lucie; I fear we will be allowed very little time here."

Lucie glanced to him, her eyes reflecting the lights of the lamp-stands like two great constellations.

"Atty, tell me: what does that mean? Over there, do you see it?"

She was pointing to the fourth wall of the temple, the one directly opposite the apothecary's rack. Here, rendered onto the marble in the very same reds and blues and yellows as the altar cross, was a large and complex fresco. It was in the form of a diagram: eleven annulets set in three columns, each one connected to its fellows by a web of criss-crossing lines."

Atticus muttered something unintelligible, and strode forward to stand before it. Lucie, in that moment, was grateful for the heavy clatter of his boots breaking the crushing silence of the place, and it was with this thought that she noticed the curious pattern of the floor at their feet. Like the temple walls, this too was faced in slabs of white marble, but unlike them it was divided geometrically into squares and rectangles. They appeared to halve progressively in size across the diagonal.

To Atticus' left were the two smallest squares, and the farthest of these, the square in the very corner, was inscribed with a six-pointed hexagram inlaid with glistening gold. Intrigued now, Lucie turned to look behind her. The slab the apothecary's rack was standing on, by contrast, was vast. It took up fully half the floor. With a start, Lucie recalled Gaspar's warning; that this place might somehow swallow them up. Might one of these squares have a hidden mechanism, she wondered, a trap designed to pitch the unwary and the unwelcome down to their doom?

"This is the Qabalah," Atticus announced and Lucie turned back to him, "Specifically the Hermetic Qabalah, which represents the path of what the Hermetic disciples call the *Divine Light,* or a follower's progression up through the degrees of Hermeticism to Enlightenment. I would imagine that Mr Gaspar may have reached a very high position on this path indeed."

"Why would you, Atticus?" Lucie asked.

"Because, by tradition, Gaspar was the name of one of the magi who visited the infant Jesus in the stable. In the ancient world, magi were regarded as exceedingly powerful and accomplished magicians."

"So Gaspar might be a title rather than his real name?"

Atticus nodded. "I believe so. And do you see those four symbols on the altar cloth? They are the Hermetic Caduceus; the rose of the inner Hermetic order known as the Rosicrucians; the Masonic square-and-compass, and an alchemical symbol known as the Baphomet. Together they mean that Gaspar will, without the slightest doubt, have the powerful friends he claims and that we, like Douglas, may just have made some equally powerful enemies."

"The Freemasons, you mean?"

"Yes, Lucie, the Freemasons, but not the ordinary brethren in the lodges, like my father or Samson Fox. These people are from the highest degrees of the innermost and most ancient of the orders. Did you notice the staff Gaspar had with him?"

Lucie nodded. "It was like a Caduceus with the Eye of Horus in the pommel."

"Exactly so, but did you also notice that it was the right eye and not the left? Whereas Horus' left eye, associated with the Moon and Thoth, is the seer of all things, his right eye is the Eye of Ra – the Sun. It is man's destroyer, which is why we must make haste to do what we must and be away from here."

Lucie glanced up to the oculus above the door, from where the ever-seeing Eye stared back unblinkingly.

"How long do we have?" she asked.

"Hermes, Hermes, swifter than the swallow," Atticus chanted and Lucie shuddered.

The white marble shelf below the apothecary's rack projected from the wall behind it without brackets, so that the headdresses it carried seemed to be floating in mid air. There were two of these, both set with horns, both made with white-metal headpieces and delicate, silver chinstraps, but each very different in style.

The first, the larger of the two, had the branched and spreading antlers of a stag, such as might have been used in folk magic for centuries by the Celts and others. The second was more exotic and much more elegant in form.

Rising side-by-side from the skullcap were two curved and slender horns, and between them a disc, struck in gold and polished to an almost mirror finish.

"This is used to represent Hathor," Atticus said, lifting up this latter and turning it over and over in his hands. "She was the Egyptian goddess of fertility, love and motherhood, usually depicted as a mother cow with the circle of the Sun between her horns."

"I don't like them, Atticus; I don't like either of them."

"Why ever not?" Atticus seemed genuinely surprised by his wife's reaction. "Just look how beautifully made they are. But of much greater importance is the fact they confirm our supposition of a connection with the autumn equinox. Both the deer and Hathor are intimately bound up with fertility and with the rebirth of the Sun.

"So now," he went on, carefully replacing the headdress onto its shelf and turning his attention to the lines of jars and bottles on the rack above, "we have work to do."

Lucie's spirits surged as she saw that each bottle and jar was neatly labelled with a gilt-metal square. That was until she realised that the labels were written out, not in English or even in Latin, but in impenetrable symbols and glyphs. Nor did it help that everything was arranged in such a higgledy–piggledy fashion. Here, large vessels were put with small ones, and there, bottles set beside jars of all shapes and sizes.

"This seems to make perfect sense," said Atticus brightly. "These are alchemical symbols and alchemy seems to be behind the order of things. Look here, Lucie; here we have the three Primes at the top: salt, sulphur and mercury. The Elements water and earth are beside them, with a striking-iron and tinder for fire. Here are the seven classical Planetary metals, together with the various Mundane Elements below."

"What about these?" Lucie asked, lifting a glass stopper from a bottle on the lowest shelf. She sniffed dubiously at the contents and grimaced.

Atticus bent to peer at the label. "I'm afraid I have no clue at all what those others might be – theurgic, most probably. We shall need to analyse them one-at-a-time and that, unfortunately, could take us a while."

In this, he was entirely correct; it proved exceedingly slow and laborious work and Atticus and Lucie had worked their way along no more than a quarter of the lowest shelf when a sudden cold breeze lifted the hairs on their necks. There was a gentle cough and then a familiar voice.

"Mr and Mrs Fox."

"Good evening to you, Hainsworth," Atticus called without looking round, "You might as well try to make yourself comfortable; we are going to be here for some time yet."

"Oh no," a second voice answered, "You are most definitely not."

It was Gaspar. He was standing, feet apart, his cane with its fearful eye planted firmly before him. "You will neither be here for any more time at all, and nor," he loured at Hainsworth, "will I allow my temple to be sullied any longer by a Catholic."

"We have been ordered to release Mr Gaspar and to leave his property immediately," Hainsworth spat, "And after that we are to have no further interest in him."

"Orders from on high I presume?" Atticus said picking up a blue glass jar.

Hainsworth nodded. "He has been vouched for by someone at the very top. Although," he turned to meet Gaspar's glare, "he needs to understand that we, at least, have the measure of him."

Atticus said: "Yes, but I fear we cannot match the measure of a square and compass."

Gaspar strode up to Atticus, the metronomic tapping of his staff on the floor growing sharper and louder as he drew near. He lifted the jar from Atticus' fingers and placed it neatly back onto the shelf.

"You will never now be permitted to bear the square and the compass. They are the tools of Hermes Trismegistus himself, the one who scribed out the Heavens and planned the Earth. And you, Catholic – you never could."

As the Foxes and Detective Sergeant Hainsworth made their exit along the driveway of Sun Villa, it was in the sullen silence of schoolboys sent down from a headmaster's study, a silence too indignant and too angry to allow them to look back. If they had, they might well have caught a glimpse of a second silhouette in the lighted window of the upstairs room, slightly less tall and a little broader than that of Gaspar, but watching them just as intently.

CHAPTER THIRTY-EIGHT

Quo Fata vocant. It was the phrase Atticus and Lucie had chosen as the motto for their fledgling business. They had borrowed it from the regiment of the Northumberland Fusiliers, since its meaning 'Whither the Fates call' seemed so very apt in their profession of privately-commissioned investigation, where so much seemed to lie so firmly in the unpredictable spinning of the Fates.

For Atticus, it seemed as if the Fates had been calling for most of his life, and for the greater part, with anguish and tribulation. It was only in his time here, at Harrogate, and with Lucie, that he had been allowed, if not peace, then perhaps a little respite, the prize-fighter's precious minute, from everyone bar the enemy within.

And yesterday, the Fates had called 'Baphomet'.

Atticus leaned into the slope of the Montpellier Hill and said the word aloud. Because, he reminded himself as he walked, Baphomet was just that: a word, and a name – a mystical name for Hermes in his role as the Great Alchemist, the ancient mediator of the conjunctions in whom all of the great opposing forces of nature come together in perfect equilibrium to purify and to enlighten.

When Alexander the Great had turned his armies to the south, towards Egypt, he discovered the entire pantheon of Hellenic gods already there. In the great Amun-Ra he had found Zeus; in Hathor, the beautiful Aphrodite. And in Thoth, revered God of Wisdom and Writing and Magic, the messenger and mediator between mankind and the gods – the Earthly and Divine, and all things opposing – he found Hermes.

When he looked east, towards the Levant and what would later become known as the Holy Land, he found Hermes there too. Revered for his wisdom, for his riches, and for the great temple he had built, there he was known as Solomon.

Baphomet, it was just a word, but the words that surrounded it, *Secretum Templi*, the secret temple, were not.

Centuries after Alexander's time, the crusading knights had come to the Holy Land and there built for themselves great churches and castles. As many were infected with leprosy, so too were they by the Egyptian and Hellenic wisdoms of astrology, alchemy and theurgy. It was there that Hermes Trismegistus, no longer Solomon but Baphomet, came to be worshipped as a god by the Poor Fellow Soldiers of Christ and of the Temple of Solomon. They were the Knights Templar.

In the year 1312, the Pope Clement learned of this idolatry and of one other. In righteous fury he had proclaimed the order disbanded and prosecuted its knights such that they were forced to flee beyond the reach of the Holy See, to excommunicated Scotland. And, as they fled, they took their secrets and their idols with them, to take fresh root, to spread and to grow strong once again, to become free-masons rebuilding the holy Temple of Solomon.

Hermetic, Rosicrucian, Masonic, Templar, secrets within secrets and orders within orders, and they, A&L Fox, like surgeons paring away the layers of foul and putrid flesh, must find the maggot at the core.

But this patient was awake. It was guarding of its wound, watchful and powerful beyond imagining, and it had snarled out a warning: 'No further interest!'

No further interest? Pah! He would see about that.

"You have a visitor I see, Mr Fox." Mr White, the donkey-ride man from the stand over the way, hailed him over the broad backs of his animals.

Shaken from his contemplations, Atticus glanced up. Across the road, Detective Sergeant Hainsworth was standing at his doorstep, apparently deep in conversation with Mrs Morris. The housekeeper had already spied him. She pointed and Hainsworth turned.

"Hullo, Mr Hainsworth," Atticus called through the traffic.

Hainsworth pinched the brim of his billycock hat. "Hullo to you, Mr Fox." He waited until a big four-wheeler had trotted past and then hurried across the road "I was on my way back to Raglan Street and I thought I'd call to tell you that I've been up to visit Father Cado this morning. He's the hermit up at the chantry, if you recall. There was no answer to my knock when we were searching on Harlow moor and it's been preying on my mind ever since, especially with Gaspar being in such an ill-humour against the church and all."

"And did you get an answer this time?"

"Yes I did, thank ye. But I can't say he looked right well, Mr Fox. He was lying there, in what he uses for a bed, not able to stand up and hardly managing to speak to me for fever. It's chilly up there, but even with him wrapped up to his eyes in a blanket, I could have broiled my breakfast on him. He refused point blank to let me have a doctor fetched."

"Would he see Mrs Fox?" Atticus asked, "She's a trained nurse, as you know."

Hainsworth shook his head emphatically.

"I can't think he'd want to see Saint Luke himself. I offered to have a waggonette take him down to the Cottage Hospital there and then but he refused that too." He shrugged. "You can lead a horse to water, as they say, Mr Fox, but at least I've given him a warning, and I can do no more than that, can I?"

"No, indeed you cannot," Atticus agreed.

"It was strange, because he already seemed to know all about Gaspar and the Hermeticists. When I pressed him to tell me more about it, he would only say that I should ask Lord Ripon."

"The Marquess of Ripon?"

That's him, the old Viceroy of India. Queer, isn't it? Anyway, I wish you a good day, Mr Fox."

"Thank you, and a good day to you too, Mr Hainsworth."

There was a second caller to Number 16, Prospect Place that day. It was in the afternoon, a far more respectable hour for a visit, and it was none other than the mayor, Samson Fox himself.

"We're pleased you've called, Samson," Lucie said after they had settled around the crackling fire in the drawing room. "Something occurred last night that we were hoping to speak with you about."

"Ah, were you indeed?" Samson seemed suddenly ruddy-cheeked above his great beard. Perhaps Mrs Morris had banked the fire up a little too fiercely. "It'll be this business up on Harlow Hill, I suppose, eh?"

"Yes it is actually." Lucie smiled at him over the twining flowers of her teacup rim. "You'll be aware that Detective Inspector Douglas and his men have been working tirelessly, trying to catch this so-called Beast of the Bogs Valley?"

Samson nodded vigorously. "Yes, yes, I'm sure."

"Well who would have believed it, but having made an arrest, he was straight-away directed to release him; this on the orders of some person unknown in the senior ranks of the police. Mr Douglas has been left very frustrated by it all, Samson. And to be quite candid with you, Atticus and I have too."

Samson grimaced and took a sip of his tea.

"Yes, yes, I can imagine, but there you are, eh? This Gaspar fellow is known to some very important folk, folk in London even, if you catch my meaning. I'm afraid the business has gone quite out of my hands."

"But you're the mayor of Harrogate," Atticus countered, "and you're a Freemason – a senior one too, by all accounts."

The reddish blotches on Samson's cheeks deepened and he rubbed a finger around his collar.

"Well, yes I am, but I'm still a good few degrees less senior than the people I'm speaking about. And it's not all to do with Freemasonry, eh; there are other…"

"There are other what, Samson?" Lucie asked him.

"Listen to me, the both of you; I'm quite sure the man isn't a murderer. He has some queer ideas, to be sure, but that ain't agin' the law, now is it? Take my word for it, Gaspar's an honest man and, by-the-by, an exceedingly generous philanthropist."

Darkness was only just falling when there was yet another sharp knocking on the Foxes' front door. Atticus looked up from his *Lippencott's Monthly* magazine and Lucie lowered her own copy of *The Harrogate Advertiser*. They stared at one another, both knowing very well that in their profession, late callers seldom brought welcome news. There was a murmured exchange of voices beyond the parlour door and Mrs Morris appeared.

"Begging your pardon, ma'am, but there is a visitor in the hallway to see you both. It's a Mr Malkin. He is enquiring as to whether you might be at home."

Atticus laid aside his *Lippencott's*. "Of course we are, Mrs Morris, Joseph Malkin is always welcome here; you know that."

"Oh no, it's not Mr Joseph come to call, Mr Fox, it's a Mr Esau."

A week had not yet passed since they had taken Esau to be admitted into the Harrogate Retreat, but in that time, he had become almost unrecognisable. Indeed, it would have been quite unthinkable that the Esau Mrs Morris showed into their parlour could ever have been regarded as a freak. Here was a sophisticated young man, shaven clean on face and pate and dressed very fashionably in a new green waistcoat and high collar. He would have passed muster in the best hotels in the town and Lucie felt obliged to beg his pardon for not receiving him upstairs in their drawing room rather than here, in their everyday front parlour.

Esau waved away both her apologies and her offer of tea.

"I am here to learn the game of chess, Lucie Fox," he explained, "And I am given to understand that Atticus Fox is a first-rate player."

"He is," Lucie confirmed. "He could easily play for the county, were he inclined. We moved here, to Prospect Place, in part to be near to the chess club. It meets in the hotel next door."

She threw a purposeful glance towards Atticus.

"And I'm quite certain Mr Fox would be delighted to teach you. The marble set from the drawing room would be the best one to use."

"I have to play against myself as a rule." Atticus lay what looked like an ivory book mark onto his page and stood up from his parlour-desk. "The chess club only runs from October until April, so it will be a welcome treat to play against a real opponent, even a novice. I've my travelling-set just here, so we can begin right away."

"No, Atticus, I believe the big set would be better," Lucie insisted, and all at once Atticus understood.

"Yes, you're quite right, Lucie, of course. The big pieces will be much clearer for a beginner. I'll fetch them directly."

Once Atticus had taken time to relate in great detail, the name, history and purpose of each of the chess pieces, he set them up into opposing ranks of black and white.

"I generally say that playing the game is the best way of learning it," he explained as he worked, "But first, let me give you this advice: One should always play for the strongest position. And do try to avoid the simple exchange of pieces; it makes for a much better and more thoughtful game." He smiled good-naturedly and settled back to contemplate his opening moves.

As Atticus Fox surveyed the board in front of him, it struck him again just how deep, and how black, were his young opponent's eyes – blacker and more lustrous even than the polished marble of his chessmen. And what was more, those eyes, and the black of his gums, were powerfully suggestive of something else – something he could not quite place.

He shrugged off the thought and focussed his mind instead onto the game. His customary opening should suffice, especially against a novice. Reaching down, he advanced a white pawn by two squares.

Esau picked up its black counterpart.

"This pawn is quite exquisite, Atticus Fox" he remarked, holding the finely-carved Belgian stone between his fingertips. And so it was; the set had been a house-warming gift from Samson Fox and it was superb.

At his back, Lucie watched him over her newspaper, and smiled.

"Tell me," said Esau, "How is it possible for you to play this game against yourself?" He placed the pawn onto the board, mirroring Atticus' own opening. "You must always know what your own next move is going to be."

Atticus chuckled as he picked up his bishop. He had been asked this question many times.

"You might well suppose it should be impossible, Esau, but you see, over the years, I have trained my mind to be able to switch its allegiance completely after each move is made. It took a great deal of effort, to be sure, but it assists me in being completely impartial at all times. That, as you might imagine, is of great usefulness in our work as privately-commissioned enquiry agents."

Esau gently sucked at his rubber gums as he considered Atticus' explanation. Then he asked: "Have you ever been admitted into a retreat, Atticus Fox?"

The bishop dropped from Atticus' fingers to clatter heavily onto the chessboard.

"Why should you ask me that?"

Esau's gaze lifted from the fallen bishop and fixed itself onto Atticus.

"Michael Roberts insists on teaching the inmates of his retreat to play rithmomachia. He said the idea came from Lucie Fox's suggestion that you learned chess in order to help you to focus your mind." He raised his eyebrows to turn his statement into a question and Atticus, staring at him, realised that they too had been shaven off. "I wondered why you might need to do that."

"Because, as I explained to you, it helps me in my work."

"I believe you have left the Harrogate Retreat, Esau," Lucie interjected, lowering her newspaper. "May we enquire where you are staying now, and what you are doing for employment?"

"I have secured rooms in the west of Harrogate," Esau replied, "on Harlow Hill, where I have taken up the study of Philosophy of Mind."

"Don't you mean the study of psychiatry? That is Dr Roberts' own specialism. He studied at the world-renowned Charité Institute in Germany."

"No," Esau shook his head emphatically, "It is Philosophy of Mind. Psychiatry is just as limiting as phrenology, since each concerns itself with just one part of the whole."

"I've worked in an insane asylum, under Dr Crichton-Browne. He is a psychiatrist but I don't believe anyone could accuse him of being limiting," Lucie said, chuckling.

"Yet without doubt he would have considered only the mental processes of his patients, just as a phrenologist looks only at the brain and its effect upon the bones of the skull. As a consequence, both miss entirely any judgement upon the heart and the soul. The Philosophy of Mind encompasses all of these. It is the only way to cast a true appraisal of man."

"Oh," said Lucie, and Atticus could not help but to agree. Esau had advanced quite incredibly from the ape that had sucked sherry from its fingers just a few days earlier.

Esau watched as Atticus picked up the dropped bishop and placed it onto its intended square. "Have you discovered the identity of this Beast of the Bogs Valley?" he asked.

Atticus, thankful for the change of conversation, exhaled sharply.

"We believed we might have done. Unfortunately, we were prevented from gathering the necessary proofs by the actions of certain, I suppose I should call them, secret societies."

Atticus explained what had transpired the previous night and Esau listened with grave attention. He reached across the board and placed a perfectly manicured finger onto the mitre of the bishop Atticus had just dropped.

"You told me that the bishop is amongst the lowliest of the chessmen, Atticus Fox."

Atticus nodded. "That is correct. They are generally reckoned as minor pieces, two pawns less in value than a castle."

"And yet, feeble as they are, they are the ones to stand on the chessboard at the shoulders of kings and queens?"

Atticus chuckled. "Why yes, upon my word, I suppose they do."

"But the castles, with their far greater power, stand away on the fringes."

"Yes, and that is quite true too," Atticus agreed.

"But the player, the real master of the game, who sees and directs every move, sits outside of the chessboard entirely. Perhaps he is a little like the grand-master of these secret orders."

Lucie laid down her newspaper and stared in open-mouthed astonishment and even Atticus clapped his hands together in something like wonderment. "Exactly so, Esau, exactly so, and may I say that I find your wisdom astounding. Now do you see the power of chess in eliciting thought?"

They played out the rest of the game in silence, save for the regular tap of the chessmen moving about the board and occasional voices passing outside the window. It played out to stalemate.

"You are already a quite remarkable chess player, Esau," Atticus commended him as he made his farewells. "It's scarcely believable that you've never played the game before, because I declare, you could beat an automaton."

The Foxes watched Esau through their parlour window, striding away, tall and proud, into the misty shadows of Montpellier Hill as if he might have been the Prince of Wales himself.

Atticus said: "Do you know, Lucie, I wasn't even going softly on him in that game, yet still he drew it."

But his wife did not hear him. She was already crouched over a black marble chess-piece, examining-glass in hand, staring at a finger-print.

CHAPTER THIRTY-NINE

Atticus Fox sits in his parlour, playing at chess. As he makes his customary opening, his mind does not focus, as it usually would, on the case in hand. It falls instead to thoughts of Esau, and of his remarkable transformation.

The September issue of *Lippencott's* lies, half-read, by his chessboard, his place kept with a bookmark. On a whim, Atticus draws this out and looks at it. At first glance, one might think it is old – carved ivory perhaps, and likely quite valuable. But it is none of these. It is Xylonite – French ivory – made by the hundredweight in a Suffolk manufactory and a prized material for souvenirs. A view of the Stray is pressed into one face, and at its tip is a tiny glass. This latter is a Stanhope: a lens which rewards the eye pressed against it with a photographic panorama of the town.

As Atticus muses, he recalls Esau's remarks on chess. He was right, of course. As it is on the chess-board, so it is in life – microcosm and macrocosm – just like the Stanhope.

He picks up a chessman, and then one other, and sets them on his palm. They are both bishops, identical, save for their colour. One is black and the other white, and it is almost as if he is holding, there in his hand, the two great sects of Christendom. For they too are alike, and they too are adversaries.

He is suddenly aware of Lucie, looking at him over her lowered book, and it strikes him that she might just have asked him something.

"What are you thinking about, Atty?" she repeats.

"Oh, only of Christianity, dearest, and how its factions, the Protestant and the Catholic, have been warring for centuries, whispering into the ears of kings, the one, by turn, having the other driven out, and for what? The answer is trifles, Lucie, mere trifles: vestments, popery and paraphernalia. They wage their wars, but in the same moments they pronounce their *pax vobiscum* and their 'peace be with you'." He sighs. "The fever of righteousness is the fever for war."

Lucie shrugs and lifts her book, and then lowers it again.

"*Pax vobiscum*," she repeats and stares, frowning, into the fire. "*Pax vobiscum*, paraphernalia, fever!"

Something in her tone causes the chill of the chessmen's lead bases to leach into Atticus' skin.

"We've been missing something obvious," Lucie whispers. "I've missed something I should have seen right from the very start. Atticus, we need a confessor, and quickly."

CHAPTER FORTY

Like some medieval citadel, the presbytery and the church of Our Lady Immaculate and St Robert threw towers and cross-topped pinnacles against the fast-darkening sky.

Atticus and Lucie, breathless despite it being no more than a few hundred yards away from their home on Prospect Place, hastened up to it. A single light was burning in the downstairs front window and through it they could see Canon William Pope hunched over a table, pen in hand, scratching at a paper.

They ran under the great Gothic arch that tied the presbytery to the church proper and pounded on the door, their hearts thumping in their chests long after the knocking-iron had stilled.

It seemed an age before a voice called: "Please be patient, I am coming as quickly as I am able," and yet another before the door was pulled open and an ancient cleric stood in front of them, peering over a pair of half-moon spectacles.

"Forgive my aged legs, my children," he said in a voice surprisingly strong and vital for such a frail and elderly man, "I am not so swift as I used to be."

"Please pardon us for calling so late, Father Pope," Lucie said, "but we need you to perform a mercy."

"You must call me Father William," the old man replied, "I am really not a Pope, and at seventy-seven years of age, I am rather beginning to have my doubts as to whether I ever shall be."

He smiled wearily.

"Nor indeed that I shall ever finish tomorrow's sermon. So then, my daughter, do tell me: what is this mercy you require?"

Esau Malkin was choked, almost completely overwhelmed, by the sheer exhilaration of life as he came to the gates of the Bogs Valley Pleasure Garden. It was as if he needed to race along these pavements, and skip and leap into the air like Harlequin. That would not do, of course. Gentlemen did not run in Harrogate, even at night, and he was so much more than a man. He closed his eyes and marvelled again at his Enlightenment, that He, Esau, was neither freak, nor wild-man, nor shit-faced monkey.

He was a god.

And then, with that most wonderful of thoughts, he was finally overcome, and he did run, more swiftly than the swallow, towards the setting sun and the very fringes of Harrogate. Here, where the town gave way to moors and to pinewood plantations, were his lodgings.

He stopped by a gatepost, dappled in shadow. There was his staff, his new and ancient symbol, and a man dressed entirely in black, waiting for him on bended knee. As Esau stood before him, he threw out his arms in the manner of the Moors and cried:

"My Lord Hermes, Thrice-Great, made manifest through Astennu, Weigher of Hearts, Master of Wisdom, Writing and Magic, I am an Adept of your Mysteries and your most humble servant."

CHAPTER FORTY-ONE

"Stop here, if you please," Atticus called out, and immediately they felt the little landau[22] slow and then draw to a stop. "If we are correct, Father, then this is the place."

"But where could a murderer be hereabouts, Mr Fox?" Father Pope asked. "There's only Widow Watson's farm and old Father Cado's chantry that I know of."

"Murderer?" the cabman exclaimed, twisting round in his seat. "What's all this about, Padre? What murderer?" One of the pair of horses whinnied at his voice and shook its head, setting the brasses of its harness jingling.

"There is nothing to be alarmed about," Lucie assured him. "No one is in any danger, barring the man we have come here to see, although it may already be too late for him."

Atticus slid open the door of his dark-lantern and lifted it high. The light within, like an eager swarm of golden bees, spilled out along a narrow track overcast by scrubby trees and overgrown with sprawling weeds and shadows.

He said: "In which case we had better make haste. Wait here for us if you would be so kind, cabbie; you'll be paid for your time."

"Very well, Mr Fox, if I must," the cabman grumbled. Perhaps anticipating a lengthy wait, he reached to turn down the carriage-lamps, fumbling awkwardly at the wick-screws and cursing under his breath. Lucie, with her nurse's eye, noticed the third finger on each of his hands, and how they were curled back tightly into his palms. *Dupuytren's contracture*, she noted instinctively – coachman's finger – the unfortunate consequence of a lifetime spent pulling on reins.

They had gone just a little way from the road, stepping across brambles and trampling through undergrowth, when the lantern light caught against the rugged face of a building. It was all but derelict with the roof sunken and bowed like an old horse's back and great cracks and ivies reaching up from the ground as if trying to drag it bodily into the earth.

"The old chantry chapel," Father Pope lamented, "I had no idea it was so decayed."

"You had better close the lantern," Lucie whispered and Atticus nodded. Instantly, the light vanished and by the stars and the waxing crescent moon, they became themselves three phantoms, shadowy and vaporous, a moorland phantasmagoria.

"Father Cado," Lucie called into the crumbling mortar of the door pillar.

What might have been a mouse or a bird scuffled in the ivy above her head.

"Luke?" Canon Pope sang out behind her, "Father Luke, are you there? It is me, William. Are you sick?"

Atticus reached up and pressed against the ancient timbers of the door. They shuddered and squealed back on protesting hinges and from the seat of an ancient pew a monster looked up. In a voice as rusted and as unused as the iron of the door-hinges, it spoke.

"Forgive me, Father, for I have sinned."

It was a little over an hour later when the door creaked open once more and Father William came out, blinking in the light of Atticus' lantern and rubbing his temples.

"Father Luke Cado has passed over peacefully to Christ," he said simply, "Thank you for waiting out here in the cold with such sufferance. You were right to fetch me, and I am grateful. So, I must tell you, was Father Luke himself.

"I performed the *Unction* and the *Viaticum* – the Last Rites as they are often, though erroneously, known – and I was able to hear his confession. It is good that he was finally relieved of the weight of his sins. He has carried it these past almost twenty years and it was onerous. But it was weakness not wickedness which burdened him and the Lord will be merciful."

He beckoned them inside, and first Lucie, and then Atticus, filed after him into the musty shadows of the chapel. There the hermit lay. His eyes were closed in peace and his hands pressed together as if he were an effigy carved forever in pious petition. A chain of silver rosary beads, as delicate as a child's, bound his fingers.

"Upon my word, what are those?" Atticus whispered, and well might he have asked.

A ragged cowl had been pulled back from the white, hairless head of Father Cado, revealing at least a dozen growths, each as big as a hen's egg, erupting from his skin and transforming him into something abhorrent and grotesque. Between them, round, pink lesions ran with the sweat of a fever they could still feel radiating from the corpse.

"Those are called gummas," Lucie said. "They, and the wounds they leave after they break down, are one of the symptoms of advanced syphilis."

The last word echoed back to them, alien and discordant in the ruined sanctity of the chapel.

"Father Luke knew exactly what it was he had contracted," said Father Pope. "In his confession, he told me that back in the seventies, when he had his own church and congregation, a young woman came to him. She seemed intent on his seduction and the Father, being born of sinful flesh, eventually obliged her. It appears the poor girl – who bore a remarkable resemblance to Hannah, whom he so violently assaulted in the bath-chair yard – was a prostitute woman on a day-trip from Halifax and that she communicated her own syphilis to him. In his reconciliation, he admitted that he took the things: the plants, the ironwood and the mercury, in an attempt to cure himself of it. That was why he forcibly seduced the nun too, God forgive him. He had some idea that relations with a virgin might reverse the course of the disease. It did not, of course. His efforts were all in vain and it has finally caught up with him this night."

"Father, it wasn't the syphilis that killed him; it was malaria."

"Malaria, Mrs Fox!" The priest threw up his hands in astonishment. "But how could he have caught malaria?

The air in here is musty and foul, to be sure, but Harrogate is hardly the tropics.”

“Malaria, contrary to popular belief, is not spread by *mal air*,” Lucie explained, “It is spread by mosquito bites and infected blood.”

“Mosquito bites? But there are no mosquitoes in Yorkshire at this time of the year.”

“Father Cado deliberately infected himself by injecting diseased blood he took from the Incurables Hospital. I’ve read in the nursing journals that the fever caused by malarial infection has, on occasion, been shown to kill the syphilis microbe. Unfortunately, with him being in such a weakened condition…” Lucie glanced down to where the compelling presence of the corpse finished her sentence.

“He should have sought proper medical help,” Atticus said.

“He was a priest with syphilis, Mr Fox. He could not have asked for help without it ruining both his reputation and, more importantly, that of the church. His sin would have been laid bare for all to see.”

He reached down and adjusted a tiny silver crucifix hanging from the rosary.

“That was how he came to attack poor Hannah. When he saw her standing there, in the entrance to the yard, he was quite overcome by rage, reminded as he was of his weakness and of how he had come to be as he was. He regretted the attack deeply afterwards and was greatly relieved to be reconciled with it.”

“But she is just as dead, Father,” Lucie said.

"Yes, regrettably, that is indeed so."

"It was the attack on Hannah – or Sarah – that made me realise what was behind this," Lucie explained. "It occurred to me that the *Abrus* peas Mr Fox found might actually be from a rosary – the attacker's rosary – and not, as we originally assumed, from her jewellery."

She reached down and eased back the corpse's right thumb. As it caught in the lantern beam, they could clearly see that the pad was worn smooth.

"And this must be Sister Agnes' rosary. He took it when he outraged her, likely to replace his own."

"I cannot think she will want it back now," said Father Pope. "One can hardly imagine it: to outrage a sister of the faith and then to steal her rosary." He bowed his head and the lenses of his spectacles occluded white in the lantern light. "Mind you, his sins were already so great, it is little wonder he wore his thumb smooth with his petitions."

"Look at this too." Atticus plucked at a threadbare patch of the hermit's worn and tattered vestment and it went to pieces under his fingers. Underneath was a coarse, roughly-woven cloth.

"A cilice!" Father William exclaimed.

"Yes," said Atticus, "a hair-shirt, made from goat or horse hair by the look of it, and do you see how he has had steel wires woven into it too? A discomfort to match his guilt."

"Or a demonstration of his remorse and penitence," said Father Pope firmly. "Father Luke Cado was no slavering beast, Mr Fox, whatever epithet the police might have put on him. You would do better to think of him more in the nature of… more in the nature of a fallen angel."

"I can understand him wishing to keep his illness a secret," Lucie interjected before Atticus could respond, "And I can even see how he came to commit such a brutal attack on Hannah; syphilis often causes uncontrollable rages once it enters the brain. But what I do not understand is how he could possibly claim to be remorseful and penitent, as you say he was, and yet contrive to decapitate those two men?"

Father Pope stared at her in open-mouthed astonishment.

"Mrs Fox," he said, "Luke Cado did not confess to decapitating anyone."

"So are we to believe," reasoned Atticus Fox, "that in the minutes before he was due to stand before his Maker, Father Cado held back on a full confession, or should we conclude instead that we have a second murderer yet at large?"

In these wee hours of the morning, the familiar streets and houses between St Robert's presbytery and their home seemed intrusive, looming even, as if the town itself were craning to overhear their words.

"It may very well be that neither is the case," replied Lucie. "Father Cado was exhibiting clear signs of what is called *general paresis*. That is a brain condition resulting from syphilis, which can cause both delusions and a kind of dementia. I really should have recognised it sooner. Dr Crichton-Browne at the asylum did a great deal of work on neuro-syphilis and I have made a point of reading all of his journals on the subject. I declare, I could kick myself! But now I think about it, it is quite possible that Father Cado performed the beheadings during episodes of deluded rage, and then simply forgot about them."

Atticus did not reply at once. After the night's moil, his mind felt like freshly-kneaded bread dough, thick and heavy, and the notion of addressing this most complex of cases anew seemed just too much even to contemplate.

"You have educed the identity of one murderer this night, Lucie. Why don't we sleep on the question and address it all again in the morning?"

In the event, it was only Lucie who was able to slumber that night. Atticus, despite his exhaustion, was plagued by a bluebottle-in-the-room feeling that he had missed something – something quite obvious. He lay awake, running the facts of the case again and again through his mind as he stared into the blackness above. And when he was finally overwhelmed, it was to a troubled and fitful sleep harrowed by dreams of mocking and bloody skulls.

CHAPTER FORTY-TWO

"Well, I'll be a monkey's uncle!"

Detective Inspector Douglas slapped the top of his desk with a blow that made the little glass inkwells jingle in their stand.

"A syphilitic priest; who would have believed it? At least His Worship will be pleased it's over with."

"I do hope so," said Atticus.

Douglas nodded solemnly. "Amen to that. So what was it that finally got the skittles falling for you, Mrs Fox?"

"It was your Sergeant Hainsworth actually," Lucie replied, "Although I dearly wish they had begun falling sooner. He happened to mention to Atticus that Father Cado had a fever he could feel even through a blanket. Few infections produce so high a fever as malaria, and malarial blood was what was taken from the hospital. I recalled that malarial infection can be used as a cure for syphilis, and that so – according to old wives' tales and a book I had from the library – can heartsease, mercury and *lignum vitae* wood."

"And mistletoe?" Douglas prompted.

Lucie shook her head. "There was no mistletoe. Advanced syphilis can result in intense pain from any light shining into the eyes. The pupils become unable to contract, you see? It can affect speech too, so his screaming out of 'packets of *Viscum*' was actually '*Pax vobiscum*'."

"Which was a standard benediction he once would have used on visiting the sick there," Atticus explained.

"That makes some semblance of sense, I suppose," Douglas said. "And what with his deathbed confession and Mrs Fox finding all those things he had thieved underneath the pew, it has all come up as neat as a butler's pantry. What about Headless Harry and the tramp-major from Ripon? How do they fit into this?"

Atticus and Lucie exchanged quick, uncomfortable glances and Douglas' eyes narrowed.

Atticus said: "That, I fear, is not quite so neat, but Mrs Fox, who has some knowledge of neuro-syphilis, believes it is perfectly possible that he killed them in some kind of a mad rage. She asks that she be allowed to examine the corpses."

"Father Cado did not confess to either of the decapitation murders," Lucie explained, "so I thought I might find something to confirm it was really him."

"I see," said Douglas. He bit his lip.

"Just to help us be sure, Inspector, and may we see a copy of Harry's coroner's report too?"

Douglas reached down into his desk drawer and fished out a single sheet of paper.

"Well I agree with you, Mrs Fox. It seems clear that it was this priest who did for them, but you may suit yourselves on proving it. It's the mayor who's paying for you, after all's said and done. I have my murderer, thank you very much, and I don't even have the inconvenience of going to court over it."

Douglas dabbed his fountain pen into an inkwell and scribbled out a note.

"The surgeon had Harry's remains taken up to the Ripon poor-house, to compare with their dead-un. He is firmly of the opinion that the same man did for them both, by-the-by. So you're in luck; they're both still lying in the morgue there, awaiting burial." He blotted the note and thrust it across his desk. "Be my guests."

Mr Turner, the porter of Ripon Union Workhouse, greeted Atticus and Lucie as long-lost acquaintances from his old, battered chair under the entrance arch. Both the master and the matron were attending a service at the cathedral, he explained, but he would be delighted, of course, to show them the mortuary himself.

"I'd have to go wi' ye anyways," he explained, neatly folding Douglas' note and handing it back to Lucie, "on account of it being kept locked. We wouldn't want folk roamin' in there by accident, now would we? No more than we'd want t' bodies taking themsens off for a night-time stroll, not at five quid an 'ead, if ye take my meaning." He tapped the side of his nose and then burst out laughing. "Oh, I forgot; they don't have any 'eads, do they?"

"Unfortunately not," said Atticus.

They followed the still-chuckling porter back through the workhouse gates and around the high, spike-topped wall which formed the perimeter of the work-yards.

"I could have taken thee through the able-bodied men's ward, I s'pose" Mr Turner explained as they walked. "It would've been quicker; it's just they're not right used wi' ladies there – 'ceptin' for Matron o' course, but she don't really count, does she?"

"I expect not," said Atticus.

"Now then, Mr and Mrs Fox, here we are; this is t' inmates' dead-house."

The porter indicated a low door set anonymously into the newer brickwork of a vast annexe, which was evidently the workhouse's infirmary.

Lucie thanked him. "Why don't you show my husband the vegetable garden whilst I'm in there, Mr Turner?" she suggested, "I shall be perfectly fine on my own, and more likely than not to be some time."

"Well, if ye're sure, Missus" The porter rubbed the side of his face and the whiskery stubble rasped against the calloused skin of his fingers. "I'll warn ye though, neither on 'em are awful pretty to look at, and the stink!" He rolled his eyes. "Ye might want to bide a minute or two after I open t' door. It'll give t' air a chance to clear a bit, afore ye go in."

Lucie watched a large blowfly emerge from the keyhole of the door and crawl away across the timber. She nodded; it was prudent advice.

As Mr Turner opened up the mortuary, Lucie began her preparations. She lifted her heavy work apron out of their investigations bag and unrolled it across the cobbles, grateful to be able to fill her nostrils with the rubbery smell of the canvass. Next, she unpinned her travelling bonnet and passed it to Atticus, who exchanged it for her little square nurse's cap. For a precious moment, she paused and held it out before her, like the photograph of a much-missed loved one. A corner was missing its starch and one of the seams was just beginning to lose its stitching. Lucie was glad to have noticed; she would shortly be called on to notice everything.

There was another waft of rubber as Atticus dropped the apron's neck-strap over her head and she felt its weight settle around her like a yoke. She turned to allow him to tie the waist strings and in that moment the stench of death caught her full in the face. What it would be like inside that basement room she dreaded to think, and the stiff, heavy fabric of her apron was already beginning to feel claustrophobic.

Lucie looked up, high above the walls of the infirmary building and into the blue-washed skies beyond. It was a big infirmary for the size of the workhouse, she reflected. Or was it? It occurred to her then how truly desperate the inmates must have been to have sought relief here; how age, frailty, starvation or disease must have so wholly overwhelmed them. No, this giant was needed and there would be ravaged flesh enough in the wards and yards around it to satiate even its appetite.

But then she had another thought, a fleeting one, and rather vulgar: If this hospital was a giant, then that door hanging ajar in front of her must be its fundament. The notion made her giggle. But it was battlefield laughter, Netley laughter, brief and nervous and couched in a yelp of repugnance.

"Smell's reached ye, has it, Missus? Aye, I said it were rank."

"Rank it most certainly is, Mr Turner. A workhouse like this really should have a separate mortuary building, with fly-screens and proper ventilation. This is all a little too makeshift. Atticus, tuck the ends in tight, if you please." Lucie was surprised by the sound of her own voice; it was brisk, professional and so very matter-of-fact. "I don't want them to trail in the slab trays. That stench is revolting."

"The stench is from the gases putrescine and cadaverine—" Atticus began.

"Yes, I'm sure, Atticus. Now, you might care to tie my pocket handkerchief around the neck strap of my apron and sprinkle it with some of my French perfume."

She was ready, or at least she could put off this thing no longer. As her husband and the porter turned away to the gently sloping ground that contained the workhouse's fruit and vegetable gardens, Lucie stepped into Hell.

Makeshift it may have been but the mortuary room of the Ripon workhouse infirmary contained two modern undertaker's slabs, both of heavy, white porcelain, separated by a narrow aisle. Across the wall opposite, the reminder 'GOD IS GOOD' was painted in thick black capitals.

Lucie flexed her fingers inside the stiff, rubberised material of her gauntlets and regarded the occupants of the slabs. Both were headless torsos and Mr Turner had been entirely accurate in his description of them; they were most certainly not at all pretty. The flesh of both bodies had begun the process of decomposition and even with her heavily perfumed handkerchief tied onto her apron strap, the foetid odour pressed down onto her almost like a physical presence.

So the divisional police surgeon had suspected the murders were linked? Here, lying side-by-side on identical slabs, both bearing the coroner's crude stitch-work across their fronts, both with grey, rotting orifices between their shoulders, it certainly seemed so. But which to examine first; inmate or guest?

The gap between the slabs was narrow. Even Lucie, a slender woman in rational dress, had space enough only to shuffle sideways along its length. A bustle would have made it impossible to work in this place, but then it was unlikely that its builders had had bustles in mind. Because she could not easily turn, the choice was made for her; she would first examine the cadaver Detective Inspector Douglas had dubbed Headless Harry.

Lucie's mama had once confided to her that a gentleman could be expected to divulge most about himself at a second meeting. She hoped now that she was right.

Lucie took a breath and leaned forward, aware suddenly of her heart beating against the heavy fabric of her apron. A blowfly buzzed in her ear, inquisitive of this new presence. She flapped it away. There were more, dozens more, a Darwinian army crawling and jostling with its own maggot offspring to gorge and to lay. For them at least, God was indeed good.

The severed vertebra was there, slightly proud of the writhing mass around it. She wiped the slime from the face of the bone and stooped to examine it more closely. Then, with her jaws set tight, she moved on to the skin of the neck, tattered and lacerated, and just beginning to darken with the onset of black putrefaction. As Lucie stared at it, she was just able to discern a mark, perhaps two, where a ligature might once have been pulled tight.

A loud plink of fluid, dripping from the drain hole into a waiting bucket, nudged her from her thoughts. She stood and with her gauntleted hands held up like the claws of a scavenging crab, sidled back between the slabs to turn and address the second of the waiting subjects.

So this was the tramp-major. Lucie was surprised he hadn't been dressed again after his post-mortem examination, but then a tramp-major is still a tramp after all, and perhaps his clothes had been needed elsewhere.

She looked down at him and here, on this first acquaintance, he told her a very great deal. The legs, thick with the gases of putrefaction were heavily bowed, a testament to a childhood of desperate poverty spent, as like as not, under the thick smog of a manufactory chimney, hidden away like a Catholic from the light of the Sun.

"Rickets," Lucie murmured aloud.

His genitals, distended and swollen, showed the early but unmistakable signs of syphilis. Unlike Father Cado he would have felt no shame in this. Rather, William Firth would likely have viewed it as a joke, a hazard of his occupation, a badge of honour even, just like so many of those she had seen at the military hospital at Netley all those lifetimes ago. The belly, bloated by drink and intestinal gasses, was already beginning to green and blister, and above it, the chest, with a crude dragon tattoo, was barrelled. Lucie saw asthma there, chronic no doubt, and another testament to his childhood.

And finally to the neck and the site of the decapitation injury that was of such relevance to this inquiry. Lucie again bent close to the cut surface of the vertebra, slick where the fluid of the lungs was oozing away, and with sulphurous, hellish breath, it too whispered its secrets.

"It will take me a month of Sundays to get this stench out of my hair."

Lucie shook off her gauntlets, one-by-one, onto the cobbles. She wiped at her brow with the back of her wrist, smearing a line of French chalk there like Death's own mark.

"There's not many folk as would go in there at all, Missus." Mr Turner was staring at her with an expression bordering on awe. "Master said to wait as long as we could afore we buried them, in case t' heads turn up. We can get five pounds each for 'em complete, but only four pounds the pair, just as they are."

His voice dropped to a whisper, as if wary of tempting fate. "Unless t' relatives claim 'em first o' course".

Atticus passed his silver water flask to his wife and reached down for her discarded gloves. "Did you manage to discover anything new?" he asked.

Lucie held the cold metal between her hands and for a few seconds allowed the blessed chill to seep into her blood.

"As far as I can tell, Harry was beheaded at the third cervical vertebra." She pointed to the side of her neck, at around the level of her chin. "And yes, there were faint but definite double-ligature marks on the skin."

"So it's *la loupe* again," said Atticus.

Lucie twisted off the cap of the flask and drank, deeply and unashamedly, from the neck.

"The tramp-major's head was also taken off at that same vertebra – the third cervical. Both heads were taken off with a knife, and I believe it was the same knife in each case."

"The coroner's inquests describe them both as having been *sawn* off," Atticus reminded her.

"They were. There are clear sawing marks in the bone but made, in my judgement anyway, by a knife – one with a serrated blade, like a cook's bread-knife – and as smoothly and as cool-headedly as you please."

Lucie took another long draught from Atticus' flask. Then she said: "These murders weren't committed by some vagrant taking advantage of a sudden opportunity, Atticus, or by a demented priest. They were carried out with cunning, time a-plenty and a very great deal of malice aforethought."

CHAPTER FORTY-THREE

Atticus and Lucie Fox stood outside a phrenologist's parlour. It was the same tiny parlour that had attracted the attention of so many schoolboys the last time they had returned from Ripon workhouse and as Atticus had remarked on that occasion too, it really was in a most unlikely place.

Lucie was inclined to agree. It was much too far from the hospitals, the hotels and the hydropathics in the heart of the town, and the only passing trade seemed to be the steam waggons, which lumbered back-and-forth from Bilton Junction with their cargoes of coal.

"I would have put it with the other fortune-tellers, down Parliament Terrace," she could not help adding.

Despite the ever-settling smoke from the stacks of the steam waggons and the clinging black dust of their loads, this window was freshly washed and the tart scent of vinegar still hung in the air. It was quite possible to read the name on each organ of the phrenological crania within, written, as they were, in a neat, round hand.

"There, Lucie, do you see them?" said Atticus, "They are utterly revolting, I know, but there's something out of place about them too. I recollect thinking exactly the same thing last time we came past here."

A street-urchin, a boy of around ten years old, pushed between them and stared through the glass.

"Atticus," Lucie exclaimed, "Those skulls are fresh."

The boy shook his hand free of his sleeve and pressed a grubby finger against a pane.

"My pal Peter said that, Missus. He's t' butcher's lad so he knows all about dead bodies. He said you could tell they was fresh on account on 'em still being pink."

"Yes, yes, I'm sure." Atticus fumbled in the pocket of his jacket and pulled out a handful of coins. "Here, here's a thrupenny-bit for you and another for your pal Peter, for his cleverness."

He pressed the little silver coins into the boy's hand and they watched him race away up the street, his ragged coat tails flapping in his wake.

"His pal is exactly right though, Atticus," said Lucie gravely, "Those skulls are very pink. Anatomical or phrenological specimens would normally be bleached white, especially if they are to be used for a display."

She pressed her own fingertip against the glass. "And do you see there? There are vestiges of gristle still clinging to the skull; that is where the tendons were once attached."

Atticus did not reply.

Beyond the tall backing-screen of the window, the parlour had a deserted air about it and a sign hanging behind the door was turned to read 'Closed'. Lucie tried the latch. It opened to her touch and a little bell tinkled overhead.

"Hullo, shop," Lucie called.

"There's no one at home," Atticus whispered after a moment. "Lucie, we can't just go in there – not without permission, or the police."

Lucie said: "No, I don't suppose we can," and stepped inside.

Atticus sighed and followed his wife into a sharp stench of carbolic acid as overpowering as it had been in the workhouse. Everything had been freshly swept and scrubbed and there was a washing-day dampness in the air that was completely at odds with the inexplicable feeling of abandonment.

Lucie pulled open a narrow door in the window-back and lifted out the nearest of the skulls.

"Hmm, I should be very surprised if this weren't the tramp-major's, Atticus."

"How can you tell that?"

Lucie rotated the skull so that the empty eye sockets seemed to be staring directly at him."

"Do you see the mandible?"

Atticus pulled his gaze from the depths of the orbits and glanced down to the lower jaw. The few teeth clinging there gave it a slightly comical appearance.

"From the sheer size of the bones we can see that this skull is from a man," Lucie explained. "But the erosion and the loss of teeth would indicate advanced age. And notice how parts of the fore-skull are very thick. We call that 'cranial bossing' and it's very common in those affected by rickets, which I know from his skeleton William Firth was."

Mercifully, mercifully, she rotated the skull, and the eyes turned away.

"And thirdly, these star-shaped fractures on the parietal bone; they are both very recent and entirely consistent with blows from a heavy object."

"Such as a lump of stone, for example?"

Lucie nodded. Then, as she turned the skull over in her hands, she exclaimed: "Hullo! Look, Atty, there's a full set of finger-prints here. Do you see them?"

"Are they Father Cado's fingertip prints, do you think?"

Lucie pursed her lips. "I don't believe so. The minutiae of the thumb pads are worn quite smooth, but not completely so."

She frowned.

"There is an *almost* full set of finger-prints here, I should have said. One of the fingers on each hand is missing. That's queer."

Atticus peered down over the screen into the window. "So might we presume therefore, that the other belongs to Headless Harry?"

Lucie set the tramp-major's skull carefully onto the thin and threadbare seat-pad of a chair, which stood with one other in the middle of the room, and then reached to lift out its companion.

"This is from an adult male, Atticus, and yes, the skull size would fit roughly with Harry's height. It could be him, but more than that I cannot say. There is the same set of finger-prints on the lower surfaces though, with the same missing fingers, but look here! Do you see, smeared against the back of the cheek-bone?"

She touched her fingertip against a thin daub of sticky, pinkish residue and gently sniffed at it.

"It's very faint, but I can definitely smell sweet oil of olives. And that looks like rotten-stone mixed in with it."

"Then it's a cleaning preparation," said Atticus.

"But an unusual one for an anatomist to be using; it would be more for leatherwork or paint or varnish, than for bone."

"Perhaps the murderer, if that is who is responsible for this, simply used whatever was at hand," Atticus glanced around the tiny parlour. "This whole place is very clean, Lucie – rather too clean, if you take my meaning."

"So what are you saying; that Harry might have been murdered here, in this room?" Lucie turned and stared at the freshly-scrubbed walls, the newly-blacked fireplace and the polished oilcloth on the floor, and she knew that he was right. "And murdered by whom? The phrenologist?"

"Well someone has labelled the cranial organs, Lucie, someone who isn't here now."

Off the little parlour-shop was a scullery, and beyond that a tiny yard containing only a rusty tin bath and a wicker dustbin, half full of ashes. An examination of the contents of this latter revealed two sets of cervical vertebrae, as fragile as dust and criss-crossed by innumerable heat fractures. The lowest, the third, vertebrae from each set exhibited clear signs of having been sawn through and the employment of their big examining glass convinced Lucie that the instrument used to do this was a knife with a serrated blade. It also revealed faint score-marks on each of the second vertebrae, suggestive, to Atticus' mind at least, of the victims having had their throats cut from ear to ear.

Along with the vertebrae they found an old and very much soiled phrenological cranium, several old copies of the *Daily Chronicle* newspaper and a certificate in a smashed wooden frame. This latter was from the Wakefield Phrenological Society granting a fellowship to one Ernest Ryan. And further, when they liberally and intelligently applied alcohol in which shavings of *lignum vitae* had been steeped for several weeks, it turned a distinct shade of blue around the seams of the bath and the handle of a bread knife they found in the scullery. This was a sure indicator of the presence of blood residues, which, it seemed, even the high tide of carbolic acid had failed to erase.

CHAPTER FORTY-FOUR

Joseph Malkin shook his head in complete incredulity. "Ernest Ryan, a murderer? It can't be; I've known the man for years."

"We cannot be certain that Professor Ryan is the murderer," Atticus was careful to remind him, "Only that we found the victims' crania at his shop, with a number of their phrenological organs accurately labelled: *Destructiveness* and *Appetite* for the tramp-major, and *Comparison* and *Causality* in the case of Headless Harry."

Malkin shook his head again. "I still find it quite impossible to believe."

"Would you kindly provide us with a detailed description of the professor, so that we may pass it on to the police?" Lucie asked him.

"Yes of course, although to be truthful, he was an altogether unremarkable man. Let me see now, he was around average height, with brown eyes, dark hair and no whiskers. I cannot think there were any especially distinguishing features about him that I can recall. But then now I think on it, how could he not be the murderer? Those skulls could hardly have got there without his knowledge, and now he has disappeared from the face of the earth."

Joseph gazed up into an ornate plasterwork ring on the ceiling.

"I recollect him asking me if he might have Esau's skull, if ever he should die. I believe he needed crania to study but had no money with which to buy them. If only he had asked me to help; I should have done so gladly. Do you suppose he has resorted to Burking[(23)]?"

He glanced over to a big, mahogany mantel clock.

"And Victoria will be back from church ere long. She's certain to be disagreeable about it when she hears; she always despised the man."

Lucie glanced to the clock too.

"We should take the skulls over to the police surgeon," she said. "He can inform the coroner and arrange to have them reunited with the rest of their bodies. The master of Ripon workhouse will be delighted."

"A full six pounds delighted," Atticus agreed.

"Yes, you must," said Joseph, "At least those poor people are with God now, and beyond suffering, although it seems they must have gone through hell to get there."

Lucie glanced to her husband, waiting for him to stand. But he did not. Atticus Fox was staring deep into the small-coals of the fire.

"Dante Alighieri journeyed through Hell to get to Heaven in his *Divine Comedy*," he said.

"He did indeed, but does that matter?" Joseph asked. Lucie too seemed puzzled.

"A German anthropologist – Hermann Welcker his name was, I recall – reconstructed Dante's likeness from his skull using clay. Lucie, is there any reason why you couldn't do the same with Headless Harry?"

Lucie stared at him for several seconds.

"Yes, you're right. He produced tables, which give the normal thicknesses of flesh across the various surfaces of the skull? Could the library obtain a copy of them, do you suppose?"

"Surely," Atticus replied, "But there's no time for that. Besides which, it's Sunday and the library is shut. Lucie, your own knowledge of human anatomy is excellent; I imagine you could produce a very fair result yourself, were you to try."

It was something of a twist of irony that the features of the poor unfortunate whose remains had been pulled from the waters of the Nidd, should be recreated beside that very same river from the sticky, yellow clay which at that point formed its banks.

Lucie worked painstakingly well into the afternoon, a new-found artist of the *Danse Macabre*, with a skull as her canvass and the clay as her paints, while Atticus, mud-spattered, and with scales of dried clay clinging to his arms, laboured Golem-like[24] to keep her supplied with material.

At last she slumped back on her stool and regarded the skull, now turned back almost to flesh by means of her knife and spatula.

"It's all conjecture and supposition, Atty, but there it is. That would be my very best guess as to the likeness of Headless Harry."

"Upon my word, it's nothing short of miraculous," Atticus commended her. "It is so lifelike it looks as if it might open its mouth at any moment to depose who its murderer was." He kicked a thick ball of clay from his boot-sole and it arced and plopped into the water. "I wonder if we could get a photograph of it put into Wednesday's *Herald,* in case anyone should recognise him."

"It's a good plan, but Samson wouldn't like it one bit," Lucie warned.

"He mightn't mind; Harry wasn't found in the visitors' part of town, after all."

Lucie stood and carefully lifted up her creation.

"Well I'm filthy and exhausted and it needs time to properly dry before we can do anything with it. All that can wait until tomorrow."

CHAPTER FORTY-FIVE

In the event, Atticus and Lucie had opportunity neither to visit the offices of the *Harrogate Herald* nor even to seek Samson's agreement that they do so. Instead, a late night knocking on their door brought news of the most immediate and grave concern. It was Joseph. His wife and daughter had not yet returned from Sunday service and given that a second and seemingly even more brutal and determined murderer was loose in the Riding, he was almost beside himself with worry.

"I've called at the houses of her friends; I've been down to the Cottage Hospital; I've even been to the police station." Joseph seemed suddenly tiny, hunched as he was over a tumbler of chalybeate water in the big armchair in their parlour. "I really don't know what else I might do."

"Joseph, try not to worry. Turning up missing people is what we do almost every week of the year and there is almost always a perfectly innocent explanation." Lucie's tone was reassurance itself and even Atticus found himself almost believing her.

"Almost always, Lucie Fox?" Joseph's hands were trembling, his fingers pressed white around his glass. "Innocent explanation? But you don't know. You cannot know!"

Atticus said: "We shall need a full list of her acquaintances, Joseph, beginning with the most intimate and running down from there – and a note of her recent movements, as you know them to be."

"Oh no, Atticus, I cannot expect you to break off from your present case," Joseph protested, the relief gushing clear in his voice. He seemed suddenly to notice the clay head, which had been left on the hearth to bake hard overnight. "Especially when you are trying to run down a murderer."

"Oh, that isn't the murderer," Atticus replied. "That is one of his victims; the one the police called 'Headless Harry'. Lucie has been working on his likeness for most of the afternoon."

"Atticus," said Joseph Malkin, "That is Ernest Ryan."

CHAPTER FORTY-SIX

It seemed that Victoria Malkin possessed an astonishingly large number of acquaintances. Atticus found a list on the floor of their hallway when he rose early the next morning, where Joseph must have dropped it through their letterbox sometime during the small hours. As requested, he had also included a note as to her movements of the previous day. It was a short note, which ended with her attendance of Eucharist at the fashionable Christ Church on the Stray, along with Alice their daughter. They had, according to the Reverend Fawkes, conversed extensively with him after the service (as, he had noted, was their custom) and had last been seen by that worthy climbing into their coach-and-four for the half-mile or so journey back to their home.

It was perturbing that Oates was also missing, despite the fact that the carriage and horses had been left, still fully tacked and standing in harness, in the driveway of Beagle House. The great spectre looming over all of this was that these new disappearances might somehow be linked to the decapitation murders, but neither Lucie, nor even Atticus, were yet prepared to acknowledge its presence. For now, they were determined to take the absence of evidence for such a link to be clear evidence of its absence.

There were also the two skulls – one of them still encased in hard-baked river-clay – together with their newly-confirmed identities, yet to be delivered up to the police. Atticus, preferring to address just one colour of chessman at a time, therefore set out for Raglan Street carrying a sturdy wooden crate securely wrapped in brown paper. Out of respect for its contents he had put on black gloves and a matching crêpe neck-tie.

Almost immediately, he met Sergeant Hainsworth bustling along Prospect Place in the opposite direction. His collar was turned up and his expression was grave.

"There has been another one, Mr Fox," Hainsworth said without a greeting, "Which confirms that Father Cado was not the only murderer, after all."

"Who is it this time?" Atticus asked. His tone was tentative; Joseph was missing three people and Hainsworth had distinctly said, 'another one'. There was hope yet.

"Mrs Victoria Payne-Malkin, the wife of Mr Joseph Malkin, at least according to the visiting cards she was carrying. I'm really very sorry for you, and for Mrs Fox; I know she was a close acquaintance of you both."

It seemed churlish to argue the point, so Atticus gathered himself and asked the question.

"Has she been decapitated?"

Hainsworth nodded. "Aye; we only knew it was her from her visiting cards. There's no sign of her head… and there's something else too, this time."

"Fragments of earthenware pot?" Atticus ventured.

Hainsworth waited until a bath-chair had rumbled past them, the chair-man and the aged invalid he was pushing both laughing raucously at some asinine joke.

"Yes, there was as a matter of fact. How could you have known that? And this time, the heart has been cut out too. Why should anyone want to do that to a fellow human being, Mr Fox?"

In two quick movements, Hainsworth drew the sign of a cross over his chest and Atticus was reminded, all at once, of a particular symbol embroidered onto the altar cloth of a Hermetic temple.

He bit his lip. "It just so happens that I may have the answer to that."

"I hope you're right about this, Fox or else we're both for the high jump and no mistake."

Detective Inspector Douglas slips his watch back into his waistcoat pocket and turns to peer through the gate with its fashionable sunburst design. The house beyond it – Sun Villa – appears deserted, a source both of frustration, and perhaps, of blessed relief.

A hired landau slows suddenly on the road opposite, the ladies inside turning to stare curiously at them, and at the line of constables at their backs.

Douglas glances round angrily.

"Go on. Get away. Get away, damn you," he hisses, flapping his gloves furiously to shoo the cab away. It draws off in a sudden clatter of hooves. "Constable Watts, take that cab's number and make sure it's reported."

He inhales deeply and composes himself once again.

"Right then, lads, we're going in, just as we've planned. So remember: on the first stroke of ten, it's up and at 'em. Watch out for Hainsworth's detail coming in by the rear and I'll have the guts of anyone, anyone, mark my words, I catch showing fear or favour."

The strident but distant clamour of a telephone bell is swallowed up by the quarter-peals of St Mary's Church, a little way down the hill. At the sound, the blue line stiffens, taut as a bowstring, and Douglas calls: "Steady, now".

They wait. The peals ring the half, and the five-and-forty, and the hour – and then, a pause.

The great tenor bell strikes.

There are shouts all around them; the gate shudders and lurches wide and Douglas' arm is a turnstile, driving them on, sending constable after constable into the grounds. The sounds are echoed as Hainsworth's party attacks the rear and all the while, the great bell beats time. Atticus and Lucie run hand-in-hand in Douglas' wake, their boots crunching and spitting gravel, into the long shadows of the house, where the alders hang low and the flagstones are slick and green.

"This way; look lively now!"

Douglas skids and catches his balance, and they round the corner, pass the coal bunker, the greenhouse, the everyday stuff of life, and then: "There it is!"

Gaspar's temple stands, pure and white, beneath the rich, mellow green of its dome. Atticus and Lucie hesitate, awed momentarily by its beauty, but Douglas, veteran of many such raids, lunges forward like a deerhound. He leaps down from the terrace and charges and shoulders the doors. They burst open in front of him, and he is in.

"You there, stop, in the Queen's name!"

Douglas stands, his revolver at a full arm's length, shoulder high and as steady as iron.

"Good day to you, Detective Inspector Douglas, and good day to you too, Atticus Fox and Lucie Fox."

It was Esau, sitting cross-legged before the emerald cloth of the altar like a Baphomet or a child at play. His fingers were spread, not across a spinning-top or a wooden Noah's Ark, but across a skull, a pinkish, human skull, resting on the marble floor by his feet. It had a conspicuously large and jagged hole in the forehead.

Esau's black eyes followed the direction of their gaze and came to rest on his own hand.

"I am engaged in making scientific observations," he said by way of explanation. "This is Victoria Malkin's cranium; I am making an analysis of it according to my own system of Philosophy of Mind, which I have named the *Astennu Method*."

He patted the cranium and Douglas adjusted his aim, dropping the muzzle of his revolver until it was sighted deliberately onto the centre of Esau's chest, where a sizeable gold medallion glinted between the edges of a short, red cape.

"I warn you, Malkin; leave that alone or I'll fire."

Esau stared at the point of the revolver and slowly moved his hands to his lap.

"The *Astennu* Method," Atticus said. "But surely the real Astennu would have made a comparison of the heart rather than of the head?"

Esau smiled comfortably, revealing a glimpse of his black rubber gums. With his dark eyes and shaven head, he looked uncannily like the skull at his knee.

"Gaspar, whose acquaintance I know you have made already, believed that too – that the heart is the clearest window on character. He believed it to be a part of the soul itself, just as they did thousands of years ago in Egypt. But I have had a *progressive revelation,* Atticus Fox. I, Astennu, I, Hermes Trismegistus, now know that the essence of character comes both from the head and from the heart – from both the *Earthly* and the *Divine*. The heart and the mental processes are the soul, *The Light Within*, the spark of divine spirit that is contained within each and every one of us. The brain, on the other hand, and the skull that encases it…"

Despite the threat from Douglas' gun, Esau reached forward and rapped the skull with his fingertips. The hollow tapping sound quite turned Atticus' stomach.

"…those together are the base, the material aspect of character. The relationship between the Earthly and the Divine, as in all things, is the basis of the Astennu Method.".

"What is he talking about, Fox: I, Hermes Trismegistus and I, Astennu?" Douglas demanded.

"It would seem, Douglas that our friend believes himself to be Astennu. He was an *avatar*, you might recollect Gaspar telling us, a manifestation, of the Egyptian deity Thoth, who became Hermes Trismegistus?"

Atticus lifted the tip of his cane towards the three golden figurines on the altar.

"There he is – the one farthest to the right. Specifically he was the ape-headed God of Equilibrium and, along with Ma'at, the Goddess of Wisdom and Truth, one of those responsible for judging the souls of the dead. This they did by ceremonially weighing the deceased's heart against a feather. If, through the weight of sin, the heart were the heavier, it was fed to a wild beast."

"Mrs Malkin's heart had been removed," Douglas said.

Esau nodded. "It was heavy with sin, so it was thrown into the pinewoods, for the birds and the rats and the stray dogs to eat."

"What sin was it heavy with, Esau?" Lucie demanded, "I know she could be a difficult woman, but that is hardly a capital offence."

Esau chuckled. It was, it suddenly occurred to her, the first time they had ever heard him laugh.

"Her sins were threefold, Lucie Fox. They were in sending one innocent beast – a horse – to a knacker's yard[25]; in barring another – a wild-man as she believed – from her home, and in her denial that I, truly, am Astennu reborn."

He pushed a finger into the jagged hole in the skull's forehead.

"We spiked her in the knacker's yard, just as she herself had poor Albert spiked, and left her body there, amongst the cag-mag[26], to be made into meat-meal for the dogs and the cats."

"I am very thankful to you for your confession, Esau," Douglas broke in, the triumph clear in his voice, "Mr and Mrs Fox are my witnesses to it."

"My name is Hermes now."

"Hermes, Esau, it makes no difference to me what you call yourself; you'll hang just as surely as a murderer."

"A three-time murderer, Douglas," Atticus reminded him. "Don't forget the tramp-major and Professor Ryan."

Esau snorted. "Professor Ryan – Ernest Ryan, the phrenologist you mean? Pah! He was a charlatan, a swine before whom pearls were thrown, and with no more idea than a swine on how to cast a judgement of character. He was given the warning, yet he chose to ignore it, and he paid the price." An angry red mottling was beginning to creep rapidly across his chest, almost as if it was bleeding out from his cape, and his black eyes flared. "The tramp-major sodomised me; he sodomised me and any other orphaned boy who happened to come into the workhouse."

All at once he was on his feet.

Douglas stepped back.

"Steady there! I'm warning you, Esau, I—"

"By his own actions he condemned himself." Esau's voice boomed around the temple. "There was no need to determine his character because I already knew it; I knew it only too well. Gaspar gave me the spell-jar and I wrote his name. The curses were read, and they were sealed for all eternity."

"What is he talking about, Fox: curses, spell-jars?" Douglas barked.

"I understand that in what they called *ceremonies of execration*, Egyptian priests would ritually mark a clay vessel with the name of the condemned before chanting death-spells over it. The jar would then be broken to ensure the curses could never be undone and only then would the victim be executed and beheaded with a knife."

Atticus kicked his heel in frustration and the hob-nails threw up an orange spark from the marble. "But I knew that. I knew it, and I should have made the connections sooner."

"You say we will be hanged for our actions." Esau stabbed his finger towards Douglas. "Yet your own Bible calls for such sinners to be put to death. Are not lips that speak falsehood an abomination to the Lord? Is not also a man who would lie with mankind as he might with a woman?"

"The Bible calls also for mercy," Lucie countered, "It tells us that God alone is our judge and that He has created everyone in His image. You must know that, Hermes."

"I know only that the Bible is but one of many sacred teachings, each incomplete in itself, each showing but one constituent colour of the pure, white light that is the Universal Truth. Progressive revelation and Gaspar have explained it to me. You see, Lucie Fox: *I* am the Truth and *I* am the judge of all mankind."

"Leeds Assizes already has a perfectly good judge of its own, thank you all the same," returned Douglas. "For now, I'll thank you to leave that skull where it is and show me your wrists. You said 'us' in connection with the murders and mentioned the name of Gaspar, so I'll take it he's your accomplice. After that you are going to tell us exactly where Mr Malkin's coachman is, and also where we might find his daughter Alice." He threw a menacing glance at the skull. "And for your sake, she had better not have been harmed."

Esau held out his arms obediently and said: "Alice, as you call her, although it would seem to me that my name for her was the more correct, is very much alive and presently with John Oates and Gaspar in the Hall of Two Truths."

"Thank heaven! That's some good news at least," breathed Lucie.

"No!" Atticus cried, "It isn't good news. It isn't a bit of it. The Hall of Two Truths is where the dead are taken for judgement."

At that instant, the temple doors swept open and Hainsworth burst in, sweat beading his forehead and a drift of white powder dusting the front of his tunic.

"The house has all been searched, sir. There's no end of heathen paraphernalia about the place but no sign of Gaspar or the missing…"

He broke off, transfixed by the grisly sight of the skull at Esau's feet.

"Well search it again then," Douglas snapped. "That is Victoria Malkin's skull; Alice Malkin and the coachman are still alive, thank God, but in the company of Gaspar in somewhere called the Hall of Two Truths. Hermes here, as he likes to call himself now, was about to tell us where that is."

Esau sank once more to the floor. He crossed his legs and stared up into the oculus above Hainsworth's head.

"I was about to do nothing of the sort."

"Then I'll thrash it out of you, damn you," Douglas snarled and Esau threw back his head and laughed, showing two full lines of his black, vulcanised gums.

"Do as you will, Inspector; I am quite used to thrashings, although my disciples may find them rather more objectionable." He inclined his head towards the Eye. "And they will know."

"In that case you can come down to Raglan Street, where you can be under the all-seeing eye of the custody-sergeant. Your disciples won't be able to help you there."

"I am, however, willing to speak with Atticus Fox."

Douglas grabbed the back of Esau's red cape and hauled him to his feet.

"I am the senior officer here," he roared, "and you can bloody-well speak to me."

CHAPTER FORTY-SEVEN

As Above, so also Below.

Alice Malkin is dreaming. It is a horrible, fearful dream, just exactly like the ones she had when she was a little girl, when she would run, screaming, to her papa.

'Nightmare', her papa would say to her then, as he hugged her and patted her hand, 'It's only a nightmare'.

She knows that this is only a nightmare, but, try as she might, she can't escape. She can't make herself wake from it; she can't make herself be at home, safe under the covers of her own warm bed.

In this nightmare, she has been entombed, buried alive in solid rock. The vicar at the Christ Church, Reverend Fawkes, had been preaching a sermon about Jacob's flight from his brother and about the dream he had had of a ladder: Jacob's ladder, the stairway to Heaven. The sermon seemed to drag on forever, and so, under her breath, she had whispered: 'Oh for God's sake, do be quiet!' and instantly regretted it. But then, when the dream moved on, she had found herself descending that very same ladder into the darkness below.

And now she is trapped.

Her head is splitting with pain, and the lights she can see in front of her keep swimming in and out of focus. Her mouth is dry, so very dry that she cannot even move her tongue. She cannot cry out for her papa to please come and help her, to tell her that all of this really is just a fearful, fearful nightmare.

In her dream she is awake now, and the lights are still. It occurs to her that there aren't five lights shining in front of her after all, but one. The others are mere reflections in the walls, the floor and the roof of this place. It occurs to her also how real this dream is, how incredibly vivid. She must make sure to remember all of it when she wakes. It would make the most wonderful tale of horror, perhaps as good even as Mrs Shelley's novel *Frankenstein*, which she keeps tucked under her pillow.

With that thought, a word comes to her, which she can use in her story of this dream. It is mausoleum.

In her dream, Alice turns her head and gazes about. Yes, mausoleum would be the perfect word to use for this place with its lustrous black walls, its single flickering lamp, and its coffin. She recognises the coffin. It is an Egyptian sarcophagus, just like the ones she has been learning about in her school lessons. How surprising, and how thrilling! She must, she really must, remember every single detail when she wakes.

But this is a nightmare, a terrifying, fearful nightmare, and it must never be thrilling.

Beyond the sarcophagus, beside the flickering light, Alice begins to make out a shape. She blinks and peers again. Yes, there is definitely something there. It is the cross-legged figure of a man… or is it a woman? Its right arm is raised and its left hangs down. And yes, it has a cross, like a church cross or a crusader's, on its chest. And then, just as the oil runs dry, as the lamp suddenly flares and dies, she sees its head, which is a goat's and the great, spreading wings at its back.

In her dream, Alice Malkin screams and screams and screams.

CHAPTER FORTY-EIGHT

"I am the Frankenstein in all of this, Atticus; I am the wretched Prometheus, who has succeeded only in bringing down calamity upon us all."

Joseph struggled with himself for a moment.

"What have I done? Upon my word! What have I done?"

"You have done nothing, Joseph and I am so sorry because it is we who have failed you." Even as he spoke the words, Atticus felt the cold steel of truth in them. He had failed his oldest friend in the very field he and Lucie had chosen as their own, that of privately-commissioned investigation.

"Joseph, you couldn't have known he would be found by these people," said Lucie, "nor that they would seek to make him into this Hermes what's-his-name."

"Trismegistus," Atticus reminded her.

Joseph closed his eyes tight and began to rock to-and-fro on his seat, as once Esau was wont to do.

"You won't allow Gaspar to murder Alice too, will you? Please, not her; she is so young and innocent. And now," he slumped forward and sank his face into his hands, "now, she is all I have."

"We will do our utmost to find her, Joseph, you know we will," said Lucie.

Joseph nodded.

"And I do forgive them, Lucie Fox; I do, even as the good Lord councils we must. It's just that I cannot stop imagining what they might be doing with her. These people have the power and the impunity to do anything. I mean, if they have murdered even Victoria, what else might they do?"

"I believe that Alice is in no mortal danger," Atticus said.

Joseph glanced up, his eyes as round and shining as a Harvest Moon. "Do you? But how can you know that, Atticus?"

"It was just something Esau said to Inspector Douglas in the temple. He said that his – Esau's – name for Alice was the correct one."

"Mary Magdalene, do you mean? But it's preposterous."

"Perhaps so, Joseph, but not to Rosicrucian adepts. Mary Magdalene will be as important to them as St John the Baptist. They will be inclined to believe the words of their new-found god that that is who she really is."

"But she's no more Mary Magdalene than I am. They'll discover that for themselves sooner or later, and when they do, they will murder her for a certainty. They will cut her beautiful, innocent head off."

"I think otherwise, Joseph." There was steel in Atticus' tone now. "You must trust my word and you must remain strong for her. We are so very sorry to have brought you this terrible news but we wanted to tell you ourselves, before the police did. Now, we must beg your leave; Lucie and I can serve you best today by finding your daughter."

"Nothing, Mr and Mrs Fox, Esau has told us nothing at all."

Detective Sergeant Hainsworth pounded the top of his little desk in fury. They had never seen him so angry.

"He refuses. He knows he's going to the gallows whatever happens. This Gaspar may have their heads and whatever else of them he chooses and be damned to us, begging your pardon, Mrs Fox. He sits there, with his legs crossed like a child at Sunday school, just as cool as you please." He hesitated. "And that's in spite of the inspector losing his patience and taking five minutes with him with the door locked, if you take my meaning."

"Is Mr Douglas with him now?" Lucie asked.

"No, a top brass came up from Wakefield – from headquarters. He's taken him off in a cab somewhere."

"Then may we try in his stead?"

"It is possible we may have more success than the inspector's fists and threats," Atticus added.

"Threats, Mr Fox, threats? I don't believe Esau could seem less threatened if he were sitting in an armchair, drinking a mug of bed-time cocoa." Hainsworth gnawed on a fingernail as he considered their request. "Very well, we're getting nowhere at present so I suppose I have little option. Speak with him if you wish, but be sure to communicate any information he may give you directly back to me."

Mr Hainsworth had been quite correct in his appraisement of Esau. Sitting, cross-legged, on one of a pair of wooden cots that lined opposite walls of his cell, and even with one side of his mouth badly swollen and crusted in blood, he showed not one atom of distress. On the contrary, he might have been holding court.

"Welcome, Atticus Fox and welcome to you too, Lucie Fox. I thank you both for coming." Esau smoothed the front of his washed-out prison jacket and cast a glance to the cell walls with their covering of blue and white tiles.

"I must apologise for receiving you here. Please sit on that cot. Thank you. It is far from being as comfortable as the drawing room of Sun Villa or your own parlour, but as none of us will be here for very long, that is of small consequence."

"Do you mean you expect to be hanged, Hermes?" Atticus asked, regardfully using Esau's preferred name.

Esau seemed puzzled by his question. "Not at all, I mean there is not a prison cell in the Empire that could keep me. I have remained here only long enough to speak with you, Atticus Fox."

"Then I'm obliged to you. Do you intend telling us where Gaspar is keeping Miss Malkin prisoner?"

"Perhaps."

"Please do, Hermes," Lucie urged him, "Poor Joseph Malkin is almost beside himself with worry."

Esau's black eyes remained fixed on her for several seconds after she had stopped speaking. He was plainly deep in thought. Then he turned towards Atticus and said: "You have not yet properly replied to the question I put to you regarding your past. It is clear that we are alike in many ways and I am curious to know why that should be. If you tell me, and if you hold back nothing, then I, in turn, will give you enough information to enable you to find Mary Magdalene, or Alice Malkin as you choose to call her. Tit for tat, move for move, just as in the game of chess.”

“This is no game and I am nothing at all like you.”

For a second time that day, Atticus Fox was obliged to acknowledge an uncomfortable burden of truth. Esau was right and they both – indeed they all – knew it. But for the grace of God and the patient devotion of a nursing-sister, he, Atticus Fox, could be sitting on that prison cot wearing those very same broad-arrows. Esau was too clever, altogether too wise, to be fobbed off by denials and protestations, and if the theory that was beginning to rise up and take hellish form in his mind was correct, time, like the inexorable swinging of Foucault’s pendulum, was already turning against Alice Malkin.

“Very well, Hermes,” he said, “Move for move, just as in chess. We have a bargain.”

Esau nodded in satisfaction. “You had little choice, in truth. So, Atticus Fox, I ask you again: Have you ever been in a retreat?”

“No, I never have.” Atticus inhaled deeply, conscious that he must hold back nothing. “Although I sometimes wish that I had. I was incarcerated for a time, not in a retreat, but in an asylum – the West Riding Pauper Lunatic Asylum at Wakefield.”

“I knew it! You were sent to the asylum.”

Esau clapped his hands together in triumph, and perhaps in glee. "I have heard of it, of course. Some of the workhouse inmates were sent there – to Stanley Royd – the ones too mad for the infirmary. Were you too mad for the infirmary too, Atticus Fox? Were you born in a workhouse?"

"I… I… Those are two questions," Atticus blurted. "We made a bargain, Hermes; question for question, move for move, just as in chess. Now it is my turn to ask you."

He hesitated, waiting for the other's protestations; Esau held by far the stronger position, after all. When they did not come, he said: "You told us that Mary Magdalene – the name you called Miss Malkin by – was the better name for her. Do you still believe her to be the Mary Magdalene of the gospels? And I'm wondering if Gaspar has a better name for her still? Might he perhaps call her Aphrodite?"

Esau considered. With his god's mind, he noted that Atticus too had just asked a double question, but then he recalled that a two-square advance was Atticus' customary opening move in chess. Graciously, he decided to allow it.

"I have told you already that the Bible is just one of many truths that make up the whole."

Atticus nodded, "The whole, the *prisca theologia.*"

"Yes, the *prisca theologia,* the one true religion. So it should not surprise you that those written of in the Bible are also written of elsewhere. Just as the Trinity of Christendom is the Osiris, Horus and Isis of Egypt, so yes, Alice Malkin is St Mary Magdalene, who in turn is Hathor, the Egyptian Goddess of Love, whom the Greeks called Aphrodite."

"I know that Miss Malkin fits the physical descriptions of St Mary and Aphrodite," Atticus conceded, "And that she is the very image of the statue at the leper chapel, but that is nothing more than coincidence."

"Mr Fox and I have known her since she was a little girl," Lucie added, "and Alice Malkin is most assuredly not a goddess."

"As I was once no god?"

Esau shifted forward on his cot.

"Now it is my move, and my question is the same as before: Were you born in a workhouse, Atticus Fox?"

Atticus shook his head.

"I was born at home – at our family house in Gateshead, which is a manufacturing town, eighty miles or so to the north of here. It was Friday, 6th October 1854. That was also the night of the Great Conflagration, which destroyed much of the town. My own father was called Joseph too, Hermes, and he was killed that morning."

"How was he killed? Do you know? Do you remember?"

Atticus nodded. He knew all too well, although he had never truly been sure whether the vignettes, which had harrowed and tortured his mind since childhood, were real or whether he had read so many accounts of the terrible inferno that they had become rooted as part of his own terrible imaginings. But memory or fancy, here again, even in this prison cell, he could smell, he could even taste the sulphur as it burned with its lurid blue flames. Once again, the air was filled with the shrieks of the victims as one by one they succumbed to the hell.

Atticus felt the touch of Lucie's hand on his wrist and he said: "When word of the fire first came, my father went up to Bensham, to check on a particular building there. It was in no danger so he continued up towards the middle of town, to see if he could offer any assistance there. Hillgate was where the flames were fiercest so Hillgate is where he went.

"Do you know what happens with fires of that magnitude, Hermes? No? Then I shall tell you. They become great, insatiable monsters, drawing in everything around them, even the very air itself. That is what happened to my father. One instant he was running to fill a pair of fire-buckets, the next he was swept up by the fire-winds and pitched into the very heart of the inferno. They found his diary two days later, scorched and charred, a full six miles away."

Through the roar of the flames Atticus heard Esau ask: "And what of your mother?"

"The architect John Dobson sent word later that morning that my father had been killed. His son was also missing, also killed, as it later transpired. My mother… My mother was so distressed by the news, and by the shock of the great explosion which followed the fire, that it put her into labour and I was born shortly afterward on our parlour floor. Father's death destroyed her. She couldn't bear to remain in Gateshead surrounded by all the memories of him, and so she eventually sold the house and moved us south, to Yorkshire, where some of my father's family were.

"She went into decline and quickly fell to liquor. When she could no longer afford her fine wines and absinthe, she took to gin. When even that could no longer provide solace, she threw herself under the wheels of a railway engine. I was the one to find her."

Esau was watching him intently as he spoke, and at that, the tiniest shadow might have passed behind his eyes.

"How old were you when you found her?" he asked.

"It was the day before my fourteenth birthday."

Another shadow, deeper, perhaps, than the first, bloomed and faded in the black depths and Esau said: "It is your move, Atticus Fox."

Atticus nodded, spent now, and sick to the bones with this game. He asked: "Where can we find this Hall of Two Truths?"

Esau threw back his head and roared with laughter. The sounds bounced back and forth between the tiles of the cell and became the cachinnation of an ape.

"But we cannot go directly to the end-game, Atticus Fox. No, no, that wouldn't do at all. This is a game of chess and it needs to be properly played as such. Surely you, of all people, must know that. All I shall give you is an opening, on a board that is not a board, and you may deduce from that how the Hall might be found. Anything less would be unworthy of both of us."

He shifted his position on his thin straw mattress, smoothed his jacket, and sat up straight and tall, like an orator about to deliver a grand speech.

"Atticus Fox and Lucie Fox, you should apply your minds to this: With the magical eye you must see, where the four orders combine to make one. There you will find the means to its location."

Atticus sensed his wife's gaze on him. She was right of course. The riddle, if riddle Esau intended it to be, seemed ridiculously easy.

"Now it is my turn again," Esau went on. "Tell me; for how long were you at the asylum?"

Atticus knew they should go, now, this instant – that they should fly up to the Hermetic Temple of the Golden Light in Harrogate and its All-Seeing Eye. But he could not. He was locked into telling his tale, as he had once told it, again and again, to one Lucie Pearson and she had been compassionate enough to listen.

"It was for a full two years of my life, Hermes, from my twenty-first to my twenty-third year, a good part of it locked in a cell, restrained and regularly electrified."

Atticus' gaze drifted past Esau, to the chequered tiles of the cell wall, and as it did, so the long years unravelled. There were tiles then too, tile after tile after tile that would merge and shift and conjure themselves into fire-dragons, and bloodied corpses and shrieking engines of death.

"Life had become too much for me, you see? I had begun to see things, terrifying things, which weren't really there."

"Breathe slowly, Atticus," Lucie reminded him, as she had reminded him then.

"Mrs Fox was a nurse there – at Stanley Royd. This was long before we were married and she, above any of the other nurses, was very kind to us, to the inmates. It was she who first introduced me to the game of chess as a way of distracting me and helping me to focus my mind away from the things that had happened. It was she who nursed me back to sanity. My cousin, Samson Fox, arranged for me to be moved to the Bath Hospital here in Harrogate to complete my recovery, and she moved there too. Samson also turned up a previously overlooked legacy from my mother and that enabled us to buy Number 16, Prospect Place and to stay in the town with its calm air and its beneficial waters."

"Then like Ma'at, the Goddess of Truth and Harmony, Lucie Fox has put order into your life, where before there was only chaos. I see that. Now, you may ask me one final question. Take my word that the girl is alive and in good health."

In the event it was Lucie who asked it.

"What does Gaspar intend for her?"

"He intends to raise her up, Lucie Fox, and restore her to her rightful place in the pantheon of gods. As a high priest, he will guide her in certain rites, which he calls rites of the flesh. We have already entered her month of Hethara and her festival, the *Venus Genetrix* is almost upon us."

"When is that held? On which day?" Atticus demanded.

"Very well, I will allow you that. *Venus Genetrix* is properly held each September the 26th."

Lucie gasped. "But that's tomorrow!"

"Tomorrow begins at midnight," Esau reminded her. "Today is the fourth day of the new moon, four being the number sacred to Hermes – to me. Tomorrow is the festival, so midnight tonight will be the conjunction of those two days, as it will also be the time of the conjunction of Mary, Gaspar…" He grinned, showing his shining, porcelain teeth, "…and me."

CHAPTER FORTY-NINE

"There it is, Atticus: the All-Seeing Eye of Horus."

The Sun had long-since passed over the domed carapace of Gaspar's temple, and the oculus that Lucie pointed to was darkened against the white limestone around it like the staring, black eye-socket of a skull.

The temple doors, thankfully, were unlocked and the interior exactly as they had left it – could it really have been in the small hours of that very same day? There was the altar, still draped in the emerald-green cloth, with the four embroidered symbols emblazoned across the face of it.

Lucie turned to look up at the Eye, dark no longer, but awakened and bright now with menace.

"*With the magical eye you must see.*" she recited. Her finger traced its line of sight down to the altar, "*Where the four orders combine to make one.* Those were his words, weren't they, Atticus?"

"His words exactly," her husband replied.

"The rose, the square-and-compass, the Caduceus and the… what did you call it again?"

"The Baphomet."

"Yes, and that. Those are the symbols of the four orders aren't they?"

Atticus nodded grimly. "The Rosicrucian, the Masonic, the Hermetic and the Templar."

"There you will find the means to its location."

They walked together across the temple floor, smooth and white as a skating pond other than for its curious pattern, and stopped before the altar. Was this why Esau's opening move had been so easy – because the next would be just as unfathomable? Or was it a gambit, some form of trap?

"You may deduce from that how the Hall might be found. You may deduce from that…"

Lucie pressed her lips together and surveyed the enigmatic array of sacred artefacts.

"So the answer has to be here – somewhere."

"Then what can we see?" Atticus asked.

"A green silk cloth," Lucie began.

"Emerald green, to represent the colour of papyrus and the fabled emerald writing tablet of Hermes Trismegistus."

"There are the four symbols of the orders," Lucie continued.

She pointed to the three golden figurines standing on the altar top. "And the statuettes of Thoth, Hermes and Astennu, together with a little stack of gold coins."

Atticus grunted. "The three principal manifestations of Hermes, together with the vulgar gold of man. Above those is what is called a Rosy Cross – the symbol of Rosicrucianism. Within that, we see a veritable rash of glyphs and symbols related to all four orders… It becomes a little harder now."

"Do you recognise any of those symbols, Atty?"

"Individually, of course, but the meaning of the whole will be exceedingly complex. Let me see now: At the centre, there is a representation of a rose. The rose can be symbolic of Mary Magdalene. This is Rosicrucian, however; it surrounds a second, smaller cross, again with the rose at its own centre. That is man as a microcosm of the whole, which is the 'Above', or the macrocosm. *As Above, so also Below,* says the Hermetic axiom. There are twenty-two petals on the rose, which are the twenty-two paths of the Qabalah, but again, I cannot see how that helps us."

"Go on, Atticus," Lucie prompted.

"Very well. The four arms of the cross are coloured for the four classical elements of earth, fire, air and water. Each arm also carries the symbols for the alchemical Primes of sulphur, mercury and salt." Atticus' pointing finger darted quickly around the reredos.

Lucie asked: "And what about the stars; do they have meanings?" Each arm carried a five-pointed pentagram, and there was a single six-pointed hexagram below the central rose. "You say that Gaspar is a magus. Weren't the magi of the Bible supposedly led by a star to Bethlehem? Could this Rosy Cross be some kind of a map?"

It was an excellent suggestion and Atticus considered it at length.

"The pentagram in this form can represent many things, Lucie: the five virtues of knighthood; the four classical elements plus the heavenly element of quintessence, or it can be a depiction of man. Do you see; there are two legs, two arms and a head uppermost?

"The hexagram might be of more interest to us, however. It is known as the Seal of Solomon – Solomon being the king of the Old Testament. See how it is formed from two interlocking triangles, one with its apex uppermost and the other pointing downward? It is the representation of the universal Hermetic principle I mentioned in connection with the rose: *As Above, so also Below*, and so itself becomes the conjunction of those two opposites."

Atticus jabbed the tip of his cane against the floor in frustration. "In the hexagram, the four orders could be said to combine but how that might help us to find this infernal hall, I cannot say."

"So what else is there?"

"I really haven't a… No, wait! These Rosy Crosses sometimes have inscriptions on the reverse."

"Atticus – that must be it! *A board that is not a board*, Esau said, and look, the Rosy Cross is painted onto a *wooden board*."

The green-painted reredos that formed the background to the cross, and to the sacred triangle beneath it, was indeed fashioned from a single, broad panel of wood. The tree from which it was cut must have been truly immense. Lucie skirted the altar table and began to examine it, methodically and in minute detail. Her fingers worked their way busily towards its edge, close to where it was set into the marble of the wall, and froze. She pushed against it; the surface depressed a fraction; something clicked below her fingertips and then the whole body of the reredos drifted open to reveal a deep black void.

"Alice!" Lucie cried and peered inside.

"There's no one here – but there are some words written on the back."

"What do they say?" Atticus called.

"It's difficult to tell; it's so dark in here. Let me see now." She leaned deeper into the cavity and her voice became suddenly resonating and otherworldly. "'The Will of the Brethren shall be the Whole of the Law.' That's queer; what does it mean?"

"It is both a reminder and a warning. It means that the orders and their adherents, whoever they might be, need answer only to themselves."

Lucie slipped from sight, climbing up bodily into the chamber.

"There's nothing else," she called out after a moment, "and anyway, it's only a tiny compartment, like a pantry or a priest's hole, hardly what you'd call a hall of anything."

She squeezed back out and brushed a cobweb from her shoulder.

"We need to try something else, Atticus. So, again now, from the beginning: *With the magical eye, you must see, where the four orders combine to make one. There you will find the means to its location.*"

Lucie stared up once more into the Eye. The colours were beginning to fade now, where the gathering dusk was darkening the sky beyond it into twilight.

"With the magical eye you must see, Atticus. So, we must see *with* it. We need to actually look *through* the oculus. That must be it. There might be – I don't know – hidden marks or something, in the glass."

"Yes, that's possible – that's very possible." Atticus turned to gaze up at it too. "But how are we to get up there?"

"I saw apple trees in the garden," said Lucie.

"So did I, now I recollect. They didn't look as if they've been pruned in years, but then Gaspar likely uses them for mistletoe."

"So there must be a ladder somewhere, which he uses to cut it."

Lucie's eduction proved correct. The apple orchard of Sun Villa comprised several large and sprawling apple trees, and with these was a gardener's bothy, full of all manner of tools and implements. It might have belonged to any one of the large villas that stepped their way down towards the middle of town, other than in one respect: Beneath a skylight, in the middle of its floor, and resting across two stout trestles such as a carpenter might use, was a mummy case. It was very similar to that they had seen standing in the passageway of the house just a few days before, although lacking, perhaps, the impression of great antiquity possessed by the other.

"This is linden – lime-wood – and made very recently," Atticus said to Lucie as they stood regarding it. He touched his finger to the thick timber sides. "Do you see? This linseed oil hasn't even properly dried yet."

"But made for what purpose, Atticus?" Lucie asked, "For an ornament?"

Atticus set his jaw and pointed to the head of the case. Here, the face of a man was depicted in the Egyptian style, with a blue-and-gold *Nemes* headdress and kohl-rimmed eyes. In place of the narrow, braided beard so favoured by the ancients, the effigy had a set of full, red whiskers. Below this and across its chest, a particular glyph also caught Lucie's attention so that as she made sense of it, she cried out in dismay.

For it was the representation of a fox.

Far too many of their precious seconds had trickled away before they could force their minds once more onto the task in hand. When they did, they found that there was indeed a set of three-legged orchard ladders laid across the roof joists of the bothy, and it was the work of only a moment for Atticus to slide them down. They were sturdy and very tall, and with Atticus footing them, Lucie was able to climb easily up to the temple's oculus and the All-Seeing Eye of Horus.

Sergeant Hainsworth had told them there would be a constable here – somewhere in this house or garden. By coincidence it was the red-headed Billy Watts, who, as part of his light convalescent duties, had been detailed to guard it against Gaspar's return. With a bitter chuckle, Hainsworth had remarked that, after his recent experience, Watts would likely be much gladder for their presence than ever they could be for his. Given that, and given what lay in the bothy yonder, Atticus made sure to keep his eyes watchful and his cane gripped, ready, in his fist.

"Do you see aught, Lucie?" he called up the rungs.

There were one, two heartbeats before she replied.

"Nothing, Atty, it's too dark in there to see anything."

"In that case, hold on tightly; I'll see if lighting the altar candles will help."

The flames of twenty-two candles, eleven on each of the lamp-stands and one for each pathway of the Hermetic Qabalah, served both to light the brilliantly white interior of the temple and to illuminate the stained glass of the oculus very effectively indeed. But Lucie, even with her remarkably keen vision, could see nothing, either through the All-Seeing Eye of Horus or within its glass, which even remotely resembled a means to their finding the mysterious Hall of Two Truths.

"You had better take a look, Atticus" she called down at last, frustration hardening her tone. The lines and colours of the glass were projected across her face like some two-shilling lantern show. "You might have a better idea as to what we're looking for."

Atticus Fox clung to the ridiculously spindly timbers of the orchard ladder and peered through the Eye. He hardly dared to move; the ladder had just three legs and it swayed alarmingly every time he did. It was all too easy to imagine it toppling, and hurling him down onto the big flagstones below.

Very slowly, he turned his head and glanced down at his wife's face peering back up at him, her smile of encouragement confuted by the deep concern in her eyes. He noticed then that one of the ladder's feet was perilously close to the black, Plutonic slots of a heavy iron grid, and his guts lurched again as he pictured it slipping and falling through.

Atticus closed his eyes and waited for the sensation to pass. In his mind however, the image of the grid, with a stylised letter 'H' at its centre, persisted. It seemed disconcertingly familiar.

But from where?

Atticus did not need to search far in his memory to find the answer. He had seen that letter many times before, and in an identical setting – at Beagle House. It was the mark for the architect, Monsieur Prêtre. But then, perhaps that was not so very surprising. After all, this place must have been designed by someone, and what was it Joseph Malkin had said? That Gerard Prêtre had designed many a fine steeple-house in his time, and a number of temples – for the Freemasons and others.

For the Freemasons.

Atticus Fox has only ever been inside two Masonic lodges. One was at Harrogate – a guided tour by Samson – and the other was a particular building in Bensham. They had very different exteriors but were, in other respects, identical. The floors in particular were laid from the same black and white tiles, arranged like a chessboard. This temple has deep Masonic connections too, but its floor…

Its floor!

"A board that is not a board," he whispered aloud, and with his words, a great rolling wave of realisation almost rocked him from his rung, and he had to grasp at the oculus and cling to the stone.

"What was that you said?" Lucie called up.

"Lucie, Esau said that he would give us an opening, on a board that is not a board. And he told us to see with the magical eye, where the four orders combine. He didn't say to look with the Eye of Horus, or with the All Seeing Eye, or any of that; he said with the *magical* eye."

"So what did he mean?"

Atticus let go the stonework and rung-by-rung, hand-by-hand, descended the ladder. As he did so, he looked through the doorway, to the temple floor and its curious progression of rectangles and squares.

'An opening, on a board that is not a board, where the four orders combine to make one.' Yes, yes of course, it had to be!

His reaching toe touched on solid ground.

"It's the temple floor, Lucie."

Atticus closed his eyes and this time he reached deep into his memory.

"The Eye of Horus was also used in ancient Egypt in mathematics, as a way to divide up unity, by which I mean the number one. If I recollect correctly, and I am certain that I do, it works like this: If the whole of the eye is one, the inner part of the eye represents the value of one half. Look there, the largest marble slab covers exactly one half of the temple floor. The pupil was one quarter, and again, do you see, the next largest slab is a quarter. One eighth was the eyebrow."

As he recounted, Atticus' finger traced the pattern of slabs across the temple.

"The outer part of the eye was one sixteenth; the tail of kohl beneath the eye one thirty-second and the teardrop one sixty-fourth. Which leaves, Lucie, one sixty-fourth remaining, does it not?"

"If you say so, Atticus."

"In mythology, the gods Seth and Horus were constantly at war. Eventually Seth, the God of Disorder, succeeded in gouging out Horus' left eye. All but the very last fraction – one sixty-fourth – was restored by Thoth, with this portion supposedly being supplied *magically*. Esau said he was giving us an opening, on a board that is not a board, where the four orders combine *to make one*. Lucie, in the last, magical, part of the eye, all of these fractions do finally add up, do combine, to make the *number* one."

Atticus' gaze crept across the floor, towards the corner between the altar and the Qabalah, where the candlelight glistened on a golden hexagram set into the marble. It was a second Seal of Solomon.

"And that, Lucie," he said solemnly, "is the solution to the puzzle."

They ran together into the temple and stared down at the large, six-pointed star set into the perfectly square slab. They could see now that it was neither gold, nor a single star at all, but two polished brass triangles, fashioned carefully so as to fit, one over the other.

Atticus said: "Do you remember what I told you about Solomon's Seal, and how the four orders could be considered to combine there? Well then, here we have it."

He pointed.

"Two triangles together; one indicating that which is Above, the other, that which is Below. The Seal itself is the *Gnosis*, the alchemical conjunction, the *means* to both. So if my reasoning is correct…"

Lucie gasped. "Then the Hall of Two Truths is directly below us."

"Yes, it must be. Now I come to think on it, I knew the Egyptian Hall of Two Truths was in the *Duat*, their underworld, so I should have made the eduction sooner."

Atticus stamped on the square and under his boot, the floor rang hollow. He crouched and began to work his fingers under the edge of one of the brass triangles – that signifying the things Below. It came up easily and grasping it firmly, Atticus pulled on what had now become an ingenious handle. The marble square, precisely one sixty-fourth of the whole floor area, hinged upwards and revealed a deep, black abyss.

"Here is Esau's opening, Lucie," he cried triumphantly, "We assumed it must be the opening move to a battle of wits. And so it is. But it is a literal opening too."

CHAPTER FIFTY

"Miss Malkin," Lucie called into the darkness Below. "Alice, it's me: Lucie Fox. Are you there? Are you alive?"

A sound like a moan rose up in response. It might have come from a young woman, or it might not have been human at all.

Lucie waved a hand towards the nearest of the lamp-stands.

"Pass me a candle, Atticus, quickly."

Atticus tugged a candle from its socket, spilling a scalding crescent of wax over his wrist, and passed it to his wife. She plunged it down through the trapdoor, where the spluttering light seemed to be swallowed instantly by the dense blackness.

"There's a ladder down there, Atty."

Lucie rolled onto her belly and slid her legs down into the emptiness. There was a dull ring as her boots caught on an iron rung. She grimaced, and dropped from sight. Atticus grasped the strap of their investigations bag and scrambled down after her.

As Above, so also Below.

The room they found themselves in was a mirror image of the Hermetic temple Above, other than it was lined, not in white marble, but in lustrous black granite. And in place of a large and airy dome there was only a low ceiling, which reflected the candle flame so deeply within itself, it was difficult to know where the space ended and the polished rock began. It was as chill and as silent as a tomb.

Lucie lifted her candle up towards its mirror twin in the ceiling, and they stared around what must surely be the Hall of Two Truths.

To their right was the hulk of a sarcophagus, or perhaps of a large mummy case, open, but with an interior strangely without depth or shadow. Lamp-stands, with oil lamps in place of candles, stood at its head and toe. Against the wall opposite was an apothecary's rack, a duplicate of its twin, other than the black shelf below it carried not headdresses but what appeared to be an earthenware jar. Beneath that were two neat and distinct piles of pottery shards.

To their left was an immense balance-scale in polished yellow metal, brass perhaps, or conceivably even gold, with its two scale pans swaying gently on their chains.

"Look, Atticus, over yonder." Lucie inclined the candle forward and a string of wax spattered onto the floor. They squinted into the beckoning darkness, to where the fourth wall of the square should be. Beyond the stabbing light of the candle, a dark and menacing shape gathered and glowered unblinkingly back at them. It was a second Eye of Horus, this one black and utterly soulless. But wait! There was something else too. Beneath it, an object laid out across the floor like some votive offering, shifted and moved.

"Alice!" Lucie's cry was loud and harsh, and skitted mercilessly by the mocking chamber. The shape moved again and whimpered. Candlelight fell across a face. It was Alice Malkin, trussed and gagged and cast against the wall, but alive.

Lucie pushed the candle to Atticus and dropped down to her, pulling and working at the twisted strip of cloth bound tightly across her mouth.

"Alice, it's me; it's Lucie Fox. Mr Fox is here too. Are you hurt?"

The gag fell free and Alice shook her head.

"Unt—" She coughed and retched and a long, glistening loop stretched down from her lip. "Untie me! Get me out of here!" Her voice was husky and dissonant, as if in the short time she had been in this place, something of it had somehow suffused her.

"Alice, you're safe." Lucie lifted her so that she was sitting upright, and held her face. "You're quite safe now. I am going to cut these ropes away with Mr Fox's knife. It is extremely sharp and so you must try to be calm and very still."

Alice, wide-eyed, nodded.

Atticus laid his cane, hesitantly, onto the floor, unsure perhaps, whether its surface was real, or if it might be fluid and insubstantial. He pulled open his pocket-knife and passed it to his wife.

Alice coughed and then coughed again. "They think we're goddesses, Mrs Fox. That's what they said. I'm Aphrodite, and they think you might be… I… I can't recall her name. The Goddess of Order and Wisdom, I think they said."

"Ma'at," said Atticus.

"Yes, that's it — Ma'at. They aren't wholly sure yet, but they believe you could be. They say the gods are being brought together in readiness for the Golden Dawn and the beginning of something called the Age of Aquarius. Mrs Fox, you and I are to take part in fleshly rites and then I am to be married to that wild-man Esau, who was in the freak show. He calls himself Hermes now. He thinks that you, Mrs Fox, if you are Ma'at, are already married to him from a former life. He's as mad as a squirrel. They all are. If you resist him, or if it turns out that you aren't a goddess after all, you are to be killed. Mr Fox, you are to be killed whatever happens. They have already said the spells for you."

"Yes, I have already had the rather singular experience of inspecting my own funerary arrangements," said Atticus.

Alice wriggled an arm free from its rope binding and pointed towards the apothecary's rack.

"Do you see that clay pot? Esau said you were sure to have the most fascinating head. They are going to cut it off and mummify the rest of you. The other man, he's called Gaspar by-the-by, chanted things, horrible things, like incantations, and wrote them on the pot, along with your name. They said they will smash the pot at the festival tonight so that the magic is sealed forever."

"Did they indeed?" Atticus set his chin defiantly. "Well, I'm glad to tell you we've upset their little plot.

Gaspar has fled; Esau is in a prison-cell, and there is a police constable waiting inside the house at this very minute, guarding against their return."

"Where are we, Mr Fox? Where is this… house? I thought I was dreaming."

"This is no dream," Lucie assured her. "We are in a chamber beneath a temple, which is in the grounds of a house called Sun Villa, but not for very much longer."

Alice stared at her for several seconds while she tried to make sense of the words.

"Beneath a temple!" she repeated.

"A Hermetic temple, behind a house on Harlow Hill." Lucie smiled reassuringly and began to tug and saw at the remaining bonds. As she worked, Atticus turned to look more closely at this most curious of places – the Hall of Two Truths.

He had read of such halls, of course; where the ancient dead were taken for judgement, to hear their deeds pronounced by Thoth and to have their hearts weighed upon the scales of Ma'at. From here they could go on to *Aaru*, the Egyptian Heaven, or else be condemned to remain forever in the *Duat*, the realm of the dead.

To the adepts, this would be a true alchemical laboratory, the very place where the material body would be transmuted into spiritual light, and now they had the Great Alchemist himself: Hermes Trismegistus, the long sought-for and now rediscovered link between mankind and the high realm of the spirits.

Atticus inhaled deeply, and then frowned, and sniffed again.

"I can smell castor oil," he remarked.

"Yes I can too," Lucie replied from behind him. "I noticed it as soon as you lifted the hatch. It's stronger over there – by the sarcophagus."

Atticus made his way forward, snuffling like a bloodhound.

"It's coming from these lamp-stands, Lucie. Well, bless me! These lamps are filled to the brim with it. At least now we shall be able to see properly."

He fished his Vesta-case from his jacket and struck a match. As each wick was lit in turn, so the light grew steadily brighter. As in the temple Above, each stand carried eleven lamps. One of the lamp reservoirs was exhausted and empty, but the flames of the remaining twenty-one swelled and were reflected infinitely, *mise en abyme*[27], in the polished granite around them.

It was to Alice Malkin's credit that she did not scream at what this new light revealed. Perhaps it was her natural courage, or perhaps it was simply because she had seen it before – that form carved into the wall above the mummy-case. It was in a dream long ago, in which a lamp had flared and died and left its image forever seared into her mind. She did not scream, but she did tremble and stare, eyes agog, and cause Lucie to turn from her work.

"God's truth, Atticus, look at that!"

Atticus had bent to examine the mummy case, which, like its twin in the bothy, appeared to be of recent manufacture. Instead of carpenter's trestles however, this was set across two great granite blocks and filled almost to the brim with a coarse, pinkish-white powder. At his wife's cry he glanced up.

"It's the Baphomet!"

"The same as the symbol on the altar cloth?" Lucie was goggling as if she might have been beholding the Great Fiend himself. "What is it? And what does that writing beneath it mean?"

Immediately below the figure and carved similarly in shallow relief was a line of block capitals.

'TERRIBILIS EST LOCUS ISTE'.

"It's from the Bible," Atticus said after a moment, "from the Old Testament and Jacob's dream of the Stairway to Heaven. It means in Latin: 'Terrible is this place'."

He hesitated.

"And as to *what* it is, Lucie: the Baphomet depicts the great opposing forces of Nature – male and female; Above and Below; darkness and light, and so on – and their coming together in a union of perfection. It is a representation of Hermes Trismegistus himself, in his aspect as the Great Alchemist."

"But why would they have that here and not the Rosy Cross, the same as they have in the temple? As Above, so also Below – isn't that how it works with these people?"

"They have it because this is the underworld. It lies, not Above, nor Below, but at their conjunction. It is a place fit only for the gods and for the dead and we need to be away from here."

"Yes, we do!"

Lucie dropped back to her work and began to saw frantically at the remaining bonds. "I'm almost there now;

there are just the leg ropes to cut through and then we can be gone."

"Hurry, please," Alice begged.

Below the looming presence of the Baphomet, the burning lamps revealed also the full glory of the glyphs which decorated the sides of the mummy case. One of these – a pictograph of a salamander surrounded by licking tongues of fire – was particularly striking. Like the fox of his own, this would surely betray some clue as to the identity of the unfortunate for whom the case had been fashioned. One of their own, Atticus reflected, as he gazed thoughtfully down at it, or perhaps an enemy they wished, if not to honour, then at least to acknowledge?

He cupped his hand into the curious powder, shimmering and sparkling now in the lamplight, and rubbed its tiny crystals gently between his fingertips.

"This is natron," he said, and when Lucie did not reply, "It was used to desiccate and mummify corpses in ancient Egypt."

He scooped up a full handful of the powder and examined it in his palm. "But intended for whom, I wonder?" As he pondered the question and studied again the salamander hieroglyph, he noticed something; a shadow or a slightly darker shape, buried just below the surface.

It was just as Lucie sliced through the very last of Alice's bonds that she heard her husband's cry. She sprang to her feet, pocket-knife in hand, and ran to him.

Atticus was standing, staring into the open top of the mummy-case. There, a pair of grotesque, grey-white objects, long and curled and slightly shrivelled, lay exposed in the hollow left by his hand.

"Human fingers!" said Lucie.

Atticus nodded. He knew it already. Those were clearly human fingernails at their tips, after all.

Lucie took the fingers and lifted them, as gently and firmly as if she might have been inviting some bashful suitor onto a ballroom floor. First a hand and then a lean, scaly arm emerged from the surface.

Atticus shied back. "It's Inspector Douglas."

"How can you know that?"

"Because Hainsworth told us that Douglas was taken off by some unnamed senior officer in a cab. And because I remember that the crest of the Douglas coat-of-arms is a *salamander in fire*."

Lucie regarded the pallid, wiry limb hanging from her fingers. "Well this body isn't long dead, Atticus; algor-mortis hasn't quite finished and the limb isn't cold. Are you quite sure it's Mr Douglas? Hasn't he much thicker arms than this, and black hair on the back of his hands?"

A sudden, chill waft of air blew through the chamber and another voice – Gaspar's – hissed as if from the very granite of the walls.

"Checkmate, Mr Fox."

There was a clash of shattering glass and then a single, thunderous, echoing report as the trapdoor above them slammed shut.

"No!"

Atticus leaped onto the iron ladder, pummelling and heaving up on the single white square above it.

"Ether!" Lucie shrieked.

A tangle of broken glass lay directly below the hatch, and a wet and shining slick was beginning to spread out steadily across the floor. Lucie, her hand clamping her mouth, screamed: "It's ether. Don't you smell it?"

"I can." It was Alice. "It's that sweet smell again. It was in my dream."

"It's sweet oil of vitriol, Atticus – an anaesthetic. Gaspar is trying to put us all to sleep."

"Sweet oil of vitriol? But the lamps, and the candle! Remember Sarah? Ether is damned near explosive!"

He bounded from the ladder, slipped, and caught himself on the mummy case. It jerked and shifted on its blocks and the dead arm inside twitched horribly in its natron bed.

"We need to cover it. Use the natron. As quickly as we can."

They worked frantically, bailing fistful after fistful of the powder onto the creeping slick. Swiftly, it was done and the ether was smothered. They had neither succumbed to its spreading vapours nor, miraculously, had they caught alight.

"How long would it have been before we were overcome?" Atticus was gasping heavily. It may have been from his efforts, or the inhalation of ether vapours, or it might have been that he had glimpsed what lay in the mummy-case beside him, which was the white and naked torso of a man, unburied now, with all but the head exposed.

"Fifteen, twenty, five-and-twenty minutes, I suppose." Lucie was panting too. "But honestly, I'm just guessing." She tugged at his arm. "Atty, come; we need to stand over by Alice, next to the Eye. The air is fresher there."

Atticus, frowning in thought, allowed himself to be led away. "So that's when we can expect Gaspar, and lord knows who else, to come for us. There's not a second to be lost in our escape."

"But how can we?" Alice's sharp retort carried the full measure of her anger and despair. "We're underground, and those walls are solid rock. There is no way out, except through that trapdoor."

"There most assuredly will be a way," said Atticus, "All we have to do is to discover it."

He stroked pensively at the whiskers of his chin and turned slowly around, scrutinising and considering everything in the room: Alice's bonds, still lying where they had been cut away; the apothecary's rack – yes, there might be something there that could aid them; the twin lamp-stands; the great scales of Ma'at; the Eye of Horus…

The Eye!

"Lucie, you're right; the air *is* fresher over here."

When neither Lucie nor Alice responded, he explained: "But don't you see? It shouldn't be. It should be stale and stuffy, especially with Miss Alice having been down here for so long with the trapdoor shut."

Lucie all at once understood.

"So the air must somehow communicate with the outside."

"Precisely so." Atticus picked up the candle, still burning by their feet, and blew out the flame. A thin stream of smoke rose immediately from the wick, and was drawn steadily to one side. He followed it, the most unlikely of capnomancers, as it led him in the direction of the black Eye of Horus.

For here it was indeed black. It was wrought in iron and set without glass or colour, not into an oculus perhaps, but into a circular aperture in the wall. Tentatively, he pushed his hand through the metalwork, and felt nothing beyond it but cool, damp autumn air.

"This is nothing more than an ornate grille," he declared triumphantly. "As Above, so also Below. Lucie, do you recall the iron grid in the paving stones by the temple doors? It was cast with a great letter 'H'. Yes? Well that must be nothing more than a cover to what is a window-well." He tapped on the metalwork with the stem of the candle. "A well to this window, which will become our way out of here."

Atticus grasped the iron frame of the Eye in both hands and shook it. It was as solid and unyielding as the Gates of Alexander.

"It's too strong," Alice groaned. "We haven't a prayer of getting out through there. They're nothing but prison bars; I thought you said—"

"Hush," Atticus snapped. He was examining the points at which the ironwork was fixed into its granite surround. There were three of these, he noted; one at each side of the great staring pupil and one other, where the iron was swept down to mimic the eye markings of a falcon. And that, he concluded, would be its point of weakness.

In this silence, the familiar quarter-peals of St Mary's church chimed and the big tenor bell counted off the hour.

"Ten o'clock," said Lucie.

"Then before it strikes the first quarter, we need to have gone." Atticus flashed his wife a defiant grin. A truly audacious plan had just occurred to him. "And what more fitting way could there be to escape an alchemist's lair than to perform a little alchemy of our own?"

"Alchemy, Atticus, what are you talking about? Alchemy is just humbuggery. It's even more nonsensical than phrenology."

"And yet, using the alchemical reagents on that rack, I shall contrive to turn the iron of this frame into gold – into golden light at any rate – and perhaps a modicum of heat too."

Atticus Fox hastened to the apothecary's rack. There was no time to lose. He worked swiftly along its shelves, muttering to himself all the while as he peered at the labels on the various bottles and jars, and interpreted their strange alchemical symbols. Now and again, he would pick up a vessel, twist off its stopper, and spill its contents into a large granite mortar.

"Mars is iron – the rusty filings at the bottom are perfect. Venus is copper. And not to forget the Mundane elements; we shall have elemental boron and zinc from those, oh, and a ribbon of magnesium to set the whole thing away."

Frenetically, he ground and mixed the contents of the mortar, cursing occasionally as a wave of powder spilled over the rim and scattered noisily onto the floor. Then he said: "There, that should suffice. Lucie, Miss Alice, I am going to ask you both to please take shelter behind the mummy case. Take care not to look! I am about to induce the most vigorous exothermic chemical reaction[28]." He lifted up the mortar and grinned like a schoolboy. "In fact, if this works as I believe it should, then I shall be reproducing here, in this chamber, the conditions of the very surface of the Sun."

"Be careful, Atticus," Lucie cautioned. She grabbed Alice's hand and ran with her to crouch behind the massif that was the mummy case, both only too mindful of what lay just the other side of the lime-wood boards.

Atticus carried his mortar to the Eye and carefully mounded its grey-black contents around its iron tail. He twisted off a length of magnesium ribbon, folded it into two, and pushed the point deep into the powder.

"Are you set?" he whispered over his shoulder.

"Yes," Lucie and Alice hissed in unison.

Atticus took out his Vesta once more, struck a match, and held its flame in turn against each leg of the ribbon. They caught and flared brilliantly white, and then, after one, two, three seconds, the powder hissed and sparked and became an inferno.

Atticus shied back and turned away, watching the spilled natron beneath the ladder for any sign of flame. It would not do for the slowly escaping vapours to be yet ignited by the intense heat and the falling torrents of sparks. But the Fates were with him, and they were not.

He turned back, holding his jacket as a shield to his eyes against the brilliant ball of light. Tears of molten metal, as fluid as water, began to run down the curve of the frame as if the Eye were suddenly weeping, and then, as quickly as it had been born, the fire faded and died, and the tortured iron was left to glow and tick.

"It has finished now," Atticus called, and bent to examine the *caput mortuum*[29] of blistered and pitted metal. He grunted his relief. It was enough, thank god. Gathering the sleeve of his jacket over his fist, he pushed it into the mortar before drawing back and smashing the heavy stone bowl, like a cestus, against the metal. The iron rang dully and a shower of blackened flakes fell away. It fractured, and sprang clear of its mount.

"Atticus, you've done it!" Lucie cried.

He grimaced. Perhaps so, but they weren't out yet. It occurred to him then that whilst he had been rummaging through the pots and jars on the apothecary's rack, his mind had registered something else on the granite shelf below. It was a pile of cloth, dark blue and neatly folded, and surely proof enough against the still-searing heat of the metal. Atticus set the mortar carefully onto the floor and reached for the cloth. It fell open as a police constable's tunic. The white-metal buttons carried the Rosicrucian – no, no, not the Rosicrucian – the rose of the West Riding Constabulary. On the collar, the light glinted off a silver number thirty. It was Constable Watts' number. So Lucie was correct; it must be Billy Watts' and not Inspector Douglas' body being slowly mummified over yonder.

A pair of thick, policeman's trousers had tumbled by his feet. Better yet! Atticus dropped the tunic and gathered up these, twisting them over and over into a kind of a rope.

Passing this quickly around the stub of the Eye, he pulled the two ends tight and pressed his boot against the wall. Lucie understood at once what he was at, and took hold too. The mordant stench of scorched and smoking cloth filled their nostrils as together they heaved. There was a creak and a splintering of mortar, a sharp squeal of protesting metal and then at last, as if closing in pain, the Eye of Horus began to twist in its sockets.

"Mrs Fox!" Alice hissed at their backs, and well might she have warned them. A square column of light, swirling and swarming with the smoke of the reaction, had appeared below the now-open trapdoor, and they could hear Gaspar's voice speaking as if in oration.

"I am informed that our Lord Hermes Trismegistus has left His prison cell and will be with us presently. Over the coming days, and to prove His identity beyond doubt to us, His servants, He has agreed to take the form of the ape Astennu, although He has advised me also that He generally dislikes that particular manifestation. The Golden Dawn has been marked by the re-birth of other gods too, in preparation for the new Age of Aquarius. Lord Hermes has himself identified both Aphrodite and Ma'at. They are sleeping at present, in that place which is Below, resting before their festival exertions."

As the chamber became filled with the sounds of sniggering and laughter, Atticus Fox stood next to the part-twisted ironwork of the Eye and took the attitude of Atlas, bracing himself in readiness for a supreme effort.

Above them, Gaspar continued: "When He arrives here, and ahead of our lay brethren, the Templars, joining us for the *Venus Genetrix*, we shall be performing the execration of the apostate, Atticus Fox. He too sleeps like a child in the Hall Below."

Atticus heaved, and the Eye groaned and twisted further.

"That's enough," Lucie whispered. "Alice, you go first. Take my bicycle and ride home, as quickly as you—"

"No!" Atticus shook his head. "They'd guess she'd be there in an instant. Miss Alice, ride to Samson Fox at Grove House. Tell him that we sent you, and that he is to lock and bar his doors. After that he should telephone Detective Sergeant Hainsworth at Harrogate Police Station. He must speak to no one else. Go, now!"

Alice stared, wide-eyed, at him, nodded her comprehension, and then scrambled up under the Eye.

Gaspar's voice, strident, triumphant, exultant even, carried down to them. "Fraters, it is time now to prepare for the festival, to purify the noble and remove the base…"

"You're next, Lucie." Atticus all but picked up his wife and bundled her bodily into the aperture."

"…to exalt the Divine and abase the flesh."

"I 'eard voices, Frater Gaspar, in the 'all below; are you certain they are sleeping?"

Atticus froze. He had heard that voice with its hint of an accent before; he knew he had.

A face, topped ludicrously by an Egyptian priest's white, feathered headdress, dropped through the hatchway. It was Gaspar, and he was glaring at him in fury.

"Stay where you are, Fox!" he howled and the head was gone. Two white and naked calves snaked down and the toe of a leather-sandaled foot reached for a ladder rung.

Atticus glanced about desperately. He needed to stall Gasper for long enough to give Lucie and Alice their chance to escape. His fingers scrabbled in his pocket for his match-case. Gaspar's feet found the ladder as Atticus fumbled out a match. He struck it. The end snapped, flared, and fell to the floor.

He cursed. "Damnation!"

Gaspar was coming quickly now, a short, ivory-handled knife in his hand. His long, sinewy thighs were bare below a narrow, white skirt, his torso lean and naked under a cloak. Atticus found a second match and with trembling fingers, struck it. This time it caught. He waited for just a second longer, for the flame to steady, then reached forward and touched it to the strewing of ether-soaked natron.

A writhing, boiling mass of wicked, blue flames sprang up and spread, silently and eerily, around the ladder. They leaped up, scattering the smoke and clawing at Gaspar's legs so that he screamed in agony and rage.

Atticus Fox grabbed his cane and threw himself up under the Eye of Horus. Something clutched at his shoulder, snatching back on his jacket. With a rending of cloth he wrenched himself free and he was out, lying on his back on a smattering of leaves and staring up at Lucie's face framed against the stars.

"Atticus, here!"

Her hand stretched down to him. He staggered to his feet and grasped it, and was half-pulled, half-clambered out.

A great crash shook the temple doors beside them, then shouts and a furious pounding on the heavy timber. The iron cover of the window well had been forced across the double-headed eagles of the door handles, imprisoning, for a time, the Hermeticists within.

"It won't hold them for long."

Lucie grabbed his arm and dragged him away.

They began to run, stumbling along the pathway and the treacherous, moss-sheened terrace beyond it to safety – or perhaps not. Lucie was right; at any moment, the adepts might break out and come swarming after them like the hosts of Pharaoh, and help, somehow and from somewhere, must be summoned.

They fell, panting, into the road, where only a single bicycle – Atticus' – remained propped against the gatepost. Thank the lord; Alice at least, had got away.

CHAPTER FIFTY-ONE

The road between Sun Villa and Beagle House was a long and gloriously smooth descent and by the time they passed the latter, the rubber tyres of their bicycle were singing against the asphalt. Every one of the windows was draped and shuttered, the house was in darkness and Atticus did not stop.

Their shadow pulsed and faded with each passing streetlamp. Lucie was kneeling on her skirts on the baggage rack and Atticus felt her arms tighten around his waist as the lamps abruptly ceased and they were swallowed up by the denser blackness of the Stray.

On this flatter ground, Atticus' long legs began to pump again. A matter of seconds later they were in Raglan Street, where just ahead, the big blue lantern of the police station burned steady and true. He rode pell-mell, right up to the station building and only at the very last second did he grip hard on the brake levers. The rubber blocks bit, and the bicycle slewed and skidded to a halt. Lucie slumped forwards against his back and he became suddenly aware of his shoulder, throbbing and stinging under the torn fabric of his jacket.

A policeman was standing by the front railings, regarding them with interest. He was holding a cigar in the fingers of one hand, with his other pushed nonchalantly into his greatcoat pocket. Only a self-assured and senior officer would dare to stand like that in front of a divisional police station and from his uniform, this was a very senior policeman indeed. He might have been an Assistant, or even a Deputy Chief Constable; it was difficult to tell in the poor light, with eyes smarting from stinging drops of sweat. Neither Atticus nor Lucie had ever seen him before.

"Officer, my name is Fox," Atticus panted. "We need to speak to Detective Inspector Douglas about a matter of the most pressing nature."

The policeman smiled and stubbed his cigar against the pyramidal finial of a pillar.

"I fear the detective inspector is indisposed." His voice held the distinctive nasal accent of the high Pennines.

"Detective Sergeant Hainsworth in that case?"

"Sergeant Hainsworth has failed to report for duty this evening. He will be placed on a disciplinary charge when he eventually does so. Your names are Fox you say – Atticus and Lucie Fox perhaps?"

Atticus nodded.

"I have been waiting for you both, and also for a young lady by the name of… Alice Payne-Malkin. It would be better, I think, if you were to speak only with me from this time onward. My name is de Molay." He pinched the peak of his richly-braided pill-box cap towards each of them in turn. "I have taken operational charge of this division and personal charge of this case. Mr Douglas has made me fully aware of your involvement."

He hesitated – perhaps it was the blue light of the station lamp that made his eyes seem so very pale, and so almost feminine – and glanced up and down the deserted street.

"I am also aware of the circumstances concerning a particular house on Harlow Hill. Given with whom we are dealing, I think it prudent that we step away from this police station and find somewhere a little more private to speak. Come, let us step around the corner; you may leave your bicycle here."

Atticus propped his bicycle against the railings and, together with Lucie, followed de Molay beyond the station building and into the yard of the church adjacent. There a police waggon stood, silent, but for the horse gnawing on the metal of its bit.

"They were planning to murder me in that house," Atticus whispered, taking care not to let his voice carry up to the driver sitting patiently above them, with his hat drawn down and his collar turned up against the cold, "And to commit all manner of outrage on Mrs Fox and Miss Malk—."

De Molay interrupted him. "I believe that the correct term is not 'murder' but 'execrate', Mr Fox." He lifted his hand from his pocket and jabbed the long, black barrel of a revolver into Lucie's kidneys.

"Please be good enough to lay your sword-cane onto the ground and then step into the back of this waggon. You too, my lady Ma'at. The magic has already been sealed and you must understand that we have no choice but to carry it out."

It occurred to Lucie in that moment that the reason de Molay's eyes seemed so strikingly odd was that he was wearing the vestiges of thick, black eye-lining.

Less than a minute later, a police waggon pulled past Raglan Street station. A casual observer might not have found it remarkable that prisoners should be transported in the dead of night. They may well have thought it curious however, that a full Assistant Chief Constable of the West Riding Constabulary should be riding upon the backboard as guard.

"Welcome back to us, Mr and Mrs Fox."

At another time and in different circumstances Gaspar's skirt and cloak, his white, feathered headdress and his kohl eye-lining would have made him seem queer, even ridiculous. Here, in this temple, at the point of a revolver, surrounded by menace and by a group of other men dressed identically to him, he appeared positively terrifying.

"We have consulted with our Lord, the Thrice-Great Hermes, and we no longer believe you to be a goddess reborn, Mrs Fox. For someone purporting to be Ma'at, you are singularly lacking in wisdom."

"I have purported to be nothing of the sort!"

"But that will not preclude you from the honour of attending, and indeed of participating in, our festival tonight. However, it will mean that before the dawn rises once more in the east, you will be joining your husband in a ceremony of execration. The Lord Hermes himself has commanded it and he informs me that he looks forward very much to carrying out a full examination of your heart and cranium too."

"You won't get away with this, Gaspar," Lucie spat back. "Too many people suspect you already."

She flinched as she felt de Molay pressing against her and whispering at her ear: "Knowing a thing and proving it are two entirely different things."

"That is wisely said, Brother de Molay," agreed Gaspar. "Mr and Mrs Fox, our Lord still wishes to honour the Lady Aphrodite. Accordingly, you will tell me now where she might be found."

Atticus and Lucie stood together, each silent in their defiance.

"We will not harm her, of course. On the contrary, she will be taken with Him along the path to Enlightenment, to take her place once again as a goddess in the great pantheon."

"No reply, sir," said Atticus curtly.

Gaspar bared his teeth and glowered at him. He lifted his sandal and turned his ankle towards them. An angry red crescent of peeling, blistered skin was spread up the pallid skin of his calf.

"See there what you did to me with your tricks of fire, Mr Fox."

Atticus shrugged.

"Have you still nothing to say then?"

Lucie said: "You were going to murder him, Gaspar. What did you expect him to do?"

The priest turned his kohl-rimmed eyes onto her.

"Mrs Fox, do tell me: what if I were to douse, not just Mr Fox's ankle, but the whole of him with sweet oil of vitriol? And then, what if I were to be clumsy enough to drop a lighted candle onto it?" Gaspar brought his hands slowly together in a clap and mouthed the word 'poof'. "Do you think that would be enough to induce you to tell me the whereabouts of Aphrodite?"

Lucie stared back insolently.

"Is she with her father, Quaker Malkin, after all, I wonder?" Gaspar went on. "I hear he is inclined against the coming together of the bloodlines, just as his wife was."

Atticus spluttered. "The coming together of the bloodlines… the Hermetic and the… and the Aphroditean! You mean the Payne bloodline, don't you?"

"Now do you see the importance of all of this, Atticus Fox? Yes, I do mean the Payne bloodline: the pure and unbroken descent from Hughes de Payens, the founder and first Grand Master of the Knights Templar, and Catherine Sinclair."

"You believe that? So you no doubt believe also that the Sinclairs are the direct descendants – the rose-line – of Mary Magdalene. Which would mean that Alice *Payne-Malkin*…"

"…is the flowering of that line, just as her mother proved to be its thorn. Women are forbidden to take up office in the *orders secular* – the Freemasons and the Templars – so Victoria Payne-Malkin joined the *orders spiritual* instead, and rose to become an adept. And we were pleased to receive her, just as we had received her progenitors into antiquity. But then she refused us her daughter; she denied that Alice is in fact Mary Magdalene – the great Aphrodite – reborn. She even tried to say that Astennu is not Lord Hermes Trismegistus at all, and fell to uttering blasphemies against him."

Gaspar angrily shook his head and above it, the big ostrich feathers of his headdress quivered.

"When my fraters called at Beagle House, they were told that Malkin was out and that his daughter was still missing. You, Mrs Fox, know where she is. So if your husband were to remain here with us, you might well be able to persuade her to a ride in a police waggon. It would be a great pity if it became necessary to find her ourselves. We would begin with a search of Beagle House, and that would most certainly involve measures to ensure our secrets remained intact. The blood of the entire household would be upon your head, and what would Brother Samson think to that?"

"Your secrets are out already, Gaspar." Lucie stabbed her finger at the men in front of her. "The police – the proper police that is; Inspector Douglas and Sergeant Hainsworth – know all about you and your ridiculous temple, and they know that we came here today."

Behind her, de Molay's laughter was harsh and utterly without mirth. He said: "Detective Inspector Douglas will trouble no one ever again. As for that redneck Hainsworth, what can he do if he can find neither a senior rank to sign his warrant, nor a judge to prosecute it? And let me assure you, he will not."

"Pass me the sweet oil of vitriol, Frater Prêtre," Gaspar ordered, "The big bottle, if you please."

One of the priests padded obediently to the apothecary's rack and returned with a large, cork-stoppered jar. The glass cast strange eddies and swirls onto the white marble below it, as if the ether it contained were pacing its lair, impatient for release."

"Merci, Frater. What is it to be then, Lucie Fox, cooperation, or conflagration?"

Without waiting for her reply, Gaspar twisted off the cork. De Molay pressed the muzzle of his revolver against Lucie's throat and dragged her away and Gaspar stepped forward. He lifted the jar and tipped it, staring without expression into Atticus' eyes as the liquid seeped down Atticus' front and spattered noisily onto the floor at his feet.

"Well, what is your answer to be?"

He handed the empty jar to Prêtre, who took it and passed back something in its place. Gaspar held it aloft; it was a pretty quartz strike-a-light.

"Be careful with that, Frater," de Molay cautioned and Lucie shut her eyes.

"Well, Lucie Fox?" said Gaspar.

"Say nothing!" Atticus was shivering now as the icy liquid sucked the warmth from his skin.

Gaspar inclined his head to the side and called out: "What is it to be, My Lord?"

From behind the priests, and from a little square in which the four Hermetic orders came together, a man they had once known as Esau rose up.

Lord Hermes Trismegistus was dressed in a full-length robe of purple and emerald-green velvet, and a hat, in shape curiously akin to a fisherman's sou'wester, but with a blunt-pointed crown.

"What has been sealed by the will of the Brethren here Below, Magus Gaspar, I will seal as law in the Above," he declared, and the priests and de Molay chanted: "Amen".

Hermes then addressed Atticus Fox directly.

"As Above, so also Below. As with the father, so also with the son. Your father died by fire, Atticus Fox; it would seem that you are about to do the same."

Atticus did not reply. He was shaking violently and his eyes, pressed shut as if he might fear to look upon the face of a god, were streaming.

"At least you will have the honour of having the Thrice-Great Lord himself to guide your spirit to judgement," Gaspar said.

He feinted, as if striking the spark that would engulf Atticus, and Lucie screamed.

"Then fetch us Aphrodite!" Gaspar bellowed the words, one after another, into her face.

"Do nothing, Lucie" Atticus croaked.

It was at the very moment when Gaspar reached forward with his strike-a-light that the great temple doors shuddered and were flung wide on their hinges and a man with a great, grizzled beard and the scarlet uniform of a colonel stood glaring at them from the night. At his shoulder was Detective Sergeant Hainsworth.

More scarlet figures, more and more, were being conjured from the darkness and these began to stream in from either side of them like twin torrents of blood. De Molay's protestations and his cries of 'police' and 'constabulary' were drowned in a chorus of shouts and oaths, and then silenced completely as a rifle butt smashed his face into a bloody mess. A phalanx of jabbing bayonets formed and pressed the priests back towards the altar.

"In Her Majesty's name, you are all arrested," the man in the colonel's uniform roared. He drew the sign of a cross over the looping braids on his chest and stepped into the temple.

"You!" Gaspar hissed.

"Yes, it is me, Gaspar, and from what I see, I have arrived not one second too soon."

"Who is this, Frater?" one of the other adepts demanded.

"Who is this, you ask? Who is this? Pah! This, my brothers, is ex-Grand Master, Lord George Robinson, His Excellency, the Most Honourable, the First Marquess of Ripon." Gaspar spat out each word.

The adept's mouth fell open. "So that's Ripon?"

"That's him. Lord Ripon, who almost twenty years ago, resigned as Grand Master of the United Grand Lodge of England to become a red-necked Roman Catholic. Lord Ripon, the man who caused such uproar in the innermost orders that we were obliged to appoint the Prince of Wales in his stead because we had no idea how far the Catholic rot had spread. He was fortunate indeed to have Her Majesty appoint him as a Lord Lieutenant and put himself beyond our reach, and more fortunate yet to persuade Gladstone to send him to India. Pah! At least we were able to have his confessor infected with the pox."

"Catholic rot?" Lord Ripon roared, his beard quivering at each syllable. "How dare you! The Order gave me no choice but to convert. I would never bow down before that abomination Baphomet and still less before that ghastly head. So let me tell you where the rot really is, Gaspar; it is here, standing in front of these men's bayonets. Yes, I am Lord Lieutenant. I am therefore Her Majesty's appointed representative here, and whether Hermetic adepts or Templar knights, you are all my prisoners."

"We shall see," Gaspar snarled. Stepping forward until he was standing against the very tips of their bayonets, he addressed the ranks of soldiers.

"Listen to me, you men. I am Gaspar, Magus of the Vault of Adepts, Guardian of the Throne of Solomon, and Chaplain-General to the Poor Fellow Soldiers of Christ and of the Temple of Solomon If any man among you counts themselves a Frater, Brother or Companion, I command you now to turn and stand with us."

"I'll see the first man who does flogged," growled an officer in the cuffs and stars of a captain.

Ripon laughed scornfully.

"Save your breath, Gaspar. These soldiers are militiamen and men of the West Riding Volunteers. You'll find no Freemasons among them. Their captain is the Earl de Grey, my own son. He's the fastest and most accurate shot in Yorkshire, so mind me when I say you've been warned."

"They are a welcome sight, thank you, Your Lordship." Atticus was swaying wildly on his feet, almost overcome now by the ether vapours rising thickly from his clothing.

Lord Ripon laid back his head and squinted down his beard at him.

"Atticus Fox isn't it, Samson Fox's cousin? And Mrs Fox, I presume? How do you do? It's Sergeant Hainsworth here you should be thanking. When de Molay there took the inspector off and then returned without him, he had the courage and the presence of mind to come up to Studley to summon me. My son Frederick, Captain de Grey, roused the troops he had billeted in Ripon and we came down on the late goods train."

"Thank you, Mr Hainsworth," Atticus was just able to whisper.

Lord Ripon frowned. "Are you alright, Fox? I think you should sit down for a while, afore you blessed-well fall down."

"Gaspar has doused him in ether." Lucie explained, running to her husband and steering him to the floor. "I need to get this jacket and waistcoat off him."

Atticus sighed and passed out.

Lord Ripon's frown twisted into a glower. "If that man has come to any harm because of this night's mischief, then make no mistake about it; I shall hold every man here responsible. Now, where is this Esau fellow Hainsworth told me about? I believe we might have prior acquaintance."

But the marble square, with its golden Seal of Solomon, had become solid floor once again and Esau was nowhere to be spied.

"The slab in the very corner is a secret trapdoor," Lucie said, fumbling at her husband's waistcoat buttons, "It leads to an underground chamber. There's a corpse down there too, in a mummy-case. Mr Hainsworth, I'm truly sorry but I believe it to be Constable Watts."

"Is it indeed? Then the Lord have mercy. I admit I did fear the worst when I saw the Hermeticists were back here," said Hainsworth.

Captain de Grey barked an order and two of his men scurried into the corner Lucie had indicated. They found the hidden handle in a moment and heaved open the slab.

"Take care, Freddie," Lord Ripon warned, "It's likely a *Sanctum Santorum*, a Holy of Holies, one of those infernal Halls of Two Truths I told you about."

De Grey nodded grimly. He drew a pistol from his belt and dropped bodily into the void. The soldiers, encumbered by rifle and bayonet, clambered awkwardly after him."

"There's a set of robes down here." Frederick's voice was muffled and echoey, as if he really had passed over into the world of the preternatural, "And yes, here's a policeman; number 30 by his collar, if that means anything to you, Sergeant. He's very badly injured, but yes, still alive."

"What?" Lucie exclaimed.

"Number 30 is my Constable Watts, Captain; we sent him over here on guard-duty," Hainsworth called back. "Thank the lord he's alive, after all."

Atticus moaned and his hand twitched.

"Send him up if you can, Freddie," Ripon called, "We'll get him to a hospital."

"He's on the ladder now, Father – as a walking-wounded. There's no sign of anyone else here though, only a rather frightful-looking carving."

"A Baphomet, I expect," growled Ripon.

"As…Above, so also…Below," Atticus murmured almost insensibly.

"Atticus, Atticus, wake up," Lucie urged, then loudly: "Captain de Grey, there should be a Gladstone bag down there, with a long strap for a handle. I need the smelling salts from it for Mr Fox.

"Your Lordship, there is a window well outside this temple, just by the door. We used it to make our escape from the Hall of Two Truths. Esau may have got away in the same manner."

Ripon waved a white-gloved hand.

"Most unlikely, Mrs Fox; I have men stationed all around this temple. They've strict orders not to allow anyone to leave."

A bloody tangle of ginger hair emerged from the floor and then a face. The smears of darkening blood and clinging crusts of natron were shocking against the lustrous white of the walls.

Unbidden, two militiamen ran forwards. They caught the revenant under each of his arms and hoisted him out.

"Constable 30, Billy Watts." Hainsworth went to him too, "The copper with the thirty-watt hair."

Billy Watts raised his blood-caked hands to his face and slumped forward. Lucie made as if to rise but Lord Ripon raised his hand to forestall her.

"No need, Mrs Fox; no need at all. These men are medical orderlies; they can take care of him perfectly well. We may well yet have need of you here."

He addressed the medics.

"There's a police waggon at the front of the house. Requisition it in my name and use it to get that man down to the Cottage Hospital. The driver will know the way. But mind you keep a gun to his head. For all his protestations, he'll no doubt be in this up to his neck. Off you go, smartly now."

There was a sudden clamour of boots on iron and Captain de Grey's head appeared, framed against the open trapdoor like a postage stamp. He lifted the Foxes' investigations bag onto the floor and said: "We've searched the whole place. It's damned queer, but there's no-one else down there. This Esau fellow's somehow got clean away."

"Did any man actually see him go down there?" Ripon demanded.

"I saw 'im, Your Lordship," a militiaman piped up, his face as red as his tunic, "Big, velvet cloak and t' queerest looking hat ah've ever seed."

"That'll be him. So he can't have escaped. Where has he hidden himself, Gaspar?"

The priest scowled back insolently. "Perhaps he has vanished into the air, My Lord Papist."

Atticus suddenly coughed and moved his head. "As Above, so also Below," he murmured again.

Lucie pulled a cork from a little phial of smelling salts and waved it in front of his face.

"Atticus… Atticus… Listen to me. Esau has gone. He was in the Hall of Two Truths, and now he has vanished."

Atticus moaned and rolled onto his side.

Seconds passed.

"As Above, so Below," he whispered for the third time and pushed his hand in the vague direction of the altar. Lucie realised at that moment what he meant, that his words had not been senseless ramblings after all.

"Of course, Atticus – the priest-hole!

"Captain de Grey, the image of Baphomet you saw, it is carved into a stone plaque. Look along the edge of that; there will be some form of hidden locking mechanism. If you press it, it should open and you will find a hidden cavity behind."

"No!" Gaspar roared, "You must not. It is forbidden for anyone below the rank of Knight Commander to open that vault. You will be cursed; you will be the last of your line; the Eye watches you—"

"Shut yer mouth, Dollymop!" The militiaman reinforced his words with a threatening jab of his bayonet.

Gaspar bared his teeth to the man and glared at the sniggering soldiers.

"Listen to my words: No man who looks upon the contents of that vault will live."

"That's enough, Gaspar," Lord Ripon snapped.

"Mr Malkin!" Hainsworth exclaimed.

Two militiamen were standing in the temple doorway with a third man shivering wretchedly between them. It was Joseph.

"We found him skulking in the grounds," said one of the soldiers.

"I had to come," Joseph sobbed, "I had to know what had become of my Alice."

"It's Joseph Malkin, Alice's father, Your Lordship," Lucie explained, "He's a Quaker and an old friend of Mr Fox."

"Which edge of the plaque, Mrs Fox?" Captain de Grey pressed.

"It'll be easier if show you." Lucie glanced towards Lord Ripon and at a firm nod of assent from him, but with her own mind screaming and screaming its protestations, she hurried to descend once more into the Hall of Two Truths.

CHAPTER FIFTY-TWO

It is sometimes said that familiarity is the greatest foe of dread.

So it was that when Lucie Fox descended the ladder and entered once again into that which is Below, the shadows, the mummy case, even the image of the Baphomet carven onto the wall before her, held a little less of the horror of her previous visit.

On the floor by her feet, the robes and the curious headgear of Hermes Trismegistus lay discarded and empty, as if for a time, the Baphomet might have transformed into flesh and blood before casting them off to become petrified once again.

Feeling the heat from the oil lamps, and the hot stares of the soldiers and Baphomet, Lucie began to examine the slab's edge, searching for any movement, any spring, any indication at all of some kind of locking mechanism. And quickly she found it: a tiny bronze key, ice-cold to her touch. She inhaled, filling her lungs with the stench of the place: castor oil, seared metal, vitriol and fear, and gathered her wits. Nodding first to the captain and then to the militiamen, all standing ready with the same grim and trepidatious expressions, she turned it.

The key turned once, and then turned once more, Baphomet glaring down at her with its eyes of a fiend, its twisting genitals tall and erect and inches from her face. It turned for a third time, and clicked.

"Here he comes!" the captain cried, "Remember, bayonets only, my lads; don't risk a ricochet in here."

And he was right. The great stone panel was moving, swinging out slowly but irresistibly on its hinges. It caught Lucie and pushed her back, forcing her cruelly against the unyielding side of the mummy case and pinning her fast.

From behind it, a man – tall, naked and unnaturally white – toppled forward, dropping onto the captain and bearing him to the floor. Shots rang out, pistol shots, one and then another and then another, each a thunderous report. The soldiers raised their bayonets and stood like spear-fishers, uncertain, not daring to plunge their blades into the writhing mass of limbs.

The gunshots, the shrieks, the yells all reverberated into silence.

"Freddie?" Lord Ripon's voice called down.

Captain de Grey kicked the corpse of his assailant away.

"I'm here, Father. Fox was right. Esau was in there. He's dead now."

The body lay on its side, stiff and grey, in the twin penumbrae of the mummy case and the gaping vault door. Lucie shoved hard against the Baphomet and as its shadow rolled back, so the full truth of the scene was revealed.

"This man was already dead." Lucie, reached down and pressed her fingers against his neck, where an angry stripe containing two, parallel, dark-brown ligature-marks was still livid against the skin, "Dead for some time. And oh, Lordy! He's been scalped."

She pointed to where the skin along the corpse's hairline had been neatly excised and the scalp of the head peeled away to expose the pinkish, blood-smeared bone of the skull beneath.

"And nor is that Esau!"

The rungs of the ladder rang again and all at once Detective Sergeant Hainsworth was standing with them.

"Strike me dead! It's Billy Watts! But how could it be? We saw him walk away, not ten minutes ago."

He gasped.

"Then it must have been Esau we sent away to—"

"Whisht!" Captain de Grey gripped Hainsworth's wrist. He pointed into the shadows behind the vault door, where it hung ajar.

"He's still in there," he mouthed, "I've just seen a face."

He motioned urgently to his men with the barrel of his revolver, and then reached forward, gripped the edge of the plaque, and hauled it wide.

Frederick Robinson, the Earl de Grey, was renowned for his accuracy in shot and eye, and in that moment, he had indeed glimpsed a face. His assertion that the throttled and scalped cadaver that had once been Billy Watts was not the vault's only occupant was correct – but not completely.

There was one other. But it was not an entire person, either living or dead. It was a head, a mummified, bearded head of great antiquity, set on a golden platter and possibly more terrible to look upon even than Baphomet.

When Sergeant Hainsworth bore the platter, rung by rung, up the ladder and raised it through the hatchway into the temple Above, it was almost as if the relic it carried, desiccated, brown and hollow-eyed as it was, had been resurrected to life.

As it emerged, the entire assemblage of priests and adepts, and even Joseph Malkin, knelt as one and pressed their foreheads to the floor. Lord Ripon himself, like Herod the Tetrarch, dropped to his knees and thrice drew the sign of the cross across his breast.

It fell to Atticus Fox to break the profound and obeisant silence He was sitting up unaided now and the searing pain in his throat had at last begun to abate.

"The head of John the Baptist!" he rasped.

"The patron saint both of the Freemasons and of the Knights Templar," declared Lord Ripon. "Yes, that is indeed his head – so it is claimed anyway. They say it was looted by the Templars during the sacking of Constantinople, along with fragments of wood from the Holy Rood – the true cross. It was that which finally caused me to convert to Catholicism: my so-called brethren bowing down in worship before it, believing that John the Baptist was actually the messenger of God and therefore Hermes – the true Messiah. I could not countenance the blasphemy that he and Solomon and that unholy fiend Baphomet were all one and the same – this so-called Trismegistus. But only the few may look upon the head, Gasper. Why is it here, in Harrogate, and not in its reliquary in Halifax?"

Gaspar lifted his brow from the floor and glared malevolently at him in response.

Atticus said: "I imagine it has something to do with phrenology." He took a sip from his hip flask and grimaced as the ice-cold water scalded his throat. "Don't some in the orders believe the head is not John the Baptist's at all but that of Hugh de Payens? I suspect that Victoria *Payne*-Malkin, his direct descendant, would have favoured that view. Perhaps that was why she so took against Esau."

"We never doubted that Esau was Astennu, and therefore Lord Hermes Trismegistus," Gaspar interjected. "He had been examined by a phrenologist and so we had a perfect opportunity to establish beyond doubt whose head it was. If it proved to be identical to Lord Hermes', then it follows that it must be that of John the Baptist, since one is the reincarnation of the other. But the phrenologist not only refused to examine it, he threatened us with the police. He suffered the *hostimentum* – the full requital – due to him."

Lord Ripon said: "Hainsworth told me he'd been murdered. So a phrenologist's shop window has replaced the spike-on-the-bridge as a place to lay out your victims' heads, has it? I can't believe for a second that the Grand-Master would allow Esau to be used as an *Exequutor*[30] though." He regarded the Assistant Chief Constable still lying prone on the floor. "De Molay there will be the relic's knight-protector, I expect, but he'd be above soiling himself with common murder. He'll have had a sergeant-companion to do the killing, but they will both most assuredly have been acting under the orders of a high knight-commander."

Gaspar cast a glance to the temple doors, and to the great Eye above them, and grinned.

"My Lord Hermes insisted on being a part of the *hostimenta* on the workhouse tramp-major, and on the traitorous Payne woman, but not the phrenologist. He sent the tramp-major's skull with the sergeant-companion, to be examined along with the holy St John's. It was to test the phrenologist's skill, since he already knew well the character of the tramp." His lips curled back in a venomous and triumphant grin. "It would seem, Lord Papist that both Lord Hermes and the sergeant-companion have escaped you."

"It's Mr Oates," Lucie said.

"What is?" Hainsworth asked.

"The *Exequutor*, the sergeant-companion of the Knights Templar," said Atticus.

"No!" cried Joseph Malkin.

Hainsworth glanced from one to the other. "Mr Malkin's coachman, do you mean? But how can that be? Hasn't he been murdered too?"

Lucie said: "No, Mr Hainsworth, he hasn't. We were told he was with Miss Alice and Gaspar in the Hall of Two Truths, but not, as we first assumed, as a captive. Mr Oates was there as an accomplice. When Mr Fox and I discovered Professor Ryan and the tramp-major's skulls, we found identical but incomplete sets of finger-prints on them. They were different from Esau's and both missing the third finger on each hand. *Dupuytren's contracture* causes those particular fingers to be twisted back towards the palm. It commonly afflicts carriage drivers through their constant pulling at the reins, hence its more common name of coachman's finger. Mr Oates suffers from it. And we found residues of a cleaning preparation too, one typically used on harness and carriages."

Atticus took up the narrative.

"Mrs Malkin, we know, is of an old Templar family and Mr Oates came with her as a servant, an old family retainer, when she was married."

"So then who is this knight-commander His Lordship mentioned?" Hainsworth asked.

Atticus glanced up to the All-Seeing Eye of Horus and held its Stygian gaze.

"It's Joseph Malkin," he said.

"Joseph?" echoed Lucie, "Surely not."

"It's Joseph Malkin," Atticus repeated. "Joseph is a high knight-commander of the Templars."

"But how can he be? He's a Quaker, and we've known him for years."

Atticus clambered unsteadily to his feet.

"Because he is the Prometheus in all of this. He even said as much himself. Isn't that so, Joseph?"

The eyes of everyone present: lord, priest and soldier, even, it seemed, of the saintly relic still resting on its platter, fell upon Malkin.

"It's true," Joseph sobbed, "It was I who created Esau. I was the one to discover him, and I was the one to tell Gaspar that he might be the missing link to the gods – that he was Hermes reborn. But, like Prometheus, I have been punished for my hubris. My wife has been killed; my daughter is in the very gravest danger. It has all run away from me – and this world is pitiless."

"So speaks the Gnostic!" Atticus said.

"But Mr Malkin is a Quaker," Hainsworth protested, "just as Mrs Fox has said."

"He is, but he is also a Universalist. Remember how adamant he has been as to the evilness of this world – its redness in tooth and claw, as Tennyson, another Freemason, phrased it? All except for the soul; he said that the soul was a spark of goodness – the Quakers' *Light Within*. It would seem that his acceptance of truth in all religions has extended as far as Gnosticism and Rosicrucianism."

"But it has, Atticus." Joseph nodded eagerly. "Of course it has; Gnosticism is the most philosophically perfect thing. Progressive Revelation has shown that very clearly to me."

"Excuse me, but aren't Quakers supposed to abhor violence?" Hainsworth interjected.

"They are," said Lucie drily, "but then he has Mr Oates for that."

"So where is Oates now?" Hainsworth asked.

Atticus frowned. "I can only imagine he was the driver of the police waggon, who was so careful to hide his identity from us."

"Great Scott! Then he must with Esau now, on his way to the Cottage Hospital."

"Two of my son's men are with them," Lord Ripon reminded them, "with strict orders to be vigilant." He sighed heavily. "I declare, I warned of this, years ago. Does anyone know if there is a telephone in this house? I can't imagine there wouldn't be. I'll call the hospital myself, to pass the message that they be detained on sight. They'll be in Ripon gaol by the time this night is out, and that is exactly where you folk will find yourselves too. The Queen herself will hear of this night's work, Gaspar, you mark my words."

Gaspar hissed and bared his teeth like the rearing cobra on his headdress.

"Frederick's men will make short work of this place with their explosive charges. The antiquities can all go to the Corporation to sell or to put into a museum as they think fit. I will have this canker cut out."

A police waggon was stopped by the Bilton junction of the Harrogate to Ripon railway line. A casual onlooker might not have found that remarkable, even at this late hour; the railwaymen kept unusual hours and a brutal thirst, and the public houses nearby were both plentiful and accommodating. Nor was it especially notable that a hand-barrow was missing from its place by the junction's coal-yard. They made convenient transports for drunken companions.

The wheel-tracks of this particular barrow were, even in the moonlight, clearly visible in the dew of the grass and accompanied by two sets of footprints. But these were not the meandering tracks of drink-sodden yardmen however; these were straight and purposeful, and they followed the railway line as far as the viaduct.

There, under the watchful eye of the crescent Moon, two figures lifted something heavy and limp from the bed of the barrow and between them, swung it, once, twice, and then up and over the low, ashlar parapet. A few seconds later, it hit the river far below and sent a duck scurrying across the water, loudly squawking its protestations.

The figures leaned and peered down for a while before turning to swing a second object, red perhaps in colour and as limp and as awkward as the first, down into the plummeting depths. Then they turned and walked solemnly into the night.

Hermes Trismegistus
Henry Wadsworth Longfellow.

Still through Egypt's desert places
Flows the lordly Nile,
From its banks the great stone faces
Gaze with patient smile.
Still the pyramids imperious
Pierce the cloudless skies,
And the Sphinx stares with mysterious,
Solemn, stony eyes.

But where are the old Egyptian
Demi-gods and kings?
Nothing left but an inscription
Graven on stones and rings.
Where are Helios and Hephaestus,
Gods of eldest eld?
Where is Hermes Trismegistus,
Who their secrets held?

Where are now the many hundred
Thousand books he wrote?
By the Thaumaturgists plundered,
Lost in lands remote;
In oblivion sunk forever,
As when o'er the land
Blows a storm-wind, in the river
Sinks the scattered sand.

Something unsubstantial, ghostly,
Seems this Theurgist,

In deep meditation mostly
Wrapped, as in a mist.
Vague, phantasmal, and unreal
To our thought he seems,
Walking in a world ideal,
In a land of dreams.

Was he one, or many, merging
Name and fame in one,
Like a stream, to which, converging
Many streamlets run?
Till, with gathered power proceeding,
Ampler sweep it takes,
Downward the sweet waters leading
From unnumbered lakes.

By the Nile I see him wandering,
Pausing now and then,
On the mystic union pondering
Between gods and men;
Half believing, wholly feeling,
With supreme delight,
How the gods, themselves concealing,
Lift men to their height.

Or in Thebes, the hundred-gated,
In the thoroughfare
Breathing, as if consecrated,
A diviner air;
And amid discordant noises,
In the jostling throng,

Hearing far, celestial voices
Of Olympian song.

Who shall call his dreams fallacious?
Who has searched or sought
All the unexplored and spacious
Universe of thought?
Who, in his own skill confiding,
Shall with rule and line
Mark the border-land dividing
Human and divine?

Trismegistus! Three times greatest!
How thy name sublime
Has descended to this latest
Progeny of time!
Happy they whose written pages
Perish with their lives,
If amid the crumbling ages
Still their name survives!

Thine, O priest of Egypt, lately
Found I in the vast,
Weed-encumbered sombre, stately,
Grave-yard of the Past,
And a presence moved before me
On that gloomy shore,
As a waft of wind, that o'er me
Breathed, and was no more.

Cambridge, Massachusetts. February, 1882.

Notes

(1) Lamplighters, who would turn the gas burners of street-lamps on and off.

(2) Charles Darwin and Alfred Russel Wallace independently developed the theory of evolution through natural selection.

(3) The House of Lords, the upper chamber of Parliament.

(4) The Royal Society is the preeminent learned society for science. It was founded in 1660 and in 1892 was based at Burlington House, London.

(5) The Blue Stockings Society was a mid-eighteenth century literary society. The term 'bluestocking' came to be used as a term for an intellectual, educated lady.

(6) The head-start given to a hare when coursed by dogs.

(7) A Scotsman, reputedly, the Victorian era's greatest athlete.

(8) A chess puzzle with the object of moving a knight to every square of a chessboard, visiting each square only once.

(9) The Linnean Society of London is a learned society for natural history and taxonomy.

(10) In the Biblical book of Joshua, Rahab was described as a prostitute or innkeeper of Jericho, who rendered assistance to two Israelite spies.

(11) The motto of the Royal Society.

(12) The McNaughten (or M'Naghten) rules are a legal defence by reason of insanity.

(13) Popular Victorian rhyme. The English satirist and writer Tom Brown, about to be expelled from Christ Church College, Oxford, was pardoned by the Dean, Dr John Fell, because of his translation, *ex tempore*, of the 32nd epigram of Martial as: I do not love thee, Doctor Fell, The reason why, I cannot tell; But this I know, and know full well, I do not love thee, Doctor Fell.

(14) See *The Eighth Circle of Hell*, by Gary Dolman.

(15) William of Ockham, an English philosopher and theologian.

(16) Lines from Alfred, Lord Tennyson's, *In Memoriam AHH.*
(17) The title of a hymn by William Cowper, 1773.
(18) If God be willing.
(19) A room in a monastery or convent where conversation is permitted.
(20) St Agnes of Rome, the patron saint of rape victims.
(21) Workhouses established under the Poor Law Amendment Act, 1834, (New Poor Law).
(22) A type of lightweight luxury carriage, used in Harrogate at this time as for-hire vehicles.
(23) Murder in order to obtain anatomical specimens. Derived from the notorious 'resurrectionists' Burke and Hare.
(24) From Jewish folklore: an animated creature formed of mud, stone or (as here) clay.
(25) A place where old or injured animals are taken for slaughter.
(26) Second-rate meat and offal, used to feed animals.
(27) Recursively, as in the effect produced by placing an object between two mirrors.
(28) A chemical reaction characterised by its generation of heat. Atticus is here using what was to become known as the thermite, or Goldschmidt, reaction.
(29) The unwanted residues of an alchemical reaction, the symbol for which was a skull (or Death's Head).
(30) An enforcer; one who carries out punishment or revenge.

THE EIGHTH CIRCLE OF HELL

In the 19th century, when the British Empire was approaching its very zenith, the Victorians began to believe that with their power and with their fabulous wealth, they could do almost anything. Some gentlemen in particular were convinced that they could indeed do anything… and get away with it.

A noted Harrogate philanthropist is discovered murdered, the victim of a brutal and frenzied attack. The apparent killer, a frail and elderly imbecile woman, had fled his house as a child.

The Eighth Circle of Hell follows strands of love, lust and revenge as they twist together across that most infernal of times: the Victorian Defloration Mania.

A chilling and utterly gripping tour de force inspired by real events in 19th century England.

RED DRAGON-WHITE DRAGON.

Atticus and Lucie Fox are summoned to a country estate in remote Northumberland, where a series of bizarre murders appear to centre on the delusions of a madman, who lives alone on the edge of the moors.

Close-by are the remains of a long-vanished castle, where, local legends say, King Arthur still lies in an enchanted sleep, waiting to be awoken at the End of Days.

The killings have all been committed using the Hallows of Arthur; artefacts long thought to have been lost in history, and the locals swear that they have seen a ghostly knight-in-armour roaming the moors for months. But how can that be? This is 1890, and King Arthur died over thirteen-hundred years before.

www.garydolman.co.uk